SOMEDAY SOON

The After War Series

Book III

BRANDON ZENNER

Library of Congress Control Number: 2019918219
ISBN: 978-0-578-60777-1

Dedicated to Hal and Natalie Zenner
"Hi Mom and Dad!"
(author smiles and waves)

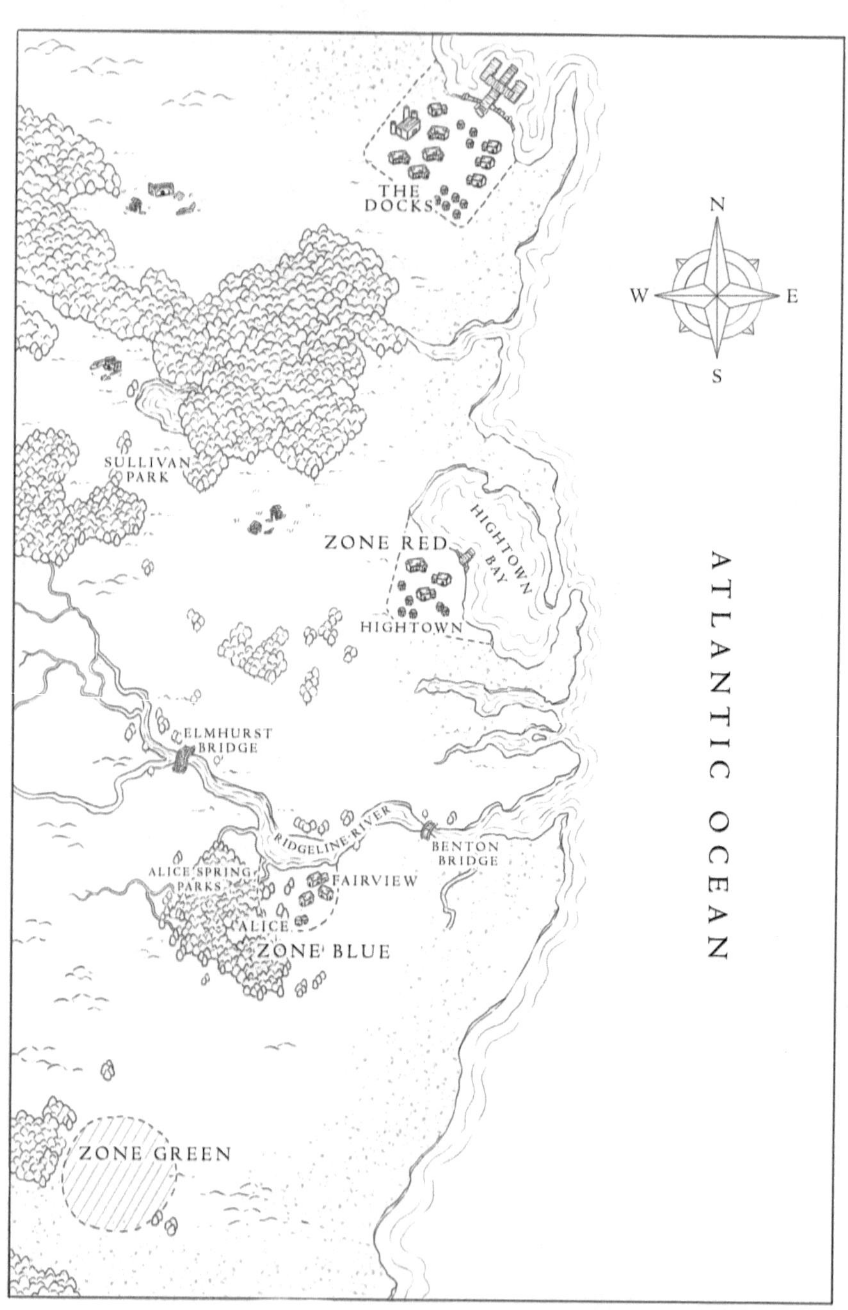

THE DOCKS
SULLIVAN PARK
ZONE RED
HIGHTOWN BAY
HIGHTOWN
ELMHURST BRIDGE
RIDGELINE RIVER
BENTON BRIDGE
ALICE SPRING PARKS
FAIRVIEW
ALICE
ZONE BLUE
ZONE GREEN
ATLANTIC OCEAN
N
E
S
W

Prologue
How We Got Here

After the virus blanketed the earth, and war reduced cities to radioactive rubble, the few who survived did not shed a sigh of relief. The unthinkable hurdle of watching friends, family, and loved ones perish was only the beginning of the struggle to survive.

Some went underground, such as Brian Rhodes and Steven Driscoll, who found safety in a bunker. Brian's cousin and Steven's sister, Bethany, along with her friend, Carolanne, endured a similar circumstance, finding themselves underground for two years as the virus ran its course. Simon Kalispell and his dog, Winston, fled to the woods in British Columbia, where they were safe from the war and disease, and well away from loathsome travelers.

There were others who did not hide. There were some who embraced the ravages inflicted upon humankind. Karl Metzger was one such person. For him, survival meant not cowering underground or in the wilderness, but gathering his fellow men to follow under his lead, and take what was left of the world by force.

Each in their own way, these men and women continued to survive well past the war, disease, starvation, and murder.

As days turned to weeks, weeks into months, and months to years, colonies were constructed and people congregated, each with a mindset that their method of survival was advantageous. The town of Alice was founded, with their ally, Hightown, in the north. They constructed walls and maintained a vast garden and working reservoirs. A foe would find it difficult to march upon Alice's walls. But the cunning Karl Metzger infiltrated the town from within, corrupting their leader, Nicholas Byrnes, and killing Nick's father, Tom Byrnes.

Brian, Simon, Bethany, Carolanne, and of course, Winston managed to endure arduous treks across the desolate United States, and became citizens of Alice. Simon's journey allowed him to witness separate spiritual paths a person could take while navigating the bleak world. He experienced fear as he was shot at and his van stolen. He experienced the crushing depression of being forced to kill with his own hands when he shot and killed a young boy who was trying to rob him. And he experienced love and compassion when encountering a gathering of peaceful monks and a young boy whose eyes lit up when he saw Winston's tail wag in happiness.

Along Brian's journey, Steven was lost and presumed dead, killed in a fit of mental anguish by Brian's own hands. But Steven survived. With help from Karl Metzger, Steven's strength renewed, and he saw survival in a new light. He would fight. He would pillage. He would become a member of Karl's terrible army, the Red Hands.

All their fates intertwined on the battlefield of Alice. Steven died in Brian's arms. Karl was presumed dead, blown up in an explosion. Karl's lieutenants, Mark Rothstein and Sultan, were slain, and Priest Dietrich was taken captive, only to be later rescued. The Red Hands were vanquished from Alice, with the help of Hightown's mighty army. Simon's friend and roommate, Jeremy Winters, was celebrated for leading the charge to free the reservoir from the Red Hand's clutches, and clean water was again under their control. Jeremy's prowess on the battlefield and quick decision-making helped save countless lives and eradicate the vermin infesting Alice.

Simon fought and took down Nick Byrnes, but not before setting the bomb for Karl and his lieutenants in an underground room in Simon's childhood home. Despite the explosion and raging fire, Karl escaped as Alice fell, helped along by his old cell neighbor, Doctor Friedman. It was a long journey to reach what remained of his force in the northern docks, where they were partnered with a Russian counterpoint. A vast army and arsenal, including warships, were maintained by the Russians, and farther to the west lay Odyssey, still harboring a number of Red Hands. Along Karl's journey to the docks, Doctor Friedman could not control his ravenous desires, and Karl had no choice but to leave the man bound to a bed in an underground bunker, which the doctor had designed for torture, mutilation, and the consumption of his fellow man.

Karl escaped. Alone. And through force, he and his second in command, Liam Briggs, overtook the Russian officers and claimed the dockworkers army as their own, to mix with his battle-hardened Red Hands. A new and terrible war would be waged against Hightown, who had suffered great casualties, and believed Karl dead and his army destroyed.

But war doesn't end.

It changes, but it doesn't end.

Chapter One
After the War

In the morning hours following the battle, Brian arrived at Alice's Volunteer Fire Department along with Simon Kalispell and his own cousin—and Steven's sister—Bethany. The lawn was awash with stretchers.

"You see her?" Brian asked, shielding his eyes from the sun.

Nobody answered. They scanned the crowd, but there were hundreds of soldiers, and nearly the same number of medical personnel, swarming around in orderly confusion. Simon had his arm over Bethany's shoulder as all three looked for Carolanne.

The sidewalks in front of the fire department were lined with the less seriously wounded soldiers needing stiches or a finger reset. They sat and smoked. Some slept on the pavement; others held soiled bandages to wounds. Most exchanged curious glances at the large white tent constructed near the garage doors where the surgeons were performing the more serious operations.

"Come on," Brian said, and began hobbling across the lawn. He'd been given a crutch back at Nick Byrne's mansion, but it did little to quicken his pace.

Brian paused when he saw a medic he recognized from Hightown sorting through a box of supplies.

"Hey," he said, "you seen Carolanne?"

The medic didn't glance up. "Who?" he asked.

"My wife, Carolanne. Blondish hair. She's a nurse."

"Look around," the medic said. "How the fuck would I know where she is? You guys here to help or just get in the way?" With that, the medic left with his arms full of bandages.

They were close to the door of the firehouse when they heard her voice above the clamor.

"Brian! Bethany!" she yelled, and as they turned, she was already there, running into Brian's arms. "Oh my God—are you okay?" She stepped back, looking at his crutch, and then turned to Bethany, and they embraced. After a minute, Carolanne tore herself away. "Sit, let me check you guys out."

"We're okay," Brian said.

"Like hell you are." She began unbuttoning Brian's shirt. "Let me get some antiseptic."

"We've been tended to. Look." Brian displayed the slip-on brace over his knee. "What we need is someplace quiet."

"Come on," Carolanne said, and turned to the firehouse. They entered the side door and went up the flight of stairs and to the door to Nick Byrnes's previous office. It was only a night ago that Carolanne, Brian, Simon, and Frank Morrow—the head of the Rangers, prior to the battle—sat in that same room, waiting for the minutes to tick by so they could begin their assault on Nick's mansion. The room was still empty, except for the throw blankets they'd left on the ground and the stack of folding chairs along the side. Brian leaned his crutch against the wall and took a chair from the pile. Bethany and Simon got comfortable on the carpeted floor, with a blanket draped over their shoulders.

Carolanne latched on to Brian's side, her arms hugging around his neck, the top of her head against his cheek. *The beach,* Brian thought. *My God, how I love you …*

"I have to get back down there," she said.

"I know."

"I don't want to."

"They need you."

Carolanne loosened her grip and wiped the wetness from her face. She smiled at Brian and brushed away a tear rolling down his cheek. "You have no idea how worried I was."

"I know plenty."

Her bottom lip quivered, and she gave Brian another hug before pulling herself away. "I'll be back as soon as I can."

They kissed again, and she left and closed the door behind her. In her absence, the room fell into silence. The uproar from outside was muted to a murmur through the window. After a long pause, Simon said, "We did it. We're alive."

Brian nodded. "Fuckin-a," he said.

It was apparent by the quiet that followed that no one was inclined to further discuss the ordeal they had endured. Not now. Perhaps not ever.

Bethany stretched out on the ground, using a rolled-up blanket as a pillow. Simon lay beside her. "I don't think there's a chance in hell that I'll be able to fall asleep," he said, "but we should try. I haven't slept in … two days?" He scratched his matted hair.

"You go on," Brian said, sitting in the chair and staring at the door, his injured leg stretched out like a log. "I'm a'right."

"Brian," Bethany said. "Lie down." She patted the floor beside her. "Come on."

He nodded and stood, flinching as he put pressure on his bad knee. After a hobble, he sat down and then stretched out. Bethany tossed a woolen blanket over him and pulled it up to his chin. Goddamn, it felt good. So good that his body shook, trembled in the simple pleasure of comfort. He closed his eyes, and then, *flash*—there was Steven. "*It's okay, Brian, it's—it's okay …*" The pool of blood spread from his cousin's body and soaked into Brian's uniform, still staining it now, and dried under his fingernails. He'd watched Steven die twice now, once in the woods, many months ago, and again in the pre-dawn.

He wouldn't cry. He wouldn't allow himself to shed another tear over his cousin. The tears he'd shed earlier were for Carolanne. They were tears of love, not loss, and he couldn't, just couldn't let misery overtake him. He would tell Bethany everything that transpired in the burning library in Nick's mansion; but not now. She wasn't ready to hear more grief. Steven killed Mark Rothstein, and for that he would be considered a hero … but he had also joined the Red Hands. He had become a member of those murderous bastards who tried to burn Alice to the ground.

Steven was dead. The Steven he knew had died a long time ago. Perhaps it was Brian's fault, all of it. If he hadn't fled after they fought in the woods under the assumption that he'd just killed his best friend with a stone, then Steven wouldn't have been captured by Karl's men. Would any of this have happened? Would the Red Hands have found them?

Brian didn't sleep. He doubted that Simon or Bethany were sleeping either, but he didn't bother to find out. They were beside him on the ground, quiet as could be. Outside of his tortured thoughts, the room was pleasant. Warm. Subdued.

Maybe an hour passed when the door opened and Carolanne appeared. She paused and said, "Did I wake you?"

Brian shook his head. She was carrying a cloth sack. Simon and Bethany sat up, wrapping the blanket over their shoulders.

"Here," Carolanne said. "It's not much." She removed three MREs from the sack, three apples, and a loaf of half-risen bread that was made in haste to feed the influx of soldiers returning from battle. "We got the seriously wounded escorted to the hospital or taken back to Hightown. They're serving lunch here, from the firehouse."

They removed more folding chairs and sat around, tearing into the food. The bread was spongy, yet hearty, with freshly ground grain.

"This might just be the best damn meal I ever ate," Brian said. "No, the second best. The first was the soup you two fed me when I showed up at your bunker all that time ago. I'll never forget the flush of warmth from my stomach to my toes as I took that first sip."

Carolanne smiled and rested her head against his shoulder. "God, I'm so glad—"

"Hey," Simon said with his mouth full of bread. "What's going on out there?" He pointed out the rear-facing window.

Bethany craned her neck to see, and Carolanne helped Brian stand. The stage behind the firehouse, last used by Nick Byrnes and Karl Metzger to deliver their poisonous deliverances, was lined with soldiers. The podium was moved to the side.

"I heard General—your uncle Al—is giving a speech today," Carolanne said. "I thought it would be tonight, but maybe since most everyone's assembled for lunch, he's doing it now."

A soldier stood on the center of the stage, addressing the crowd. Whatever he was saying was lost to them.

"Should we go out there?" Carolanne asked.

"Probably," Brian said.

But nobody moved from the window.

A moment later, more soldiers walked on stage.

"Oh, Jesus," Simon said. The soldiers were forcing along five … no, six men, their hands tied before them, cloth bags over their heads. Some were limping, and all had red stains on their frayed uniforms. They were forced to kneel, and two toppled over before being brought back up again. One by one, the bags were torn off, displaying the battered faces of Red Hand officers. They paused before the last, the soldier addressing the audience. The condemned man's leg was fastened with a splint around his knee, and he was held by the shoulder to remain upright. Then his mask was torn away.

"Oh my God," Simon said, looking away. Carolanne opened the window to hear the pandemonium.

The battered and snarling face of Nick Byrnes looked over the crowd, his dark hair slick with blood and sweat, his eyes bruised to slits. A rock crashed into the stage floor beside him, and then another. The guards yelled at the crowd. Nick was struck once, twice; a third rock grazed his forehead.

"You fools!" Nick shouted. "You terrible fools! I have only *ever* had your best interests at heart! I was going to give you everything—all the power in the world! You think you're any different than me? You're nothing more than a pack of animals fighting for scraps! I gave you the world on a silver platter! The fact that none of you can comprehend—"

A guard stepped forward, grabbed the top of Nick's slick hair in his fist with one hand, and slid a blade across Nick's throat with the other.

No … Brian thought.

"Christ in heaven—*no*," Simon said, peering through cracks in his fingers.

Nick's eyes went large, his poisonous words taken from his mouth. He began to fall forward, but the guard reached out and yanked him back up to face the people he had betrayed. As the last flicker of life dimmed inside him, the guard pulled a dark brown Smith & Wesson revolver from his belt— Nick's own pistol with a deep groove cut into the handle from Simon's machete—and pointed it at the back of Nick's head. The gun recoiled as it shot, and Nick's body crashed face-first to the stage floor, where it bounced and then lay still.

Bethany turned away.

"Nothing changes," Simon said. "We're going to go on killing each other until there's nobody left to slaughter."

Brian wrapped his arm around Carolanne's shoulder. "Don't look."

But she looked. They all looked as the rest of the prisoners were executed before the roaring public, one after another, all with Nick's shiny brown pistol.

Chapter Two

Deer

Simon closed his eyes and inhaled, feeling the bottom of his lungs expand against his lower rib cage. He imagined the oxygen traveling through his lungs and into his bloodstream, pumping life into the far reaches of his organs: his brain, feet, even hair. He exhaled slowly.

Breathing in I know that I am breathing in. Breathing out I know that I am breathing out.

I am the wind. I am the rock. I am the tree, and my roots grow deep …

The mantra played over in his thoughts for several breaths until his awareness was reestablished. His fingers moved off his knees and touched the grass beneath him, feeling the dirt floor, centering himself in time and place.

Less than a yard away was the track. A depression in the soil no wider than an inch, with the same depth going down. Simon exhaled and moved to inspect the indentation once more. The soil was wet to the touch, but not so wet as to suggest the animal remained in the vicinity.

The shock he first felt when seeing the print still surged through him. As he'd neared the shallow line of impressions, his footing went off balance, and he stepped on a scattering of crisp leaves that should have been avoided. Before proceeding, he stopped, sat, and attempted to slow his racing heart.

A deer …

Half of Alice's revolving guards reported seeing movement of deer in the brush, but none of the reports ever turned up true. A Ranger would be sent to investigate only to find scattered tracks of rabbits, possums, or racoons. Deer had become so fabled that anything brown and blurred was recalled as being one. But all sightings were false. The small game would be stalked and killed nonetheless, and brought back to the town's kitchen.

Just an hour ago, a breathless Ranger came running up to Simon, still camouflaged with mud and charcoal, and exclaimed, "We got one. A real one." Simon was led to the edge of the woods to investigate alone.

Once readjusted, and feeling the print again with his mind cleared, Simon moved. Each slow step deliberate; touching down from the ball of his foot, to the outer arch, and then to his heel. He wore shoes made from single strips of leather to protect his skin, yet remain as quiet and soft-footed as possible. He scanned the horizon, taking stock of the entire distance through the wood line, looking for the slightest disturbance. A bent blade of grass indicated the direction of the animal, winding further into the woods toward the shade of large pine trees where the lawn was thick and dense.

The sun flickering through the overbrush indicated that the early morning had made way for noon as Simon crawled over rocks and around the bases of tall maples and oaks. Always, he kept the horizon in view.

Then he saw it by a small runoff creek from the reservoir. Its long neck craned down as its slender lips touched the water's surface. The animal lifted its head, looking off in the distance. It was alone. A solitary deer in a world that had become inhospitable to its existence. Its ear flickered; sunlight reflected off a trail of water on the animal's nose and mouth.

Simon felt the stock of his rifle, envisioned his cheek against the cool wood grain, his vision down the barrel. Where had this animal come from? Were there more? Did it have a mate? There were no additional tracks, but that didn't mean another wasn't around.

He breathed in and out, long and slow breaths.

***

It grew late into the afternoon when Simon returned to the waiting scouts. Ben stood upright as he approached. "Well?" he asked, handing over a canteen.

"Thanks," Simon said, unscrewing the cap. "It was a deer all right. Followed it to the creek north of here." He took a long sip, savoring the cool water as it coated his throat and filled his stomach.

"And?"

Simon shook his head. "The tracks vanished by the water."

Simon considered that Ben would know the soil near the creek was soft, and a deer's hooves would sink easily. "I followed the trail to a field a quarter mile past the creek," Simon added. "The ground was rocky. I lost the tracks."

Simon handed Ben his canteen, and the men walked to the north road, leading to Alice. Ben was an able hunter, but he appeared to believe the story, despite it seeming odd that the senior member of the Rangers, Simon Kalispell, had lost the trail of the most elusive and sought-after source of protein roaming the woods.

As they neared Alice's southern border, Ben called in their approach from his handheld radio. A few yards further, a guard waved them over. "So?" the guard asked.

"No luck," Simon said. "But there were tracks."

The guard's eyes shot large. "My God," he said. "They're back?"

"One's back. We'll have to wait to see if a herd is nearby."

The guard nodded. "Did you see it for sure?"

"No. But the guard that reported the sighting was right, and Ben here, who'd been first sent out to investigate, was correct. The tracks belong to a deer."

The guard smiled. The news would spread fast, and Simon would have to stifle the men's urges to hunt the animal. The deer was not a dragon of lore. It was not a fabled beast. Yet, he knew the hunters desired to claim the animal's death as their own achievement. What chance did an endangered species have against the violent aspirations of humankind?

More guards awaited Simon's report by the gate. None were saddened by the news of the deer's escape. Verification alone was enough to satisfy their craving, which was what Simon hoped. Some of the workers repairing the destroyed wall in the rear stopped to hear the story. "Tracks?" one said, wiping sweat from his forehead and leaving a greasy trail. "I'll be damned." The workers dispersed, talking amongst each other about the triumphant return of the deer.

Many of the men were from Hightown, helping Alice recover after the battle. Only a few weeks ago, this same line of trenches had been manned by Karl Metzger's vile soldiers. The people of Alice and Hightown were forced to destroy what was rightfully theirs—the guard towers, security gates, and walls—to eliminate the vermin infesting it.

The process of returning Alice to a formidable and defensive town was going well, although proper healing was still far off. The people were betrayed. Their own leader, Nicholas Byrnes, had deceived them into allowing Karl Metzger's Red Hands into Alice, to rot it from within. Both Nick and Karl were now dead. Simon himself was responsible for Karl's demise, tricking him into the basement of Simon's old house and blowing it to rubble. The fire that consumed the building left nothing more than ash. Sultan, his trusted officer, was also killed.

Ben took an offered cigarette from the guard in the trench and asked, "Any news on the election?"

The guard flashed a silver lighter. "Nothing yet. But you might want to head to town, results should be in any minute." He gave Simon a knowing smile. "You'll want to be there, I presume."

"Thanks," Simon said.

Ben accompanied Simon into town, then the men split up to clean themselves in their respective homes. Simon could hear the commotion in his apartment before he opened the door. The clacking of nails against the hardwood floor, a swinging tail banging into walls.

"Hey, buddy-buddy," he said to Winston as he stepped inside. His dog's tail swayed in wide arches and his tongue lapped at Simon's hand. Winston followed Simon to the bathroom, his rear torso limping along, and his nose pressed firmly into Simon's thighs, smelling the trees, dirt, and faint animal scents from Simon's foray.

Simon scratched at Winston's head as he washed the dirt and charcoal off his face and used a washcloth to scrub his chest and what he could reach of his back. He was careful not to splash any dirty water on Jeremy's and Bethany's toothbrushes. When he was reasonably clean, he dressed in a military jumpsuit and opened the front door for Winston to join him outside.

"C'mon, boy," he said, letting his dog hobble in front of him to sniff various patches of grass and greet the occasional resident.

Lunch was served from the buffet line in the garage of the firehouse, but few people were waiting with trays in hand. The gathered crowd seated or mingling on the lawn awaited news of the election to be delivered on the same stage where Nick Byrnes had been brutally executed.

Simon veered through the crowd, sidetracked by the many hands that wanted to pet at Winston's fur and tell him what a good dog he was.

"You're a good boy, aren't you?" a young soldier said, kneeling next to Winston and scratching behind his floppy ear. "He's such a good listener," the young man said to Simon. "My old dog, he'd never be able to stay off leash like Winston does. I'd of lost him by now in a crowd like this."

Simon wished he'd brought the leash; not out of fear of Winston getting lost or running away, but despite what the young soldier said, in Winston's older years he didn't always listen like he used to. The war had aged his dog, if that were at all possible. Winston had been taken from his apartment by the Red Hands and locked in a room in Nick Byrnes's mansion when the fighting broke out, where he'd endured the explosions and gunfire. When Simon found him, he was indeed the same dog; happy, smart, yet in the weeks following, Winston seemed to nap more frequently, and his energy level waned after shorter walks and hikes than he'd previously been accustomed to.

Probably has nothing to do with the war, Simon thought. Winston was an old dog, after all. His years would add up … eventually … Simon shook the thought out of his head.

"C'mon, boy, let's find Jeremy and Beth."

"Jeremy's near the stage." The soldier motioned with his chin. "Good luck, sir. You have my vote."

"Thanks," Simon said, feeling his cheeks redden at being called sir.

He gave a short whistle and Winston snapped his head around to face him. As he neared the front of the crowd, he could see Jeremy sitting at a picnic bench not far from the stage.

"Simon," Jeremy said, seeing him approach. "Got Winston there?" He smiled and let his hand get licked.

"He was locked in the house all day," Simon said. "He needs some air."

"Of course you do, don't ya, buddy?" Jeremy scratched all over Winston's head, making the dog's tail sway in a frenzy.

Simon looked around. "Beth here?"

"Haven't seen her."

Simon nodded. She was probably still working on the western wall. She'd recovered fast from her terrible ordeal: being taken prisoner, drugged and chained to a bed deep in the depth of Nick's mansion during the fighting.

She'd seen the Red Hand's method of interrogation firsthand. Made to watch the slow and methodical torture and dismemberment of her friend, Will Holbrook, and thinking it was her turn next on the surgical gurney. In the days following her release, once the strength returned to her body, she began laboring with the workers to repair the defenses. At night she would come home, blistered and worn thin, and sleep in the bed beside Simon. They would stay up late, holding each other tight, recounting the horrors they had endured, and then after a few hours of troubled sleep, she would be out the door, tools in hand.

"You ready for your official title?" Jeremy asked.

"I think the only reason anyone voted for me is because of Winston here. No one in Alice is more popular than him. He's probably the reason my name got added to the ballot in the first place."

Jeremy smiled. "Ha! Your name got added to the ballot because you were next in line after Frank Morrow. And you're going to win because of your abilities, not because of your dog." Jeremy looked down at Winston's alert eyes. "But you certainly help, don't ya, buddy? Plus, Simon, the people look up to you."

Simon shrugged.

"Don't be modest. It was you who led the battle on Nick's lawn. The people know that. They respect you. They saw you fighting alongside them— or, from what I've been told, way in front of them all, charging headfirst into bullet fire, as stupid as that is. You were put in charge of the Rangers after the battle for a reason. You're the best scout in Alice. Hell, you're the best scout I've ever met, and I've worked with hundreds of Navy Seals and special ops when I was deployed."

"Simon, Jeremy," a voice called out from behind them. Simon turned to see Brian cutting through the crowd.

"Hey, Brian. Carolanne with you?" Simon asked.

"Na, it's her shift at the infirmary."

Jeremy stood as Brian neared. His limp was minor, but he was still using the cane to get around. Winston ran up to greet him, his tongue bouncing out of the side of his mouth.

"Don't get up, I'm fine standing."

"I've got to stretch my legs anyway. I'll be making a speech, either to thank everyone for their vote or to accept resignation, and still thank the crowd for their support while I served as acting general."

Brian took Jeremy's offered seat. "You can go ahead and throw away that second speech. There ain't a chance of you losing."

Jeremy found his pack of cigarettes and offered them around. Brian accepted one and borrowed Jeremy's lighter. They were halfway through their cigarettes when three of Hightown's ranking officers walked onto the stage. The crowd near the front turned to watch as the podium was moved to the center, and Lieutenant General Casey Edmonds adjusted the microphone. He tapped a finger on the windscreen, making a muffled noise over the speakers. The din of conversation lessened, and the man before the microphone spoke.

"Hello," he said. "I'm sorry to keep you all waiting. General Driscoll apologizes for not being able to attend the ceremony, but he's needed in Hightown. He offers his blessings. Alice has and will continue to have the full support of Hightown so that both colonies continue to prosper."

Casey scanned the audience as he shifted the notes on the podium.

"Before we get to the election results, I want to remind everyone that the ceremony on the battlefield of the Dragoons will take place tomorrow evening at seven o'clock. All residents are welcome to attend."

"Long overdue," Jeremy whispered to Simon and Brian.

"Couldn't agree more," Simon said. Nick's mansion had stood as a derelict heap since the hours following the battle. A whole wing had burned to blackened beams during the fighting, and the rest of the home was near collapse. Following the battle, the casualties from Alice and Hightown were gathered and placed ceremoniously in the trench line before the mansion. Backhoes filled in the graves with soil, and bags of wildflower seeds sat ready on the sidelines to cover the soft earth. The corpses of the Red Hands and Dragoons, along with undetermined limbs and parts, were dumped in heaps inside Nick's mansion. Plans for the ceremony were to douse the structure with gasoline and set it ablaze. Once the timbers cooled and were bulldozed over, the seeds would be planted in lieu of tombstones.

"Without further ado," Casey announced over the speakers, "let's keep conversation to a minimum until all the results are given."

An officer beside him rifled through a stack of folders and handed a sheet to Casey. The lieutenant general glanced down and quickly spoke out the names of the newly appointed officials. Supply and management. Master gardener. The new head of urban planning, Ricardo Ruiz, had worked under Martin Howard on the previous administration and was an advocate of Martin's project for solar power.

"Rangers," Casey bellowed, looking down at the paper. "Simon Kalispell."

Brian reached out and patted Simon's shoulder. Simon could feel a thousand eyes staring into the back of his head, and he got the urge to be far away, out in the woods, alone, scouting for the deer.

Casey continued with the Guards, and then he said, "And that brings us to our final position. General in charge of Alice." He paused for dramatic effect. "I am happy to announce that the same man whom General Driscoll gave temporary power to after the war will continue to lead. Jeremy Winters, will you please join me on stage?"

The audience began to clap as Jeremy walked up the stairs leading to the stage. Once the applause died down, Jeremy reached in his pocket for a folded piece of paper and began smoothing it out on the podium. Near his feet was the deep red stain of blood, soaked into the dry wood platform, from where Nick and his officers were executed.

***

In the weeks it took for Alice to begin to heal with Hightown's help, many surviving Red Hands had fled and managed to escape the combined colonies' armed forces. Some perished in the woods, injured from the fighting, or lost, starved and dehydrated, without the aid of a map. But many had made it to safety far in the north, where a large force remained, veiled from the prying eyes of enemy scouts in an area known simply as the docks.

One such survivor had endured explosions, fires, bullets, and betrayal. He marched to the gates surrounding the docks in good health and appearance, bewildering the guards who had presumed him dead, and stood gawking in amazement as if the man were a mythical deity returned to life.

It did not take long for Karl Metzger to regain his control over his Red Hand army and add to their numbers the dock workers, who were eager to follow his command so they could reconquer the colonies of Hightown and Alice, to pillage, eat; survive. If not for Karl's reemergence, they would have starved under the prior command, withered to skin and bones. All cheered as the rightful king took his throne once more, and proclaimed to the crowd that their troubles were over. Full rations were to be issued at once, and soon, with Hightown and Alice under their control, there would be no need to fight further for food, water, and fuel. They would possess it all. The world would be theirs.

As Karl walked down the trident-shaped pier extending from the mainland, he cut through the cluster of soldiers examining their gear, counting munitions, and cleaning their weapons.

"You smell that?" he called to Liam walking beside him.

"Smell what, sir? The smoke?" Liam spat a trail of tobacco juice to the floor and pointed his chin toward a circle of men gathered around a small flame in a metal bucket where something long dead was cooking. "Want me to tell them to cut it out?"

"No, Mister Briggs." Karl raised his palms in the air, inviting the scents. "Fire. Grease. Sweat. Adrenaline. The filth of soldiers ready to fight." The odor of gasoline stung at his nostrils. "Victory. That's what it smells like." His memory brought back the marches his army had endured. The battles, the slain enemies, the dry desert wind coating his dangerous hoard in a fine gray dust.

Various military ships were anchored on either side of the two-lane dock, and at the end of the trident point, the largest warship of them all floated like an island city. The men onboard were busy readying the munitions in the missile chambers and testing the various electronics and navigational equipment.

Karl looked to his side, his face stern as a group of soldiers said, "Sir," as he passed. The gathering were shaving each other's heads into mohawks, cigarettes dangling from their lips. He turned to Liam. "They're ready," he said. "They're strong."

"Yes, sir," Liam responded. "Been doing drills since your first day back, and eat'n plenty."

"Hasten departure by four days."

"Sir?" Liam said. "You sure about that, sir?"

"Yes, Mister Briggs." Karl turned to his second in charge, his gaze scolding the man for questioning a command. "The men are ready. The longer we wait, the more anxious they will become; the greater the chance for second thoughts, cold feet. They're ripe for it now."

"Sir, I'm sure you're right …" Liam fidgeted with the buckle on his gun belt.

Karl sighed. "What is it, Liam? Spit it out."

"It's just that, well, you've had a rougher journey than most. And since you've been back, you've barely taken a moment to rest. Hell, you get more than an hour of sleep a night?"

"Yes, Mister Briggs, I certainly do."

Karl bumped into the back of a soldier on his path who was in the process of lighting a cigarette. The man turned with a scowl. "What the fu—" He saw Karl and Liam breeze past him. "Sir," the man said, his eyes snapping wide, standing straight and saluting.

Karl let out a laugh as they neared the massive wall that was the side of the warship. "I've never felt better in all of my life. That much, I can assure you."

Liam nodded.

"Give the order," Karl said. "Dole out the amphetamines. Let's get this show on the road."

"Yes, sir." Liam unclasped a handheld radio from his belt and began delivering commands over the crackling airwaves.

Chapter Three
Beaded Necklace

The crowd standing before the stage at Alice's firehouse was quiet as Jeremy cleared his throat and began his victory speech. He was no more than a few words in when a soldier came pushing through the crowd. "Simon," the man said in a whisper, his breathing labored. "Simon, sir."

Simon turned to the man, saw his weathered face and graying hair wet with perspiration.

"Yes?" Simon said.

"You're needed at the hospital."

A flash image of Bethany hurt stung him, and the same terrible feeling he'd endured during the battle pitted in his stomach. "What is it? Is everything okay?"

"Yes sir. It's, umm, a person, sir. Someone's here to see you."

Simon was about to ask Brian if he could watch Winston when Brian said, "Leave him here. I'll bring him to your place later," and patted Winston's back.

Simon thanked Brian, scratched his dog behind his ears, and followed the soldier through the crowd and out to the road, distancing themselves from Jeremy's boisterous speech from the loudspeakers. When it was quieter, Simon asked, "How did he get here?"

"He was found, sir. About a mile and half west."

"Is he all right? Is he injured?"

The soldier shrugged. "I dunno, sir. I was stationed in the hospital when he arrived. Looks skinny, malnourished. Dirty. He asked for you. Even out in the woods, he knew your name. You and Winston. Carolanne is with him now."

Simon nodded and picked up the pace. "Was he alone?"

"Came to the hospital alone."

The three blocks between the firehouse and the hospital were deserted, with everyone gathered before the stage. A half dozen injured, yet healing, soldiers stood before the sliding doors to the hospital, smoking cigarettes and scratching at bandages. The furniture from the lobby had been taken outside and heaped in a pile, replaced by occupied stretchers which now lined the entry room from one wall to the other. Simon was again taken aback at witnessing carnage on such a large scale, the little clinic of a hospital overflowing with the victims of warfare.

"This way," the soldier said, weaving through the stretchers to an open door in the rear. Simon followed, trying not to stare at the injured, but unable to resist. Their faces blackened with soot, their clothing charred and torn, the floor splattered with dried and fresh pools of blood. One soldier looked Simon right in the eyes. "Sir," the man said, lying on a gurney, half of his face bandaged up. "You did a hell of a thing back there at Nick's house."

Simon nodded and walked on.

The hallway was packed with more stretchers, and the medical staff were everywhere. They went further into the recesses, through a labyrinth of corridors, until they came to the door of an examination room. The soldier turned the handle, and there he was. The monk. The boy. Wrapped in a blanket and sitting on an examination table, with Carolanne standing before him.

The child's eyes went large. "Simon!" he shouted, and jumped down from the table. Carolanne moved to stop him, but then relented.

"What happened?" Simon asked, kneeling down and squeezing the young boy, feeling the tickle of his shaved head against his chin. The boy smelled ripe, unwashed for what might have been weeks. "Are you all right?"

The boy didn't answer. They stayed where they were, and it became apparent that the child was crying. His back heaved up and down, his frail rib cage rubbing against Simon's fingers. Simon looked at Carolanne. Her lips were pursed.

When the tears subsided, Simon again asked, "What happened?"

Carolanne stepped forward and touched Simon's shoulder. "He was just about to take a bath." Turning to the boy, she asked, "Would you like to do that now? The water is nice and warm."

The boy nodded and looked to the floor. Tears fell, the dirty water streaking down his cheeks. A nurse came and took the boy's hand. "Come with me, love."

"I'll be right here, waiting for you," Simon said. "Go on."

As the nurse and boy left the room, Carolanne spoke to Simon, "They found him alone. Thought he was a small animal at first, crouched by a stream."

"There were others with him. A group of monks. What happened to them?"

Carolanne shook her head. "They got to them."

"Who?"

"The Red Hands. Judging by his current state, it must have happened a while ago. He said they were camped in a clearing, when, from what he's saying, a whole army's worth of soldiers emerged from the brush. I'm guessing it was when the bulk of the Red Hands marched into Alice."

Simon instinctively felt in his pocket for the beaded necklace he still kept with him at all times, given to him by that same young boy.

"How'd he escape?"

"A woman in their group hid him under a blanket when the soldiers entered their camp. The boy couldn't see anything, but he heard their voices. Says he heard arguing, and then a scream. And then more and more screaming. Someone picked him up, blanket and all, and dropped him down an embankment. He fell out, tangled in the brush, and the woman stood at the top. She said, "Run," and he did.

"Were they all killed?" Nausea rose in his stomach.

"He has no idea." She paused. "However ..."

Simon looked to her.

"Those beads. The boy had a pair just like the ones you carry. And I've seen them before, just recently."

"Where?"

"An injured soldier I stitched up was playing with them, trying to keep his mind off the pain. I thought it was a rosary, so I asked him about it, trying to keep his thoughts away from the needle, and he said he found them in battle. Taken off one of the Red Hands."

"Christ," Simon said. "Is the boy injured?"

"All in all, he's healthy. He's dehydrated and near starved, but he's all right for what he's been through. He was drinking stream water, unfiltered, so we'll have to see if his stomach cramps up, but there's no indication of poisoning. I don't know what he was eating, or if he's eaten anything at all since his escape. He mentioned finding some cattails, but I don't how long ago he's eaten them."

They were quiet for a moment, and then Carolanne said, "I have to head back to the ward."

Simon nodded. "Of course."

As Carolanne left the examination room, Simon asked, "What are we going to do with him?"

She shrugged. "Put him in the orphanage with the other kids, I guess. I don't know. He asked for you, so maybe you should talk to him."

Simon nodded as Carolanne left. He sat in a chair on the opposite side of the room and thought in silence for a moment. Then he called to the soldier who was still in the hallway. "Hey, you mind doing me a big favor?"

"What's that, sir?"

"You think you could run back to the firehouse, or find someone available to go?"

"I'm on duty, sir, but I'll find someone. What do you need?"

"My dog."

Chapter Four
New Life

Brian stood at the edge of the paved lot as trucks from Hightown rumbled past the gates and parked on the trade grounds. Following the war, little changed in the way of commerce. Hightown still needed water and food, and Alice still needed fuel. Now more than ever. The cranes, backhoes, and power generators were working twenty-four hours a day. Rebuilding the defenses was a priority, and the machinery drank combustibles like hot desert sand evaporates dew.

"Brian," a soldier from Hightown said. "I hear the votes are official. Guess you'll be keeping your post."

"Reckon so. But the trade delegate wasn't cast to a vote. Jeremy asked me to fill the post on my uncle's—General Driscoll's—suggestion. I probably would have kept the job regardless of who's in charge."

"True enough. Ready to start pumping?"

Brian nodded, and the soldier went to the rear of the petroleum truck and began attaching the unload coupler and hose. He wiped his palms on the thighs of his uniform, where the grease buildup had turned the material black.

"Hey, Brian." He turned to the voice, and saw Bethany coming his way.

"Beth, there you are."

"Sorry, sorry. I know. I'm late."

"The trucks just got here. I was worried, is all."

Bethany pulled a cloth from her rear pocket and rubbed at her grimy fingers.

"Worried?" she said. Before Brian could respond, she continued, "Got a sheet?"

He passed her a clipboard with the trade ledgers. She adjusted the rifle sling over her shoulder and pulled the pen from the clip.

"You're doing a hell of a job," Brian said. "Just make sure you don't work yourself to death in the process."

"I don't aim to."

They walked to the back of the truck unloading fuel into underground vessels. Three of Alice's own liners were waiting to depart with Hightown's convoy once the fuel was deposited.

"How's Carolanne?"

"Busy," Brian said. "Always busy."

"Yeah. Who isn't? We've been working such opposite hours; I haven't seen her in days."

"Opposite? Seems like you're both working all hours. We need more nurses and medics. Sometimes she stays the night in the ward, catching a few hours of sleep on a cot when possible. She was hoping to see you at the ceremony at Nick's mansion."

"Yeah." Bethany paused after taking note of the gallon stoppage. "I didn't need to see that."

"Might have brought some closure."

"Closure?" She turned to face him, her cheeks flushing red.

"I'm sorry. I'm not trying to get you riled. I know …" He wasn't sure what to say. There was nothing to say. There was no way to understand the mental torment she'd endured in that basement. Carolanne, along with a doctor, inspected her for signs of rape while she'd been unconscious, and according to Carolanne, she had been spared that brutality, but it was difficult to be a hundred percent certain. The thought that those men—those filthy, vile men—might have touched her, this woman who was practically his sister, made his blood pump hot in his chest.

Bethany turned around and exhaled. "No, I'm sorry, Brian. Maybe watching the mansion burn to the ground would have brought some relief. I just … don't want to see any more destruction. I don't want to talk about it—not Nick, not Karl, not the Red Hands, the fighting, or even Tom Byrnes. It's all in the past. I want to move on."

"Moving on sounds about right." Brian wasn't so sure Bethany was ready to get over her ordeal. It seemed that whenever peace was at hand, a new wickedness emerged to further threaten their survival.

They went to inspect their own trucks, double-checking the water fill and the haul of produce going out. Luckily, the gardens had remained unharmed during the fighting. They were somewhat depleted, with the Red Hands devouring more than enough to feed five times their numbers, but the citizens in Alice were not in danger of starving. The livestock took the largest hit. Eggs were still coming in, but it would be a while before they could afford to slaughter an animal.

All at once, Bethany looked to Brian with a smile. "You heard Simon saw a deer, right?"

"Sure," Brian said, happy to see her face brighten. "Who hasn't?"

"They're coming back. I know it."

"Where there's one, there's bound to be more. It's a shame he lost its trail."

Bethany glanced at him knowingly. "He didn't *lose* its trail."

"No?"

"He followed it to the creek."

"Right. He told me as much."

"He could have killed it, right then and there."

"He let it go?"

Bethany nodded.

"I'll be damned. Why? A deer's the trophies of all trophies."

Bethany shook her head. "If you think Simon wants any sort of trophy, you don't know the man well enough."

Brian had followed Simon into battle on the front lawn of Nick's mansion. He'd seen the man fight in a manner he'd never seen before, and doubted he'd ever witness again. The way Simon flowed down the trenches, shooting, slicing, chopping with his machete, all the while shirtless, covered in the blood of his enemy. He was an animal, tapped into some wild part of his subconscious.

But after the fighting, once they got Bethany and Winston out of the mansion and found their way to the firehouse to recover, Simon doubled over in sickness. When the three of them found solitude in a room upstairs, as the sea of injured soldiers were tended to on the lawn, Simon wept. He and Bethany held each other tight, curled up on the carpeted floor with a blanket draped over them. It was evident that whatever he'd done—the bloodshed, the trickery he'd devised to kill Karl Metzger—was not part of who he was at his core. Simon was not a soldier. He was not a killer. He was a peaceful man who only accepted his rank as the leader of the Rangers because he genuinely believed that he could help others. He knew more about wilderness survival than anyone, and through his teachings, he imparted both knowledge and a form of awareness that bordered on meditation.

Brian returned to the conversation. "Still though, why would he let the deer go? We need as much meat as possible."

"He let it go because it was one solitary deer facing the flood of humankind. There isn't another soul alive that wouldn't have killed that animal. But until there's enough to shift the population balance, Simon won't kill it." She paused, and Brian glanced over to see Bethany smile. "It's decisions like this, to not kill when given the opportunity, that make Simon a leader."

"I agree." It warmed Brian's heart to see his cousin happy.

"Where is he now, you seen him today? I left home early."

"He's at the graves. They're planting the wildflower seeds."

Bethany nodded. "That's right."

"You going to help?"

"I got to get back to the line after the transports leave. We were raising a beam for a watchtower when I left. We want to get two more set in concrete before evening. You?"

"I'll be heading to scatter the seeds."

"Tell Simon I'll see him at dinner."

"Will do."

The hoses on the fuel trucks were disconnected and the ports resealed. The engines of the convoy came to life, and the procession left the gates. Brian said goodbye to Bethany and left to find Simon among the workers spreading seeds of new life. He smiled, thinking about Bethany's cheerfulness, completely unaware that far out over the bounding swells of the ocean, a darkness was approaching with the ambition to eradicate everything the people in Alice held dear, and trample the seeds before the sprouts had the opportunity to taste the sun's rays for the very first time.

Chapter Five
Ante Bellum

Simon held a bag of seed in one hand and scattered the tiny grains with his other. He stood up straight and stretched his back, looking over the two dozen or more people out there in the field along with him, spaced out so that most were alone or talking in small groups, and seeming to enjoy the easy work and the sun on their faces. Winston was a few yards away, getting his head scratched by a smiling worker. Compared to fixing the trenches and reconstructing the guard towers, this task of spreading seeds was welcoming.

Simon didn't know many of them, since about half belonged to Hightown's colony. Despite them living together in Alice since the war, he still hadn't met all of the soldiers. Following the battle, a large force of Hightown's military stayed behind, helping repair the front line and sending out expeditionary patrols to capture any escaped Red Hands. The town of Masterson was discovered, where a large enemy regiment remained. The patrol fell back, and a full-on assault rumbled into the town, tanks, artillery, and ground troops. However, the enemy had disappeared before their arrival, and little was left behind to suggest the town was ever inhabited. Scouts were sent to follow their trail.

Now weeks later, and a branch of Hightown's armored wing remained in Alice. Their soldiers mixed in with Alice's citizenry on the lawn of Nick Byrnes' mansion, helping spread the wildflower seeds. Simon looked up to see Brian's slow approach over the soft field. His knee appeared to be acting up, making him stop and lean into his cane every few minutes.

When Brian was close, Simon said, "Why don't you go get some rest?" He reached into the burlap bag for more seeds. The tiny grains felt nice in his hand, a living thing not yet come to be.

"Nah," Brian said. "I've spent enough time in bed or on the couch the last few weeks. I need some air. The ground here is bumpy is all. I'm a'right."

Simon shrugged. "Suit yourself."

Off in the distance, Winston left the worker and had his nose pressed deep in the soil. Simon looked up to see him digging. Dozens of bodies were underfoot, in no logical order, and the ground was soft, freshly turned over. It was impossible to decipher where a corpse may be.

"Winston!" Simon whistled loud and his dog's ears perked up. He whistled again, and Winston came trotting over, his tongue bouncing out of the side of his mouth. "Come on, boy. No digging." He scratched at the dark spot of fur on Winston's head, and then said to Brian, "I should have left him at home with Bethany."

"He needs fresh air too. And Beth's working on the front line, helping raise a guard tower."

Simon didn't answer to that. He let the tiny seeds drift from between his fingers, scattering with the breeze. The radio attached to his belt made a muffled noise, and then a voice spoke. *"Simon, come in. Over."*

Simon unclasped the radio. "This is Simon. Over."

"You're needed in North Ward Five. Over."

Simon looked at Brian, and before he could say anything, Brian laughed and said, "I'll look after Winston. Go on."

"Thanks." Simon scratched Winston's head and reached down for his rifle, which was leaning beside a gardening rake. As he walked off the lawn, he turned to see Winston lapping at Brian's hand as his head was ruffled, his tail in a frenzy.

He still has so much life in him.

Simon left the lawn quickly, then took up a jog down the street toward the northern section of town. The air expanding his lungs felt good. North Ward Five was a checkpoint close to the trade grounds, just slightly above it.

Two other Rangers were waiting along with the guards near the checkpoint. "Simon, sir!" one called out. No matter how many times Simon was called sir, he couldn't get used to it. He was the logical next in command after so many of the other Rangers had died in combat. Especially with many of the residents looking at him as if he were supernatural after the battle on Nick's front lawn. There was so much death that day … Simon had killed so many … and he barely remembered doing it. The night was like a dream. He fought in the trenches like an animal, his body moving and slicing the machete of its own accord. At night, when the nightmares came, it was like watching a horror movie.

"Jack," Simon said, reaching the scouts. "What's going on?"

Jack shook his head. "I don't know, sir. I think it's best you see for yourself. I'll explain on the way."

A jeep was waiting outside of the gates, and Simon sat in the passenger seat as Jack took the wheel and turned onto the pavement.

"There were three of them, sir. Just came wandering out of the brush. It's—it's a sight."

"What is?"

"Our hunters were near Partridge Lake, and they saw the first of 'em. The guy came stumbling out of the brush, his wrists tied before him."

"Who is he?" *Jesus Christ, I hope it's not one of my Rangers, sent on my orders …*

Jack swallowed visibly. "A scout from Hightown. It's his eyes, sir. He doesn't have any. Eyes, ears, tongue, nose … they've been cut away. He's near dead, starved and dehydrated."

"Dear God … there are more?"

"Three, including the one scout. But he's the only one still alive. The hunters called in a medic and reinforcements—"

"Why wasn't I notified immediately?"

"I don't know, sir. This all just happened. I don't think the hunters knew what they were coming upon, or what was happening."

"Okay, go on."

"They found the second man dead in the woods about a half mile away, swarmed with flies. His face cut up the same. The third man was nearby, sitting against a tree. He was unconscious, but alive. When the medics came and started removing his binds, cutting away his clothing, there was a gash on his side, stitched up, and a bulge. Then all at once, the guy fucking blew up."

"*What?*" Simon's eyes shot large.

"Two medics died."

"Holy shit. What about the other two?"

"The same. Both the one alive and the one dead, they got big bulges in their sides. The medics aren't touching them until a bomb unit arrives. They've been called in, and should be there before us."

"Does the general know?"

Yes, sir."

Jack turned onto a gravel road, the bumps and potholes in bad shape.

"Any idea who the men are?"

Not the one who blew up, or the other who's dead. It's hard to tell … you know, with their faces how they are. But one of the hunters says he might recognize the one alive. A scout from Hightown, a mapmaker of some sort. Don't know his name."

Jack turned again down another gravel road, the woods growing thicker on either side. Three jeeps were parked ahead. Jack maneuvered behind them, and a soldier walked over.

"Simon," the soldier said. "The bomb squad is there now."

"Is he still alive?"

"Unconscious, I think." The man pointed into the woods, where a dozen armed men stood about. "Just up there. Stay behind those trees."

Simon stepped to the broad side of a maple, and the soldier passed him binoculars. Through the circular peripherals, a man sat with his back against a tree, his hands on his lap. Two men in full protective gear stood before him. The man's face was red with blood, and black with grime. It was difficult to see the extent of his injuries from their distance, yet the dark voids where his eyes and nose should have been were unmistakable.

"One more thing, sir," the soldier said. "His chest is all cut up. Looks like someone tried to write something on him with a knife."

Simon looked away from the scene.

"Here." The man passed Simon a slip of paper. "Whatever it means, it's beyond me."

Simon studied the words. *Ante Bellum.*

All at once, his radio, along with everyone else's radio, issued a high-pitched alarm. Simon grabbed it from his belt. *"All forces return to Alice. Hightown is reporting an attack. I repeat, all forces return to Alice."* The alarm repeated.

Simon turned to the car and ran to the passenger door. Jack started the ignition and turned in the road.

"Take us straight to the general," Simon said.

The window was rolled down, and the warm breeze played over his skin.

Please, Simon thought, feeling as if he couldn't breathe, *let this be a false alarm …*

He thought of Brian, injured from fighting. Of Bethany, whose nightmares rivaled his own, and of Carolanne, Brian's wife, who had sewed and patched up hundreds of wounds. He thought of Winston, who now was so old that it took him a pause to sit and stand, yet still had so much youthful eagerness to smell and experience new things. He thought about Tom Byrnes, and the hundreds of people he called friends who were brutally slaughtered during the battle for Alice. All for nothing. He himself had killed dozens, and he would never be at peace with that. Then there was the monk boy, who was so broken by all he had witnessed that it took several hours for Simon to get him to tell them his real name, Connor.

We can't take any more … No more fighting, please, for all that is holy …

But deep down, Simon knew that something terrible was on the horizon.

Chapter Six
Futile Gestures

A coughing fit woke lead engineer John Zur from unconsciousness. A foggy wave of uncertainty rolled over his mind as a thick blanket of dark smoke engulfed his body and shot upward. His eyes teared a steady stream, and he blinked over and over, trying to keep them open long enough to see where he was and what had happened.

He remembered an explosion from outside the mobile command truck. A terrible blast from the artillery yard, followed by others in fast succession. At first, he thought it was the cracking of the cannons unleashing at the approaching vessel in the bay, but Sergeant Turner, the battery commander, had not given the order to fire live rounds. Before John could radio a query, his world turned black. Like a train ramming into the side of the command center, the rectangular structure was ripped in half, and his little corner was sent twisting to its side.

He turned onto his stomach to shield his face from the overwhelming flood of smoke and crawled upward, toward the hazy rectangle of blue sky. Still unsure if he was injured, and on the verge of fainting from lack of oxygen, he clambered over broken computer monitors, shards of glass, and an unrecognizable plethora of burning debris. The heat inside that small piece of trailer was like a vortex oven. Something sharp dug into his chest and snagged his uniform. Still, he pulled himself forward.

He was close to the jagged, torn-open end, his eyes engulfing the outline of the outside world, when hands were on him. He was pulled outside fast, and he collapsed on his back, inhaling fresh air, wheezing and coughing. Each breath felt like daggers poking at his lungs. Hands dragged him farther from the wreckage, and then left him to lie on his back. Through the succession of coughing, he became aware that the soldier kneeling over him was speaking.

"John! John! Mister Zur, sir!" The soldier splashed water from a canteen over a cloth and wiped at John's eyes and mouth, and put the nozzle up to his lips. John sipped and spat out the water, then drank a mouthful. "Are you okay, sir?"

His vision cleared to see the carnage around him. The artillery yard was on fire. Pockets of twisted metal burned in blackened craters. A swarm of soldiers and medics were tending to dozens of men on the ground. Somewhere in the distance, beyond the roaring clamber, was the undeniable popping of gunfire. John pushed himself up on his elbows. "What-what the fuck happened?"

"Sir, I don't know," the soldier said. "I was on my way to the bayfront when all of a sudden there were explosions in the artillery yard. I ran over and saw you coming out of what's left of the command center."

The soldier had unbuttoned John's shirt, which was torn and red. Beside him, lying in the grass, was a portion of someone's arm ending before the elbow, with three fingers intact. He lay back down and allowed the soldier to check his wounds as he attempted to rationalize his thoughts.

What was the last thing he'd heard over the radio? It was his job, along with two other men who'd been in the mobile command unit, to relay information from central command to various points along the line, as well as the artillery.

"We're under attack," he told the soldier.

The young man nodded. That much was apparent. "Who's attacking us, sir?"

"I have no idea." His chest stung as the soldier washed a fluid over it and wiped his skin with a cloth, again and again. John craned his neck to see his injury. "How bad is it?"

"You'll be fine. Big scratches and bruises."

It felt like he'd broken a rib. The radio on the soldier's belt was abuzz with clatter. "What are they saying?"

The soldier placed a long bandage over John's chest and began tearing strips of medical tape. He paused to pull the corded microphone to his ear.

"All men to their posts," he said, and then, "Units Charlie and Delta to the bayfront."

John began buttoning what remained of his tattered shirt back up. "I have to get to command," he said.

The soldier didn't protest. He helped him to his feet, then said, "The boat … there's more of them. Dozens of small craft reported. They're landing."

A dart of terror struck at his heart. "Who?"

The soldier held the radio to his ear, shook his head uncertainly.

"Give me your radio," John said, and reached to grab it. He switched the channel. "Command, come in," he said. "This is John Zur, post two. Over."

Voices continued giving orders, then one said, *"Zur, report to HQ, immediately. Over."*

John gave the radio back to the soldier and turned to leave without saying another word. He ran up and over craters where explosions had left deep scars in the field, and past injured men wailing as medics swarmed around.

He was just past the yard when pain in his legs became apparent, and his lungs felt like they were on fire. The wound on his chest pulled with each step, but still he continued. A platoon of near fifty soldiers came running from around a corner toward the bayfront, nudging John to the side of the road.

Jesus, he thought. *What the hell is going on?* A few years ago, in what might have been another lifetime, John worked in telecommunications. He was one of the few members of Hightown without a military past. He was a technician and engineer. He knew how to make electronics work. He knew how to make radios give and receive messages. How to make computers relay information. Using a gun was a skill he'd only recently become acquainted with.

A dozen armed men stood before the door to headquarters, in the center of town. John reached them, holding the bandage on his chest, barely able to speak with his lungs on fire. The soldiers recognized him, and two ran to meet him as he approached. "Sir," one said. "Are you okay, sir?"

"Where's the general?"

"Inside, sir."

They held the door to the warehouse-turned-office open, and John entered into a sea of officials. Dozens of men before a row of computer monitors, shouting orders into microphones, hunched over tables, pointing at maps and charts.

He pushed around them, toward the executive offices.

"John!" a voice shouted.

He turned to see Lieutenant Turner walking hurriedly toward him, his usual grim demeanor darker.

"Lieutenant," John said. "What's going on? Where's the general?"

"What happened to you?" Lieutenant Turner said, looking at John's torn and soot-covered uniform. "What happened to command two?"

"It's gone." John shook his head. "The whole yard, all of the artillery. It all blew up."

"Come with me," he said, and turned toward the offices. He entered a door and John followed. Inside the quiet room, he said, "They've landed." His composure wavered through a crack in his voice. "Hundreds, maybe thousands."

"Jesus Christ—*who*?"

"We don't know. We sent two detachments to the bay, but with our armored wing still in Alice, they've managed to climb the embankment. General Driscoll just ordered initiative *Dire Straits*."

John felt his knees get weak. If this were true, then whoever was attacking was gaining ground, fast, and Hightown was in desperate trouble.

"You're going, now, John." Lieutenant Turner reached out and gripped John's shoulder. "You're carrying the torch. Report to the western gate."

"Where am I going?"

"You're on the Texas convoy."

"The Lone Stars? We'll never convince them. Albuquerque, maybe, but Texas—"

"Look, I know." The middle-aged lieutenant squeezed John's shoulder. There was empathy in his eyes, deep under his somber gaze. John knew the man had lost four children and his wife to the disease, and there was no coming back from a loss like that. "We don't have the luxury of time to debate this," he continued. "You're going to have to try. Those good ole boys in Texas are clinging to their fierce individualism like it's a birthright, but we've all signed a pact. Whether they want to acknowledge their responsibility to that agreement is yet to be seen."

"The pact was all but voided when no one responded to Albuquerque's call. Not even us."

"That was different. We couldn't help back then. Alice was still in its infancy, and it was difficult enough to keep them up and running, even with our support. John, this is an order from the general himself."

John nodded. He was frightened. Terrified. He was leaving Hightown. He was leaving safety, security, to journey for days to some distant settlement of people he'd never seen. "I understand," he said. "I'll go now to the gate."

"Godspeed," the lieutenant said.

"And you, sir?"

"I'll leave with the last of them."

John shook the man's hand, and turned to the door.

***

Hightown's western gate opened, and a flood of vehicles and men on foot raced out. The caravans were preloaded and ready for the journey, each set to snake the land in opposite directions; south, north, and west. The bulk of the army was ordered to fall back to Alice, where they would regroup, man the line, and await further instructions for a counteroffensive.

General Driscoll remained behind along with five officers and what remained of company Charlie, Delta, and Omega. They would pull out once the invaders neared the headquarters and the rest of his men had run to the woods for safety.

John Zur sat in the back seat of a Hummer, a medic re-examining the wound on his chest. He found a change of uniform from one of the boxes of supplies in the rear of the truck and held the crisp, new shirt in his hand, waiting for the medic to finish. He looked out the rear window at the line of trucks following behind. In the southwest, he would face his greatest trial yet; convincing the people of Texas, the Lone Star colony, to journey to the East Coast in defense of the federation. He had many miles to cover, and more than enough time to contemplate just how futile the task would be.

Chapter Seven
Burning Reeds

Smoke rose from the steep northern embankment and drifted in light swells until they dissipated into nothing more than a floating dance of cinders. The shore was awash with corpses, bobbing with the rhythmic pulling of the sea. Farther south, the sounds of war prevailed in contrast to the light lapping tide.

In a shallow depression, lost among the thicket of towering reeds blanketing the steep hill, a young soldier named Luis sat with his knees tucked tight to his chest. The view of the bay was magnificent from his perch. The warship he had departed from earlier was anchored still and silent like a solitary island. At the shoreline, the swell of landing vessels drifted driverless and heedlessly among the dead and dismembered. A memory came to Luis as he meditated upon the calm yet ghastly scene, one that brought a bit of warmth to his inner pit of cold despair. His mother, oh so many years ago, sitting before her easel … the hardwood floor speckled with the many layers of paint that composed her dozens of paintings, closely resembling a piece of artwork itself, akin to something Jackson Pollock might create. His mother turned to him, a child awoken in the night, and smiled. "What are you doing out of bed?" she asked, and brushed a loose strand of hair out of her face, leaving a smear of crimson red on her forehead. That paint, that shade, was identical to the battered shoreline where the bodies piled and the landing ships drifted.

The popping of distant gunfire slowed. His perch had shielded him from the onslaught of bullets that had rained down from Hightown's soldiers, causing the reeds to ripple like a raging sea. Luis had scaled the hill among his brotherhood, those of the Red Hands. He'd been a dockworker before Karl Metzger took charge and integrated the men into one solitary force. They belonged to those who would survive the days to come, to flourish, to eat and drink, and abolish those who stood in their way.

Karl had told them, had bellowed out over the loudspeakers while standing before the podium on the docks, that these people of Hightown and Alice had secured enough water, fuel, and food to feed ten times their own number. But would they share with their fellow man to see humanity spread? No. They would not allow any more into their fold. So men like themselves, those who had survived the epidemic and war, were now left in a depleted world without the aid of their fellow man. The Red Hands would not allow that to happen. Under Karl's rule, they would take what they needed to ensure their own survival, and the continuation of humankind in the coming decades. The army was promised, as they were gathered together on the docks listening to the tall and grave man deliver his sermon, that following the battle, those left alive from Hightown and Alice's population would be allowed to join in the brotherhood if they were no longer deemed a threat.

Under Karl's leadership, humanity would endure, and the compensation would be great. Already, the stores of food had been opened, and more was delivered from his neighboring colonies, one named Odyssey in the south, and finally, after weeks of eating nothing more than a few bites of boiled rice crawling with maggots and bread so old the threat of ergot poisoning was a real and normal experience, they were issued warm rations. Sealed MREs— seasoned beef, spicy chili, crispy crackers. Fresh stew, thick with vegetables and unidentifiable chunks of meat, ladled from vast cauldrons. Strength returned. A clear mind followed. Karl's words rang true, and the idea of following him into battle, to ensure that life would continue to be so sweet, never sounded more palatable. The people of Hightown and Alice, hoarding their resources so that only a select few could thrive in the years to come, had to be eliminated to ensure mankind's continued survival. Keeping others away, scratching at the thick walls while starving to skin and bones, was not only cruel, it was inhumane on the scale of mass genocide.

The exhilaration of warfare was captivating as Luis first stormed the hill. Then the bullets rained down and explosions plumed in the air like fiery pillars from hell. It was an explosion that rocketed him on his side, a blanket of dirt shrouding his body, grinding between his teeth, suffocating his nostrils, blurring his vision. The army advanced, but Luis did not. He could not. He was stuck to the earth as if glued, bullets striking the ground around him, wavering the reeds, further cementing him down like a crouched stone, overwhelming his mind and perception with terrible things. He stared at the shade of red on the shoreline, time lost from his awareness.

Now silence prevailed. At first, once the battle moved from the hilltop and farther into town, a blanket of serenity enveloped him. But now, the silence of the dead was causing a clamor. He stood on shaky legs and turned upward, pulling on rocks. Large portions of the dry reeds burned, and the fire was fast spreading. He scrambled for the top, out of breath, his hands and fingers torn and bleeding. Bodies scattered the ridge and settled in piles.

"Hhh-eey …" a voice croaked. Luis recoiled and aimed his rifle at the noise. A body lay covered in ash and charred from feet to torso. The eyes strained to open and lolled about behind blackened lids. "Hh-h-elllp."

Luis turned and ran, jumping over blown-about debris and avoiding flaming sections of homes that lined the top of the hill overlooking the bay. He continued toward the sporadic sound of gunfire. When he arrived near the front gates, he could hear the rancor of his brotherhood. Happy voices. Celebratory tones. A layer of anxiety peeled back from his heart. He passed the medics tending to men on the ground and moving the wounded in something of an orderly procession. Some soldiers sat solemn and smoked cigarettes with trembling fingers. Others uncapped bottles of liquor and took long swigs. A tall man whose uniform was torn and sullied came charging out the door of a small home, pulling behind him one of Hightown's soldiers by his hair. The tall man's eyes were lost in madness and narcotics, and he tossed the soldier as if he were a toy down onto the dust. Luis moved on, and went around a bend to come into a clearing. Hightown's massive wall stretched in the opposite distance, and among the top were members of his brotherhood, hollering as if they'd scaled a mountain. Some were shooting precise shots at fleeing soldiers; others were lighting cigarettes and cigars.

A gathering of enemy combatants stood against the base of the wall with their hands tied behind their backs. They were bloodied and beaten, their heads looking down in despair as they were made to kneel, and more were being roughly added to their numbers. Their pockets were searched, their identities discovered. The more desirable and high-ranking officials were pulled out of the assemblage and brought out of sight. The other less worthy were systematically led to the side of an adjacent home and made to stand in front of a firing squad.

General Karl Metzger was there, watching the execution, Liam Briggs at his side, shouting orders to the officers. "C company, report! Man the walls!" Another stood among them. Tall and lean, filthy, with a full head of gray hair.

Luis remained motionless, catching his breath, when Liam turned to him and they made eye contact across the short expanse.

"You there," he shouted. "What the fuck is wrong with you?"

"N-nothing, sir."

"You look like the ass side of a dying dog."

Karl produced cigars, sharing them among the officers as he watched the line of prisoners grow. "No more live ammunition," he instructed. "Save the bullets. Find easier implements."

"Yes, sir," an officer replied.

Liam took a swig from a bottle, then turned back to Luis and walked his way. "Here," he said. "Have a drink. Try to fucking smile—this is a victory, after all. Then get yer ass moving, man the line."

"Y-yes, sir." Luis took the bottle and drained back a gulp. The liquor stung hot in this throat. He coughed and felt his stomach twist. He doubled over, turning away from the officers, and stumbled. Behind him, he could hear first Liam and then the other officers laugh.

"Give him a minute," Karl's deep voice bellowed. "If he's not right by evening, add him to the line."

Chapter Eight
Movement in the North

The first of Hightown's fleeing soldiers entered Alice; a dozen at first, and then a steady column of trucks and transports rumbled into the trade grounds.

"They came from the water," a soldier with a bloody cloth tied around his forehead told a guard. "A warship steered into the bay. You got a smoke?"

The guard gave the soldier a cigarette, and the man proceeded into town. The gymnasium in Alice Elementary School was lined with cots to hold the overflow of troops, and the officers met in a classroom turned office. Simon sat next to Jeremy at the round table, looking over the photocopied map of Hightown and ledgers with estimated numbers of troops and statistics.

"Any word from General Driscoll?" Jeremy asked the table.

"He was adamant about staying until the last minute," a lieutenant in a clean-pressed uniform with short-cropped hair responded.

"Are you sure it was them?"

The officer rested his elbows on the table and clasped his hands together, displaying a hulking ring from some branch of the military. "They have red handprints on their chests. Saw it myself."

"Jesus … where the hell did they get a working ship? And how do they have so many numbers? These guys just keep coming. Who's leading them?"

"We don't know." The officer sighed and rubbed the bridge of his nose. "They must have known the layout of Hightown; they were strategic with their areas of attack. Our artillery was hit before they advanced. Our forward observation post, out on a jetty of land overlooking the ocean, never reported the ship and didn't respond to radio communications. They must have been dealt with before the invasion."

The table was silent, each member observing the papers before them. "We need to muster the men and attack at once," the officer continued.

Lieutenant General Casey Edmunds placed the papers on the table. "We wait for General Driscoll," he said.

"There's been no word from the general. The longer we wait, the more prepared they'll be for a counteroffensive."

"As able as they were for the initial attack, I expect they're anticipating us to strike. Hightown's defenses were left intact; we would have a tough time breaking the line."

The lieutenant picked up the papers and pointed to a line of numbers. "Between our armament left behind and the vehicles that have escaped, we maintain three-fourths of our armored division. The general might be captured, or worse. If we—"

"Which would make me acting general in his absence." Casey paused, making eye contact with the lieutenant, then continued, "We don't know the munitions carried in their vessel, but by all indication, they have an abundance of artillery. If we attack head-on, their missiles could wipe us out a half mile from the front line. We need to wait on word from General Driscoll, and from the other settlements."

The officer nodded. Casey was Hightown's senior officer, and his decision was the final say.

"And if there is no word," Jeremy said, "a plan will be needed. We cannot let those monsters remain in Hightown. We have to reach out to the fuel convoy before the next shipment, and have them veer course to Alice. If the ship reaches Hightown, it could have catastrophic consequences. They could renegotiate the pact. They could steal our supply. They already have a huge surplus of fuel from Hightown's storage tanks, enough to outlast our own. We have to attack before the shipment arrives."

"This is true," Casey said. "We can't let the Red Hands learn of the other settlements, negotiate, and establish their own lifeline for fuel. If no word comes from the other settlements before the next convoy is expected, we will invade."

"So," the officer said, rubbing his ring with the thumb of his opposite hand. "We need to come up with a logical plan of attack."

"Agreed," Jeremy said. "We need to be precise. Simon," he said, turning to his side. "What are your thoughts on scouting their line? Do you think we could sneak some scouts past the wall, into Hightown?"

The weight of a dozen eyes burned on Simon. He swallowed. "I, um ..." He cleared his throat. "It's, ah, possible." He breathed in and out, attempting to clear his thoughts. "They'll be on high alert," he said, "which goes without saying. I have confidence in our scouts' abilities, but we lost a lot of qualified Rangers in the battle."

"So, what are you saying?" Casey cut in.

The man's direct nature brought back a degree of uncertainty, but Simon focused on what he knew of the men he was responsible for. "We could scout the line, check for any of their forwarding patrols, but as far as getting in ... that's uncertain."

I'm sending more men to their graves, Simon thought. *By my own hands or by my orders, more will die because of me. My friends. My Rangers. Trying to save lives, save the people of Alice and Hightown, spells death for those I order to defend us ...*

The battle on Nick's lawn had changed Simon in ways he was still trying to understand. Before the fighting, Simon had taken a personal oath to never kill a human. Not again. Not after the boy ... the gas station from another lifetime. The events were becoming a distant memory, yet certain frames still burned bright in his thoughts. He saw himself kneeling beside the manhole to the gas tank below ground ... The boy appeared before him, rifle in hand. Rifle so large the boy's small hands had trouble holding it steady, his fingers barely reaching the trigger. Then the gun fired, either by accident or not, and the shot went wild. Simon grabbed his rifle and fired as the boy chambered another round. A freeze-frame image of the child suspended in air, a puff of red and shirt fabric before him, brought terrible pangs of guilt. After all of the deaths he was responsible for, the dozens he'd slaughtered with his own hands in the trenches before Nick's home, it was the boy that brought him the most remorse.

But now Simon was responsible for the lives of others. His decisions had consequences for the men ordered to obey his command. *They're soldiers,* he reminded himself. Tried to rationalize. *They fight. They kill and die ... they know this.*

"I might be able to get behind their line," he said. "But it won't be easy."

Ever since the night of the battle, when his mindset switched from a focused intent into something almost animalistic, he was having difficulty remaining in the attentive state needed to scout for long durations. Images of the gore he was responsible for popped into his thoughts like appalling bubbles.

He continued, "We need to learn their patterns and numbers—"

The door opened and a young female soldier with her hair tied back in a tight bun said a collective, "Sir. There's movement to the north."

There was a pause, and then all the officers stood at once. The soldier walked through the throng of officials, straight to Jeremy, and spoke to him softly. Jeremy's gaze remained unflinching as she gave her report, and then he said, "Jesus Christ. Simon, come with me."

Jeremy walked fast out of the office, nudging around the officers, with Simon and several officials in tow. From behind, Jeremy's movements suggested that he found a pack of cigarettes in his front pocket, pulled one out with his teeth, and snapped his lighter open. A waft of smoke followed as he said, "I don't even know how to explain this." A guard ahead opened the doors leading outside, and a shaft of blinding sunlight stung their eyes.

Chapter Nine
The Truck

Brian and Bethany were in the trade grounds, awaiting word on the truck spotted due north of the gates.

"It's from Hightown, right?" Bethany asked. "I mean, it has to be."

"I would think so," Brian answered.

Bethany paced on the blacktop, rubbing her hands together. "Why did they stop?"

"I don't know."

"You think it's Uncle Al? It's got to be, right?"

"Beth, I have no clue."

She looked at him, unsatisfied with his answer.

"Look," Brian said. "I don't know … but I don't think it's Uncle Al. It's been hours since the bulk of Hightown's men poured out of the city. If it were Uncle Al, the truck wouldn't have stopped outside the gates."

"You don't know that, Brian," she said with a scowl.

"That's what I've been saying; I don't know. We have to wait. That's all we can do."

"That's not good enough." Bethany turned fast toward the gate.

"Beth!" Brian shouted, limping after her. "Where are you going?"

She didn't answer. When she got to the sliding chain-link fence, she said to the guard standing before it, "Open up," and swung her rifle into her hands.

"Ma'am?" the guard said.

"Open the gates. I'm going out there."

The guard shook his head. "No, ma'am, you're not."

Brian caught up to her. "Beth, c'mon. They sent a detachment; we'll get word soon."

"Brian, if you're not going to help, you can kindly fuck off."

Brian scratched the back of his neck and exchanged a glance with the soldier. A few more guards wandered over.

"If you don't—" was all Bethany got out before two soldiers came running out of the woods from beside the road.

"Open up!" one shouted.

All faces turned toward him. The gates were opened, and the first soldier ran right past the guards. "Where's General Winters?" he asked.

"On his way from the school," the guard replied.

The second soldier doubled over, out of breath, and said, "Bethany Driscoll, Simon Kalispell, and General Winters—they're all needed, *ASAP*."

Brian felt a moment of reluctance at hearing Bethany called for by her last name. After the many months of keeping her identity a secret and struggling to remember to call her by her made-up surname, Rose, her identity had come out after the battle in Alice.

Bethany stared at the guard with a sour demeanor. "Well?"

"Yes, ma'am. Go ahead."

The guard raised a hand to stop Brian, but Bethany said, "Let him through. He's coming with me."

The guard shook his head and said, "Go on."

"I'll escort you," the soldier said. "Simon and the general can meet us."

He turned, and they passed the entry gate. Brian had been getting around well without the use of his cane, but now with Bethany and the soldier several steps ahead of him, and having to stop on occasion for him to catch up, he wished he'd brought it along.

"What's going on?" he asked the soldier, partially so he and Bethany would slow down.

"We spotted the vehicle over a mile out, and had it pull over when it neared Alice." He shook his head. "I don't know where to begin."

"Is Uncle—General Driscoll there?"

"Y-yes, ma'am," he said. "But it's not what you're expecting." He explained the situation as they walked.

"Jesus Christ …" Brian said. "That's sick. That's plain sick."

Soon, a detachment of soldiers were seen standing at the side of the road, weapons at the ready. "We're close," the escort said.

Then the vehicle became clear. It was a standard military cargo truck, with a walled bed in the rear covered in an olive drab canvas stretching over the top. Two soldiers in protective bomb gear stood beside the open driver's side door. As they neared, Brian saw the driver, his left wrist still handcuffed to the wheel. The soldier had explained on their way to the truck that the driver had been holding an envelope addressed to Jeremy Winters. The letter was now under transport to the general.

"Stop there," one of the bomb squad members said. "We have gear for you." He pointed to a pile of equipment and helped Bethany and Brian with the cumbersome pants and jackets. As a helmet was placed over Brian's head, the weight became apparent, and he had to lean on his good leg.

"Where is he?" Bethany asked, her words barely audible behind the thick mask.

"This way," the soldier said.

Brian's breathing came out fast, and the faceplate was fogging up.

Jesus Christ, what the fuck am I doing out here?

"Beth," he said, putting his hand out to stop her. "Wait, hold up. Doesn't this seem fishy to you? I mean, why ask for you, Simon, and Jeremy only?"

She shrugged and walked past his hand. "Don't know how the minds of sick fucks work."

He stepped in front of her. "Wait, just hear me out. Something ain't right. They want you out here for a reason."

"No shit, Brian. Whatever the reason, I'm here."

"Beth, just hold up. Let's not give them what they're asking for on a silver platter."

"What are you saying, for me to turn back? Not gonna happen. If Uncle Al is in there, I'm getting him out."

"Just let me take a look first. Please. Keep a few steps back."

She stared at him through the faceplate.

"C'mon, Beth. If this is a trap, let's not walk right into it."

"It's not any safer for you."

"No, but if they don't see you, Simon, and Jeremy beside me, well, it might be safer. Let me just take the first look, see if it really is Uncle Al."

There was a pause, and then she nodded. "Fine, but I'm not going back any farther. I'm staying right here."

"Agreed."

Brian turned and began walking to the truck. As he passed the open driver side door, the driver called out, "I'm-m sorry." The man's face was dripping sweat. "I didn't want to do this. I-I didn't have a choice." His uniform was soaked.

"Calm down," an engineer said, inspecting the wire weaved through the chains on the handcuffs to the remotely controlled bundle of C-4 strapped to the man's chest. The wire snaked to another bundle of explosives visible on the passenger side seat. The wire continued to the rear cargo area, which Brian was told led to more explosives.

He turned the corner, and a man in army fatigues stood from sitting on the bumper.

"Ah," he said. "I see we are beginning to arrive." He smiled a wide smile and flung a cigarette to spiral away. He pointed at Brian's chest. "Those suits—ha! What good will they do?"

Brian spotted a slow and lazy drip of red from the rear gate of the truck, pooling below the tire. At the side of the road, off in the trees, were a dozen armed soldiers, aiming their rifles at the truck.

The man continued smiling and brushed a hand over his smoothed-back hair. He was unarmed, and carried a single handheld radio attached to his belt. The red handprint on his chest was fresh. "Please let me introduce myself. My name is Walter Ryder, Sergeant First Class in the Red Hand army. I am here as a messenger." Walter's ever-present smile and smooth mannerisms reminded Brian of a man he once knew back in Nelson, who owned the used car lot in town. Walter continued, "Once we are all gathered, I will proceed. Mister Kalispell, I presume? And is that Miss Driscoll back there?"

Brian realized the man couldn't see him properly through the faceplate.

"Let me remind you that I check in over the radio every seven minutes. If I fail to answer, the explosives will be triggered without a delay. The letter was clear: we would like to speak with Simon Kalispell, Jeremy Winters, and Bethany Driscoll, alone."

"Yeah," Brian said. "I'm Simon."

"And why is Miss Driscoll standing back there? We asked—"

"She'll follow after you get on with what the hell this is all about."

Walter flashed his friendly smile. "Let me give you a reminder of how dire the consequences are." He turned to the truck and unlatched the rear gate, then grabbed the cloth cover and yanked it back, displaying the interior.

"Dear God," Brian muttered.

***

Simon followed Jeremy and the officers out of Alice Elementary School, and they walked fast down Maple Avenue toward the trade grounds. Jeremy issued commands to soldiers and scouts as they proceeded. On the way, he explained what little information the soldier had told him in the meeting room.

I hate this, Simon thought. *I fucking hate this …*

They turned the corner, and four soldiers came running toward them. "General Winters!" they shouted, and waved their arms. "General!"

One soldier was so out of breath he could barely speak. "Sir," he said, and then paused, taking in lungfuls of air. "I've come … come from the truck." He took another breath and straightened up. He held an envelope in his hand. "Sir, this is for you. The driver was carrying it. We have a situation."

The soldier further described the truck full of explosives. The driver, one of Hightown's soldiers, was captured and chained to the steering wheel. There was an emissary from the Red Hands to deliver further instructions. The general, Simon, and Bethany were ordered to go to the truck; otherwise the explosives would be remotely detonated. Jeremy read the letter as the soldier spoke.

"Dear God," Jeremy said, not taking his eyes off the page. "Impossible. This is impossible." He paused, and no one spoke, waiting for Jeremy to explain. His eyes remained glued to the paper for another minute, and then he folded it into his breast pocket. "Where's Bethany now?" he asked.

"Sir," the soldier said. "She was escorted to the site, along with Brian Rhodes."

"They've been what? Under whose authority?"

The soldier's eyes shot large, and he stepped back. "Sir, I …"

"There's a truck full of explosives, and you sent members of our establishment out there? This is obviously a trap."

"Sir, they have one of their own out there. They won't detonate—"

"Like hell they won't. We're being called out there to be killed, plain and simple."

Jeremy brushed past the soldier. "Call them back," he shouted over his shoulder. "Call them all back."

"But, sir, General Driscoll is—"

"It's a trap, goddamn it. Call them back, now!"

"S-sir. Yes, sir." The soldier unclasped his radio.

"Jeremy," Simon said. "How many soldiers were sent out to the truck?"

Jeremy looked to an officer at his side. "How many?"

"Fifteen," the officer said without hesitation. "The bomb squad is present at the vehicle, and thirty men are waiting as backup less than a quarter mile down the road."

Simon looked back to the man on the radio. "Is Bethany there yet? Is Brian there?"

"They're being recalled," the man said.

"Have the reserves meet them, now," Simon said, and turned in a sprint toward the trade grounds.

Chapter Ten
Duplicity

The trunk swung open, the canvas cloth pulled back, and a wave of nausea nearly overwhelmed Brian. "You're sick sons a'bitches, you know that?"

Walter Ryder looked from the rear of the truck to Brian and smiled. The truck was full to the walled sides with the severed heads of Hightown's executed prisoners; a bloody jumble of unmoving eyes and open mouths. Three fell when the trunk opened, and rolled to a halt on the ground. In the middle of the pile was General Albert Driscoll, tied to a post secured in the floor, the gore drowning him to his shoulders. A ball gag was stuffed in his mouth, and his face was bruised and bloodied, his eyes swollen shut. He tried to speak as he saw Brian, tried to wiggle free.

"Uncle Al!" Brian called out, and moved toward the opening. The guard from the bomb squad grabbed his arm.

"He's strapped with explosives. Don't go near him!"

Another soldier came from around the front of the truck, not wearing protective gear. "Brian Rhodes, come with me," he said, motioning for him to follow.

Nobody moved.

"Brian?" Walter said. "Your name is Brian, not Simon?"

Brian stepped to meet the soldier.

Walter Ryder said, "Stop." He unclasped the radio from his belt. "All it takes is one word, and this will be over, fast."

"And you'll be blown to pieces too," the soldier said, aiming his rifle at Walter.

"Death finds us all, one way or the other."

"General Winters and Simon Kalispell are on their way, but they won't be meeting you at the truck. Brian," the soldier said. "Follow me." He stepped forward and grabbed Brian around his bicep.

Walter sighed and clipped the radio back on his belt. His hand went to his rear, and when it returned, it held a pistol.

"Beth!" Brian shouted to Bethany back by the trees. "Get down!"

And with that, a volley of bullet fire erupted from every direction.

The soldier beside Brian was shot in the chest and fell over. Walter aimed the pistol at the other guard in the bomb suit and fired point-blank into his faceplate. A ripple of gunfire erupted from the tree line, and bullets plunked the side of the truck while torrents of dirt shot up from the ground. Brian dove to the earth and looked up to witness the horrendous sight of movement … the heads, the hundreds of severed heads were moving, rising. "Oh, Jesus!" was all he got out as a man birthed from the gore, rifle in hand. Another emerged, and then another. Uncle Al was struggling from his confines as bullets tore into the canvas cloth and popped into the severed heads. A bullet pierced Walter's shoulder and he stumbled forward, attempting to jump in the rear of the truck. He called out, "Your general is in the truck! Hold your fire!" He was partially in the cab when a volley of bullets struck him, and he fell beside Brian.

"Beth, move!" Brian shouted, and attempted to roll to the opposite side of the truck, tearing away the helmet and bulky equipment that was making escape nearly impossible.

The soldiers hidden in the back of the truck were firing out from flaps in the canvas covering. Above the roar of gunfire, another noise came rumbling from the road, and two and then a third Hummer came rushing toward them. Machine guns mounted to the tops fired bullets of such large caliber that the tree line where the soldiers hid was torn to sawdust, and smaller trees toppled.

The vehicles screeched to a halt, and men poured out, exchanging fire with the reservists who were approaching from the rear.

"Brian!" Bethany shouted from the tree line. A soldier grabbed her around her waist, stopping her from running to him.

Brian stood, but a terrible jolt crashed into his back as a bullet hit the protective plate in the suit and ricocheted off, sending him down face-first.

"Christ," he said through gritted teeth. Another pain walloped his side, and then another in his leg. A deep, hot pain. Then hands were on him, grabbing his arms, his shoulders. A bag was pulled over his face, and darkness followed.

His feet were off the ground, but still he tried to push, pull his way out of the arms of the men shoving him. Then he was in the trunk of a Hummer, his hands tied with zip-tie handcuffs. His body bounced as the Hummers fled back the way they'd come. He couldn't hear anything over the roar of the machine gun mounted on the roof and the loud plunks of returned fire bouncing off the armored truck. The boom of an explosion was evident. Loud, yet not as loud as all the C-4 in the truck would have suggested.

The bullet fire became less and less until it stopped completely, and all Brian could hear was the rumble of the engine and his own heart beating heavy. *Jesus,* he thought. *I can't breathe.*

The Hummer must have been driving fast, and each bump in the road caused his body to bounce violently, and his mouth was sucking in the fabric of the hood with each inhalation.

I'm a dead man, he thought. *Where the hell are they taking me?*

Chapter Eleven
The Butcher Returns

The rumble in the sky was evident, even with the foghorn blaring in the distance. Simon shielded the sun with his hand, looking for the little black dot.

"Jesus Christ," Jeremy said to no one in particular. "Where is it coming from?"

A soldier beside him was calling into a radio. Jeremy looked at him and the soldier said, "I'm working on it, sir."

They were in the trade grounds, where a large brigade of Hightown and Alice's soldiers had just departed to secure the site of the cargo truck. A guard stationed nearby said, "Are we under attack, sir? Is it them?"

Jeremy remained looking into the sky as he replied, "Yes, we're under attack. And yes, it's them." He turned to an officer. "I don't think this is the main assault; get reports from the scouts."

"Sir," the man said. "There's no indication of—"

The bullet fire was heard in the distance, from the direction of the cargo truck.

Simon ran to the gate, but a guard put his arm out.

"Simon," Jeremy said. "Wait."

"They're out there. Bethany and Brian, they're both out there!"

"I called them back. Just wait."

Simon yearned to shove the guard aside and run past, but he suppressed these feelings, swallowing them into a tight ball in his stomach.

"Sir," the officer said, looking at both Jeremy and Simon with a sober expression. "We have reports of movement, north of the cargo truck. Vehicles …" He pressed his ear to the speaker. "Five or six, moving fast … and a helicopter, north west, nearing Checkpoint B."

Simon turned to face the noise in the sky, and saw the black dot appear. High up, it sailed toward the checkpoint closest to the heart of Alice. Jeremy removed his radio and issued commands. "Ready large-caliber munitions for an air assault." A crackling voice spoke back to him, and then Jeremy responded. "Report on the whereabouts of Brian Rhodes and Bethany Driscoll, and pull every soldier back behind the line, away from the truck!"

Simon exchanged glances with Jeremy, both knowing full well who they were leaving behind in the cargo truck.

"Here," Jeremy said, removing the folded paper from his breast pocket. "Read this, fast."

Simon took the paper, his vision burning bright with adrenaline. The message was short, written in fine black ink from a meticulous hand.

Dear General Winters,

I offer you my sincere congratulations on becoming general. You will serve in a better capacity than your predecessor, Mister Nicholas Byrnes, and that stout old man whom you were all so fond of. I apologize wholeheartedly for having to kill him. It was not personal, just a matter of necessity.

Now, it would appear that the two of us are locked eye to eye. Make no mistake about it, I plan on delivering upon you the same inferno that you so recklessly unleashed on my men, and attempted to turn into my funerary pyre. Alice will burn. Oh Lord, I swear it. Full retribution is at hand. The might of my Red Hands will see you all dead, in due time. For now, I leave you with a taste of things to come.

I look forward to making your acquaintance.

Sincerely,

Karl Metzger

Karl Metzger … Simon looked up from the paper.

"Ka—" was all he got out before Jeremy said, "Don't say his name out loud." He snatched the paper from Simon and folded it back into his pocket.

In the distance, they heard an explosion, and all the men on the line recoiled. At the same time, the first tracer rounds emitted from the line, aiming at the helicopter and missing. More bullet fire erupted, and the helicopter turned sharply, swooping back toward the way it came. Something dark dropped from the sky as it turned. Something small and round. And then more. Dozens.

Jeremy shouted into the microphone as the helicopter continued its loop. Tracer rounds followed in pursuit, but none brought the vessel down.

All eyes were on the mass of black falling objects, awaiting the detonation. But then they disappeared from view, and no explosion followed.

Chapter Twelve
Behind the Gates

Jeremy returned to command in a rush. Simon remained in the trade grounds with five high-ranking Rangers hunched over a map spread out on the pavement. He pointed to locations away from main avenues and roads that would offer the best vantage points. There were already a dozen Rangers settled around Alice, high up in trees or in the crevices of rocks, but their numbers would need to be doubled. Lieutenant General Casey Edmunds stayed in the trade grounds as well, awaiting reports from his men returning from the skirmish at the cargo truck. As the soldiers returned, Simon left his Rangers and ran up to the front gate. He scanned each face for Bethany and Brian.

"What happened out there?" he asked the first and then the second returning soldier.

Casey Edmunds touched Simon's shoulder. "Give them a minute," he said. "Let them get inside."

"Bethany Driscoll was out there, and her cousin, Brian," Simon said.

"So were a lot of good soldiers. Let them get behind the gates."

Simon fought back the urge to grab the next returning man and berate him with questions. Instead he asked, "What dropped from the helicopter?"

Casey Edmunds answered without the slightest show of emotion. "Heads," he said. "Severed heads. Maybe a hundred in total. Most were smashed beyond identification when dropped from that altitude, but they're all presumed to be our men killed or executed in Hightown."

"They dropped *heads*?"

"Are you shocked?" He looked at Simon. "These people, these monsters, they're capable of doing things humanity wouldn't dare dream of. It's a tactic. They want us afraid. They want us to leave our posts when their army storms the gates. They want us to know they'll have no problem adding our heads to the pile."

Before the truck appeared outside the gate, when the officers from Hightown and Alice had convened inside Alice Elementary School, Casey Edmunds had presented a document outlining the armament and personnel lost in the battle with the Red Hands. On top of that, he detailed the munitions and fuel that was believed to be left behind intact, and now in the hands of the enemy. The first barrage of artillery from their war vessel had destroyed much of the airstrip outside the hangar where the helicopters were stored. But the hangar itself was not targeted, and was believed to be in the enemy's possession. Simon noted that if they were willing to send one lone helicopter into enemy fire, they must have more at their disposal.

Even more terrifying was their sudden acquisition of a working navy. Not just the one warship, but the dozens of landing vessels. The shallow depth of the reservoir bordering Alice would make it impossible for the destroyer to stay afloat, but the smaller ships could navigate their waters.

Simon wanted to ask the simple question during the meeting, "Is this a war we can win?" but he didn't. This was something they were trying to decipher, and Simon wasn't sure if he wanted to know the answer. It had become apparent that they knew nothing of the Red Hands' numbers. By all accounts, Karl's army had been wiped out during the battle in Alice, but now here they were, a thousand more infesting Hightown like a plague.

And if—or rather, when—they came marching to Alice's gates, would they be able to defend themselves against such an onslaught? An invasion from the air, land, and sea? Alice's line was still in repair. There were sections of the trenches manned by a thin line of men behind makeshift sandbags as the pits were redug and the towers reconstructed.

By all accounts, Simon didn't believe they could endure another battle. Even with the might of Hightown's armored wing, if they were to be attacked by landing vessels, helicopters, and a direct assault, the bulk of the defenses would be spread thin.

There was some hope, though.

A revelation was presented to Alice's officials from Casey Edmunds, who showed a degree of humility that he had kept the information to himself for so long. He said, "There are … other colonies. Large colonies, equal in power to our own, and in alliance."

"Where?" Jeremy asked. "And how do you know this?"

"We have always known." His answers were matter-of-fact as he told of each settlement in turn, and pointed them out on a map. He continued by saying, "Tom Byrnes was aware, and it was his design that we kept the information private."

"Private? For what good?"

"It was his belief that in Alice's infancy, little would be accomplished if the people knew there were other lands to seek sanctuary. Alice was to become fully operational before word of the other colonies spread. Although we didn't see eye-to-eye with this approach, General Driscoll respected his wishes. By all accounts, he went so far as to keep this information from his son, Nick."

"These colonies, why weren't they informed when Alice was under attack?"

"They were."

Silence followed. Casey Edmonds cleared his throat and continued, "This is not easy for me to say, but I believe full transparency is needed at this crux." He sighed. "We sent scouts to the closest colonies when Alice was attacked. Their response was universal: that they could not supply troops or help at that juncture."

"If they wouldn't help then, what's to make you think they'll help now?"

"Because—and you won't like this reason—they don't consider Alice of the same value as Hightown, despite our reassuring them that Alice was and is a major producer of crops and filtered water. It's no surprise that the relationship between the colonies has been strained since their inceptions. Each colony has asked for help in the past, and not once did any of the others answer their call. Even ourselves. The distance has been cited as too great. The risk too large. There are always reasons, both to go to war and to refrain from it. But now, with the Red Hands showing they are more than a limited threat—that each and every colony is in danger of their ruthless pursuit—it's possible the colonies will see the importance of a unified front."

The officials in the room remained stunned as Casey Edmunds further described the colonies. If not for the possibility of help, Simon would have urged Jeremy to consider a full withdrawal from Alice. But now, as Simon inspected the faces of each returning soldier for Bethany and Brian and saw the injured and killed men brought in on stretchers, his anger toward the Red Hands grew.

"Simon," Casey Edmonds called out and motioned for Simon to approach. "Over here."

Simon joined him, where he was speaking to three soldiers.

"It was tactical, sir," one of the soldiers said. "The whole thing was rehearsed and planned. The truck, it was there to lure you, Bethany, and General Winters."

"Where are they?" Simon asked impatiently. "Where's Beth?"

Before the soldier could answer, Simon looked up to see the final assemblage of soldiers appear from the thicket beside the road and come running toward the entrance.

"Beth …" Simon left Casey Edmunds and the soldiers and met her a few steps inside the perimeter.

"Jesus, Bethany, are you okay?" Her cheeks were flushed, and her lips set in a scowl.

"They took him, Simon—those sons a bitches took him!"

"Who, Brian? Where?"

"I don't know. Hummers came speeding to the truck and grabbed him. Jesus, it was their plan all along to either kill us in the explosion or take us back as prisoners. But Brian didn't have to be there, he wasn't supposed to be there."

"Are we following them? We need to follow them!"

"They're being taken back to Hightown, no doubt about it," she said. "My cousin … my uncle … God damn them …"

Simon reached out and wrapped his arms around her shoulders. She let her guard down and embraced him back. "Did you see your uncle?" he asked. "Was he taken back to Hightown too?"

She wiped her eyes on his shoulder. "He was in a truck. I didn't see him. Brian went in my place." She shook her head. "They blew it up. The whole truck."

"Then we need to attack—"

A voice cut in, "What we need is more information." Simon turned to see Casey Edmunds beside him, listening to Bethany's report.

There was a pause, and then Simon turned back to comforting Bethany. "I'm going to go get Brian. I'll do everything that I can."

His vision was a pulse of red. This wasn't possible. It couldn't be. They were just beginning to heal. Bethany was broken enough … this was just so unfair. A part of him wanted to scream. A part of him wanted to cry. The vision of Karl Metzger danced around in his mind, and he pictured tearing the man limb from limb. The thought gave him a sense of pleasure.

"I'll get into Hightown," Simon yelled over his shoulder. "I know I can. I'll get past the line."

"And then what are you going to do?" Casey Edmunds replied. "Alone, nothing. Maybe you'll get in—I believe that you can. But wherever they've taken him, you'll need help. You need a plan. You need soldiers; the same soldiers that are relying on you here. You go running off on some crusade, and the Rangers will lose the best scout in Alice. I'm not telling you to let your friend go, I'm asking you to accept our help. Please. Come back, we'll go to Jeremy and figure out how to clean up this terrible mess."

Simon paused. He looked down at Bethany, her face looking at his.

"I hate to agree with him," she said. "But he's right. We can't run in alone."

They split their embrace and walked through the busy trade grounds, urgently toward Alice Elementary School.

Chapter Thirteen
Solitary

The moment the world turned dark, Brian was certain death would soon follow. Unable to see, with a cloth bag wrapped tight over his face and the feeling of hot suffocation around the bend, he swung and kicked viciously at whoever was before him, striking soft objects, stomachs and thighs, and harder cheekbones and helmets. Hands grabbed his arms, his legs, his torso. A forearm wrapped around his throat, and as he shouted out, "Beth—" his windpipe closed and the word came out in a hiss.

Bodies pressed against him, tossing him hard on his side; a terrible sharp kick to his stomach and the air in his lungs deflated. Gasping to suck in air, he was lifted and thrown on the cold floor of a vehicle, and then came the sensation of movement and the sound of an engine. His ankles and wrists were bound, and the more he twisted his hands to free the binds, the more the ties cut into his skin.

"Beth? *Beth!*" He managed to call out.

A force struck him hard on his side, and then another, as strong hands held him down.

"Keep yer fuckin' mouth shut!" a voice shouted.

The fabric of the hood sucked into Brian's mouth as he took large inhales, fighting against the spasming pain on his side. He remained quiet for the duration of the trip, expecting a blade to find its way into his flesh at any moment, or for a bullet to tear through his hooded forehead. Would he hear the gunshot?

As he regulated his breathing, with each inhale sending stabs of pain from the battered side of his rib cage, it occurred to Brian that he should be paying attention to where the vehicle might be going; he should take note of when he felt sudden turns, or the heat of the sun through the windows, to determine which direction he was being taken.

Since he wasn't yet dead, the Red Hands had other plans in store for him … but what? If anything, they'd thrown away their greatest bargaining chip—Uncle Al. So what did they want with him? No doubt, they'd made the connection that Bethany was related to Uncle Al, but if so, why ask for her and not keep the general alive?

Did they capture Bethany too? Was she in another vehicle, speeding alongside their own?

Uncle Al, his eyes bruised shut, drowning in the sea of heads …

The soldiers emerging from the gore like deathly apparitions …

The bullets striking the dirt around him in a torrent …

… Uncle Al, his face battered unrecognizable, his thinning white hair a frenzied nest …

… the heads that rolled, plunk-plunk, to the dusty road …

The thin air filtered through the cloth bag—not air at all, but a diluted steam—lacked the proper amount of oxygen to keep his mind functioning. Panic and anxiety followed. At each bump in the road he felt for Bethany, yearning for their bodies to bump into each other, to know she was still alive, but hoping to God that he wouldn't feel her, that she was safe back in Alice.

The vehicle came to a sudden halt, engine running, and just as a gust of cool air sucked in from an opened door, hands grabbed him and pulled him from the trunk. He fell to the ground on his injured side, and could smell the cloud of kicked-up dirt as the vehicle sped off. Again, hands grabbed his shoulders, yanking him to stand, pulling and pushing him onward. Many voices spoke at once, all around him. He said, "What do you want with me?" but none answered.

His toes hit stairs, and he was pulled up, past the creaking of an opened door, and down hallways. Boots squeaking on polished floors. The air temperature dropping. Doors clanging open and shut. Then he was shoved hard and fell to his knees on a hard cement floor. The binds cut and the bag ripped from his face. Cool air welcomed his senses, filtered fast down his nostrils.

The door behind him shut with a loud clang, and he rubbed at his wrists, staring at the only two pieces of furniture in that dismal cell: a cot and a toilet.

***

The cold made the pain worse, not better. The refreshing air that was so relieving at first crept under his sweat-soaked shirt, into his skin, aching his bones. He laid on the cot, his knees tucked into his chest. His side hurt something fierce, but as the hours passed, it was the cold that worried him more than any of his injuries.

He stood and walked in circles, warming his joints. The cell had a musky, almost electrical smell, like old, corroded metal. The walls, floor, and ceiling were concrete, and radiated such a chill that it was noticeably warmer in the center of the room than near the sides.

A strip of dim light came through a solitary slot in the door; otherwise the enclosure was pitch-black. Brian sat on the cot and leaned back, the wall damp against his head. Did they capture Bethany? What were they doing to her? Oh Christ, they killed Uncle Al … these men were demons. Wretched, horrible monsters. Brian dropped to his knees before the toilet as a wave of sickness gurgled in his stomach. The moldy water in the stainless toilet-sink combination reeked, and Brian couldn't keep his face above it without feeling even sicker. He fought back the nausea and gathered himself off the floor.

He sat on the cot. Lay down. Shivered. Got up and walked in circles. Rubbed his palms together to gather warmth. Massaged his temples as images of severed and battered heads, skulls cracked open, crossed his listless eyes. Blood, all the blood. His uncle in the middle of it all.

Hours might have passed. The only way to tell the time was by his growing thirst and hunger, despite the ever-present nausea. He looked at the toilet bowl and knew he would rather die of dehydration than stoop to that level.

Steven emerged in his thoughts again. The torment of losing him came crushing back. In movies, he'd seen people locked in solitary going crazy, hallucinating amid their torment. But Steven's form did not join him in that room, only the ghostly images in his mind. Perhaps it would be better to face affliction in company with a hallucinatory form rather than face it alone … Brian wasn't so sure.

A noise from outside. Footfalls. Creaking. A voice. Brian sat up in bed … had he dozed off? He rushed to the slat in the door, peered out, but couldn't see anything other than the opposite wall. His chest beat heavy against the cold metal, and as the sound grew closer, he moved back to the bed. A key scratched at the lock, and a voice said, "You still alive in there?"

More dim light flooded the interior; enough to make Brian shield his eyes. A man stood before him, keys dangling in his fingers. "Ah, so you are," he said. In his other hand was a tray. "Haven't been ordered to git rid of yer ass yet, so eat up." He dropped the plastic tray to the ground. The food splattered, and a plastic water bottle bounced and rolled to the corner.

Brian didn't move.

"I'll be back to git the tray later."

"Where-where's Bethany?" The sound of his voice was thin.

"Who?"

"Beth."

The shadowy man shrugged and left, closing the door behind him with a thud. A moment passed, and Brian went for the water, taking the whole bottle down in fast slugs. A liquid trail trickled down his chin as he caught his breath. His stomach twisted at the sudden fill.

The slop on the floor, whatever it was, covered the ground and splattered over the wall. There was some left on the tray, but Brian didn't inspect it any further. He tossed the plastic bottle and sat on the cot.

"Christ," he said out loud, and his head fell into his palms. *What do they want with me?* Torture, maybe. Execution. Names? Places? He didn't know much. Not more than Uncle Al would know, that was for sure. And Beth … he couldn't think about it. Not after seeing her in the basement, all that time ago. Drugged and strapped to the bed, dissected bodies in the room opposite the hall, flayed and ritualistically taken apart.

Brian held back tears. Tears for the dead. Tears for the living. Tears for his family, friends, the sheer injustice of it all. The *whys* of the world. *Why* were the Red Hands doing this to them? *Why* did the world have to end, just so the living would go on in fear and terror? There were so many questions. More questions than answers.

In that cold cell, deep beneath the surface of the earth, Brian tried to accept his fate. He tried to accept that death was inevitable. He hoped it would be fast and painless. Would he see Steven again? Did he even believe in an afterlife?

Alone in the dark, his thoughts turned dismal.

Chapter Fourteen
Future Uncertain

There was no consoling Carolanne. Not that Simon could offer much in the way of comfort. They found her in the infirmary and took her to an empty examination room.

"Is he dead?" she asked.

"I don't know." His words were raw against his throat, and when he tried to speak again, nothing came out. Carolanne faltered, and he stepped forward to help her, but Bethany was quicker, and they held each other tight.

There were so many things that Simon wanted to say, but it was pointless. Only action presented a solution, and it was action that Simon both yearned for and dreaded. When he thought about fighting—of having to fight the enemy once again—it brought a deep pain. He could still feel the sickening sensation of his blade slicing through sinew and bone, vibrating his fingers, aching his hands. He wasn't sure if the nightmares would ever cease. But with the terrible realization of Brian abducted, locked away in some dungeon to be tortured, killed … he yearned for the vibration once more. He wanted to feel his blade sink deep inside Karl Metzger. He wanted to cut down the entire sadistic army, hack away until nothing was left but a mountain of bodies. And although it was hard to admit, these violent urges were not the result of Brian's abduction alone; it was the pain and torment inflicted on Bethany that made him want to rip the heart out of the Red Hands. Watching her suffer, witnessing her uncle murdered and her cousin abducted, further delaying the prospect of the two of them residing in peace, content, happy to be together; that was what made the heat in his chest rise with rage.

Carolanne got to her feet and Bethany said through tears, "Come on, let's go home." Only a few feet out, a doctor took a look at them and said, "Dear God, what happened?"

Carolanne shook her head, tears falling. "B-Brian ..." she squeaked out. "I'm gonna-gonna be sick." She held her stomach. The doctor found a chair for her to sit, and Simon told a rushed tale. The doctor listened, then told them to remain there until he returned. A minute later, he appeared with a bottle of benzodiazepine. "Take one and go home," he told them. "Both of you." He exchanged glances with Bethany. "Try to rest."

Carolanne took two pills and offered the bottle to Bethany, who shook her head. "I'm going to get him back," she said. "I swear it, Carolanne."

"Beth," she said. "We-we have to leave. We can't stay here anymore. They're coming. The Red Hands. They're going to kill us all. They're going to murder everyone." Her chest was bobbing up and down and her cheeks flushed red. Simon hoped the pill would kick in soon.

He put an arm over her shoulder and helped her to her feet, with Bethany on the other side. "I'll do everything in my power to stop them," Simon said.

"You're one man," she said. "Did you hear what they did to Uncle Al? Oh, God, we have to run."

Simon felt her body weight dip, and thought for a moment she was going to faint, but she remained walking past the hospital door, and pressed on through town until they arrived at the apartment. Winston greeted them at the door in his usual frenzy.

Simon gave a short whistle and said, "Relax, boy."

Connor appeared at the kitchen and stopped short when he saw Carolanne and Bethany, their faces red and wet with tears. "What happened?" he asked.

Simon took Connor aside, his hand resting gently on the boy's bony shoulder, and gave a quick explanation as Bethany got Carolanne to the couch. Her eyelids were droopy, and Simon guessed that a combination of the pills and the shock and stress were kicking in. A part of him wanted to collapse beside her. A portion of his brain wanted to shut off, allow for sleep to shield him from his anguish, at least temporarily. But the better part of his mind was consumed by a cocktail of adrenaline, fear, and anger.

Jesus, he thought, *I need to focus. I need to calm my thoughts.*

Connor stood by the doorway to the kitchen scratching at his growing hair, his eyes large. He'd traded in his monk robes for jeans and a flannel, and he was beginning to look like another boy altogether. A frightened boy. A boy growing up in a world filled with dread, and an uncertain future with little prospect for change.

"Christ," Simon said. "I'm sorry. Come here. It's going to be all right." He motioned for Connor to come to the couch.

Carolanne's eyes were open to slits. "Tell him the truth, Simon," she said with a slight slur. "He's old enough to know. He's seen the state of the world. The Red Hands are coming, Connor. We're at fucking war again."

Connor walked to the couch, his eyes wet.

"The same people who killed my family?"

He was referring to the monks, Simon knew. He shook his head and gripped Connor's shoulder. "Come here," he said, not wanting to give an answer.

"Is it them?"

Simon hugged the boy, felt warm tears on his shoulder.

"I—" was all Simon got out as he heard footfalls leading to the door, followed by a fast and loud knock, and Winston barking.

Thank God …

Simon stood, and Carolanne resumed hugging and consoling Connor. Simon pushed Winston back from the door, where a member of the Rangers was waiting.

"Simon," the man said, out of breath. "Where the hell have you been? We've been calling for you."

"I … um." Simon felt his belt for his radio and realized it wasn't there. He remembered taking it off at the hospital. Did he leave it behind?

I'm not a leader, he thought. *This is too much pressure, all of it. Surviving, it's just too much.*

"You're needed back at HQ," the Ranger continued. "Jeremy's looking for you."

Simon nodded and turned. "Carolanne …" Her eyes were closed. The pills appeared to be working. "Connor, keep an eye on her, okay?" The boy nodded and wiped his eyes with the back of his hand.

"Hold up," Bethany said, standing from the couch.

Simon was about to recommend that she stay, that it was her cousin who was taken, so maybe a bit of rest would do her good. But Bethany wasn't the type to be swayed.

Outside, Simon asked the Ranger, "What's going on?"

"Some of the scouts have returned."

"Which scouts?"

"From the other colonies, sir. A few have returned."

Chapter Fifteen
Compulsion

The army was restless. Normally, Karl would share in that restlessness, and not feel peace until the final bullets were exchanged and victory was certain, but events were transpiring so smoothly that he remained calm. The army would march—soon—and Alice would fall. It was no longer a question of *if,* it was a question of *when.* And at the present, Karl was content to rehash the plans with Liam and the Priest as they inspected the defensive line.

A young private with a limp approached. "Sir," the man said, "Captain Briggs has sent me to inform you, they're back, sir."

Karl turned to him, eyebrow raised. "And?"

The soldier swallowed visibly. "Perhaps, sir, you should speak to Captain—"

"Do you not know the outcome?"

"Sir, it's …" His eyes cast to the ground. "It didn't work, sir. We didn't kill Jeremy Winters or Simon Kalispell, and the girl wasn't captured."

The sting was worse than he could have predicted. For nights, weeks, and months, he'd envisioned the raven-haired Bethany, played out fantasies in his mind of her chained to his bed. She would have to be broken and rebuilt, see her loved ones perish, know that all hope was lost. Over time, she could be turned to see the magnificence of his form of governance. She could become a lieutenant, an officer, the one and only female allowed into their ranks, to be treasured, adored, and feared by the soldiers. If she could not be broken, she would be chained away nonetheless, a hidden plaything. Both options piqued his arousal.

A fleeting thought crossed his mind, that his obsession over Bethany was not unlike the other girl, from his childhood. That girl had not arisen in his thoughts for decades. She had been sufficiently blocked from his mind, hidden away with all the other abuses, losses, and crimes of his past. It was something in Bethany's persona, her straight dark hair, that managed to bring the memories of his lost love back to the surface of his repressed memories.

The private continued, "We got one of them, a soldier—"

"Is it not Bethany?"

"It is not, sir."

"Is it Jeremy Winters or Simon Kalispell?"

"N-no, sir."

Karl thought he would have his trophies that day, right now, that he could play with them into the late hours. The feeling of loss was worse than expected. He turned to leave, discuss plans with Liam, when the young soldier flinched away at his sudden movement.

"What?" Karl asked. "You going to stand around all day?"

"N-no, sir." The man turned to leave.

Karl eyed him as he left, the sweat mark down his back, the way his voice trembled and his body shook. Coward. The man couldn't even address him without showing fear. He felt the cool handle of his sidearm in his palm, unholstered the dark metal revolver. He inspected the cylinder despite knowing that it was loaded. He could feel the hot stares of Liam and the Priest standing at his side. He reholstered the pistol.

I'm getting soft, he thought, and moved away from the line.

Chapter Sixteen
In the Night

Footfalls. Voices. The creaking of a lock turning. Dim light.

"Not hungry?" a voice said. Not the same voice as before. "Trust me, in due time you'll be hungry enough to lick shit off a toilet." He laughed and picked up the tray. Brian had stared at that tray for many hours, thought that maybe the plastic side could be ground against the cement to sharpen it. He thought about making a triumphant escape, slashing his way across an army of Red Hands. But common sense prevailed.

"You gonna kill me?" he asked from the cot.

"Me, personally?" the man shrugged. "Probably not. Maybe."

If this was to be his end, Brian decided then and there that he was taking at least one of them out with him. He would not go quietly into the night. He would raise hell. He'd burn down the heavens.

"What do you all want with me?"

Again the man shrugged and turned to leave.

"I don't know a damn thing. You gonna kill me, get on with it. Give it a fuckin' try."

The man paused and looked at him.

"Aren't you fiery." He laughed. "The only reason you're still alive is 'cause we haven't been ordered to kill you yet. Give it some time. Eventually Karl will remember that you were taken, and realize he has no need for you."

"Where's Beth? Why did you ask for her?"

"Not my job to know."

"No? It's just your job to clean my shit up, huh?"

"You got some spirit, I'll give you that. Tell you what, if the cell doesn't whittle that spirit down a notch, I'll be sure and help out. See this here shit food you left on the floor to rot? You'll be scraping it up with your teeth when we *forget* that we're supposed to be feeding your sorry ass. We got a bad memory, all of us."

The heat rose inside Brian's chest, and for a moment he thought he might leap at the man, if not for his sore knee.

The man began closing the door. "I don't know anything!" Brian called out. "There's no use keeping me around!"

The man peered in one last time. "Ain't that the truth. I know perfectly well we don't need you. Hell, I probably know the layout of Alice better than you."

The door shut, and Brian called out, "How's that?"

The lock creaked shut. The guard's voice came from the open slat: "I lived there long enough to know," he said. "It's a regular paradise you got going on there."

The footfalls faded until they disappeared behind the sound of a closing door.

***

Brian guessed a full day went by, judging by his hunger. The dim light casting through the slat never changed, and the silence was near deafening. If Brian focused enough, he could just make out the low murmur of a mechanical buzzing coming from the hallway outside.

His mouth was so incredibly dry, and the deep bruise on his side throbbed in pain. The walls of the cell were damp to the touch, and Brian's thoughts stirred madly thinking about how long he might be stuck in this horrible little room. Would he die here? What would happen to Carolanne? Would she fight against the Red Hands with the rest of the army? He hoped not.

The cold was so all-consuming that he no longer noticed his shaking, just felt a general sense of misery. He thought of the boy with the springy red hair that he'd killed all that time ago, when he had left Bethany and Carolanne's bunker in Aurora. Brian had acted without thinking, out of pure adrenaline, and something else ... a sense that after all of his travels, from Nelson, all throughout the Smoky Mountains, losing his best friend along the journey, that he'd hit a wall; he would rather die than accept Bethany was about to be taken to be raped, killed, perhaps boiled in a stew. After shooting two of the men, Brian lunged at the trembling, filthy boy holding Bethany with a vile blade pressed to her throat, and shoved that same blade into the boy's neck, saw the shock and terror cross his eyes as blood gurgled to his lips. Death was inconceivable, impossible, even to the mortally wounded.

So, who was Brian at that moment? He wanted to muster the same strength as he had that day … but he felt more like the wide-eyed boy. He felt like the damned. Death was coming. It was inevitable. He'd done so much, survived for so long; to spend his remaining time going mad underground before dying was preposterous, absurd, impossible … a sure thing.

Footfalls returned and stopped before the door. The lock didn't click, but a shadow cut across the dim slat of light. A tray was placed on the shelf below the opening and the footfalls grew distant. His water came in a cup this time, just a few sips of metallic-tasting fluid, which he drank in two gulps. He dipped his finger in the chunky porridge and licked the gravy-like substance off. Rancid. Sour. Brian was again reminded of his travels from years past. Despite Steven's protests, they had stopped at a gathering where an old man and a mentally challenged younger man had set up camp. With some convincing, the old man ladled them both a heap of the stew he'd been stirring with a knife. The meat, raccoon meat, the old man had told them … fatty … tough … they found the remains of a girl in the woods the next day, butchered like a deer.

A wave of nausea returned, and Brian sat down before the little water he had in his system evacuated. It was that night, after finding the girl, that Steven went mad. That night the demons in his mind came out to play, and Brian kept them at bay with a large rock that he used to bash in his cousin's head.

Brian lowered his head into his palms again and fought back tears.

The same demons that possessed his cousin—that made him go mad— they were never extinguished. They were not killed in the woods, or later when Steven died in Nick's mansion. They resisted the pull of hell to walk the mortal earth and lay claim to humankind. The demons spread their venom-wings into the minds of men such as Karl Metzger and his malignant army. They existed wherever greed made men turn to murder. They thrived when a person was not repulsed by rape and torture. To witness an execution with delight. To spectate starvation with no trepidation. To feel delight when striking a child, abusing a child. These were the workings of demons with fire in their eyes. Evil spread its shadow over the frail earth. It existed in that cell, deep underground, just as it had infested the bunker in Nelson, when Steven had his first taste of insanity. Devils slept on the cot beside Brian, offering false shoulders to cry upon, for temptation is often most appealing when under true despair, and the only way to block the roots of evil from infesting the mind is by fighting back, no matter how unwinnable the battle.

***

The tray was taken away by a stout man with jet-black skin and a chipped front tooth.

"Not hungry?" the man said.

"I can starve a bit more."

"I'm insulted." The man smiled his broken smile, and his eyes sheened a yellowish hue from the hallway light. "Made it special for you and the others. Put some prime cuts in there."

"There's others here?"

"Of course. We don't kill everyone we come up against. Shit. We ain't monsters, now are we?"

The man left.

Time again slipped by. Brian walked in circles to keep his body temperature up and his muscles from atrophying, and fought the urge to speak to himself as he made his loops. All the quiet, the lack of contact, was making the conversations in his head want to escape his lips. He slept for minutes at a time on the thin mattress, hugging his knees into his chest.

He stood to walk, and as he did, his head felt like it was spinning out of control and he had to sit for a few moments before his balance returned. The empty pit in his stomach was to blame, Brian was sure of it. He couldn't remember the last meal he'd eaten.

When the next guard arrived, it took a moment for Brian to realize it was the same guard who'd first brought him food.

"Hear you're not eating," the man said. "Shame-shame."

"I'm a dead man anyway, so I might as well go out without that rotten slop in my belly."

"Aw, come on now. You look plenty alive to me." The man put the tray on the cot and turned to leave.

"You figure out what Karl wants with me?"

"Like I told you, I don't think the man gives two shits about you. It was the other three he wanted: Jeremy, Simon, and the bitch. You're just a bonus. He's a tad busy at the moment getting ready to march to Alice, but I'm sure when he remembers you're down here we'll end your suffering mighty quick. Or maybe not. Maybe he has a plan for you. Maybe he wants to march into Alice with your head on a stick to show 'em the nature of our hospitality."

Brian shook his head. "How do you live with yourself? Any of you—but you most of all. You lived in Alice, and yet you have no qualms murdering them all."

"Murder?" The man paused at the door. "Is that what you think we're doing? Murder? You got it all wrong; but that's what they teach you in the academy, isn't it, that the only ones permitted to do the killing are the soldiers."

"I ain't a soldier. Never been."

"No? Well, you're a good-ole-boy just the same. You think that when one side decides on rules, the others must obey."

"I never made rules."

"But you live by them. You protect the same people who were to have me killed—executed—for doing nothing more than trying to protect the values that *they* set forth."

"I don't know nothin' about that. I wasn't in Alice when you were there, and I don't know or give a rat's shit about whatever injustice you're claiming." It felt good, great, to be speaking frankly. Brian could see the wall, practically feel its hard side. He knew the closer he was to reaching it, the farther the demons would be kept at bay. "The fact that General Driscoll was my uncle is irrelevant. I came here, traveled across the US, for one reason and one reason only—to survive. The same reason Alice came together. For survival. How are our situations that different?"

The guard shrugged. "They're not. After I was imprisoned inside Alice, then banished from the front gates, I did what I had to do to survive. Tom Byrnes can rot in hell. I had to—"

"And that justifies you taking Hightown and Alice for your own? That justifies you murdering men, women, and children by the dozen?"

"Again with that word. We're not murdering anyone. We're surviving. Just like you. And justifying?" He shrugged. "Perhaps. Or perhaps it's just the way of the world now. Perhaps it's all the injustices I've suffered that has brought us to this place and time, with you behind bars and me on the outside, tossing in scraps."

Brian ignored his comments. "Tom Byrnes is dead. So is Nick. The Alice you knew has changed, mostly because of what your people have done; the fighting you've created."

"Created? Ha! We didn't create hostilities; they were always there, they never ceased to exist. And whether Tom and Nick are alive or dead is irrelevant. Alice *is* Tom Byrnes. It is everything he stood for. The people, their methodology and governing, their system, is what threw me to the wolves."

"You're wrong," Brian said, although he wasn't so sure if he was correct. "They would take you back. That's the type of people they are. That's the type of system we have. They would forgive you if you showed true remorse."

"They'd never—"

"They would. They'd have taken most of you in, given you water and food, a job and a purpose. But instead, the Red Hands blindly follow a man who doesn't care if you live or die."

"Tom Byrnes didn't care if I lived or died."

"Tom Byrnes is dead. He's dead and buried. Whatever you did, you said you were protecting Alice's values. They would accept you back. You could continue to survive by living in peace, and not be forced to murder by the hand of a psychopath you obey without a second thought."

The guard opened his mouth to speak, but then shook his head slowly. Then he said, "Not all of us are as blind as you think."

Before Brian could respond, the guard turned and left.

***

Sleep was pulled away as quickly as it set in. Brian developed a cough, which only added to the miserable feeling in his head, chest, and body. Everything ached. When the pain and the cold didn't keep him awake, his overactive mind didn't help. The conversation he'd had with the guard played out over and over again in his thoughts. And when his mind stumbled into full exhaustion, his eyes would snap back open in a half-dream-like sensation of terror.

But this time, it was a noise that caused him to stir. Footfalls, and then a shadow covering the open slit. Something was pushed through and fell to the floor soundlessly. Brian waited for the footfalls to recede before reaching out and pulling the wool blanket over his lap, feeling the bristly fabric between his fingertips. Nothing had ever felt as comforting as the sensation of the rough, warm material in his hands. He pulled it over his shoulders and smiled, knowing the demons had lost a round.

Chapter Seventeen
Forty-Eight Hours

The operating landing ships were driven to the dock. Any beyond immediate repair were left to drift along with the corpses of those who did not make it ashore. Karl sat before a table on the second floor of a home along the steep bank that led to the water, watching his men inspect the idling vessels. From his vantage point he could see his marvelous warship in the distance, shimmering in the sun like an island of steel. In the other direction, the yard of the property gave way to pavement that stretched on throughout Hightown. The town center was a series of warehouses, each outfitted for a different task. Some housed soldiers; others garaged armored transport vehicles. They found a surplus of fuel and stores of canned preserves and military rations. Karl himself had entered the building turned into an office complex, and wove through the maze-like halls. Papers remained scattered atop tables, and computer monitors were still alive. The officials had fled before the Red Hands reached the vicinity.

Once Hightown fell and the defenses were secured, he claimed a home along the shore to reside. Here he sat, bottle of dark liquor on the table before him. He grabbed it by the neck and refilled the glasses belonging to Liam Briggs and Priest Dietrich.

"Not much greenery here," he told them.

"Reckon not," Liam replied and drained back half the glass.

"Rather drab, if you ask me," Karl said.

An assortment of dried meats, canned smoked clams, and sardines were on a plate on the center of the table, and the men used their combat knives to cut at the meat and spear the seafood. They faced the large window and leaned back on their chairs. In the town center, the men had taken to a restrained revelry, waiting for Alice's army to counterattack. If given the choice, Karl hoped that they would. It would be much easier to cut them down before Hightown's walls rather than stage another invasion, even with his armored superiority.

But Alice did not attack like he hoped. Those bastards were hiding behind their walls. Even with a little coaxing, they didn't seem ready to budge. Karl had thought that fear would be enough to make them march, as often, fear turns to anger. He'd dropped a busload of severed heads along the line, and risked one of his helicopters to do so. At the same time, he'd used his second tactic: General Albert Driscoll. Upon finding him on the battlefield, he was brought before Karl, bound, gagged, and beaten. Karl unholstered his pistol and aimed it at the old man's head, when Liam said, "You might want to reconsider. He's valuable."

"I'm not here to play games, Mister Briggs. No longer will we wait and plot. Killing them all as fast as possible is our best recourse. Blitzkrieg, I believe it is called. Lightning war."

General Driscoll's white hair was wild and streaked with red, and he looked up at Karl defiantly.

"True enough," Liam said. "I agree on all accounts. But him, he's their leader. Might be worth holding on to."

And so, General Driscoll's life was spared.

When the truck full of severed heads and C-4 was brought outside Alice's gates, Karl said, "They'll never go to the truck themselves. You're wasting your time."

"They probably won't," Liam replied. "But if they do, we can make the battle a little easier. And maybe we'll snag one of them."

They were referring to the slim chance of Jeremy, Simon, and Bethany falling for their far-fetched ruse. At this, an image of Bethany rose in Karl's mind. Her dark hair fanned out on the bed down in Nick's basement, her hands restrained. The way she cursed and fought the guards.

But Liam's plan had failed. Neither Jeremy Winters nor Simon Kalispell had been killed, and Bethany escaped.

Karl picked up a manila envelope taken from the office complex.

"Well," he said, then finished his glass. "If what we have here is correct, the next transport of fuel is scheduled in two days. That throws off our timeline a bit."

Liam refilled their glasses. "Two days ain't nothing," he said.

"By all accounts," the Priest added, his good eye hazy with alcohol, "it would appear that our steps are guided. We attack as the Lord has prepared."

Liam snarled his lip, but then shook his head and laughed. "You know, I sorta missed you talking all crazy." He turned his head and spit a trail of tobacco juice to the floor.

"You missed me?" the Priest said with a smile. "Oh, by God, we've made a soft one out of you."

"Don't get ahead of yourself." Liam raised his glass, and Karl and the Priest raised their own. "It's good to have you back, Dietrich."

They clinked glasses and sipped.

"Even more," Karl added. "You're much more fun to be around now that we've made something of a drinker out of you."

The Priest laughed. "If the Lord's blood is wine, then whiskey must be his tears."

"Well," Liam said, and paused to drain his glass. "He can go on crying then."

***

There was no doubting that Alice had scouts snaked throughout the woods. Invading unannounced would be impossible. Now, days after Hightown fell, it was apparent that there would be no counterattack. The Red Hand's own scouts, led by a man named Bishop, who had such an ability to walk undetected in the wild that he could traverse a lawn of crisp, newly fallen leaves without making a sound, had not detected the indication of movement from Alice's line. They were staying put.

"Perhaps," Karl said to Liam as they inspected a box full of munitions in one of the warehouses, "they want a war of attrition. They do maintain enough water and food to last indefinitely."

Liam shrugged and scratched at the developing beard on his wide chin. "Maybe."

"We, however, cannot endure indefinitely. Not without ownership of

Alice. Think of it now … all of the water, food to last millennia … and we won't have to lift a finger. There will be more than enough prisoners to keep the gardens prosperous. All the battles we've fought together, all the people we've conquered; it all comes down to this. One last war to claim our fruitful home."

"So," Liam said, inspecting the sliding mechanisms of a brand-new assault rifle from a crate, "let's get on with it."

Karl smiled and laid a heavy palm on his shoulder. "Oh, Mister Briggs, I do appreciate your enthusiasm." Karl checked his watch. "Make sure the men are mustered and waiting. We proceed as planned. I'll meet you at the gates."

"Yes, sir."

Karl turned and left, navigating the maze of stacked boxes toward the exit. Outside, the lots before the warehouses were scrambling with activity. Bright spotlights illuminated the droves of soldiers, all checking and rechecking their supplies. Rifles, sidearms, knives, grenades, and explosives. Some strapped axes over their backs, many had machetes, and a few dozen were responsible for carrying sharpened spears bearing strips of torn red cloth to flutter in the wind as they were held aloft.

The army never looked better. His legion of terribles. They fed well on Hightown's plundered goods, and their spirits were high. As Karl walked the perimeter of the lot, the men nodded or saluted. "General," they said.

Back at his home overlooking the bay, Karl found the Priest sitting in the kitchen along with the chief medic, Alexander Pearl, and Bishop.

"Gentlemen," he said. "What are you still doing here? The men are waiting."

"General," the Priest said. "Going over some last-minute numbers."

Karl's eyebrow rose. "Oh? Do fill me in."

"Yes, sir," Bishop said, clearing his throat. "I was just relaying the last reports from the scouts."

"And that being?"

"The men positioned on the opposite side of the reservoir have a fair advantage in places, overseeing the shoreline. There's been nothing to suggest activity by the water. The scouts to the south, east, and west are too far out to see the town, but there have been no reports of movement. Everything suggests Alice is sedentary."

"When did the last communication come in?"

"The scouts changed shift at seven ... so"—he checked his watch—"six hours ago. I'll have the men radio in before the assault."

Karl nodded.

The Priest spoke up, "And Doctor Pearl here has something he would like to add."

Karl turned to the young man. Long beard. Uncombed hair. His uniform was ruffled and hung loose over his meager frame. *Oh, Doctor Freeman ... why did you go and try to kill me in that bunker of yours?*

"Yes," the doctor said. "We were going over supplies. We have an excess of basic medical goods: scalpels, scissors, and bandages. Our number of antibiotics is also good, thanks to Hightown's infirmary, which was well stocked. I have a limited amount of amphetamines to dole out to the troops prior to the battle, but our surplus will be meager at best following the attack. We used most of what we had prior to invading Hightown. As far as blood, every man filled a bag two days ago, and we drained the dying in the hours following the invasion of Hightown."

The doctor went on to give precise numbers, and Karl found his mind wandering. It was time for action, not preparation.

The doctor was saying, "Plasma is—" when Karl stood from the table. "We're in good supply then, Mister Pearl." The other men stood on Karl's cue. "Mister Briggs will be arriving at the gates about now. The time has come. Ready the men."

The doctor gathered together the loose papers on the table, and the men all said, "Yes, sir," before turning to leave.

Karl waited for the front door to open and close, and the air to be still.

He closed his eyes. Felt his blood beat hot in his veins. Then he opened his eyes, and turned to the hallway on the other side of the kitchen. He followed it up the stairs and past bathrooms and bedrooms, to a closed door in the rear. He knocked gently and pushed it open. "Good evening," he said.

Chapter Eighteen
Menu Twenty-Four

Hunger was gnawing its way through Brian's stomach, and his senses were dulled. If he stood too fast, his head grew dizzy and his knees felt weak. Still, he refused to eat. The slop they were feeding him, the rancid and chunky brown gruel, it was likely made from corpses butchered after the battle. The Red Hands weren't so generous as to feed him something proper.

"What puts you at odds with Alice?" he asked the guard as the tray was taken off the cot.

The man paused, then said, "Killed someone."

"Don't seem that strange, these days. Must have been someone important for them to commit you to execution."

"No one important."

"I killed plenty of unimportant people. Never brought me to the gallows. Well, except for this predicament." Something strange happened. Brian felt a tickle from deep in his stomach, and he let out a laugh. A small, yet undeniable laugh.

The guard looked at him from the corner of his eye. "Something ain't right with you," he said.

"There's a lot not right with me. Shit, it was my own cousin who brought you all to us, here in Alice. At least, he's partially to blame."

"That so?"

"Sure is. You want to hear what's more?" Again, Brian laughed. "*I'm* the one to blame."

"How's that?"

"I smashed his head in with a stone out in the woods …" He was laughing so hard tears came to his eyes. "I bashed in his head with a fucking rock! Left him there for dead. He was picked up by you all and made into a monster."

The guard let out a stifled laugh. "Ain't that some shit. You've gone plumb mad, haven't you?" He took the tray and turned to leave, leaving Brian alone to laugh in the dark. "But he wasn't the only one who brought them here. I told them about Alice, shit … right after I left. Your cousin had little to do with them invading."

***

The next meal was placed on the cot, and Brian looked up through foggy eyes. He hadn't bothered getting up to do his walking rounds since … yesterday?

"What's your name?" he asked the guard.

"Here," the guard said, reaching into his pocket. "I'll be back in a half hour to take the wrappers. They'll kill me if they find out."

He passed a rectangular brown plastic pouch. Brian knew what it was before taking it; an MRE—Meal Ready to Eat. The pouch was cut open at the top, and the inside felt slim, about half-full. Brian opened his mouth to speak, but the guard spoke first. "The war has begun to the south of us. Alice will fall, I'm sure of it, and I don't know what Karl will do with you after, if he remembers you at all. If he doesn't, you'll be stuck down here until craziness overtakes you or the guards are reassigned, and your meals and water are long forgotten. Either way, your future doesn't look so hot."

Brian swallowed and said, "Why not just kill me and get it over with?" The words weren't mocking. "I'm dead no matter how this plays out. Why waste your time coming down here? Karl don't need me, and we both know it."

The guard sighed. "I've killed plenty enough. I don't make a habit of murdering without justification."

"Justif—" Brian cut himself off from sounding hostile. Then he said, "None of the others seem to care much about justification. I've seen what the Red Hands are capable of with my own eyes."

The guard shrugged. "Some," he said. "Not all." After he spoke, a silence filled the room, as if those simple words held a great weight and were not to be told; an accident leaked from his lips. He looked up at Brian, his shadowy eyes locked with his own. "I've been with Karl for many miles. We've conquered towns together, survived for years, fighting as a well-organized machine. After the first battle in Alice, we lost, well, I don't know how many of our men. Over half our numbers, I would guess. We recruited a colony up north—dockworkers, near-starved soldiers. Karl killed their Russian superiors and took charge. It was a blessing to them. They were fed, made strong, and told of all the plunders to come. But Karl made a mistake …"

In the pause, the guard swallowed visibly and looked to the ground. Brian was about to speak, but worried that if he did, the man would snap out of his revelation and remember he was not supposed to be sharing such intimate details.

Finally, the guard continued. "Well, not so much a mistake, but a misjudgment. Those of us fighting with him since the beginning, we never questioned his orders or ambitions. Karl's leadership has kept us alive. More than alive—healthy, well-lubricated with alcohol, methamphetamines, and pills. On the docks, Karl gave a speech, his hands still stained with the blood of the Russian commanders. He claimed leadership to wild approval from the mass of spectators. He spoke of Alice and Hightown's villainous ways, and he promised that prisoners taken from Hightown would be looked after. Offered amnesty. You"—the guard pointed to Brian—"you are the villain, Karl told us, and after the battle, we would rebolster our numbers by allowing surviving enemies into our ranks. His misjudgment was that he thought the people believed him. And worse yet, that they wouldn't care when those promises turned into lies."

"What are you saying?"

The guard shrugged. "Don't really know. When Hightown fell, the dockworkers began organizing the prisoners, but Karl ordered their immediate execution. Shot. Hung. Hundreds were decapitated. These sights …"—the guard shook his head—"have become such an accustomed ritual that it was peculiar seeing the looks on many of the new recruits' faces. Shock. Horror. They'd never seen such a bloody spectacle, and it reminded me of days, years past, when I myself was not yet accustomed to the ease with which we kill each other."

There was a pause, and the guard turned to leave. "Why are you telling me this?" Brian asked.

The man paused, looking back. "Because it doesn't matter much what you know, or what I tell you. I left you something in the bottom of the bag. Just remember, it's up and down, not side to side." He pointed to his wrist.

Brian felt the slick, comforting side of the plastic pouch. The thought of sinking his teeth in an actual piece of meat, savoring the protein and fats on his tongue, nearly brought him to tears.

"What's your name?" he asked again.

"Jacob," the man said.

"You can come back, Jacob. They'd let you back in Alice. Unlike Karl, you—all of you—would be given amnesty."

Jacob huffed a quiet laugh. "No. No. We wouldn't. And besides, there's an element I left out of that tale. Many of the dockworkers might have been horrified by witnessing the executions, but others, probably most … they lusted for it. Their eyes sparkled; they savored the exhilaration of striking down those who opposed them. Bloodshed has a strange effect on humans; we either fear it or lust for more."

With that, Jacob turned and walked beyond the open cell door, closing it with a bang behind him.

Brian wasted no time sliding the two pouches of food out, and marveled at them on the mattress. One read: *Applesauce, Carbohydrate Enhanced.* The other read: *Menu Twenty-Four, Southwest Beef and Black Beans.*

He reached in the brown plastic bag, feeling something small and flat. He removed and examined a singular razor blade, the sharp point illustrious in the dim hallway light.

No wonder you told me so much, he thought. *Up and down …*

Chapter Nineteen

Years Prior to Humanity's Collapse: Soft Rebellion

A hypnotic swirl of cotton ball-like snowflakes drifted in the wind and scattered over the pavement. The row houses of the Washington suburb appeared magical at the late hour, with shafts of the blustery white flakes luminescent in the streetlights. General Albert Driscoll's car pulled to the curb, and the driver was about to get out to open the rear door for the general.

"No need," Albert said from the back seat, opening his own door.

"I'll be parked nearby, sir. Call when you're ready to be picked up."

"Thank you, Tom."

Albert held the collar of his overcoat tight against the wind and walked fast up the stairs of the brick townhouse. The door was opened before he could knock, and Senator Jeffries welcomed him into his home. "Come in, come in," he said. "Let me take your coat."

Albert brushed the flakes off his shoulders and stepped inside. "Thank you," he said. "I'm sorry I'm late. The highway's a mess."

"No problem. We're still waiting on General Davis. He should be here any minute. Everyone's gathered in the living room; can I get you a drink?"

"Please." Albert followed the senator out of the entryway. Just a few steps beyond he met the familiar faces of what at first would have been considered a resistance movement, but with recent developments, they were now perhaps the only people left in the United States with a genuine plan to ensure humanity's survival. The ten members consisted of high-ranking military brass and a few senators and congressmen. The world was on the brink of a disastrous war, with

89

the president brushing his finger aloft the nuclear button, and these men and women shared similar opinions and strategies on how to weather the inevitable storm. However, the events first reported in the Middle East, and now throughout Europe, China, and Russia, split their priorities to not only surviving nuclear annihilation, but how to rebuild society after the unrelenting disease would soon blanket the earth. As the current administration was keen on escalating the threat of warfare, and largely disregarding the scientists' foreboding of the disease, having these meetings in secret was a necessity.

The group turned and nodded to Albert, and he shook hands with his comrades as he made his way across the room. It was strange seeing his fellow service members out of uniform. He himself felt odd in his plain slacks and wool sweater, as if this were a casual affair, a relaxed social event. But the Rolex watches, pearl necklaces, shiny loafers, and high-heel shoes did little to mask the grim expressions and sense of dread blanketing the officials.

Senator Jeffries returned with a rocks glass filled with a dark liquor. "Thank you," Albert said, sipping at the rim. Scotch. Good scotch, with a vibrant earthy aroma. The senator left to wait by the door for the last arrival.

A middle-aged man wearing a tan sweater and holding a tumbler of liquor shook Albert's hand. "Any reports from the border?" he asked, holding his firm handshake for a moment.

"I'll go in detail during the meeting," Albert replied. "But yes, I'm afraid there are reports. It's reached our shores. The quarantine has done little to nothing. And if it's airborne, well, closing our borders won't make a lick of difference. What about you, General Barnett? Any word on your end?"

"Please," the general said. "Call me Nelson." He pinched at his sweater. "We're not here on official terms. But, no, there's been no reports of the disease in the Southwest, or anywhere along the southern border."

Albert nodded. "That's good."

Nelson sipped his drink. At forty-two, the slim and graying-haired man was the youngest among them, and responsible for so much. His colony would be one of the three that was landlocked. And with the harsh temperatures of New Mexico, his people would have to rely on an elaborate hydroponic system to ensure crop production. The only other member still in her forties was congresswoman Laila Beaumont, who would be heading the Montana initiative. Albert noticed her when he arrived, speaking to General George

Clifton, who was in charge of the largest of all the settlements—California. Albert was eager to hear General Clifton go into detail about the bunker he'd constructed, which could hold upward of ten thousand. The California initiative was the boldest construction in development among them.

Albert felt a light buzz creep in from the few sips of scotch when Senator Jeffries returned to the room with Senator Davies in tow. The old senator navigated the plush carpet with a mahogany cane and offered a thin smile. "I'm sorry I'm late," he said. After the man was offered a drink, the rest of the gathering found seats in the parlor, and Senator Jeffries stood center beside the spectacular marble fireplace. The talking subsided to a few murmurs and a subdued cough as the senator first turned his attention to the fire burning in the mantle, placing another split log atop the blaze.

Then he turned and smiled, his palms held upward, just like he'd been known to do when speaking at forums and debates throughout his long career.

"Ladies and gentlemen," he said, "here we are, once again. It saddens me that this may be the last time we're all together in one place at the same time for quite a while, and in such pleasurable comfort. But because of the work we've accomplished, I'm confident that we will meet again, in one capacity or another. No one in the world has worked harder than this gathering. Each of you is responsible for directing hundreds, if not thousands, of men and women, to ensure that at least a fraction of our civilization will endure to see the world repopulate and once again thrive."

Albert felt the weight of the world crush upon him. At times, he wasn't so sure any of their projects would work. He had to direct dozens of architects and laborers to construct the elaborate bunkers needed to house his men. Sadly, most of those responsible for the construction would not make it through the coming days. As the senator finished with his opening remarks and gave the floor to Doctor Hopper, Albert was reminded of the last time the doctor had addressed the crowd. "The Middle East is expected to fall within a month," the man had said. And he was right. The disease killed indiscriminately, finding the soldiers that bullets could not: senior military, officials and clerks included. It was hailed as a victory to those already at war with the region, but soon the epidemic spread.

"I'll get right to business," the doctor said, passing out a stack of manila envelopes. "Please take one and hand them back." He waited a moment for the papers to be dispersed, and then resumed, "On the first sheet, you'll see the estimated tallies and figures of the contaminate thus far, beginning with the Middle East, and ending on the last page, with the US."

Albert scanned the numbers and statistics. His eyes fell and stuck on one: *Estimated Mortality Rate: 87.69%,* and he thought, *That's from the disease alone.* He tried tallying together the other estimated mortality rate he'd read in other reports, from the inevitable war, nuclear fallout, rioting, and looting. The combined statistic was catastrophic.

"We have made progress learning how the disease operates and spreads. We know that it is highly mutable, and did not begin airborne. We are still trying to trace its origin, but we have reason to believe it was transmitted via touch at first, which explains the slow spread in the beginning stages, and the recent explosion we're seeing in Europe now. It's changed and adapted as needed, making it difficult, if not impossible, to treat."

"Have there been *any* developments on a vaccine?" Laila Beaumont asked from the crowd. Her voice had a pleading quality, a hope that perhaps they could scrap everything they'd been working on if only a cure could be doled out in time.

The doctor's chest expanded in a large inhale, and he closed his manila folder. "To put this as bluntly as possible, the answer is no. But to be more specific, if we had sufficient time, I'm convinced the scientists working tirelessly at the CDC could concoct a cure. But going back to the outline presented in the report, the disease is spreading too rapidly for a treatment to be produced in quantity. A limited batch is possible, but by then I fear the majority of America will already be experiencing ill effects. The virus operates by staying dormant for upwards of thirty-six hours, and then, when it appears, it comes in full force. The body gets eaten from within, and the infection does everything in its power to populate. The sufferer will experience severe stomach and intestinal ruptures, which is the bacteria's way of freeing itself from the confines of the body so that it can find new hosts."

At previous meetings, the group had been shown images and videos of the afflicted. Similar videos had recently become widespread, despite the media's attempt to stifle the grotesque nature of what they projected, and help to qualm the panic pervading the general public. But with nearly the entire population of the earth having high-quality cameras in their pockets at all times, and an easy means to share anything online, the videos made their way out.

"I fear the only way to proceed at this juncture is to continue in the direction we've been planning. The best we can do is hope that the small percentage of those left unaffected will manage to survive until the disease runs its course."

The doctor took his seat, leaving the room in silence. As Senator Jeffries retook the stage, Albert was reminded of all the dates and statistics the doctor had shared over the months. He had confirmed what Albert had been told by other high-ranking government officials—that the virus would die off in about thirteen months. After fourteen, it would be safe to venture out again, as long as the scientists gave the all-clear. For anyone without the scientific instruments needed to detect the disease, two years was a safe amount of time.

The doctor finished his presentation and gave the floor back to Senator Jefferies. "It might do to brighten our spirits by reporting on the current state of the colonies. Let's begin on the East Coast and work westward." The senator looked to the general from Maine, and the frail old man stood on wobbly legs.

As the man spoke, Albert was reminded that not everyone in that room would make it through the coming years. There was a statistic shared early on, as the bunkers were in the midst of construction: a third of the settlements would fail. Either at the onset, because of the disease, or in the later years to come. Surviving the apocalypse was step one; enduring the aftermath was phase two.

The general from Maine was quick to give his report, and a full rundown of the amount of fuel and supplies still needed.

Albert was next to take the stage. After giving a report, he added, "I've developed plans to spread my colony to a second location following our rebuilding stage. Several miles to the south of Hightown is a fertile park called Alice, with a running reservoir. You've all met Tom Byrnes, who's been perhaps my biggest asset in developing our strategy. He will lead Alice to produce, in time, enough food to feed not only our settlement but any others who need it. First, though, we will need to get the reservoir back on line." Albert gave a quick estimate of the number of people needed to keep Alice in working order, and then sat so that the delegate from Louisiana could speak.

Out of all the colonies, Louisiana, led by General Greg Ubel, was perhaps the most important for Hightown's continued survival. Greg and his soldiers were geared to populate a naval base alongside the Mississippi River. His armada would be responsible for fuel transportation to the eastern colonies. The petroleum would begin its journey in Texas, and make its way to the South and then the East. California was also to benefit from Texas's production, as would New Mexico and Colorado. Montana would be responsible for producing fuel for the northern colonies.

In order, after Greg, the following colonies gave their reports: Kansas, Texas, Montana, Colorado, New Mexico, and finally, California. Afterwards, their glasses were refilled, and the men and women mingled in sober conversations. Albert checked his watch and rubbed the bridge of his nose. He finished the glass and stood off to the side of the room, peering out through the window at the dancing gusts of snow as it fell in the shafts of streetlight, and called his driver to pull the car around.

Chapter Twenty
Deluge

The gates groaned open and a buzz filled the sky. Boats swarmed from the dock, following the canal that would bring them to the ocean, and then down to the snaking channels connected to Alice's reservoir. The warship would offer artillery assistance from the open sea, far enough away so the hull was not in danger of scratching the bottom of the shallow trenches.

Karl's transport led the procession, with Liam in the front passenger seat and the Priest on his side, humming a hymnal tune. Hundreds upon hundreds of soldiers followed, with the might of the armored division acquired from Hightown.

Victory was far from certain. Despite Alice's defenses still in shambles, the soldiers manning the line maintained formidable munitions and were battle hardened. The attack would have to be precise and well executed, which was not something the bulk of Karl's men were accustomed to. The infrastructure of the gardens and the reservoir were to remain intact, requiring artillery to be called in as needed. They would destroy Alice much the same as they had defeated Hightown—breaking the line and flanking it from the sides, with the aid of air support.

Karl played out the various scenarios in which the battle might proceed, reveling in the images of droves of prisoners bound and kneeling before his feet: the line on fire, Jeremy Winter's head on a spike, Simon Kalispell hung from a lamppost.

Oh, Bethany, just wait until I show you a conquered Alice, and your pathetic little toy of a man defeated and lifeless. I can't wait to break you, Simon Kalispell.

The men were instructed to take prisoners, spare as many as possible. Karl told his army the captives would be offered redemption, a chance to join the brotherhood. The dockworkers were a soft bunch. Able fighters, but not hardened by the years of warfare and strife that his long-accustomed soldiers had grown accustomed to. And they would need prisoners, not to join in their ranks, but to man the gardens, produce the food and water for the Red Hands. The able bodied would be spared. The desirable would be taken. The elderly, children, disabled—they would be eliminated. The dockworkers had to become seasoned to Karl's methods, especially when sharing in the spoils of war, the abundance of food, water, and fuel that made taking the settlements and risking their lives so well worth it.

He patted his front pocket for his cigars and offered them to his officers. The Priest waved his hand dismissively, but Liam was eager to take one.

"Give me—" Karl said, sucking a flame into the end of the cigar as he spoke, "a full report from the scouts."

"Quiet to the north," Liam said. "Nothin' from across the water. Same goes in the east and south. The scouts to the west were discovered and killed in a skirmish. They have since been replaced, twice. Don't know what happened to the last batch; might have been captured."

Karl knew all of this. The news was a day old. His scouts got too close to the line and were spotted. The western border was lightly wooded after Hightown's invasion had toppled many of the trees and thicket as its armored division rolled into Alice.

"They'll be expecting us," Karl said, offering Liam news that he already knew.

"Yes, sir. They will."

Despite Liam's expertise in navigating the vessels, Karl had decided that his second in command was best suited at his side during the battle. Perhaps it was superstition, but the last time they were divided, the fighting did not go in their favor.

Karl exhaled a large plume of smoke to trail outside the window. In a bag at his side was a bottle of scotch, the foil waiting to be peeled back in celebration. His mouth watered for a sip of the peaty liquor. He longed to feel the sting on his tongue, the warmth spread from his stomach into his head, feet, and hands. He yearned to be sitting beside the reservoir's edge, in quiet contemplation, washing the blood of his enemies from his hands.

Hours, not weeks or days. Victory was hours away.

I'm coming for you, Jeremy Winters. I'm coming for you, Simon Kalispell. With my own hands, I'll strike you dead, oh Lord, I swear it.

Karl smiled listening to the buzz of his trailing army, like a legion of monsters called out of the depths to destroy all who stand in their way.

Alice would be his.

In Karl's mind, it already was.

Chapter Twenty-One
United Colonies

It was late as the officers gathered in Alice Elementary School. Simon walked fast down the eerily dark hallways, with only a few emergency lights running and long stretches of shadow in between. His shoes squeaked on the polished tile, and from down the hall he could see the luminous outline of the office's glass window projected on the far wall.

He opened the door on a meeting already taking place. A few looked up at him, and he caught Jeremy's quick gaze before sitting down. Being late for a meeting of this magnitude was unacceptable, and there was only so much that his and Bethany's despair over Brian's capture would excuse.

When this is over, when this battle is won … I'm handing in my resignation.

He tried to focus on his breathing and listen to the scouts speaking to the gathering of officials, reading numbers and tallies off sheets of paper, but his thoughts wandered to Bethany and Carolanne, the sadness in their eyes, the torture of not knowing their husband's and cousin's fate. Was Brian still alive? Did Simon have the capability of sneaking into Hightown? Jeremy would surely not authorize it, but still … could he? So many had died, was it worth risking his life to save just one?

Simon returned to the conversation, listening to a scout who'd returned from Albuquerque. "There's no way they'll send their entire force," the man said. "Jackson is still with them, so maybe he'll sway their decision, but while I was there, they agreed to send two hundred soldiers." The scout speaking, an older man named Glen Spears, had left with two others, traveling nonstop to Albuquerque, carrying the fuel needed for their journey. Glen remained in

Albuquerque for a few hours before making the return trip, along with one other soldier, driving as fast as the roads allowed. A relatively straight path was established a year earlier, with stalled automobiles moved aside, and areas of utter destruction marked. The complete journey took under four days.

Three other scouts had taken a similar journey to one of the other United Colonies, near Gunnison, Colorado. However, they arrived at a deserted location. The long strip of buildings that comprised the territory was reduced to blackened skeletons. Glen told the gathering that the Colorado colony fell during the winter months after succumbing to a massive fire. After a desperate attempt to rebuild, despite the frigid temperatures, the remainder of the citizens migrated south to Albuquerque. A fraction of their numbers survived the fire, starvation, and journey afterwards.

Jeremy sat at the table, pen in hand but not writing, looking weary. "Two hundred is a good number," he said. "I wasn't expecting them to agree to send any aid, so I'm astonished. When will they depart?"

"They were mustering the convoy before I left."

Jeremy rubbed his eyes. "Good," he said. "That's good." Simon wondered if the man had slept at all since the first reports of the Red Hands invading Hightown came in. He hadn't been home, Simon knew that much.

"All right," Jeremy continued. "Sergeant Rayne, you're up."

"Sir," one of the other scouts said, and tapped his papers together on the table. "Yes, sir. Louisiana didn't delay. They've already sent ships north to our aid. Before I left, they were around the panhandle. I imagine their progress would have them near Charleston at the moment."

"What about the fuel convoy?" Lieutenant General Casey Edmunds interrupted. "Hightown had a delivery scheduled that we couldn't intercept."

"There's been no word, sir. The officials in Louisiana have been trying to contact the vessel as well, and promise to send word once they hear back. It's gone radio silent."

"All right," Jeremy said. "What numbers are they sending?"

"Four cruisers," Sergeant Rayne said. "Equipped with sea-to-land missile systems. The Red Hand's warship will be no match for them. They're pledging four hundred additional troops, all onboard the cruisers, with landing vessels."

Jeremy sighed. "Things aren't looking so bad," he said. "However, there's no guarantee that we'll receive any of this backup before the Red Hands attack our line. If they do, we'll have to hold them back for as long as we can. Has there been any word from California or Texas?"

There was a moment of silence as each member looked to one another. Texas and California were the largest of all the United Colonies, and maintained an arsenal unmatched by the others.

Casey Edmunds broke the silence. "Nothing yet," he said. "We sent our lead engineer, John Zur, to Texas as Hightown fell. I expect we'll hear back shortly, but I wouldn't hold your breath. Texas is the rugged individualistic type. And both of the colonies are a long journey away. This is the first time we've sent scouts straight to California without a holdover in Albuquerque or Texas. The likelihood of either of those settlements coming to our aid is slim."

"So that brings us to a total of six hundred soldiers, an armored wing from Albuquerque, and four cruisers."

Casey Edmunds nodded. "The biggest concern we face is our lack of intelligence," he said. "If the Red Hands strike with the same numbers they maintained when they attacked Hightown, we can be reasonably sure of victory. However, just a few days ago we knew nothing of their reserved army and their ship. Hell, we thought Karl Metzger was dead. We've sent small drones for miles around and haven't found whatever naval yard they came from. There's no way of knowing what we face."

The group was silent.

Simon wanted to ask what the plan was to rescue Brian, but he didn't. He knew the answer—there was nothing to do until the war was over. A rescue mission was out of the question. All of Alice was at stake; the fate of one man did not weigh heavy on any of the official's shoulders. Deep down, Simon believed that Brian was still alive. Jeremy believed it too, and had told Simon as much. There was no practical reason for the Red Hands to go so far out of their way to trap him without some nefarious reason.

There was nothing Simon could do now, and waiting was torture.

Chapter Twenty-Two
Cutting the Fog

The bright moon high in the sky projected the outline of the living room window onto the far wall. Carolanne slept soundly on the couch beneath the window, deep in a medicated fog. Winston lay curled at her feet, occasionally letting out a whimper and a muscle twitch as his dreams played out.

Connor had been granted permission to stay at Simon's apartment whenever he liked instead of Alice's orphanage, which consisted of five other children. The boy had fallen asleep on the couch along with the sleeping household, wedged behind the round side of Winston's curled back, and his head atop Carolanne's legs. Simon scooped him up and brought him to his own bed, laying him beside Bethany, whom he was happy to see was fast asleep. She needed it. No one had slept much recently, and she least of all.

Simon closed the door behind him and returned to the living room. Carolanne woke up with a start. "What's happening? Has there been any word?" She looked around the room as if trying to decipher where she was. Her hair was flat and matted on the side.

"Nothing new. Go back to sleep."

"I can't sleep," she said.

"Try. Just try. I have a meeting with Richard. We'll be in the kitchen. You can sleep in my bed if you like. We'll be quiet."

"You have a meeting now?" She looked at the window. "What time is it?"

"Late," he said.

He left fast to the kitchen, not wanting Winston to wake up and start barking when Richard Jarrett came in. He opened the front door, where the second Ranger in command waited with his hands in his pockets.

Richard entered. From the living room, Simon could hear Winston's tail beating against the couch cushions. But a moment passed and his dog didn't muster.

He's getting so old, Simon thought. *A year ago, he would have come running at the notion of a sound from the front door.*

"Take a seat," Simon said. "I'll put coffee on."

"Coffee?" Richard said. "Isn't it a bit late for that?"

Simon didn't check his watch. He knew it was well after midnight.

"Water then?" he asked.

Richard nodded.

Simon poured two glasses and sat across the table from his second in command. The man was close to Simon's own age, just a few years older. His dark hair didn't yet display the grays that came along with aging, and his muscular form still moved like the wind when out on a hunt.

"Richard," he said, looking down at the still water in the glass. "This isn't easy for me to ask."

Richard took a sip and placed the cup on the table.

"I, well, I'm just going to come right out and say it; I'm not going to stay here waiting while Brian is held captive …" He trailed off, then looked up, catching Richard's stare. "It's not fair. It's just so goddamn unfair. Not only for him, but for his family, Carolanne and Beth. He's a citizen of Alice, and we owe him at least an attempt of a rescue mission."

Richard nodded and tapped the tabletop with his fingertips. "I know how much this ordeal is troubling you, but it won't be easy getting in. You'll be risking your own life and the lives of the rescue team trying to save one man, when we're about to be at war with the whole of the Red Hand's army." He paused, and Simon was about to respond, but Richard continued, "Still though, if you say the word, I'll get a team assembled. We'll leave before dawn, stake out Hightown's perimeter, find the best way in."

Simon took a sip of water, then said, "No, Richard. That's not why I asked you here. It's no secret that I'm at odds with my position in Alice. The rest of the Rangers, except for two or three, Shepard and Jensen, are all military." He shook his head. "I have no right leading you or anyone else. I'm not a soldier. I don't deserve to pretend that I am."

"Boss," Richard said, patting his front pocket for his cigarettes. He opened the pack and offered one to Simon, who waved his hand dismissively. He struck a match and tossed it in a trailing descent of smoke in the ashtray on the table, half-full with Jeremy's cigarette butts. "You need to get over that shit. You're in charge of the Rangers because of your skill and ability. Because you have something to teach. You know things that the rest of us need to learn in order to survive."

Simon wanted to argue that he was largely put in charge because of his performance on Nick Byrnes's lawn. All of the dead he slayed, shot, hacked into pieces. But he didn't. "I'm going alone," he said. "I'm leaving tonight, and I will not risk the lives of anyone else. I'm sorry to put this burden on your shoulders, but I don't have a choice. You'll have to lead the Rangers, which you are more than capable of doing."

Richard inhaled and let out a large cloud. "I'll come—just you and me. We can get past the defenses, no problem. Near the water's edge is my best guess."

"No, Richard." Simon let out a sigh. "You're needed here."

Richard took a last inhale and ground the cigarette out. "All right," he said, swatting at the trail of smoke. "Do you have a plan?"

"Other than getting myself behind their line, not really. Either I will—"

The radio on the table made a squelching noise, and a voice said, *"Mister Kalispell, report. Over."* The line was designated for communication to Simon only. Each of the officials had their own frequency, so that they wouldn't have to sift through the ongoing communications between the various posts.

Simon picked up the radio. "This is Simon. Over."

The voice said, *"Report to HQ. Over."*

Simon looked to Richard. "I'm sorry to place this burden on your shoulders."

"Simon, I—"

"Do you copy? Over," the voice asked.

"I copy," Simon said into the microphone. "What am I needed for?"

"Scouts report enemy activity, less than a klick northeast. Scouts along the riverbank are reporting the same; vessels approaching. Over."

Simon remained motionless, and then he stood. Richard did the same, taking another cigarette out of his pack. Once outside, Simon spoke again into the microphone.

"How large is the advancing force? Over."

"*Sir,*" the voice said. "*Initial reports are in the hundreds, maybe thousands. All scouts north of Alice have been pulled back. Over.*"

Simon swallowed against the dryness in his throat. He was about to speak again, but then the foghorn blared, rattling the dew from the leaves.

Chapter Twenty-Three
Twisting Descent

Jeremy burst through the door to the office in Alice Elementary School, greeted by the thick aroma of coffee and a fog of cigarette smoke. A few officers looked up as he entered, then cast their eyes back to the maps and ledgers. Casey Edmunds was already there, the collar around his neck unbuttoned. A steaming mug of coffee sat on the table before him. A soldier handed Jeremy a cup, and he stood next to the lieutenant general.

"Where are they?" he asked, letting the steam meet his nostrils.

Casey's finger trailed the map and stopped on a location in the woods above Alice. "Here," he said. "Scouts report the bulk of the army approaching from the southeast." His finger trailed along the reservoir, and to the bay leading into the ocean. "Last reports spotted the vessels in the water, going at a slow speed. No doubt to match the army's progress. By now, they should be along the bank here."

"How many ships?"

"Hundreds. All small vessels, enough to carry a handful of troops each. Here, at Alice's banks, is where they are presumed to land. If they go any farther the coast grows steep, and we'd pick them off easily from the vantage."

Jeremy studied the maps as he pulled a cigarette from the pack with his teeth and snapped his brass Zippo open. Earlier that evening, the first good news in days reached him: forwarding scouts from Albuquerque's detachment arrived by motorcycle. They were less than a day's ride ahead of the main force. They came with a full report of the armament, which was impressive. In private, tears came to Jeremy's eyes knowing that the bonds established at the colony's beginnings were not cut. A sizable army was coming to Alice's aid, including three attack helicopters strapped to the back of flatbeds. Jeremy spoke at length with the scouts, and sent one back to give word to the officers of everything learned of the Red Hands up to that point. It was likely their army would arrive in the thick of battle.

And now, it seemed certain.

Jeremy glanced at the wall clock above the door.

"All we need is time," he said. "Just a little more time."

Casey nodded. "We'll get some," he said, pointing to two locations along the Ridgeline River bordering the northern shore of Alice's perimeter. "Everything's in place. The men await our command. It should buy us at least a few hours, and halt their progress until Albuquerque arrives."

Jeremy nodded. It was all they could do, as futile of a plan as it was.

"Any word from Louisiana's frigates?"

Casey shook his head. "Nothing yet. We've been attempting to contact them over the Ham radio, but to no avail. Possible radio malfunction. We'll try the CB frequencies when they're within range."

"All right," Jeremy said, grinding his cigarette out in the ashtray. The room was so loud with voices that he didn't hear the soldier beside Casey was speaking to him.

"Sir?" the soldier said. Jeremy looked up. "They're within range, sir. The forward scouts have a visual. What's your command, sir?"

Casey looked to Jeremy. "Well," he said. "Do you want to make the call, or should I take lead?"

Jeremy pulled another cigarette from the pack with his teeth, and reached out to take the radio.

***

The excitement of the troops' voices was noticeable radioing in over the airwaves. They were within a mile of Alice, their minds ripe with amphetamines, their bodies eager to surge from their transports and trample down Alice's gates. Karl had no delusion that their progress went unnoticed. The element of surprise was out of the question. Priest Dietrich sat behind him in the Hummer, muttering his gospel tune.

"Mine eyes have seen the glory of the coming of the lord;

He is trampling out the vintage where the grapes of wrath are stored;
He hath loosed the fateful lightning of His terrible swift sword;
His truth is marching on."

Fond memories of the entourage on horseback crossed his mind, with the Priest singing loud and the men mumbling along as they raided and sacked countless lands. In the back of the Hummer, the song lost much of its might. The confinement was displeasing, and Karl was eager for the battle to be underway and his army to be free of their convoys. The soldiers operated best when out in the open, like one giant living organism hell-bent on consumption.

A report came in over the radio: *"We're at Benton Bridge. Over."*

That was good. The bridge was the marker for the assault. Once crossed, it was a swift western turn to Alice's gate. Soon, his ships would pass below the bridge to anchor north of the land assault. Over the roar of the engines, Karl heard the thumping sound of the helicopter blades high above. They had been instructed to keep their distance far in the rear until the army crossed the bridge.

Karl found a cigar and struck a match to the end, rolling the tip in the flame.

"Light 'em if you got 'em, boys," he said. "Once over the br—"

A plume of fire and smoke shot high in the near distance, and the cab of the truck rattled with an explosion. The driver came to a halt, and Karl lost the grip on his cigar.

"Jesus," he said. Rocks and debris rained down on the hood in a heavy downpour. "They blew the fucking bridge …. Fan the column!" he ordered to no one in particular.

***

The corded radio crackled in the scout's ears. *"The operation's a go. Enemy contact less than a half mile out. Over."*

The three dozen scouts were in position along the shore, scattered high in trees or behind cover as the sound of the coming army grew loud. When the first truck came into view the radio again spoke, *"We have visual. Get ready for contact. Over."*

Richard Jarrett was given battlefield command. Besides this being a full-on military operation, it was only hours ago that he'd learned Simon had every intention of leaving Alice to make some suicide mission alone into Hightown, and leave him in charge. Did Jeremy know of Simon's plan? Did Jeremy know that Simon wanted to step down as head Ranger? If the Red Hands hadn't arrived when they did, Simon would now be on his way to Hightown instead of relaying communications in the headquarters.

Those thoughts would have to wait. Richard knelt behind the broad side of a boulder, feeling the cold of the stone penetrate his uniform. He peered through the night-vision scope of his rifle, watching the first two armored vehicles proceed onto the bridge. Far in the rear of the procession, he could hear but not see the drumming blades of the helicopters.

God, he wished that Albuquerque and Louisiana's army would arrive. If they had, this operation would be much different. Instead of a small brigade—only to stall the enemy—they would have the manpower for a full-on showdown along the riverbank, and end this nightmare for good.

The full might of the enemy was hard to determine through the limited view of the scope. All Richard could see was the side of the bridge and a small portion of the road beyond. The first vehicles on the platform were Hummers, two and then four, and then two more. Next were tanks. US-issued Abrams tanks. His pulse beat fast knowing that those tanks belonged to Hightown's arsenal, and were commandeered by those vile men.

The first Hummer made it to the opposite side, followed by two more, and then all six were on land. The treads of the tanks were close to the end of the bridge when Richard said, "Now." A soldier beside him didn't hesitate. He typed a code on the keypad of the remote, flipped the safety switch, then squeezed the trigger beneath. The transmission was instant, and the firing pulse ignited the small batch of C-4 and dynamite planted on the beams behind the supports on both ends of the bridge, hidden on the undersides.

The explosion turned night into day for a flash as columns of fire shot high. Prior to the threat of invasion, every bridge connecting Alice to the north was wired with explosives in a ten-mile stretch. For this mission, the explosives planted in the middle of the bridge were hastily removed. It was not the intention to blow the structure to rubble. With a terrible creak, the metal and stone collapsed, and the lane holding the tanks and armored vehicles disappeared behind a gust of smoke and a plume of water as they fell into the Ridgeline River below, effectively blocking the canal from the oncoming boats, if at least for a short duration.

Gunshot erupted from either side of the road as Richard's brigade opened fire on the six Hummers that had made it safely across the river. Machine guns mounted to the tops of the vehicles fired back, indiscriminately cutting down the brush in the woods. It wasn't long until a medic was called for over the radio.

Three of the Hummers sped off the road, and one crashed into the side of a tree. Grenades were lobbed from the shadows, and pillars of dirt rocketed high. The doors opened on two of the vehicles and men emerged, running and shooting wildly, but they only made it a few steps before the snipers and machine gunners mowed them down.

From across the river, the Red Hands' procession had begun to spread out along the bank, and a volley of bullets and tank shells began to rain down.

"Fall back to position two," Richard told the solder beside him. His message was relayed, and Richard waited behind the boulder, seeing his men emerge from various foxholes and dug-in positions. Bright tracer rounds tore at tree branches as explosions became more frequent. A shell burst into the side of a massive oak tree, and Richard was momentarily entranced as he saw the middle section burst into splinters, and the giant tree topple like a boulder falling, the crash as loud as thunder.

The drumming of the helicopter blades increased in volume, and Richard could now see the dark outline of the aircraft moving steadily toward them. His heart thumped heavy against the rock as he thought, *Come on! What are you waiting for?*

High-caliber machine gun fire strafed the ground, and with terrible shrieks, missiles came tearing out from the heavens. He saw his men run for cover as the munitions tore up the ground. Another tree a few yards before him burst at its base, sending a torrent of shrapnel and fire, and Richard dropped down behind the boulder.

Fuck! Come on!

All at once, doubt plagued him. The shoulder-mounted stinger missiles should have been fired by now. The plan was a simple bait-and-eliminate. The helicopters weren't supposed to make it across the river. This wasn't the war, this was only a skirmish, planned to slow the Red Hands' progress and eliminate, reduce, or frighten their air support.

But now the woods all around him were boiling with bullet fire and explosives, and he doubted that half the men would make it back if he called for a full retreat—which was exactly what he needed to do. "Private!" he yelled. "Call for—" He looked over. The man beside him was motionless, his back against the rock, half his face missing. Richard reached for the radio, when he heard it. The sweet roaring of rockets fired from the rear of the formation.

The cacophony of explosion came first, and then he peered over the edge of the rock, seeing fire blazing in the sky and twisting, around and around, as the helicopter lost control, its rear tail burning. More rockets streaked into the air, and there was a deafening explosion from high above.

Bullet fire continued from both sides as his men fell back. Far in the distance, the buzzing sound of a lone helicopter grew distant as it retreated, but there was no doubt that it would soon return, with backup in tow.

Chapter Twenty-Four
Reposition

Karl met Liam behind the defensive perimeter hastily constructed along the riverbank. On the opposite shore, pockets of fire burned, the brightest belonging to their own Hummers blown to pieces in the melee.

"I've sent outriders to check the bridge west and—"

"No bother," Karl interrupted. "They're all wired. I'm sure of it."

Liam scratched at his beard. "We can begin construction of a new bridge ASAP. I suggest going a mile downstream, where the distance between the shores is minor."

Karl looked over the sea of his men digging trenches and setting up machine gun turrets behind sandbags and fallen trees. He bit his cigar and spoke behind clenched teeth. "No, Mister Briggs. It would be a foolish pursuit. They'll pick off the workers one by one with snipers."

Liam rested his palm on his holstered pistol. "The armada is held up a half mile down the river. They can clear a path enough to pass through the debris in no time. We have enough ships to load the whole army, if needed."

"And then, Mister Briggs, we would leave our armored wing behind. Without the tanks, the battle would go quickly in Alice's favor."

"All right then ... what's the plan?"

"If you were them, what would you do?"

Liam shrugged. "Probably wait behind the line."

"Maybe. But right here, where we are, we appear to be in a place of weakness. We're stranded at the riverside, with a thin defensive perimeter."

"Exactly my point."

"But we are *not* as weak as we appear, now are we?"

Liam shook his head. "No, sir."

"If I were them, I would muster the troops and have our battle right here, along the bank of the river. Line the opposite shore with artillery and snipers, and attack us head-on with a ground assault. Drive us into the river."

"We could move the army closer to the bridge, strike them down as they came across, just like they did to us."

"Staying close to the ocean is a priority." Karl dropped his cigar and ground it out with the toe of his boot. "Going further inland will lessen our firepower. This is but a game of chess. Pieces move and strategies alter."

"Yes, sir. What is the plan then?"

Karl took in a big inhale and let it out slowly. "We wait. See if they attack." He paused in contemplation. "Strike that," he said. "They *will* attack. Sooner than later. Get me a radio. I want to get this show on the road."

Chapter Twenty-Five
The Verdict

The officials stuffed in the meeting room in Alice Elementary were exhausted, yet listened to the presentation with focused intent. Wafts of cigarette smoke layered in murky drifts, and the stale odor of coffee permeated the fog. Simon's stomach was sour and twisted with anxiety, yet he sipped from the mug.

A briefing of the attack and reports from the front line were presented. It was followed by an assessment of everything gathered about Karl Metzger, Liam Briggs, and the Red Hands at large. Much of the information was accumulated by interrogating the prisoners acquired following the battle in Alice; the intel included the locations of Haddonfield Maximum Security Prison and Odyssey, which were the birthplaces of the Red Hands. They were still controlled by Karl's men, yet believed to hold limited resource or strategic value, and some of the prisoners spoke of Karl as once being an inmate of the penitentiary. The personal information presented offered a wider perspective of Karl's thought process. Although it was hard to decipher reality from fiction in the prisoners' accounts, some information was correlated with records kept in Alice's public library.

Karl was, by all accounts, a murderer before the fall of civilization. The library kept limited documents of newspapers from around the United States on microform, and after hours looking over films from Houston and Dallas, one article came to light. It told the tale of a vagabond. A ruthless and sinister criminal. The article was written upon his arrest, which subsequently put two police officers in the hospital, battered and maimed. The full scope of his atrocities was still under investigation at the time the article was written, but he was on trial for nine murders, and suspected of at least eight more. Men. Women. Children. Police officers had followed his trail of arson, robberies, and murder from coast to coast. At first, it was believed that one man was not capable of committing all these horrific crimes alone, such as in the case of a former small-town delegate and wealthy benefactor, found with his wrists tied behind his back and a bullet shot through his temple in executionary form. The same fate befell his family, which included three young and robust sons. The strong boys were beaten and subdued before being killed. The mafia was blamed before the connection to Karl was established, who had acted alone with only a pistol and a baseball bat.

Karl never remained sedentary, leaving a wake of carnage as he drifted from state to state. He stole everything in his sight and formed two false companies which employed four gullible employees, who were all subsequently robbed and murdered. A police officer interviewed in the report stated, *"The man holds no semblance of human emotion. When we told him of everything we knew of his crimes and offered a plea deal that might spare him the death penalty in exchange for his cooperation in discovering more of his victims, the man laughed and asked how the chow is over in Haddonfield Max. He doesn't care about anything, including his own life. He's the most dangerous man our department has ever encountered."*

The presentation was given to a quiet assemblage, with Jeremy sitting behind the desk, bleary-eyed and chain-smoking cigarettes. The officer at the podium was using a projector to display an image of the article on a roll-down backdrop.

Then the door swung open, and a soldier walked straight over to Jeremy and whispered something in his ear.

"All right," Jeremy said, and twisted his cigarette out in the ashtray. "We've received word from both colonies. Albuquerque's army will be arriving within an hour, and Louisiana before dawn." He checked his watch and stood. For a moment his legs seemed to falter, then he said, "We march when the ships arrive. Everyone, get what rest you can." He turned to the soldier who'd just arrived. "I'll be in my office. Alert me on any developments."

"Yes, sir."

As Jeremy left the room, the officials all began speaking at once. Maps were unrolled on the table and ledgers were produced. Simon stood, and squeezed past the throng of activity toward the door. The air in the hallway was cool and refreshing. He rubbed at his sore eyes, not sure which was making them more bloodshot, the sleeplessness or the room full of smoke.

Jeremy's office was along the same hallway, just a few doors down. Simon knocked, and Jeremy's voice was quick to call out, "What is it?" Simon turned the handle and entered. "Oh," Jeremy said, taking a seat behind his desk. "Simon, what's up?"

There was a cot with a ruffled blanket in the corner. "Jeremy," Simon said. "You getting any sleep?"

"A few minutes here and there."

"You need more."

"I'm fine. I learned a trick during boot camp, that if you get a few twenty-minute naps in during the day, you can keep going without a full night's sleep. The brain goes into REM faster when it knows it won't be getting much rest."

"You getting any twenty-minute naps?"

Jeremy shrugged, took his cigarettes from his front pocket, and pulled one out before tossing the pack on the desk. "What is it you need?"

Simon looked to the ground. "Well, first, I wanted to check on you. Make sure you're resting."

The Zippo lighter snapped open and flicked to life. "Right," Jeremy said, closing the lighter. "Which is just what I'm planning on doing."

"Good."

"Simon." Jeremy flicked an ash into an overflowing ashtray. "What's wrong?"

"There's no easy way to say this, so I'm just going to say it."

"You want to go try and save Brian, right?"

Simon looked up at him. "Richard talk to you?"

"No, but I'm not surprised," he continued. "I tried putting myself in your shoes, thinking about what I'd do if the person I loved was in as much pain as Bethany." He took a large inhale, then blew the smoke out. "You willing to risk your life in the process? What happens if you fail? This is only one man, remember, and we're about to go into battle."

"What happens if I do nothing?"

Jeremy offered a thin smile. "Look, I get it. But I'd be lying if I told you it wasn't foolish. As good of a scout as you are, sneaking in past Hightown's line and finding him—and then bringing him out safely—is impossible."

"I can go during the battle, when they're distracted."

"You mean, while the men on their defenses are on high alert?"

Simon didn't answer.

"Look, I know that if you've made up your mind, there's nothing I can do to stop you. But I would much rather have you fighting at my side when the battle begins. Once the colonies arrive, we'll catch the Red Hands by surprise and squeeze them from both sides. They'll pop like a grape. The men need you. The soldiers respect you. You took down Nick Byrnes, after all."

Simon shook his head. "I'm not … I'm not a soldier. I'm not a fighter. I don't think I can do that again, fight the way I did on Nick's lawn."

"Damn it, Simon." Jeremy ground his cigarette in the ashtray and leaned across the desk. "You've been going on about *not* being this, *not* being that, since the day I met you. I'm starting to realize that you're completely full of shit. You need to recognize that who you are, the real you, is the person you are every day. A fighter. A soldier. A compassionate human. If you go off and die on some suicide mission, what's going to happen to the boy … what's his name?"

"Connor."

"Yeah, him. The kid survived terrible ordeal after terrible ordeal, to wind up in your care, if at least partially. He doesn't need more people in his life dying a pointless death. And what about Bethany? Does she know your plan? Is she going with you?"

"No, she doesn't know. If she did, she would want to come along, and I wouldn't be able to stop her."

"Just like how I can't stop you?"

"Look, the way I see it, I have just as much of a chance—more of a chance—dying in the battle as I do sneaking into Hightown."

Jeremy was quiet for a moment and sat back in his chair. He began unbuttoning the front of his shirt and said, "Your chances of saving him are better with us than alone. Not to mention that your Rangers need your leadership."

Simon was about to mention his plan to hand the position over to Richard Jarrett, but decided it was best to wait.

"Look," Jeremy said. "I would order you not to go if I thought it would do any good. But like I said, if you've made up your mind, there's nothing I can do to stop you. But if you haven't made up your mind, if there's a seed of doubt, know that you will fare better invading Hightown with the full force of our soldiers once we take down and kill Karl Metzger and his invading army while they're camped by the waterside." He unclasped his watch and tossed it on the desk. "Go think. Meditate. Sleep for an hour, which is what I'm planning to do. I promise you this; when the time is right to reclaim Hightown, you can personally lead a brigade to find and rescue Brian. Scout's honor."

Simon nodded but didn't reply. After a pause, he said, "Get some rest," and closed the door after him.

***

Winston greeted Simon at the door, his tail in its usual fervor. Carolanne was there, awake, and so was Connor, both on the couch under blankets.

"Beth still sleeping?" Simon asked them.

"I think so," Carolanne said. They stared back at him. "Is this it?"

Simon reluctantly nodded.

She sat up on the couch, her eyes puffy slits. "I'm ready. I can't just sit here, waiting. I'm going with you."

He couldn't tell if Carolanne's hoarse voice was excited or terrified. On one hand, Brian might be saved. On the other hand, in doing so, a battle would be fought that would see many of their friends die.

"Carolanne," he said. "You're needed here, tending to the wounded that will come pouring in."

She shook her head. "I don't think I can help anyone. I can't think straight, knowing Brian is out there, somewhere"—she swallowed visibly—"probably dead."

"We don't know that. We don't know anything. No one will blame you if you can't help the wounded, but you're in no shape to fight. Get to the fire station before dawn with the other medics, children, and elderly. They're setting up a transmitter on the stage, and information from the front line will be relayed. The army is marching as soon as Louisiana's ships arrive, and Albuquerque will be here any minute now. The battle will begin early in the morning."

"I have to do more. I should be out there fighting for Alice. For Brian."

"Me too," Connor said. "I can fight." He looked terrified just saying the words.

Simon and Carolanne exchanged glances, and their expressions seemed to reach a mutual understanding.

"Connor," Simon said and rubbed the boy's shoulder. "I know you can fight. I have no doubt about it. But I need you to do something for me. Something important, more important than fighting."

Connor looked at him, his face half-covered under a blanket, his eyes huge, hair growing out from the short monk's crop. He was curled up against Carolanne's side, his body less than half her length. Back when Simon had first met him, all that time ago in the woods, the boy seemed so much older than he was. Wise beyond his years. But it was evident that despite the treacheries the world threw at him, the terrible ordeals he faced, he was, after all, still a child.

"I need you to look after Winston while I'm gone."

Connor's lip wavered, and he said, "Will you be okay?"

Questions like this, Simon thought, *shouldn't have to be asked by a kid.*

"From what I'm told, with the colonies fighting together, the Red Hands are vastly outnumbered. By this time tomorrow, the Red Hands will be gone for good. Finished."

The boy nodded.

"But I'm not going to lie to you … I don't know. If things go badly, the three of you need to leave—immediately. Don't wait around. Be ready to leave at a moment's notice."

"I'm already packed," Carolanne said. "I have a duffel bag with some supplies and clothing for Connor and myself."

"Good," Simon said. "That's good. If Alice is about to … well, collapse, the fallback colony is a long journey, all the way to Albuquerque. So be prepared. And please, get Winston there safely."

No one answered, but Connor nodded and Carolanne rubbed her eyes. *All out of tears,* Simon thought.

He got up from the couch and went to his room, gripping the door handle gently, not wanting to wake Bethany. But as he entered, the light of the study lamp greeted him. Bethany sat before the desk, her assault rifle half-assembled, a grease-stained cloth and brushes beside it. "Simon," she said with a thin smile. "How much time do we have?"

"We're out of time."

She nodded and turned back to the rifle, continuing the reassembly. He had a flashback of the first time he'd met her, when she was injured in the woods, and he came to her aid. Yet, she cursed him out, not wanting any help. Her dedication and persistence was inspiring, even in the face of pain and exhaustion. It was in that moment, watching her assemble her rifle, that all plans on leaving her behind to fight in the battle so he could make a desperate attempt to save Brian vanished. He would fight by her side, and later, when the bullets slowed, they would march into Hightown together and discover the fate of her cousin.

Across the room, Simon opened his bedside drawer and removed his Colt .45. It felt cold and comfortable in his hand. He holstered the pistol and swung his M1A rifle over his shoulder. Bethany put the magazine in the port of her assault rifle and stood.

For a moment they remained speechless, looking at each other across the room. Then they met in the center and embraced. She rested her head on his shoulder, and they were quiet. A million words tried to escape the tip of his tongue, but there was no need to say any of them.

Holding hands, they left the room.

Chapter Twenty-Six
United

Six Hummers rode into a clearing outside of Alice's perimeter and came to a halt. The doors opened and anxious-looking soldiers stepped out, scanning the bordering wilderness and calling communications in over their radios. A tall man emerged and removed his helmet. He slicked back his graying hair and walked to meet the delegates from Alice. Simon stood at Jeremy's right side, Casey Edmonds on the other.

"Jeremy Winters, I presume?" He smiled and extended a hand.

Jeremy reached out and shook. "General Nelson Barnett. It's an honor to finally make your acquaintance." They were of similar age and stature. Years of warfare and survival under dismal circumstances had hardened them both and embedded lines of worry among the scars.

"Likewise. I would like to offer my condolences over the loss of Tom Byrnes. I had the pleasure of meeting him on several occasions. He was a born leader and a great man."

"He is missed every day. I believe you already know General Casey Edmunds." Jeremy motioned to Casey standing beside him. "He is the ranking officer from Hightown after the loss of General Driscoll."

"Yes," Nelson said. "Of course." They shook hands. "We've met, many lifetimes ago. It's a terrible loss, what they did to Albert. He was the greatest military man I've ever had the privilege of serving alongside."

"Thank you," Casey said. "He thought highly of you as well. He would have been elated to know the colonies have not failed, and that we stand together, united."

"I couldn't agree more. With the collapse of Colorado, Maine, and Montana, our old bonds need to be strengthened. To that extent, has there been word from Louisiana?"

Jeremy nodded. "They're out at sea, waiting on our command. Their vessels are manned, and a landing zone has been established. They'll flank the Red Hands from the rear while we face them head-on."

"So here we are," Nelson said, scanning the faces of the officers and soldiers from his colonies and the others, "together, at long last. In hours, we will celebrate victory, friendship, and renew our bonds. My men are eager to ride into battle and see this band of criminals turned to ash."

The gathering nodded, and a few said, "Hear-hear."

Simon didn't budge.

"Jeremy," Nelson continued. "This is your land, and your show. We've been over strategy on the journey, but please catch us up on any new developments."

Jeremy motioned to his side and said, "General, no one in Alice knows the lay of the land better than this man, Simon Kalispell, the head of our Ranger division." He exchanged a quick glance with Simon. "We're lucky he's with us."

The general looked up and nodded. The officers asked Simon questions about the terrain outside Alice, the bridges and wooded areas. Maps were unfolded and laid out on the hoods of the Hummers. The officers studied the markings and paths, and copies were given to Albuquerque's ranking officers. Not a half hour went by before the soldiers rolled up the maps and shook hands. Jeremy said, "This is it. We'll radio Louisiana. To a swift victory."

***

A brigade set up on the bank beside Elmhurst Bridge with long-range mortars, ten miles west of the destroyed Benton Bridge where the bulk of the Red Hand army remained, just in case the enemy gained an upper hand and pushed the advancing army back in retreat. Scouts related that efforts were being made to remove the debris fallen in the river so that the stalled armada could pass.

Jeremy took a final drag of his cigarette and flicked it out the open window of the Hummer as it crossed Elmhurst Bridge, where it spun to the water in a twisting descent. He had no delusion that the Red Hands would be caught unaware by their attack. This war, which began with deception all that time ago when Karl slithered his way into Alice, had become all-out open hostility.

He often wished that Tom Byrnes was still alive to head this terrible new dawn of their continued survival. The old man never faltered, never missed a step. He'd envisioned Alice's formation before the war and disease reduced the world to rubble. This battle would be a cakewalk for Tom Byrnes. But for Jeremy, it was his first major action as general in charge. He wasn't taking orders; he was writing his own.

If it weren't for the colonies coming to his aid, victory would have been near impossible. Somehow, the Red Hands had grown in numbers and acquired a navy. They were strong, but now with Louisiana's fleet, the tide of war would change. The Red Hands' fleet of smaller landing crafts were sitting ducks for medium-range ordnances, while they were still held up in the river. They would be wiped out in a matter of minutes, just as Louisiana's own landing crafts anchored their army ashore. The Red Hands would be squeezed like a grape.

As the last of the army now crossed the bridge, the assault was officially under way. Jeremy found his pack of cigarettes. One more. Just one more before his hands would be needed for the trigger.

He flicked his Zippo open and shielded the flame from the wind of the open window. The vehicles were picking up speed as the army went into tactical formation. The bulk would strike east, following the river. Casey Edmunds and Nelson Barnett were branching off with a large portion of the armored wing. As the main army targeted the front line, they would attack to the north, and Louisiana's soldiers would take up the rear. Cruise missiles would be called in from the armada to precise locations, and the Red Hands' force along the riverbank would be set ablaze in record time. And then, the army would proceed north to free Hightown and eliminate the vermin who infested its walls.

Jeremy flicked his cigarette butt into the wind and took a deep breath of fresh air before closing the window. The operator in the back seat manning the CROWS remote-controlled M240 machine gun atop the roof said, "Movement reported."

Jeremy rechecked the chamber of his machine gun and peered to the horizon, trying to see past the several rows of armored vehicles preceding him.

His hand was on the radio, waiting to give and receive communications. Bullet fire erupted, mixed with the booming of tank shells. He was glad that Simon was sitting beside him, although he could feel the trembling from his leg as they were packed in the back seat. Jeremy knew the boy could fight; he just had to tap into that animalistic portion of his brain once again and become the warrior he was born to be.

Jeremy looked out over the horizon as best he could see and hit the receiver, calling to the armada to begin the assault.

Chapter Twenty-Seven
Offering the World

Shallow trenches and large-caliber machine guns sat behind sandbag fortifications. Mortars and artillery were in the rear, along with the helicopters that were roaring to life.

"Here they come," Liam said, looking through binoculars.

Karl checked the chamber of his rifle and looked out over the horizon. From his slight vantage point, he could see past the defensive line to the straight road ahead and the wooded sections at either side. Farther up the line, his men had infested the dilapidated homes in a residential section to gain high ground.

"Artillery, sir?" Liam asked, and spat a dark trail of tobacco juice to the brush.

"Hold," Karl instructed as he listened to the helicopter blades grow louder. "Ground explosives first. Wait until their vehicles are past the mark, and then unload the artillery on what's left of the advancing party."

"Yes, sir." Liam shouted orders into a radio.

A twinkle appeared on the road ahead, moving toward them, and a crunching noise came from the distant woods. Reports over the radio described brush and small trees toppling in the far thicket. The first pop of gunfire was followed by another and another. Which side had fired first, no one could tell. Explosions followed, some close to Karl's position, many distant. Reports came in from various sections. *Shots fired! Shots fired!*

"They're coming right at us," Liam said.

"Yes, Mister Briggs, they are." The twinkle on the road came to full fruition, and through the binoculars, Karl made out a line of Hummers and what looked to be a tank leading the advance, coming fast, right at them. Machine guns atop their roofs flashed, unleashing torrents of high-caliber rounds. His defensive line was getting peppered, with debris of all kind ricocheting wildly. Bullets were finding their way farther ahead, striking the leaves and branches over Karl's head. The officers crouched, using the side of a fallen tree for cover. "Ground explosives," Karl issued.

Liam called in the order. All at once, a line of fire shot upward in a semicircular formation, as the hastily planted C-4 detonated beside trees, boulders, and on either side of the road. The approaching vehicles were cut off from the reserves as a blinding wall of smoking flames consumed the horizon.

"Short range," Karl commanded.

The order was repeated, and the artillery in the rear of their position opened fire. Dozens of shells fell in unison. Karl watched a tank take a direct hit yet keep its approach with the top on fire, shooting a shell into the side of a tree on the line, exploding a torrent of splinters and shrapnel. Three of his men evaporated into mists of red. More artillery fell, and the tank took two more hits until it crashed into the side of a massive oak and remained motionless. More Hummers and transports exploded, adding to the hellish landscape, with troops trying to escape their fiery incinerators. Machine gun fire riddled the colonists not consumed in the blazes.

From behind the wall of flames, Alice's reinforcements bounded through, crashing into the stalled vehicles and proceeding onward into the melee. Reports came in from across the line that The Red Hands' positions were falling. Alice's army was gaining ground, and a second battalion was attacking their northern fortification in force, attempting to cut off their route back to Hightown in the case of retreat, and further push them toward the sea.

"Position two," Karl said, and turned, not checking if Liam and the officers were following, but knowing they were. The front line was issued the command, and many tried to fall back as the bulk of Alice's armored wing crashed through the defenses, and their troop transports began unloading. Swarms of the enemy were in short-range combat with the forwarding Red Hands. The houses to the north were either blown to rubble or flooded with troops, and the fighting spread from room to room.

"Release the rest of the air support, and radio for long range, on my mark," Karl said, running for cover to their second line of defense. He showed no sign of emotion, worry, fear, or exaltation.

***

The tanks and armored transports tore past the wall of flames, and as Simon's Hummer accelerated into the inferno, the air became stifling, singeing his throat. They burst through to the other side and into a smoky landscape, their lead vehicles burning in craters, and their troops running from the back of the transports, many consumed in fire.

"Christ," Simon said out loud. Jeremy had the radio to his ear, shouting orders and listening for reports. The rattling from the remotely controlled turret overhead shook the entire cabin. Bethany sat beside him, her knuckles white as she squeezed her rifle. Her other hand remained on the door handle, ready to run into battle, or escape the Hummer if it became damaged.

I'll never be as brave as her, Simon thought.

A dozen armored vehicles preceded their Hummer, fanning out in either direction, and firing into the Red Hands' defenses. They were breaking the line. As they approached the fighting, they passed demolished remains of the enemy's machine gun nests and fortifications. Their own short-range artillery was raining down, and tracer rounds exchanged fire with a helicopter above. Any minute now and Louisiana's armada would unleash as the enemy clustered close together while falling back.

The Hummer came to a halt and Jeremy said, "Why are you stopping? Move!"

"Sir," the driver said, "I was ordered to keep you behind the front line."

Jeremy opened his door to run into the melee ahead, before a heavy hand grabbed his shoulder.

"I'm ordered to keep you safe," the driver said, reaching to the back seat.

"We're sure as hell not safe sitting idle—a perfect target for their helicopters. And I can't call in orders if I'm away from the front! Move us into position—that's an order!"

The driver remained motionless, his hand still on Jeremy's shoulder, then he turned around and put the vehicle in drive. "Yes, sir," he said, and maneuvered with the rest of the fast-approaching reserves. Simon jolted back and forth as the truck rebounded over bumps. It was hot enough without the uniform and gear, and Simon wished he had gone with his first instinct—to scout the land alone to sneak into Hightown—and wasn't squeezed into the back seat of a truck while dressed in a bulky flak jacket, thick boots, and cumbersome helmet. He'd undergone drills and training with the gear, but he'd never liked it. Dexterity was impossible to maintain.

He breathed in and out, in and out, trying to focus his thoughts. Whatever mindset he was able to tap into that night so long ago on Nick's front lawn seemed impossible to reclaim, almost like Simon was a bystander watching a stranger hack across the trenches. Each time a small munition ricocheted off the Hummer's bulletproof armor, he flinched as if the bullet had found its way to his heart.

Reports came in that the Red Hands were falling back from every position, cramming together close to the river's edge and the ocean behind, although it was hard for Simon to decipher most of what Jeremy was shouting to the officers with his own pulse vibrating in his eardrums. Alice's armored wing was approaching the collapsed bridge when Jeremy took his ear away from the microphone and announced that Nelson Barnett's brigade was making fast progress to their location, having effectively cut off the enemy's fallback route. Casey Edmund's division was setting up a defensive line to eliminate the possibility of enemy reinforcements coming out of Hightown, and awaiting the order to proceed north to liberate the city.

Jeremy studied their position against a map and called in for Louisianan's armada, which had reported they were in firing position, ready to unleash their missiles on the enemy's location. The ships reported no signs of the Red Hands' destroyer.

Jeremy opened the door to the Hummer to follow the rush of ground troops, when again the driver again put a heavy hand on his shoulder.

"Sir—"

"You want to keep me safe? Pick up your rifle!"

Jeremy ran from the Hummer, and for a moment, Simon sat there, staring out the open door. Then Bethany said, "Move your fuckin' ass!"

Bethany was kneeling outside the Hummer, scanning the area ahead, and Simon came up beside her, his rifle at the ready. A sergeant called for soldiers to form a perimeter around their general, much to Jeremy's protest. Simon's toe hit something and he stumbled, looking down at a torn and dismembered leg. There were bodies everywhere, both from Alice and the Red Hands, along with shredded machine guns, vehicles, and crater holes. In a world full of death, witnessing corpses was nothing new; the fear came from their freshness, knowing that he could easily join their numbers.

Come on, Simon told himself, *Get it together. Stop fucking shaking.* He tried repeating mantras like he had during the battle at Nick's mansion—*Bethany, Bethany, Beth*—but it was no use. It wasn't coming naturally, subconsciously.

They fell to a crawl inside a crater as they neared the front line, with explosions raining down nearby. Simon's cheek hit the dirt, his sweaty skin turning it to mud.

The collapsed bridge was in view, with the Red Hands' flotilla somewhere behind. Bullet fire peppered the rim of the crater, and Simon pressed up against the side, wishing to meld into the soil and disappear from sight. The Red Hands were across the highway, where they seemed to have a secondary hardened defensive line in place.

Bethany lay beside him, her rifle and head peering just over the rim, firing into the distance. Simon took a deep breath and glanced over. From his vantage, there were no enemy soldiers visible, but still he aimed and fired into the wooded area across the road. A portion of Nelson's armored wing was mixing with their own to the north, on the opposite side of the enemy's flank, further crushing the Red Hands into a crevice. Jeremy shouted to the sergeant, "Stop all advancing troops before the bridge! The armada will be targeting east of the road! Call in the strike, now!"

Overhead, one the Red Hands' helicopters streaked across the sky, trailing a cloud of black smoke. Tracer rounds followed its retreat, and the smoke grew heavier and heavier, until the aircraft burst in a flower of fire high in the air.

"Holy hell!" Bethany shouted. Simon pressed the side of his body up against hers as they watched the flaming debris trail to the ground.

The noise of the explosion was overtaken by loud and terrible shrieks from Louisiana's missiles, and the first explosion rattled the ground so fiercely that Simon's vision blurred. More missiles fell, and a wall of dirt blanketed them in the crater. A burst of firelight came from Nelson's armored wing, followed by smoke so thick that the rest of the squad fell over in coughing fits, rubbing at their eyes. Simon spat dirt out of his mouth and rubbed it from his nose as more and more missiles fell, and bright strobes became blinding. Bethany pressed in tight against his chest.

"Ca—" Jeremy tried to say, coughing and shielding his head as another wave of dirt fell over the officers, along with wood fragments and rock particles. A soldier's body careened backward into the crater, shot like a cork from a bottle. "Call the armada!" Jeremy yelled. "They're firing on us! Call—" He grabbed the sergeant's shoulder, but the soldier's head lolled to the side, dripping red.

***

Louisiana's ships navigated as close to the shore as they could before hitting the bottom, and the convoy ships released. A swarm of landing vessels rebounded over swells as they reached the eastern shore, and close to four hundred troops made landfall. The general and founder of Louisiana's naval colony, Greg Ubel, traveled in the second reserve of soldiers, rather than wait on the destroyer and send an emissary in his place to make contact with their allies.

Officers called out orders, assembling tactical formation. His men were hardened, genuine military, not unlike the soldiers from Hightown. Many of Alice's population were also trained soldiers, but most were not, making them the weaker of the two forces. From everything he'd gathered, the Red Hands were something of an enigma. The vast majority were common lowlifes with the knowledge of how to point and fire weapons. However, they had conquered Hightown and brought a new age into the colony's existence.

Through sheer brutality and anger, Karl Metzger had transformed bands of deviants into a capable fighting force. Not just capable, but dominant. They fought with disregard for their own safety; they fought with a passion to see their enemies slaughtered. They were terrifying.

The clamor of warfare echoed to the landing area, and trails of smoke blended into each other to form a semicircular wall in the distance. Loud shrieks tore overhead from the missiles fired from Greg's vessels, and the explosions were loud.

If the plan was succeeding, as he was led to believe, the Red Hands would be less than a mile from the shoreline. His men formed a bulky formation with reinforcements in the rear, and it didn't take long until he heard over the radio, *"Soldiers in sight."*

This was the first assault that Greg was personally overseeing, and it felt good to be holding a rifle again. His legs were aching already, and his hips weren't as limber as they had been all those years ago when he'd been in active combat, but still, the rush of warfare was euphoric.

He spoke to his lieutenant, "We get a bead on 'em yet?"

"Yes, sir. Right on target, less than a half click."

His men held up, assembling in mass behind derelict homes and buildings.

"They're spotted, sir," his lieutenant said, and offered a pair of binoculars. Greg didn't take them. He could see the movement across the short expanse in a dense row of homes.

"Advance," Greg ordered and stood from his crouch. The lieutenant spoke into a radio, and all at once, the army emerged from the woods and behind the homes into full view. The opposing line of Red Hands turned and pointed to their procession. More men appeared at various window openings and from behind corners of buildings.

The distance between them was short. A tall man stood in the center of the line of soldiers, a cigar clamped between his teeth. Greg took lead, and as he neared, the man with the cigar stepped forward.

"General Ubel, I presume?" The man had a deep, baritone voice.

Greg nodded. "Karl Metzger." The men reached out and shook. "It's a pleasure to make your acquaintance."

"The pleasure is all mine, Sir General."

The two armies met in the field, looking each other up and down. Some nodded, a few shook hands.

"Time is of the essence," Greg said. "Catch me up to speed."

"Yes," Karl said. "Your missiles are doing just as planned; Alice and Hightown are being shredded to pieces. And even more, their confusion is causing further disarray."

Greg followed Karl with his army in tow. Various faces permeated his thoughts, all the people he'd known prior to this terrible mess and the people he'd met or heard of since: General Albert Driscoll; Nick Byrnes; Jeremy Winters. He had turned on them all, and had done so with an ease he would never have thought possible.

But Karl had offered him what the colonies could not. The age of hiding behind walls was over. The disease had done its damage, and with help from the war, humanity had become threadbare. But that did not have to continue to be the case. In the past, Greg had used examples of famous conquistadors and colonizers, Cortez, Magellan, and Dias, when trying to persuade the other colonies to venture out from behind their walls. What if these famous explorers had never taken the leap to find new worlds? Humanity must progress with a swift and forwarding movement at all times. But the colonies wanted to remain sedentary. They didn't want to expand to new locations, to once again cover the earth.

They refused to explore this new world.

There were two types of people left: those who were content to wait in hiding, guarding what little they could maintain, and those who were ripe to explore it to new advantages, be it by force or not. Greg's pleas to the other colonies for growth had been ignored—and there's only so long a person can go neglected. In the end, his colony was being used for their fuel, and nothing more. Karl told him as much. They spoke for hours on end over the radio, after the fuel ships docked, unaware that Hightown had fallen.

Karl greeted the apprehensive sailors with a full smile and no weapons raised. He offered them a drink, and although they refused to deboard the ship, Karl was permitted to address Greg via radio. It then became clear that there were others out there who saw the world much the same as he did. Together, they could spread their wings and cover every corner of the world, if they so wished. The time was ripe for further colonization. Together, General Ubel and General Metzger could lead a new dawn. One that they dictated.

After hours of consideration, along with tallies of numbers, armaments, and past victories, Greg returned to Karl after holding a meeting with the officers. They would join the Red Hands to see Alice fall, and after, they would help it rise back up again. In the end, Greg knew that betraying his alliances was the best course of action to ensure humanity's continued survival. As it were, the United Colonies did nothing to help one another. Never once did they come to each other's aid. The Colorado territory died screaming for help, but did Albuquerque offer them assistance? No. Under Karl Metzger's rule, under the methods of the Red Hands, a true alliance was formed. The next step in humanity's continued evolution was at hand. This was the era of exploration. Of growth.

Karl offered Greg and the Louisiana territory a proposition that they could not shy away from. He gave him an invitation to turn his back on the other settlements, and realize it was time for change.

Karl Metzger offered Greg Ubel the world.

Chapter Twenty-Eight
Realization

A strong hand grabbed Simon's shoulder and pulled him to his feet. Before he could clear the dirt from his eyes, he was shoved, dragged, voices shouting in his ears, cutting through the roar of explosions and terrible screams.

"We need to fall back!"

"We're getting torn to shreds!"

"What do we do, sir?"

"What do we do?"

Simon halted, rubbing his eyes, and making sure Bethany wasn't injured. Weary faces stared back at him, recoiling at each succession of blasts. They were speaking to both Simon and Jeremy, but Simon could only stare back. The world around him was on fire, the air stifling, twisted, and burning scraps of armored vehicles streaming dark smoke like spilled ink.

"Fall back to the bridge!" Jeremy shouted, even though the soldiers were already falling back without his command. "Call the armada! Find out what the fuck is going on!"

The huddled group began to move, running away from the front line. An officer said, "They're not responding, sir."

"Keep trying!" Jeremy replied.

Back on the road, a Hummer idled, waiting. The back door was open, and Simon was shoved inside, followed by Bethany, Jeremy, and a crush of men. The vehicle accelerated fast over the pavement, in a convoy escaping the hellish bombardment.

"How did they get the wrong coordinates?" Jeremy yelled to the occupants.

An officer sitting in the passenger seat held a radio to his mouth, calling the boats to no avail. Once they got to the bridge, they could reevaluate their position, try to find out what had happened, and hopefully get the armada to start firing on the correct position.

A half a mile out, the wooded section disappeared into a neighborhood of derelict homes. As the army fell back, a ball of fire erupted ahead of the line, and the Hummer swerved around a massive crater in the pavement and the burning wreckage of a troop transport. Unrecognizable bodies and parts littered the ground.

Another bomb fell behind them, followed by another, and then several all at once.

"Fan out!" Jeremy commanded, and the driver jerked the Hummer onto the lawn of a home and crashed through a fence onto the adjacent property. *They're following us …*

"They're following us," Simon said to no one in particular. "The bombs, this is no accident … Jesus Christ. Louisiana and the Red Hands, they're working together."

Jeremy looked at him with a grim demeanor. A streak of smoke trailed downward across the sky, followed by a boil of machine gun fire. Simon didn't have to look out the window to know they were being strafed by the helicopters. How many of those damn things did the Red Hands have? Every time they blew one up, another appeared. By previous calculations, they had acquired three from Hightown's arsenal. But what about Louisiana? What terrible toys did they possess?

The bridge came into view, and a procession was already passing swiftly to the other side. *Please, God, in all that is holy, let us cross this bridge before the bombs find us.*

The robotic machine guns on the rooftops fired back at the helicopters, along with dozens of small arms from soldiers on foot, and rockets were discharged from shoulder-mounted launchers. Jeremy gave the order for the bridge to be blown once their army made it over, as there was little doubt that the bulk of the enemy's forces were following their trail.

As the Hummer crossed to the other side, the soldiers in Alice were ordered to open the gates for the coming army to make a swift entrance, and for all defenses to be manned. A combined air and land assault was expected, and those helicopters had to be taken down if they were to keep the walls intact.

"Is everyone over the bridge?" Jeremy asked the officer in the passenger seat.

"It's believed so, sir."

"Give the order for detonation. Have we heard from General Edmunds or General Barnett?"

The man shook his head. "No, sir."

Simon looked at his friend—his best friend, other than Winston—and knew that numbers and tallies were going through Jeremy's head to such a degree that he must feel lightheaded. How many men were lost? Were Nelson and Greg dead? How many officers survived … did they have enough of a force left to ward off an assault from both the Red Hands and Louisiana? Could Louisiana's armada target locations inside Alice?

"Sir," the man in the passenger seat said, looking over his shoulder. His eyes were huge. "Alice is under attack, eastern section, near the trade grounds."

Simon's chest tightened, and he saw Jeremy's lips purse. The small vessels must have gotten through the fallen bridge.

"Jesus … how many?" Jeremy asked.

The man held the corded headset for Jeremy to take. Before he could speak, a voice on the opposite side shouted so loud that Simon could hear it, "… *breaking the line; they're breaking the line!*" Jeremy's mouth was open, but he didn't say anything. "… *hundreds of them …*" the voice continued. "… *we're falling back to secondary positions … the helicopter …*"

The explosion from the bridge never occurred, and Simon didn't have to hear a report to know that something went wrong. With the enemy now infested inside Alice's walls and fast on the heels of the retreating army, they would be crushed before the day was done.

Jeremy gave a visible, dry swallow, and said to both the passengers and into the headset, "Code thirty-five, one-o-six."

The officer in the passenger seat looked back and said, "Is that your order, sir?"

"Yes, Lieutenant." Jeremy removed his headset and handed it to the officer. "Give the order to everyone who can hear it." The man nodded and took the receiver. The Hummer halted, and the vehicles all around him veered fast to the south.

Simon caught Bethany's distressed gaze. Her eyes were large, glassy, but she didn't say a word.

Carolanne … Connor … Winston …

Jeremy sat back in the seat rubbed the bridge of his nose. Then he removed his pack of cigarettes and offered them to the car. Every grim-faced individual took one, including Simon. It was entirely possible that no one in Alice would make it out alive, but they had a better chance fleeing to Albuquerque than they did trying to fend off the invaders. The thought that it was gone—all gone—was too much to bear. The Red Hands' filthy fingers desecrating the gardens and water, which had taken so long to build. So many lives lost over a piece of land. And just like that, it was taken from them by force.

Alice was lost.

Chapter Twenty-Nine
Moon over Water

The food turned into energy the moment it passed Brian's lips. A mental image formed of the protein, vitamins, and calories on a molecular scale, sucked in like a sponge on his tongue, to his blood, and delivered to every inch of his body with each heartbeat.

The calorie count was substantial, and Brian debated whether to save half of the pouch for later, but then thought better of it. A full MRE would have consisted of more side items, perhaps tortillas for the spicy beef, bean, and vegetable mixture he was sucking out of the package. It also would have included a dessert of some sort, like a cookie, but the entree portion alone was enough to refuel him at least for a while.

A funny thing happened as he swallowed the last bit of food and licked a trail of gravy off his finger: he got tired. Not just the ordinary sleepiness after a big meal, but an all-out exhaustion. He gathered the plastic wrappers and placed them under the bed, in case a different guard would check on him. A pleasant dizziness overtook him. His knees buckled, and he fell onto the mattress. His mind swam fast to the void of unconsciousness, when a thought occurred to him that it was entirely possible he had just been poisoned. Jacob's kindness could have been veiled in an attempt to either help him out by letting him die a peaceful death in sleep, or a more malicious motivation—that he simply wanted every member of Alice dead. But the razor blade? It didn't add up. Why offer a way out if he was planning on doing it himself?

These thoughts were only fleeting, as the draw to sleep was overwhelming.

Brian pulled the blanket to his chin, his hands barely able to hold the weight, and let his mind wander to the depths.

***

A voice awoke him.

"Ain't dead, I see."

Brian didn't open his eyes.

The crinkling of the wrappers followed, and he was halfway between worlds when the voice returned. "It's a pity. There's not much more I can do for you." The door creaked shut and locked.

There was no way to decipher how long he'd slept, but despite his grogginess and lethargy, Brian felt better than he had in days. His mind was sharper, his muscles had regained some strength. Even his knee felt better than it had in weeks, but that was probably due to the inactivity. He was hungry again, but nowhere near the starvation madness he had experienced.

Slowly, he turned and sat up, letting his tingling feet dangle over the side of the bed before standing and stretching his back long and tall. His spine popped and cracked, and he envisioned the same going on in his brain and organs, things crackling back to life.

There was no way he'd kill himself, that was a certainty. Not as long as Carolanne and Bethany were still alive. Not as long as there was a sliver of hope of ever seeing them again. Back when he'd reached their bunker in Aurora, Brian swore he would do everything in his power to protect them. For their survival. It was what sustained him on their journey to Hightown, and it was what compelled him to fight on during the battle on Nick's lawn. No matter how bad his situation got, if the girls were alive, he would do everything in his power to stay the same. If they did not survive ... he shook the thought from his mind.

***

That hippie shit that Simon Kalispell preached wasn't his thing, but Brian had to admit, maybe there was something to all that lecturing about meditation and being at one with nature ... not that he really knew what that meant. This ordeal might be a bit more livable if he could find an area of his mind to help him escape his immediate confines.

Carolanne's strawberry-blonde hair fanned out on the bed played in his thoughts, bringing just as much torment as pleasure. Her natural scent, like the ocean; her mischievous smile as his hands explored her stomach, thighs, and breasts … it was taken away from him. There was no way to process the Red Hands' intentions. There was no way to understand their brutality. He had to get out of there. He had to escape, somehow. The things they would do to Carolanne if Alice fell, if they got their filthy hands on her. *Oh, Christ …*

This room was his tomb. He was going to die here. His heart jumped every time he heard footsteps from the hallway, thinking that Karl Metzger was on his way to torture, maim, and kill him. Instead, he was starting to believe that Karl had forgotten him entirely. Soon enough, the rations and water would stop arriving. He'd wither away and die, alone and insane, far below ground. He had no way of knowing how much time had passed, or if it was day or night. The only indication of time passing was his developing beard and his body's increasing fatigue. If given the chance, he wasn't so sure he'd be able to fight his way out. His muscles were becoming soft, consumed to maintain his brain's functioning.

He swallowed against the dryness in his throat, and let his head fall into his palms.

Footfalls from the hallway caused him to recoil. They grew louder until stopping at the door, and then the lock turned.

Jacob entered, half his body bathed in the dim hallway light.

"Here," he said, handing across a hiking backpack. "Let's go. Hurry up."

Brian didn't move. "Go where?"

"Alice is about to fall. You've lost."

An awful pang struck inside his chest. *Carolanne …*

Brian opened his mouth to speak, but nothing came out. It couldn't be over. They couldn't have lost … everything they'd fought for in the last conflict, all of the death, people slaughtered, just so a select few could go on living …

"Look," Jacob said, "I'm never going to forgive your people for sending me to the wolves. Tom Byrnes can rot in hell, for all I care. But Nick, he had enough compassion to sneak me out."

Compassion … Compassion! The man was solely responsible—along with the naivety of the townspeople—for letting Karl inside Alice and murdering countless numbers of his own people. He was a monster, and not a compassionate one at that.

Jacob continued, "When we move out, you'll be left down here for days or maybe weeks. Some of the dockworkers are organizing the release of other prisoners kept near the line, who were to be used as leverage if the colonies had won the last battle, and were approaching Hightown's walls. When Karl finds out, he'll be mad as hell. However, your name hasn't been mentioned in days, so I'm going to give you the same opportunity that I was given. Follow me." He turned and headed out the open door.

For a moment, Brian didn't follow, thinking that certain death lay outside. Jacob's friendliness must be a ruse. But then he stood and shouldered the heavy bag. His legs felt the weight, but the spike to his adrenaline had him forgetting his body's fatigue.

The hallway was narrow, and as he proceeded a few feet behind Jacob, they passed the sole light that illuminated the cell. The bulb appeared it would die at any given moment. Through another doorway was pure darkness. A flashlight came to life, and Brian followed close behind the beam of light. His heart was now beating so heavy it felt like it would burst free of his chest.

"Quiet," Jacob said. Brian didn't respond.

They paused at the doorway of the police station, and Brian could now see that it was nighttime. "Most everyone's stationed at the defenses or mustering to move out, but still, keep your head down. If we pass anyone, just keep on walking like you're one of us."

The door was opened, and a cool breeze greeted Brian's skin. The shock of fresh air invigorated his mind and body, washing away some of what the solitude had done to his psyche.

Brian was familiar with this area of Hightown, from his time living in the colony. They were far from the front line, among stretches of vacant buildings, with the warehouses nearby. They were traveling east, to the bay, and they saw no one along the walk. It was difficult to make out the rough trail through the wooded section that brought them to the old path running the length of the waterside, close to where the Red Hands had begun their invasion. Sticks crunched underfoot, and he used his hands to shield his face from the branches; yet still, his face was stung by thorny brush and pine needles. Jacob's flashlight did little to help.

Once on the trail, they veered right, continuing to the easternmost section of the bay. A few minutes later, Jacob stopped and crouched down. "This is it," he said, and felt around in the brush.

Brian dropped to his knees, helping remove leaves and debris from a small rowboat.

"Don't return to Alice," Jacob said. "By the time you'd get there, the battle will be long over, and the town will be ours. This is as far as I'm willing to help you. Row your way past Hightown's defenses, and dock well out of sight."

They pulled the rowboat to the water's edge. "Come with me," Brian said. "You can leave this all behind and rejoin Alice. You broke me free, and I can't thank you enough. Please, leave with me. You'll see that we're not the monsters that you think we are." Brian dropped the backpack inside the boat and began pushing it beyond the breaks. The water was cool as it filled his shoes and soaked his pants.

Jacob shook his head. "I can't go with you," he said. "My fate was decided a long time ago, when I took the life of my fellow man and was excommunicated to face the crumbling world alone. Karl might be the leader now, but one day the power could shift, and the Red Hands might be led by a more compassionate general. Alice and Hightown will be at peace."

"That will never happen. You'll all be dead before then. Karl Metzger will send you all to your graves."

Brian stepped inside the boat, and Jacob pushed it gently out to sea. "There's something …" he said, and then trailed off, shaking his head. Then he continued, "There's something you should know. Inside Karl's home, he has … a trophy of sorts."

Brian grabbed an oar, using it to keep from floating further off as Jacob told him a dark tale. When he'd finished, Brian said, "Jesus Christ … save him, please. You can save him." The boat was drifting farther, and Brian didn't want to shout.

"There's nothing I can do."

Brian opened his mouth to speak, but Jacob continued, "Move on. Don't come back—it will be the death of you."

At that, he turned and left. Brian watched the flashlight beam return the way they had come. He found the second oar at the bottom and began paddling. The boat cut across the rippling reflection of the moon cascading across the water. Despite his fatigue, he felt strong, better than he had since first being taken. He was alive. There was hope.

Chapter Thirty
Thunder and Lightning

The western gates leading to Alice were thrown open, and a flood of residents streamed out through the wooded sections in Alice Springs Park, following the rapid retreat of the army. Simon's Hummer had made a full turn and was in fast evacuation.

"Stop!" Bethany shouted from beside him, looking back through the rear window at the vehicles and people escaping on foot, terrified as the Red Hands broke through the northern defenses on the opposite side of the town. Most of the vehicles were used in the battle at the bridge, and any transports with room were stopping and becoming overrun by desperate residents clawing their way inside or on top. One truck—with people holding onto the roof, the side, the hood—accelerated fast, and two flew off to become broken among the rocks.

"Stop!" Bethany again yelled.

The driver glanced into the rearview mirror, and Jeremy took a pause in his hasty relay with a lieutenant.

"We can't leave without Carolanne and Connor," she said. "Stop the truck. Let me out!"

"Everyone's been ordered to retreat," Jeremy said. "If they got out safely, we'll see them when we stop to refuel, or in Albuquerque."

Simon envisioned his dog, his ears pulled back, his fur raised in fear at the sound of the explosions. He envisioned Carolanne, who had already lost Brian, now taking on the weight of both Winston and young Connor, who had also lost everything and everyone dear to him. Then he thought of

Bethany, her cousin missing, her best friend in mortal danger, perhaps already dead … he began to open the door as the Hummer still moved.

"Damn it, Simon." Jeremy reached over and grabbed Simon's shoulder.

"Sir," the soldier in the passenger seat said, holding out a long-range communications radio. "You have to take this."

Jeremy held firm to Simon's jacket and looked at the radio, then back to Simon. "Where the hell are you going? You're in charge of—"

"Put Richard in charge. I'm getting out, one way or the other."

"Sir," the soldier repeated, "it's urgent. It's John Zur, sir."

Jeremy's eyes shot large. "Fine then, Simon. Pull over. You want to leave so bad, so be it!"

The driver came to a fast halt, the vehicles in front and behind that protected the general stopping as well. Simon opened the door into a swell of kicked-up dirt and grabbed his backpack. Bethany jumped out beside him.

"Do whatever the fuck you want, Simon," Jeremy said with scorn. "Just keep a radio on you if you still give half a shit about any of this—any of us."

Simon understood Jeremy's frustration, but he couldn't let it bother him. He said, "We'll meet you at the refuel stop or in Albuquerque. I have not, and will not give up on you." He shut the door before Jeremy could respond.

The Hummers peeled out, and Simon and Bethany took off running headlong into the flood of people escaping Alice's downfall. In the distance, thick trails of smoke leaped into the sky, dark as storm clouds, lapping at the heavens like devilish tongues.

What am I doing? he thought, sprinting into the woods, clutching his rifle to his chest and feeling the weight of his backpack pulling him down by the shoulder straps. *What if they're already out? What if they're in a truck, speeding away at this very moment? I'm leading Bethany to death!*

Still, he ran, scanning the faces of the scared and weary as he passed.

"Carolanne!" he yelled. "Winston!" and he whistled, loud. Bethany shouted the same, "Carolanne! Connor!"

They ran past an older man clutching a cane with a younger soldier practically dragging him through the woods. The old man tripped, his feet moving like stones, and was pulled back up. Simon passed a gazebo used as a forwarding lookout, now with the machine guns and rifles facing Alice, and a few soldiers manning the guns while the residents fled, yelling, "Come on!

Move it!" The guard towers came into view over a cluster of bushes. One was in the midst of reconstruction, blown to splinters during the last war. The other was manned, the soldiers making a foolish stand against the onslaught of the Red Hands, who, judging by the racket of warfare, were somewhere in the middle of town.

A half dozen soldiers remained by the entrance, and as Simon pushed through a cluster, one said, "Where the hell are you going?" Simon didn't answer. He scanned the faces, yelled, "Carolanne! Connor!" He gave high-pitched whistles above the shouting and screaming and explosions and gunfire. There were people holding bandages to wounds, both soldiers and residents alike, some on stretchers, or held by their shoulders and dragged along. A soldier wailed as two of his comrades hoisted him up, his right arm ending halfway down his forearm and a bundle of red cloths wrapped with what looked like duct tape.

"Carolanne!" Simon yelled, sidestepping bodies, people who had bled out and were abandoned before they could make it outside.

A bullet whizzed by, striking the dirt. Soldiers just out of sight around a strip of buildings were emptying their clips.

"Connor!"

Simon whistled over and over. The Red Hands' advancing line couldn't be far off. Those of Alice's and Hightown's soldiers who either stood their ground, or couldn't escape in time, were keeping them from overrunning the town in a flood; but still, the tide was overwhelming.

Through the thick air came a sound that pierced his heart. A bark.

"Winston!" Simon whistled again and ran diagonally across the properties. "Winston! Carolanne!" And then he saw his dog bounding from behind a home, his tongue dangling out of his open mouth. His leash trailed behind him. "Oh, buddy!" Simon ran and embraced Winston, grabbing him around the scruff and feeling the dog's trembling. Carolanne appeared from around the same corner, running with Connor in her arms, a duffel bag swinging from her shoulder.

"Beth!" she yelled, closer, her face flushed. The boy lifted his face from her shoulder, his cheeks red and wet. A waft of smoke like a shadow encompassed them.

Simon slung his rifle over his shoulder and took Connor from Carolanne's arms, then unholstered his .45. "Here." He passed it to Carolanne handle side first. "Keep your finger off the trigger unless you're ready to shoot."

Bethany tried to grab Winston' s leash as they took off, but the dog ran ahead. Simon was worried about the leash getting tangled in something, but he didn't call for Winston to stop. Every few yards, the dog would turn, checking on their direction, which was opposite of the never-ceasing gunfire. Onward they ran to safety, with certain death fast at their heels.

Chapter Thirty-One
Moonlit Shores

The boat cut across the long rippling reflection of the moon over the gentle swells of the bay. After rowing for an hour away from the shore, out of range from any wandering eyes along Hightown's perimeter, Brian turned inland.

Blisters had formed on the pads of his hands, and he was reminded of summers spent working at old Frank Meyer's farm back in Nelson with Steven, all those years ago. No matter how calloused their hands were at the beginning of the season, blisters were quick to appear after a few hours of holding rakes and spades. It was Frank who took the rake out of Brian's hands and showed him how to properly hold it. The old man gripped the handle, his hands so weathered they seemed a part of the wood, with his thumbs on the pole and facing down instead of wrapped around in fists. His trick worked, and now as Brian gripped the oars, he attempted to do the same. But the back and forth movement was different, and it didn't seem to matter how he held on to the wood; blisters formed and popped, and stung fierce.

The opposite shore didn't seem to grow any larger as he continued to row, and he paused for a minute, letting the boat drift. The moon was bright enough, and his eyes adjusted to the dark. He took a moment to inspect the backpack that Jacob packed. Right on top was a canteen, and Brian nearly tore the cap off before taking large gulps. The cool water absorbed into his stomach the moment it was swallowed and quenched the burning in his throat.

Most of the backpack was taken up by a sleeping bag, stuffed in a smaller sack, but there was also a folding knife, two loose apples, a compass, and at the bottom, a pistol. Brian removed the clip and felt the top cartridge, making sure all fifteen rounds remained. He slid the clip back in, chambered a round, and double-checked the safety before placing it on the bench beside him. He then snapped the pocketknife open and cut away two small sections of the backpack's inner, second layer of fabric and wrapped them around each hand. It made the oars a bit slippery, but his palms were protected and the pain subdued.

The shore grew larger at the slowest pace imaginable. His back was sore, and his neck muscles ached, but he didn't stop paddling until the horizon was overcome by shoreline and the gentle surf propelled him toward a sandy bank. There was a slight grating as the hull hit the soft sand, and Brian let go of the oars with an internal sigh of relief.

He removed his shoes and socks and rolled up his pants before stepping out into the water. They were still wet from when he'd walked into the water in Hightown, and he wished he'd thought ahead to how miserable it would be to hike for miles with soaked shoes.

After tucking the pistol in his rear pocket and shouldering the bag, Brian moved inland. By moonlight he rechecked the compass and proceeded in a southern direction, toward Alice. Like hell he wasn't going to return home—war or not. He had to make sure Carolanne and Bethany were safe.

Chapter Thirty-Two
United

An immense pine tree in the wooded section of Alice Springs Park burned, from base to crown, in a torrent of flames leaping to the heavens, scouring neighboring bark and boughs. Simon carried Connor through the woods with Carolanne a foot behind, occasionally bumping into his back when they came to hard terrain, and Bethany remained close to his side. There were four others with them who had escaped as the Red Hands overwhelmed Alice.

Winston remained in the lead, and Simon kept an eye on the horizon, but relied on his dog to keep vigil on upcoming hazards. When scouting or hunting, Simon had trained himself to let his field of vision broaden, so that he could notice slight movements in the woods. If he were hunting a deer, a flight of birds from a neighboring tree might suggest a disturbance up the trail. In that manner, he also watched Winston—noticed the way his head turned and sniffed the air, if his fur would begin to stand on end.

The mass of the townspeople had a solid lead on them and were nowhere in sight, but on the side of the trail they encountered bodies scattered in the brush, mortally wounded or bled out. Simon gave fast, high-pitched whistles as Winston trailed over to investigate, diverting the dog's attention. They also passed a Hummer resting low on the tires of its broken frame.

Connor's weight became difficult to bear the farther they fled, and by the time they were close to the border of Alice Springs Park, Simon's biceps were stiff and cramping up. The boy had kept his arms wrapped around Simon's neck the entire journey, and his face buried in his shoulder.

When they neared the edge of the woods, with homes and once-manicured lawns taking over the trees and brush, the group slowed and stopped, dropping to their knees. Everyone was out of breath and dripping sweat.

The four guards escaping with them were all injured in some capacity. One, Jay, appeared to have escaped the melee with some minor bruises and scrapes. He said, "I'll take Connor for a while. You take point." Jay was about Simon's height, but with wide, thick forearms. Two of the other soldiers had more serious wounds, with bandages and rags wrapped around arms and legs. One man held a thick rag over his stomach, with both arms bleeding, and a host of scrapes and lacerations covered his face. Carolanne began inspecting the wounds and bandages. The other soldiers, Ellen and Jack, insisted they were okay. The wounds on their hands and arms were superficial.

Simon attempted to hand Connor over, but the boy's grip remained firm around his neck. "Connor, buddy," Simon said in a whisper. "Jay here's going to take you, okay?" Connor didn't budge. "I'm not going anywhere. I'll be right here." Reluctantly, Connor pulled away and nodded. He kept his eyes down, his face crimson and wet with tears. "You okay?" Simon asked. Connor nodded. "You hurt?" Connor shook his head. Jay reached out and took the boy.

"Hey, kiddo," Jay said, "I got you."

Simon shook out his stiff arms and removed a folded map from his breast pocket. He traced the area with his finger over the page. Ellen, tending to the bandage on her forearm, said, "We need to move." She peered behind her, as if a force of Red Hands would appear at any moment, which was entirely possible. "We can follow the tire and foot tracks, at least to the paved road."

Simon nodded. "Keep a look out to the north as we go; their scouts could be cutting a similar path. Beth, take point with me." The group reshouldered their bags and readied their rifles. Simon pooled some water from his canteen into his palm for Winston to lap up and looked at Carolanne, who was switching the pistol he'd given her from hand to hand. "We'll be okay," he said.

She nodded and swallowed visibly. Her jaw trembled open, and she said, "It's … we can't keep going on like this." A tear dropped as her eyes clenched shut.

Bethany turned fast to her. "It's not like we got a damn choice, now do we?" Her voice held a hint of anger.

Carolanne met her gaze, her eyes watery. "We've been running, hiding, watching our friends die for years now."

"I know," Bethany said in a softer tone. "It's not fair. Never was, never will be. We can't think of these things. We can't think of …" She paused in contemplation, then continued, "…the ones we lost. Not now."

Carolanne wiped her eyes on a sleeve and nodded.

"I'll take up the rear," Ellen interjected, holding her rifle and rechecking the chamber. She was shorter than Simon, but wide and strong, hardened by years in the military. Ellen had been stationed in the trade grounds, protecting the access door. She was there when the Red Hands advanced upon the gate, and she'd told them that in her estimation, less than a dozen of their soldiers stationed there had escaped the onslaught.

Before leaving, Simon took the handheld radio from his bag and turned it on now that they were far enough away to have the volume on low. He typed a passcode to access the encrypted frequency and the airwaves came to life with voices speaking fast, back and forth, a bit fuzzy with distortion.

Jack put his arm under the more seriously injured soldier's shoulders, and they began stepping out, following the dozens of zigzagging tire tracks implanted in the dirt. Then Simon froze and put the radio closer to his ear.

"What is it?" Bethany asked.

Simon put a finger in the air as he listened to the report. After a moment he looked up at the group, meeting their combined gazes, and said, "We need to hurry to the refuel point. They're forming a perimeter."

"Who?" Ellen asked, "Alice? It's a half-day's drive to get there."

Simon shook his head. "It's California and Texas. They've joined the battle."

Chapter Thirty-Three
Human Semblance

Dew collected like crystalline pearls on the thin complexity of a spiderweb, each orb reflecting the transparent morning sky. Brian crouched in a thicket of branches, leaning against the base of a maple tree with bright green boughs. Two Red Hands soldiers were stopped in the road ahead, hunched over the open hood of a pickup. They were far from the fighting in Alice, which, if what Brian had been told was correct, might be long over.

The lack of additional voices urged Brian to creep closer and closer, staying low and going slow, gripping his compact Ruger pistol before him. When movement was visible, he stopped and watched. The sun rose in the sky, and the two men spoke loud, yet muffled, laughing at times, and taking breaks from fixing the stalled vehicle to smoke cigarettes.

The dew droplets grew smaller and then evaporated altogether as the sun broke free from the morning confines, producing a dazzling and vibrant blue. The men wore a disarray of army fatigues of no particular origin, the dark hues stained darker in patches with various rips, holes, and frayed edges. They were bearded, filthy, yet appeared strong and in good health. They leaned against the truck, assault rifles nearby, and smoked cigarettes as they spoke and peered upward, admiring the weather.

The more Brian stared, even from his distance, the more he could make out nuances in their personas. One had a minor limp, barely noticeable. The other might be missing fingers, or just held his cigarette in an odd manner. Both wore pistol belts with long combat knives and pouches for spare magazines and radio receivers. And both had red handprints painted over their hearts.

The men ground their cigarettes out on the pavement and turned to the open hood. One wiped his grease-stained palms on his pant legs and picked up a wrench before leaning his head into the cavity.

Brian closed his eyes and inhaled deep and exhaled slow. What was that meditation thing that Simon had told him about months ago? Something about breathing in, being a bird or a rock or some shit? A plant or a tree?

With open eyes, he clicked the safety off his pistol and stood slowly, his back against the rough bark of the maple, his backpack left at the base. He peered out and then took a step, and then another and another. He approached from behind, taking each footfall with care, cautious of sticks and leaves. He heard their radio crackle. Heard the men say stuff like, "Can't reach the bolt … not till this afternoon … give it another hour …"

Then he squatted, aimed between the shoulder blades of one man, and pulled the trigger. The pop was loud, and the sudden evacuation of birds from the neighboring trees seemed to make the whole atmosphere come alive. The soldier rocked further into the cavity of the truck, and Brian aimed the pistol fast toward the other man, who barely had enough time to jolt before Brian pulled the trigger twice. Both bullets struck the man in the back, and he made a huffing sound as the air escaped his lungs. Brian sprinted toward them as they toppled over. A flash of memory crossed his mind, the cell walls in the dark basement, the feeling of the damp cold entering his skin, his stomach consuming his muscles to keep him alive. He fired two more shots at close proximity.

Brian stood over them, reining in his heavy breathing. The air grew quiet once more, except for the occasional report coming in over the radios. He went to the driver side door and found a canteen on the front seat. The liquid smelled clean, and he took a long pull of water. The men's backpacks were in the back seat, each with food rations, sleeping bags, and plenty of ammunition. He consolidated what he could, then dragged the men into the brush, one at a time. A stain of red trailed behind; hiding their bodies wasn't worth the effort.

Before leaving, Brian took their pistols and knives and examined their boots, but neither was large enough to fit him. It was a tough decision between his damp shoes or their tight ones, but he decided to keep the ones he had. He hoped to swap out his wet socks, but the dead men's were so well-worn, carrying an undeniable stench, that he opted to keep his. After tossing the boots, he used a combat knife to cut strips of a blanket and fashion them into something resembling gloves. The blisters from the oars had burst while he was paddling, and his palms stung. Brian took the last apple that Jacob had left for him and bit into the sweet, crisp flesh as he walked back into the wild.

***

His heels were raw from rubbing against his wet socks, his toes like squashed fruit, and the handle of the assault rifle bothered his burst blisters, despite the material wrapped around his palms. Starting a fire would do wonders to strengthen his resolve and dry out his clothes, yet Brian knew how foolish it would be to bring attention to himself. If he'd learned anything from his journey to Alice all that time ago, it was that he could override comfort if it meant survival. So onward he went, toward Alice.

He used the position of the sun to guide him south, along with an estimate of where the ocean resided. At least he no longer experienced the pangs of starvation he'd suffered in the prison cell. The soldiers he'd killed each had a hunk of stale bread, a sack of dried fruits, a pouch of smoked meat, and four high-calorie survival bars. He'd already peeled back the vacuum-sealed silver foil of one of the wrappers and ate a full bar, which tasted like chewy wood sprinkled with cinnamon and had the calories of a full meal.

Keeping close to the water's edge, away from the main road between Hightown and Alice, Brian managed to avoid seeing more Red Hands, or anyone for that matter, aside from birds and squirrels. Every ten minutes or so, he clicked on the slain soldier's radio to save the battery life, keeping the volume low. The radio was small and handheld, and the programmed frequencies were mostly silent. Occasionally he heard someone asking for reports on the vehicles, so it was safe to assume the men he'd killed were limited to a mechanical detachment. He scanned other channels, but aside from two that came in scrambled, there were no other active lines. And now, only a few miles further south, he was losing the short-wave distance from the other relays, and conversations were choppy.

Again, he tried to remember Simon's meditation: *I am the animal, the wind … shit … the rock, the tree?* It would have come in handy down in the jail cell … *Don't think about the past. Don't dwell on thoughts that can harm your mind, dull your senses. Remember what it was like in the woods after you left Steven for dead?*

He shook the memory away.

Insanity was close at hand back then, along with a terrible fever. If he hadn't found Bethany's bunker when he did, he surely would have perished out there among the pine trees and wavering brush, lost with the scattered bones of the departed.

After the battle at Nick's mansion, the faces of the slain and the cries of the dying haunted him for weeks. He'd often thought that he could never aim and shoot a gun at another human again, no matter their crimes. But less than two hours ago, he'd shot and killed two Red Hands without the slightest trepidation. He moved as if in a dream, aware that he was doing the things he'd done, but it was as if he were watching himself do it. He tried to remember the faces of the men he'd just killed, their eye color, jaw structure, the way their mouths dropped open moments before death as if in disbelief, the things that used to haunt his dreams, but the details were blurred. And it didn't bother him in the slightest. Those men deserved to die. All of the Red Hands deserved to find death in the most horrifying of conditions. They were not human. They had no semblance of a soul, and lived with such reckless abandon that they would leach the blood from children just to see them die. They were insects. Vermin. Monsters, and Brian had no hesitation to swat as many as he could. The thought gave him a warm embrace, a pleasant tingle. Without realizing it, his lips cracked into a smile.

Chapter Thirty-Four
Smoke and Ash

Ellen told a rushed tale of the Red Hands' invasion of the easternmost section, where she'd been stationed along with Andrew, the man with the stomach wound. They were both members of Alice's Guards division, and among the first to deal with the onslaught.

"It was those damn helicopters more than anything else," she said. "We heard them before we could see them, and then when they appeared high up in the air, they were already unloading their ordnance. We were expecting the ground assault, but their numbers … Jesus, where did they get so many soldiers? They came like a flood out of the woods."

"Louisiana," Simon said, despite being aware she already knew. "They betrayed Alice."

"If it weren't for Andrew getting hit early on, I don't know if either of us would have made it much further. I started dragging him back behind cover after the shrapnel tore him up. Another Guard helped us, but a bullet hit him plumb center." She lifted her camouflaged military cap by the visor and pointed to the center of her forehead. Simon noticed she too had some scrapes on her cheek, behind the layer of grit that seemed to cover everyone who had fought. "I got him to the medics, who were beyond saturated with the injured coming in from the fighting up north. I was about to turn back to the line, leave him on the grass, but with him slipping in and out of consciousness and no one able to hold the bandage to his wounds, I stayed. Then we heard that our line was broken. The sound of bullet fire grew closer. We got the order to retreat, and luckily I found Jack and Jay, who were able to help me get Andrew out of Alice."

Simon was half listening to Ellen's story, but trying to focus more on the sounds of the wild and the broadcast coming in over the radio. It was doubtful that the Red Hands had any men stationed this far west of Alice, but it was possible. It was more likely that a division was following the trail of the retreating army to finish them off, and would soon be at their heels.

After a brief silence, Bethany asked, "You think they know about California and Texas?"

"The Red Hands? I'm not sure." Simon had been wondering the same thing. "There's no doubt that they have our radios in their possession, but who knows if they have the access codes." The frequencies were all encrypted, and a code had to be entered into the receivers for them to broadcast. As the leader of the Rangers, Simon had codes to access frequencies used only by officers. "If the Red Hands captured an officer, it's possible they have the cipher in their possession."

Bethany nodded.

"Alice just fell, and they have a lot to do on top of interrogating prisoners," Ellen added. "We might have some time until they get the code."

Silence followed as Simon remembered what interrogation by the Red Hands entailed, and that many of his friends were under their control.

Up ahead, Winston inspected a tree, sniffing the bark, his tail wagging. He dug up the earth at the base with one paw and smelled the soil, searching for something. He looked up at Simon, dirt on his nose, his tongue bouncing out the side of his mouth.

If only I were a dog … War, loss, the devastation of human decency, none of which can eliminate the simple pleasure of an enticing scent in the grass.

"Hey," a voice said in the rear. "Hey, hold up."

They all turned. Andrew's eyes were half-open, his feet flipped around so that his toes were dragging along the ground. They placed him down and Carolanne felt for a pulse.

Simon kept vigil on the perimeter, but relied more on any subtle nuances in Winston's behavior.

"He all right?" Simon asked.

Carolanne didn't answer, still holding the man's wrist. "It's faint," she said. "I can barely feel it." She rechecked his bandages. They were loose and desperately needed to be changed, but they didn't have any medical equipment. During their last break, when the man was conscious, Simon offered to cut a portion of his shirt to use as a dressing. Carolanne had said, "You'll give him an infection. The bandage he's got will hold." Now, the material was saturated.

Jack opened his pack and ruffled through it. "Here," he said, displaying a roll of duct tape. He tore long pieces and handed them to Carolanne. "Let's keep moving," she said. "His best chance is to make it to the doctors, sooner than later."

"You need a break?" Ellen asked Jack.

He shook his head and began hefting the unconscious man up by his shoulder, with Carolanne holding the other shoulder.

"What about you?" she asked Jay.

"I'm good," he said, and patted Connor's back.

"And you, little man, you okay?"

Connor didn't answer.

"Hey, buddy," Simon said. "You all right?"

The boy looked up. His face was red with an indent from Jay's jacket. "I'm all right," he said. There was nothing in Connor's expression that indicated he was okay. Numb, perhaps, but far from okay. His eyes were bloodshot, his skin pallid.

"Hey, I have something for you," Simon said, and reached into his pocket. "Here." He held out the cord of thick beads.

Connor looked from them to Simon. "They're yours," he said. "I gave them to you."

"I know. I remember. But how about you keep them safe for me, just for a little while?"

Connor hesitated, but Simon moved his hand closer. "Please," he said. "They won't do any good in my pocket."

Connor took them in his small hands, rolling the beads delicately between his fingers, as if they were each a tiny egg about to hatch.

Simon turned and checked his compass while Ellen held a map, and the group trekked onward toward the west.

***

When they rechecked Andrew's pulse a half hour later, he was dead. They placed his body at the base of a pine tree, and Ellen marked the spot on the map so he could be given a proper burial if the opportunity arose. Carolanne washed her hands with a splash of water from a canteen, and rubbed them against fallen leaves to try and scrape the dried blood from her skin, to little avail.

When they began walking again, Simon asked her, "You okay?"

"No," she said.

"I'm sorry," he replied.

"None of this is your fault."

"Still, I'm sorry all the same."

"Are you okay?"

He looked over to her for a moment, but when she looked up with her big, wet eyes, he looked away. "No," he said.

"You'd think by now we'd have become accustomed to losing people."

"We don't know if Brian's lost."

She shook her head, her lips pursed. "He is."

"You don't know that."

"Simon, they took him … he's been gone for days."

"He could still be alive."

"He's gone, Simon." He spied a shimmer of light reflected in a tear falling from her cheek. "Dead, alive, it doesn't matter. For his sake"—she paused and took in a shaky inhale—"it might be better to be dead. Whatever those monsters did to him, are doing … Christ, I can't think about it."

Simon fought back a tremble in his chest, imagining Brian in Will Holbrook's place, strapped to a gurney with parts missing. He felt lightheaded, and anger rose like boiling water in his chest.

"I met my husband, Robert, when I was twenty-three, at school. We started dating, and two years later, we married. I loved him so much. He was my world. Now"—she shook her head, more droplets falling—"I can barely remember his face. I don't want that to be the same with Brian. I-I … I don't want to keep doing this, running from one terror to the other, waiting for life to become normal, hoping that one day it will. Forgetting faces …"

Simon wanted to tell her that everything would be okay. He wanted to share his own grief—the death of his parents, his missing brother, Winston on his last legs. Yet everything seemed to be all right as long as he had Bethany—hope, desire, something to keep fighting for, someone to make the day seem never-ending in delight, and the nights warm, her body against his. All he said was, "I'm sorry."

"My parents died young," she continued. "I was a teenager."

"I'm—"

"You don't have to keep saying you're sorry. It was a car accident. I was at school. The principal called me to the office, and I knew right away that something was wrong. He opened the door and said my name. There were two cops holding their hats and they asked me to take a seat. The principal didn't sit behind his desk like he normally did, but rather leaned against it in front of me." She took a long inhale, then continued, "I had pictures of my parents to keep my memory sharp, and I looked at the albums every night in the bunker in Aurora. But I don't have any pictures of Robert. We meant to bring our wedding album in the bunker, but it was one of those things; I thought he grabbed it, he thought I did. But it wasn't a big deal; we still had each other. Then he died, and his face… I don't know if my memory is playing tricks on me, if I started remembering him differently as the months went by. I don't have any pictures of Brian, so I expect the same will happen. In time, we'll all be lost, smudged from existence, only to be remembered as dull shadows of our former selves."

Simon was about to apologize again, but he didn't. The pictures he'd kept of his own family, which kept him going on his journey from British Columbia to Alice, were now left behind in the filthy grip of the Red Hands, more than likely tossed to the ground as their home was ransacked.

Ahead, Winston stopped in his tracks and his ear perked up, the other permanently flopped to the side. His head cocked at an angle. Simon gave a light whistle, but Winston didn't budge. The rest of the traveling party noticed the interaction, and everyone was quiet, weapons shouldered. Simon approached Winston, walking slowly, and Ellen and Bethany followed, crouched low. They peered across what they could see of several fenced backyards as Winston sniffed at the air, his fur raised. "What is it, boy?" Simon whispered.

Then there was movement, and two, three, then five soldiers stepped out, weapons drawn.

"Stop right there!" one of them said. They fanned out, and Simon observed the dark windows of the surrounding homes. At least two of them were open, and human forms were silhouetted in the shadows.

No one lowered their guns; then Simon looked closer at their uniforms and said, "It's me, Simon Kalispell, head of the Rangers." *At least I was head of the Rangers.* He lowered his rifle on the sling and displayed his open palms. "We're from Alice."

The guards approached hesitantly. "You steal those uniforms?" the closest one said, his gaze sharp on all of them. Then one in the rear said, "Wait, Patterson, that's him. I know Kalispell."

Simon recognized the gray-haired man. He'd been posted on the eastern entrance, and they often chatted when Simon returned from a hunt, him always asking, "See any deer today?"

Weapons were lowered. "You guys made it out, huh?" the lead man said. "C'mon, let's get you behind the line."

"I was going to call in when we got closer," Simon said. "We're still a half mile away from the rendezvous."

The soldier nodded. "We're moving out in under an hour. I'm sure General Winters will want to speak to you. I'll radio ahead."

Ellen, Jack, and Jay recognized the soldiers and stopped to shake hands and give hugs. Jay put Connor on his feet, who seemed to brighten up once he'd seen the troops.

"That a kid?" a guard asked. "You'd better hurry, they're sending all children and elderly to Albuquerque, if they haven't left already."

Simon reached down and took Connor's hand, and they began walking away from the front line. When out of earshot, Connor asked, "Where is everyone headed to in an hour?"

After a moment of hesitation, Simon said, "I believe we're going back to war."

"And I'm going to Albuquerque?"

"It would appear so," Simon answered.

Connor walked beside Simon, gazing at the ground. "I don't want to go."

"It will be safer there."

"I want to stay with you."

"Connor ..."

"I want to fight. I can fight."

Simon exchanged glances with Bethany and Carolanne. "We'll see," Bethany responded.

"Connor." Simon crouched down and looked the boy in the eyes. "When I first met you, all that time ago when you were younger, I was told a few pieces of advice that have not only stuck with me, but have helped guide my path. The words were spoken by the old man who told you to give me those beads." Simon pointed to Connor's hands, as the boy rolled the beads back and forth between his fingers. "He said there are many paths that we can take; some of us are warriors and some of us are monks. He told me that I am a teacher, but there is a fierceness inside me, and I must be careful of that fierceness, because there are two types of violence: one that causes damage and another which causes it to cease. I took his words seriously, and when I became the warrior and fought and killed, I thought that perhaps I was on the side of ceasing violence. I thought that I would be alleviated of guilt, of mental sorrow, if I fought for the right cause. I wish that were the case."

Simon paused and placed his hand on Connor's shoulder. Then he continued, "I'm still deciphering who I am. My path in life might veer in many directions, but I see something in you that I believe the old monk would have seen as well. You, Connor, are a teacher. You will be a teacher. You've learned so much about survival, at such a young age, that by the time you're as old as I am, you will be needed to pass the teachings to future generations. That's a big responsibility to hold. Perhaps the most important responsibility that there is."

"I don't know that much," Connor said, his voice wavering.

"You know more than you're aware. And once this is over, once this war is finally done and we're settled as back to normal as possible, I will make it my sole ambition to pass on everything I know about hunting and stalking in the wild to you, so that you can light the torch for future generations."

Connor's eyes cast to the ground.

"Deal?" Simon asked.

"Yeah." Connor nodded. "Deal."

They followed the spray-painted markings of an arrow on a stop sign, and once they turned a bend in the road, they saw soldiers walking toward them. When they were close enough, they shook hands. "Glad you guys made it," one of the soldiers said, and repositioned the sling of his rifle over his shoulder. "Follow me, camp is around the bend."

They continued behind a property, and then around another home and across the street, an impromptu staging area had been erected in a large soccer field beside a school. Hundreds—thousands—of troops had settled in, sitting on their rucksacks and cleaning their weapons. There was a paved track with dozens upon dozens of vehicles parked somewhat in order—Hummers, tanks, and troop carriers.

Seeing it all at once was stunning, hopeful, that this war was still far from over.

"General Winters is in the rear, in the tent to the left." The soldier pointed to where a half dozen camouflage tents were erected. "He'll be with General Schafer from California. The rest of their army is stationed a half click to the north."

"Wait," Simon said. "This isn't everybody? How many soldiers did they bring?"

"Who, California or Texas?"

"Both."

The soldier smiled. "Just you wait and see."

***

Simon found Jeremy in a tent the size of a bedroom, standing hunched over a table with a cigarette dangling from his lips. A dozen more officials were jammed into the space, some around the table, dropping ashes to scatter over maps and ledgers. Others sat before a table to the side, in front of radios and relays, headphones over their ears, broadcasting orders and receiving information.

Jeremy looked up as Simon opened the tent flap, casting an outline of sunshine along the table. A voice from the table said, "Simon, you're okay!" Richard Jarrett broke away from the gathering and came to greet Simon at the doorway. "Jesus, man, we were worried about you."

"I've been worried about you too."

"We're making preparations now. Your men will be happy to see you."

"No, Richard—they're your men now."

Richard narrowed his gaze. "You sure you want to do that?"

"I can help the people hunt. I can help them in the woods. But leading them in battle is another matter. I've come accept that I'm not cut out for that line of work."

"Still though, they look up to you. You can change your mind; nothing's been made official yet."

"He's sure," Jeremy called out from the table. "Told me as much when he fled from the caravan."

Simon felt the eyes of the officers burning into him. "Jeremy—"

"But all the same"—Jeremy paused to ground out his cigarette in a full ashtray—"he's right. You may not be the person to lead the Rangers into battle, Simon, but we need your expertise all the same. Come over here while we finish up, get acquainted with the plan."

Simon followed Richard and nudged his way to the table. A brief introduction was made, which included the officials from California and Texas. A middle-aged man with pursed lips and sunken cheeks reached out and shook Simon's hand. "George Schafer," the man said with a gruff voice. "General in charge of the United Western Federation." A tall woman with blonde hair, maybe a few years older than Simon, reached out after General Schafer. "Ariel Taylor," she said, offering a firm handshake, "General in charge of the Lone Star Republic." She didn't smile as they shook. No one in the room smiled.

Everyone's attention was focused on maps and papers. Simon repeated the names in his head to remember them: *Schafer, California; Taylor, Texas; Schafer, California; Taylor, Texas ...*

The big map on the table was covered in lines and dots in different colored ink, and scattered with cigarette ash. The outline of Alice's defenses was represented in the half-circle formation from the edges of the Ridgeline River. Hightown was outlined too, beside the bay. Simon tried to make sense of the various colors and designs, and followed the conversation that was nearing completion. "... Delta Company will take up the rear after Fox, zone seven. Artillery dispatch twelve will set up in zone nineteen ..." None of it made sense to him. Richard was studying the map as General Schafer continued, and Simon felt relieved he'd made the right decision by giving him control.

"That's that," General Schafer said, and gave his watch a cursory glance. "We're running behind." Everyone nodded their acknowledgment, and Jeremy slid another cigarette from the pack with his teeth and flicked open his brass Zippo, yet no one moved from around the table. Once they left, the plans would begin, and the weight of thousands of lives would rest heavy on their souls.

General Taylor was the first to break the silence: "I got a regiment of eager soldiers out there waiting to rid this planet of those vermin, once and for all. This is it, people—the last battle. The final war. Let it be swift."

Everyone nodded, and a few repeated, "Let it be swift."

And with that, everyone turned to their respective officers, and a flurry of information was given to the radio operators. Simon turned to leave, following Richard, when Jeremy called out, "Hold up."

Simon turned back to the table, a sense of apprehension tangible. This was his friend—his best friend, after Winston—and whatever lecture or discipline he was about to receive for disobeying his command and relinquishing his title was going to be ten times worse coming from him.

Simon spoke first. "Jeremy, I wasn't trying to disobey your order, or—"

"I'm not mad." Jeremy's tone was light.

Simon exhaled a sigh of relief.

"I realize not everyone in Alice has a military background, and I don't expect the same level of commitment to authority that comes from people in the service. Come closer, look at the map."

Simon looked down; Jeremy was pointing to rectangular outlines in the ocean, close to the shoreline. "This battle, it's not going to be … what you think. I need to explain a few things to you, quickly. This"—he again pointed to the rectangles—"is Louisiana's fleet. And this"—he pointed to another group of rectangles, farther south—"is the fleet from Texas. They've brought an aircraft carrier and warships."

"They have air support?"

Jeremy nodded. "No one, not even Louisiana, is aware of just how mighty their navy and air power truly is. The same goes for California. They've acquired a vast arsenal, unmatched by any of the colonies, and in the period when communication between the territories was limited, they decided to keep their numbers secret."

We're going to win … we're going to win this battle …. The urgency to attack now became pressing. *I'll find you, Brian. Dead or alive, I'll find you.*

"Here's the thing," Jeremy continued. "The first stage will be a two-pronged attack, eliminating their navy while striking Alice at the same time."

"All right," Simon said.

"It's been decided and voted on that the only way to eliminate the Red

Hands once and for all is to make a large and sudden all-out bombardment of Alice and Hightown now, while the officers and the bulk of their army are stationed together."

"What do you mean by all-out bombardment?"

"Simon … we're writing the zones off."

"Wait—you're doing *what*? What about the prisoners, what about Brian?"

Jeremy held his palm out. "You have to understand that this is not an easy decision."

"But still, it's a decision that you made—all of you."

"And that's why I asked you to stay. We're—" He paused, grounding out his cigarette. "We're friends, Simon," he said while rubbing the bridge of his nose. "Everything that we fought for, everything Tom Byrnes and General Driscoll did to ensure our colonies' safety, it's over. If we made a tactical assault, more of our people would die—hundreds, thousands. The ones held captive would be bartered with and executed. As of now, there's no reason to believe Brian has been moved to Alice, if he's still, well …"

"Alive?"

Jeremy cleared his throat. "Yes, Simon. If he's still alive. After the planes eliminate Alice's defenses, the army will deploy in mass. The air force will land to rearm, and then the assault on Hightown will begin in earnest. The colonies sent up drones, searched for miles, and we've come across a naval yard far to the north where we believe their warship came from. And there are other lesser-manned posts, such as Odyssey in the south. One by one, they will all be destroyed, until every Red Hand is eradicated. But tonight … tonight, the bulk of their army will be crushed."

"What about Alice? Our home? We're just going to burn it all to the ground and walk away?"

"Our people are invited to help populate the other colonies. Albuquerque has suffered a great deal of causalities; I expect the bulk of our numbers will end up there. But that will be decided on later."

"We've lost so much already to just let Alice fall."

"Simon." Jeremy pulled another cigarette from the pack and checked his watch. "We need to get moving. The army will be marching as the first planes drop their missiles. Listen, in war sometimes, you lose a battle. Again, I know this isn't something you've experienced. As for the soldiers, the ones who have been fighting since the disease first came around and Chicago was decimated with a nuclear strike, we've been waging war since the beginning. We've won some battles. Many we've lost. One day, we'll reestablish the Zones, but for that to happen, the Red Hands have to be wiped out. Eliminated."

"Jeremy." Simon shook his head, feeling anger rise. "I can't accept this. I can't let Brian and all the captives be killed by our own bombs. They are members of our colony, our family. They've dug trenches, planted in the gardens. Put yourself in their shoes. Imagine your friends and allies giving up on you."

"We will do everything we can to save captives. The police departments will be spared from the bombardment. We will attempt to rescue any prisoners there. But my guess is that the captives will be moved to the line, used as shields to help persuade us to stop the air assault. There is little we can do."

Simon's heart was beating so fast that his vision pulsed red.

"And you're okay with this?"

"No, Simon, I'm not." Jeremy rubbed his weary eyes and continued, "Alice is no longer, and everyone will have the opportunity to do and go where they choose. I'm giving you the option now. You don't have to fight if you don't want to. Or if you prefer, you can be stationed with the ground assault which will liberate the police barracks. I hope to see you on the other side, but if you decide to leave, then this is goodbye." Jeremy reached out to shake.

Simon felt a spike of adrenaline as he met Jeremy's hand. He could leave. He could take Winston and go back into the wild, to forage and travel, grow old in the forests and parks. But Connor and Carolanne … Bethany … What would she choose if given the same opportunity? She'd fight. She *will* fight. Even if Simon left, she would fight, at least to determine her cousin's fate.

"Jesus," Simon said. "How about you give me one of those cigarettes you're famous for sharing?"

Jeremy laughed and took two from his pack, striking open his brass Zippo.

Chapter Thirty-Five
The Shadows

The evening turned homes into shadowy figures, and trees into dark dancing patterns. Brian sat on the front steps of a home and peeled back his socks, now much dryer. His heels were a mess. Using strips of cloth cut from the blanket, he wrapped his feet as best as possible before tying up the laces and getting back on the road.

Hours earlier, he'd come to the bank of the Ridgeline River. It didn't take long before the destruction of recent battles became visible. First, the trees bordering the road leading to the bridge were splintered, and thin ones were fallen over or missing large portions. It was eerily quiet, the only sound the melodic wind playing with the leaves. A few steps onward, he came upon a half dozen vehicles riddled with bullets or blackened by exploded shells. Bodies were left where they fell, some missing parts, others in vigorous stages of rigor mortis, stiff as the fallen branches.

Brian looked past the carnage to the bridge itself, and in the dim evening light saw the twisted metal frame jutting out over the water several feet, where it ended.

He continued parallel to the river as it grew darker, using the water as his guide. He crossed backyards, around fences, patches of woods, and overgrown parks, with idle swings and playgrounds overtaken by vining plants. He tried not to compare this current journey with the one taken from Nelson to Aurora, but nonetheless, he did. He was healthier this time around, despite his aching feet. His determination was set in stone, just like last time, only now something felt different. He wasn't traveling out of duty to complete the task Uncle Al had bestowed upon his shoulders. There was more now, an aching, terrible sense of love and loss. A deep affection for the people in Alice and Hightown, and of course Carolanne and Bethany. Did they make it out of Alice before it fell?

It was agonizing knowing everything he valued in the world might be wiped away. What would he do? He couldn't think about it, yet the thought crossed his mind in unceasing intervals. *Jump in the river at the highest point,* he thought, envisioning the swift plummet into the water. *Shoot myself under the clear morning sky. Maybe travel to Albuquerque … to do what? Start over again, fight the Red Hands next month, next year, forge new relationships and lose them again …*

The next bridge was intact, with a few bodies on either side, and two broken-down vehicles. Hundreds of spent bullet shells twinkled in the moonlight, and he nearly slipped on them as he walked across to the opposite bank. Far in the distance came a powerful noise: thunder. A deep roar, high in the clouds and off to the east, possibly over the water. Alice wasn't far now. And when he got there, what would he do? Had it really fallen to the Red Hands? Was Jacob telling the truth?

The thunder didn't take a moment's pause, but at least for now, the sky was a clear and dazzling display of stars in such quantity they would be impossible to count.

There came another noise, something moving … many things moving.

He dropped to his knees and crawled to the side of a house, pressing his back against a wall. Footfalls. A lot of footfalls. He breathed in, tried again to remember Simon's mantra. *Breathing in … just keep breathing in, out, breathe out, you dumb bastard …* His heartbeat steadied, but Brian knew the mantra had nothing to do with this. The answer was far more nefarious: he was becoming accustomed to war. He was familiar with confrontations, shooting and killing. The thought was troublesome, but he'd have to reflect on it later.

He craned his neck around the edge of the building, and with the land candescent in pale form, he first saw three and then four, and then a dozen men walking out in something of a line, all carrying rifles, the moon casting crescent illuminations atop their helmeted heads. He studied them as they neared his side, going in the direction of Alice. He looked for the red handprint, but couldn't decipher anything. They were passing now, their backs to him. Three were visible as the others went around the side of the neighboring home. Then there was more noise, footfalls, on his opposite side. He stared straight ahead at the road, and more dark silhouettes crossed from the neighboring property to the street. One was close, a yard or two away. The make of the man's sidearm was decipherable from the handle alone.

His pulse was beating fast now. In a few steps, he could be at the man, or the man could be at him. None of the soldiers spoke, and they walked cautious of the terrain, scoping out the area, like dark apparitions. The soldier's uniform appeared neat, his gear organized, with pouches attached to his belt and vest. His clothing wasn't pieced together like the Red Hands', which belonged to various branches of military and civilian attire.

The words came so quick and quiet, he wasn't sure he spoke them at all. "Don't shoot," he said. The man froze midstep, looking around in the shadows, and snapped down a night-vision scope attached to his helmet. "Don't move," the man said in a whisper after spotting Brian, and pointed his rifle.

Brian lifted his hands shoulder height. "You're from Hightown, aren't you? I recognize your uniform."

"Who are you? Why are you out here?"

"I'm Brian Rhodes. I was the sous chef in Hightown under Chef Remo for a duration, then transferred to Alice."

"Brian?" the man said, flipping up his night-vision scope and taking a step closer. Two more forms appeared, stepping cautiously toward him, rifles raised. "I'll be damned. I remember you from the kitchen. What the hell are you doing out here?" He lowered his weapon and motioned for the approaching men to do the same.

"It's … a long story. Have you seen Carolanne and Bethany? How's Simon Kalispell?"

"Haven't seen Carolanne. Simon's alive, I hear. Not sure. He's not in charge of the Rangers anymore, I can tell you that. Listen, you need to move back to the HQ, fast."

"Did Alice really fall?"

"Not for long. We're scouting ahead, looking for booby traps mostly, explosives in the road. Before morning, the Red Hands will be nothing more than dust."

"What—how?"

"Texas, California—they've brought thousands, full armored divisions." His voice rose a pitch, then he continued in a whisper, "They're coming up two clicks in the rear. I'll radio ahead, make sure no one fires at you. Head due west. You won't be able to miss them."

"You're attacking tonight? Holy shit … there's a storm coming in from the east. Be careful. You can hear the thunder; listen."

They were quiet for a moment, then one of the soldiers standing in the rear said, "We got to keep moving." The man nodded in response and said, "That's not thunder. It's a different kind of storm. Take care, Brian."

Brian stood and watched the man walk across the street, whispering into his radio as he crossed. Now standing and looking over a fence between the properties, it was easier to witness the line of soldiers crossing from one side of the road to the other. Dozens were coming out of the shadows, silent and cautious. Brian shouldered his bag and turned west.

Chapter Thirty-Six
Locked Away

Alice fell just as Karl had expected. Fear more than anything else pushed the lousy peasants to flee. Thanks was given to Louisiana's fleet, whose missiles instilled panic and confusion. Invisible until detonation, loud and proud upon impact.

As the citizens fled from Alice, leaving it high and dry, Karl issued the command for his men to arm the defenses. Looting was fine, but the normal degree of celebratory damage was halted. The same went with executing the prisoners. Less were captured than expected, and those still alive would be needed to work the gardens and repair the trenches.

The decision to not follow the fleeing soldiers weighed heavy. The men would sleep sounder knowing their enemies were vanquished into oblivion, yet at this juncture, Karl went against his overwhelming desire to chase and cut down the escaping residents without discrimination. They had no hope of issuing a counterattack that would break the defenses, even if they marched all the remaining residents from Albuquerque along with the army. Their numbers were depleted, and the warships anchored offshore maintained an arsenal of long-range missiles, capable of hitting Alice's border and beyond.

The bodies of Jeremy Winters and many of the ranking officers, including Simon Kalispell, were not yet found. Deciphering and numbering the dead would take more time, but it was possible their corpses were yet to be discovered. At the present, Karl had to believe the enemy's leadership was still intact.

An assemblage of officers inspected the defensive line, and then the town's inner workings. Karl pointed out familiar points of interest to Liam and the men who had not been there for the first infiltration, such as the schoolhouse-turned-offices with the communications relay in the gymnasium. As it became evening on the first day of victory, the officers took quarters in a magnificent colonial home near the soldiers' barracks, confident that their men were manning the defenses. Celebratory bottles appeared. The scrambled radio frequencies used by the enemy were still an enigma, but it was hopeful that one of the prisoners would give the access numbers during the interrogations that were fast underway.

Karl struck a match and rolled the end of a cigar around the flame to produce an even burn, and then stood from the chair and looked out over the lawn of the property to the road ahead. A line of his army marched with bound prisoners toward the makeshift cells in Alice Elementary School, since the jail in the police department was full to capacity.

"Casey Edmunds is dead," Liam told the group, having just received word. "They found him twisted up in wreckage by the bridge. They're bringing 'im back now, see if that won't demoralize the prisoners a bit."

The officers laughed, all except Karl and the Priest, who instead raised his glass and issued, "Praise be."

Karl faced the window, clamping the cigar in his teeth. He'd taken back the first glass of whiskey in a slug, and now sipped at the second, letting his nerves dissolve and his limbs relax. The men were happy and loud, yet Karl felt the taste of the bourbon was not as sweet as it should be. Something was missing. A key to the celebration was left behind, in Hightown.

"When's the next transport heading out?" Karl said, cutting off conversations mid-sentence.

"It's, ah"—Liam checked his watch—"little over an hour. It'll be the last until morning."

"I'll be joining the procession. Schedule another to return from Hightown shortly after."

"For what purpose?"

Karl didn't turn to face him, yet Liam's voice betrayed his insubordination as he said, "Sir. I'll call it in now."

The glasses were drained, and the officers left silently, aware that their leader was deep in some trance and that it was best not to disturb his thoughts, lest they be added to the long list of the dead. The Priest and Liam were all who remained, sitting on lush recliners opposite Karl.

When the cigar burnt low enough to radiate heat on his lips, Karl took a last puff of the velvet smoke and ground the burning nub out on the wooden floor. With that, he finished his glass, placed it on a dresser, and walked from the room. The Priest and Liam followed.

"You intend to join me?"

After a brief pause, the Priest asked, "Should we?"

"You stay to mind the men. Liam, you come with me. If the soldiers in Hightown are lacking authority, you may be needed to stay."

"Yes, sir."

***

Evening turned to night as the convoy arrived in Alice with the last of the supplies for the day. Karl and Liam stepped out of the Hummer as boxes of produce were removed from the pickup trucks and delivered to the kitchen.

"What's on the itinerary?" Liam asked. "The escort back to Alice is scheduled in two hours."

Karl walked fast from the trade grounds, eager to be away from the clamor of the men and the roar of the vehicles. He thought back to a time when his battles were fought from the saddle of a horse, and how afterward he did not have the headaches that now plagued him. "Cancel the escort."

"You're not planning on traveling back alone, are you? There's still plenty of 'em about."

"No, Mister Briggs. I intend to stay the night." He rubbed his temple as they walked.

"Yes, sir." Liam brought a bottle of brown liquor on their journey, taking back the occasional swig. Karl had taken a few slugs, but it did little to ease his headache.

"Keep an eye on the line, would ya?" Karl said. "I'll be in my quarters. Wake me only if needed."

"Yes, sir." There was trepidation in his voice. Never before had they not celebrated a victory until the bottles were dry.

Liam turned back the way they'd arrived, and the commotion lessened to a few soldiers carrying supplies. Then a voice said, "Sir?"

Karl turned, seeing a skittish soldier standing a few yards away. Liam stopped as well.

"What?" Karl asked.

"It's the prisoners, sir. It's, um, they're …"

"What about them? Get the fuck on with it."

The soldier cleared his throat, and said, "The ones tied up by the wall. They're gone, sir."

"Escaped?" Karl's eyes widened. "Which regiment was responsible for guarding them?"

"Third regiment, of the dockworkers, sir." His fingers played with the rifle sling over his chest. "They, um … it doesn't appear they escaped. They were freed … sir." The man looked at the ground.

"They … were … *what?*" Not once had those words been uttered by a member of his army. Freed. *Freed!* The pain in his temples radiated across his skull, and his vision throbbed crimson strobes. "Liam?" he said, looking across the way to his second in command.

"Sir?"

"Find out who exactly is responsible. Tie them up in the"—he spat to his side—"*freed* prisoners' place. Give them a few hours to think about how their actions brought them to that juncture, and give the rest of the troops an opportunity to witness their punishment. Then string them up to the wall."

"Yes, sir." Liam turned to the shaky soldier. "Come on, lead me to 'em."

Karl left and walked across Hightown, rubbing the bridge of his nose, until he neared his home overlooking the bay and the wide ocean beyond. He was quickly through the front door and up the steps. For a moment he paused outside his bedroom and closed his eyes, hand wavering over the handle. He breathed in the familiar warm scent of the interior, then turned to the door opposite the hallway and felt his pockets for the key to the padlock. The plan was to bring his trophy back to Alice before morning, but the throbbing in his temples called for rest. Tomorrow he would parade the prisoner down the streets. What he would do after, Karl didn't know. Execute him, perhaps. Force him to work the gardens, although it was best to keep the man's wicked tongue away from the eager ears of the fellow prisoners. The last thing Karl needed was for the detainees to have any sliver of hope. The jails would suffice for now, keeping his prize locked away deep down in the dismal underground, alone in the pitch-black.

The thought brought a thin smile to his lips.

With the padlock removed, Karl opened the door. It was cavernous inside. He groped the wall for the light switch, happy that the house still had flowing electricity, warmth, despite his preference for sleeping outdoors. The prisoner's chains had been purposely made short enough so that he couldn't reach the light switch, or come close to the door or barred windows. With the lights on, Karl inspected the bolt attached to the floor, trailing the chain locked around the man's ankle. The wood around the thick nut was scratched, stained with pale streaks of red. A futile task, with the thick screw extending all the way past the downstairs ceiling and clamped on tight.

A sweet fragrance hit his nostrils, and he saw a food tray with a browned apple core on the dresser nearby. Another smell was obvious: that of the bedpan and stale sheets.

"Did I wake you? You look well," Karl lied in a meek tone. The man stared back at him from the bed, his eyes hollow and dark, his hair wild, his cheeks sunken.

Exhaustion was taking away from this moment which Karl had longed to savor, but still he said with a smile, "It pleases me to inform you that Alice has fallen, and rather easily so. The town is now under my control, and in the morning, I will personally lead you down the avenues so you can witness the takeover firsthand, and the townspeople can witness yours. Sleep well, sir."

The man said nothing. The red wound around his ankle from the cuff was visible from across the room. Karl turned and left, first shutting the lights, and then padlocking the door shut.

Chapter Thirty-Seven
Full Speed

Simon found Bethany, Carolanne, Connor, and Winston after dark. They'd been taken to a medical tent, despite Carolanne arguing that they were fine, and given cots beside each other. They were eating MREs from a tray as Simon navigated through the orderly rows of bunks. It occurred to him that more than half of the mattresses were vacant—a sure sign of things to come.

When he got closer, he gave a quick whistle and his dog's head spun around, a plate in front of him licked clean. It was tough watching Winston struggle to his feet, and his heart broke as his old dog's tail wag so frantically at seeing him.

There's so much love inside him.

He scratched Winston behind his ear, and after a dozen licks at his palm, but mostly hitting the air, Winston curled back up in a ball, going around and around like a corkscrew before tucking his face near his hind quarters.

"Hungry?" Carolanne asked. "You can use my tray; I'm finished."

Simon nodded and took a seat beside Connor on the cot. He took an MRE from a box and opened the various pouches. "You want my cookie?" he asked Connor.

The boy looked up. "You're not going to eat it?"

Simon shook his head. "Nah, not that hungry." He squeezed a pouch of beef in barbeque sauce on the tray and found a miniature bottle of hot sauce packed along with it. He took a bite. Horrible stuff. The thought of roasting wild game over a fire made his stomach ache for real food … roasted acorns … maple syrup dripped straight from the tree … those tomatoes in Alice's garden, so red and warm, the juices exploding from the skin when bitten into.

Bethany sat beside him, her gaze burning into the side of his face. He didn't want to say it; he wished someone else had already told them of the colony's plan.

Finally, Beth said, "*Well?*"

He placed the tray on his knee. "It's begun. A large scouting party left a few hours ago, and the rest of the army will be following around midnight. They'll attack Alice first and then Hightown."

"What about us?" Bethany asked.

"How are they going to rescue the prisoners?" Carolanne asked.

He paused, and then said, "They're not going to rescue the prisoners—"

"Wait, what do you mean?" Bethany's tone was almost accusing.

"It's …" Simon sighed. "They're writing off the colonies."

"Writing them off? What the fuck does that mean?"

Simon turned to Bethany. "The decision was made before we arrived. I had nothing to do with it. Alice and Hightown … they're going to be destroyed. Bombed and burned to the ground. Their ambition is to kill each and every member of the Red Hands, indiscriminately. Karl Metzger and all of the officers are believed to still be in Alice, so that will go first. The colonies will surround them from the north, so any of their retreating soldiers will be dealt with. Once Alice falls, they'll turn northward and raze Hightown."

Carolanne stared at him with wide eyes, her mouth agape. "They're going to let Brian die … they're going to kill him."

"I-I don't know. The police stations in both towns will be avoided during the bombings. If he's been captive in the cells, there's a chance he'll be rescued."

Simon took a last bite of the MRE, leaving about a quarter of it on the tray. He placed it on the ground for Winston, who was all too happy to lap up the remaining slop. The rush of calories was making him feel sleepy, and his body was overcome by weariness.

"And they expect us to sit around and do nothing," Bethany said. "Fat fucking chance."

"No," Simon replied. "We have a choice to make. The injured, children, or those unable to fight will begin the trek back to Albuquerque under escort. Jeremy gave me the option; we can leave, either with them or on our own. Or we can fight, and be there as the soldiers liberate the prisons."

"Then that's right where I'll be," Bethany said.

Simon nodded. "I told him as much. And I'll be right beside you. They're assembling an hour before dawn. I suggest we all get some rest, if that's at all possible. We have a few hours before deployment." Rest was entirely possible, for Simon at least. Despite the adrenaline, fear, and anxiety coursing through his veins, his mind and body were on the verge of shutting down.

Simon looked at Connor, sitting on the cot opposite him, beside Carolanne. "I'm going to need you to do me a favor," he said.

The boy looked at him with his large brown eyes that had witnessed so much pain and destruction, a mouth covered in cookie crumbs that belonged to another era when happiness could exist, and children could enjoy simple pleasures unhindered by the horrors of the world. "You want me to watch Winston?"

Simon nodded. "That's right. I need you to keep him safe."

Connor nodded and wiped his mouth with a sleeve.

Simon stretched his legs out.

"I don't know how you're going to sleep," Bethany said, yet she lay beside him and rested her head on his chest. The cot was narrow for one person, let alone two, but being forced to hold her tight made him relax even more.

"I may not," Simon said. "Just going to shut my eyes."

He recited his mantras, trying not to imagine what the day ahead would bring. He might be dead before the afternoon. Bethany could die at his side, in which case, he didn't know what he would do. After the battle on Nick's lawn, he knew he was capable of doing terrible things to people. What if he snapped? What if she died?

… he couldn't think about that.

He'd rather die first than see anything happen to her. At least Winston would be safe and well cared for. Connor would be all right too. Carolanne, though … she would never recover from losing Brian and Bethany, and the home she'd become accustomed to.

As these terrible thoughts crossed his mind, he attempted to rein them in, for at least a short duration. *Focus on your breathing,* he told himself. *In and out, and in and out …*

***

The weariness of the fighting, the traveling, had done a number on him. His mind had delved into a deep state of REM when a noise woke him, snapping him from the depths of unconsciousness. Shouting. He sat up fast, saw two people fighting beside him, wrestling. The generator had been extinguished, but the lights from the surgical wing shone out from the distance over the sea of awaiting cots. Simon grabbed his rifle from the ground beside him. Connor was sitting up in bed, watching. Winston was standing, his tail wagging, and he was … licking someone? Wait … they weren't fighting, they were hugging, crying …

Brian!

Simon stood. "Brian, is that you?"

Bethany stood, her hands covering her mouth.

Brian embraced Carolanne, both of them crying into each other's shoulder. They remained that way for many minutes, then began to kiss. They kissed more and more, and Simon wondered if he should take Connor away to give them some space, but then they went back to hugging.

"I never thought I'd see you again," Brian said, and then acknowledged Bethany and Simon. He stood and grabbed Bethany, then reached out and pulled Simon in, hugging them both tight. "You have no idea how good it is to see you."

They separated, and Brian went back to Carolanne.

"I-I'd said go-goodbye," Carolanne said into her palms.

Brian shook his head and tried to lighten her sadness. "They couldn't kill me if they tried. And believe me, they tried plenty hard. If I was a cat, I'd of lost a few lives by now."

She hugged him tight. "How?" she said. "How are you here? Are you injured?" She began inspecting his face, chest, despite Brian protesting that he was fine.

"I met some scouts on the way here; they said the battle is set to begin."

Simon looked at his wristwatch. "We're assembling in a little over an hour."

Brian stood, reluctant to break Carolanne's embrace. "I have to see Jeremy."

"Now?" Simon asked. "Why?"

"It's a long story. Come with me, I'll tell you on the way."

Carolanne stood, wiping her face. Brian's mouth opened, but she spoke first. "You just came back; I'm not staying behind."

He nodded. "All right. Simon, you know where he is?"

"Probably the HQ tent. Come on."

On the way, Brian told them a rushed tale of his confinement, and quickened to the part about meeting Jacob and what the man had told him on the bank of the river.

Bethany shook her head. "It's not possible."

"Sure it is."

"No, it's not. I was there, I saw the explosion."

"It was a ruse. They tricked us."

"But didn't you see him?"

"What I saw could have been anybody."

Soldiers were gathered around the front of the headquarters. Lieutenants and lower-ranking officers, going over maps and details. They squeezed past and entered the tent. The inside was even more packed, and cigarette smoke fogged the air. Simon led them through a throng of people, to a table in the rear. Jeremy was in the corner, speaking to General Schafer. As the group neared, Jeremy noticed them.

"Simon," he said. "Brian, is that y—"

"He's alive," Simon blurted out.

"I see that," Jeremy said, reaching out to shake Brian's hand.

"No, not Brian—General Driscoll. He's alive, in Hightown."

The cigarette on the edge of Jeremy's lip sat there, looking ready to drop, then he said, "Wait, wait, wait … *what?*"

"It's true, sir," Brian said, and told a rushed story.

Jeremy ground his cigarette out in an ashtray. When Brian finished, Jeremy said, "I remember Jacob. He murdered his roommate, and then escaped from prison. Not surprised that he joined the Red Hands. I wouldn't necessarily call him a reliable witness."

"He didn't escape; Nick let him go."

Jeremy seemed to think it over, then said, "Not surprising." He exchanged glances with General Schafer. "Still though, there's no way to know if he's telling the truth."

"I believe that he is, sir. He freed me. I would have died if not for him.

And he told me more. Many of Karl's soldiers, the ones recently acquired—it appears that they're not following his orders as blindly as we've been led to believe."

"How so?"

"They fell under Karl's lies. But now they're seeing past the smoke and mirrors. Jacob told me that they're releasing more prisoners, without Karl's authorization."

There was a pause, and then Jeremy said, "This could be a trick. They might have released you with all of this information to press us to attack Hightown and fail against the defenses. Maybe they have a trap set up. Who knows?"

"The attack on Alice will be underway in less than an hour," Simon interjected. "But it's not too late to at least try to save the general."

"Simon," General Schafer cut in. "It *is* too late. The bombardment begins in a half hour, and the troops are mustering for the ground assault. Albuquerque's ships will be targeted first, along with the warship anchored in Hightown's bay."

"So, begin there," Simon said. "Sink the ships—just halt the invasion into Alice and Hightown, for at least a short while. Give us time to send a detachment in to rescue General Driscoll. Let us see if the prisoners were actually released."

"Releasing the prisoners could be a diversion, a tactic of theirs," General Schafer said. "And a direct assault to rescue General Driscoll is out of the question."

Jeremy pulled another cigarette from the pack with his teeth. "But a smaller operation is possible."

Simon nodded. "I'll go in, alone."

"Like hell you are," Bethany said, stepping forward. "He's my uncle. I'll be damned if I'm expected to sit aside while there's a chance of saving him."

Jeremy nodded.

Brian sighed audibly and looked to Carolanne while holding her hand. "I'm sorry—" he began to say, but Carolanne cut him off. "I know what you're going to say," she said. "You're going."

He nodded.

Jeremy lit the cigarette and said, "Let's make the plans then."

Chapter Thirty-Eight
Drowning in Flames

Someone was saying his name. Shouting his name. Calling him out of the deep unconsciousness. Dreams swam in his mind, flashed before his eyes, and turned into a nightmarish arm of some mythical god entering from above in the dark void, ripping him from the comfortable womb of the subconscious and back into the world of the living.

Karl's eyes snapped open, but it took a moment for him remember his surroundings. A mattress lay beneath him. The room was dark. The voice calling his name … *Liam?*

He sat up in bed, his head dizzy with fatigue; the years of fighting, marching, scrounging for food, surviving, all led him to succumb to weakness in that bed at that particular time. "What?" he said, his deep voice choppy. "What is it?" The light from the hallway shrouded Liam, casting him in shadow.

"Sir, we're under attack. We have to move—*now.*"

It crossed Karl's mind that he might still be sleeping. This could be a dream. His weary muscles yearned to lie back down on the warm mattress, pull the blanket up to his chin.

"Sir!"

Karl snapped to reality and threw the covers off. "What's happening?" He pulled on his pants and slipped his feet in his boots as he met Liam at the doorway.

"We're under attack," Liam said. "We have to go."

"I understand, Mister Briggs." He turned and closed the door. "What's happening?"

"Warplanes, sir. They—"

"Warplanes?"

"Jets, sir." They walked fast down the hall to the stairs. "We heard them before we knew what it was we were hearing. Sounded like thunder, a bad storm over the water. But the thunder never stopped; it grew louder."

"Jesus, where the hell did they get jets? Where are they attacking?"

"Louisiana's fleet got hit first, and now they're aiming at select locations inside Alice."

Karl eyed his watch; he'd only slept a few hours. His listless brain tried to rationalize the sudden entry of warplanes. "Why wasn't I summoned at once?" he asked.

"This just happened, sir. There was no warning."

Liam's balance faltered for a step, and Karl knew that the man had been drinking, probably up until a few minutes ago. Celebrating with the men, despite the command to remain vigilant. This would be dealt with later. Without saying another word, they exited the house, cut across the lawn, and were quick to the communications station set in one of the warehouses. The signal had been given that an attack was imminent, and men swarmed around in urgency, their faces weary.

Karl nudged aside a radio operator and said, "What's happening?"

The man looked up, trouble written over his expression. "The ships, sir—"

"Damn it, I know they've attacked the ships. What's the damage report?"

The man shook his head. "The planes came out of nowhere, sir. The men on the boats weren't prepared for an aerial attack. None of the surface-to-air missiles were in place."

The anger coursing through Karl's veins was waking him up faster than a pot of coffee could. "Speak plainly, damn it! Are they still operational?"

"No, sir." The man was sweating, trying to avoid eye contact.

"What's going on in Alice?"

"They reported hearing the planes less than ten minutes ago." His words were dry and he swallowed visibly. "Since then it's been radio silence from all their relay stations. We've received dozens of communications from men on their line—some targets are being bombarded with pinpoint accuracy; others are carpet-bombed. There are reports that all of Alice is surrounded."

Footfalls resounded across the open warehouse from behind, and Karl turned to see General Greg Ubel rushing toward him, followed by four of his officers.

"Mister Ubel," Karl said. "Your ships—"

"They're gone." His voice was sharp, angry. "Alice will be gone soon too."

"They've acquired an air force, somehow."

"They haven't acquired jack shit. It's California and Texas. Goddamn it, they've marched. Never in a million years would I think … where were they when Montana fell? Or Maine? Where were they when Albuquerque pleaded for help? None of us mustered our armies to support one another; why now?"

"When we first spoke, before an agreement came to fruition, you promised me the other colonies would not come to Alice or Hightown's aid."

"They never so much as moved a muscle for anyone before; why would I think otherwise?"

Karl felt an impulse to unholster his pistol and deal with Greg Ubel. The world had grown larger, it appeared, and not to their benefit. Before speaking to the delegates from Louisiana, he'd had no prior knowledge of the colonies on the West Coast. And because of those early chats, Karl was put to ease that they were of no consequence. Too many miles away, and little was expected from Hightown and Alice. They didn't produce fuel, just some water and food, and the other colonies produced enough on their own to survive. They wouldn't protect these lesser colonies when more productive communities, such as Colorado and Montana, were allowed to crumble without the slightest show of support.

"How many men did they bring?" Karl asked.

"How the hell should I know?"

Karl waved his hand dismissively. "We have surface-to-air missiles." He turned to Liam. "Have them armed, now."

"Yes, sir."

Greg Ubel shook his head. "They'll be flying high and fast and will have the town in ruins before daybreak. They're going to erase Alice and Hightown, and us along with them."

"They'll never—"

"They will. Get out of here, now. Abandon all posts. Have your men flee."

"Flee? Flee! We don't *flee* from anything. We stand and fight."

"And lose. You're going to lose. I've called for a complete departure of my men."

"You've done what? Where will you go? Your fleet has been annihilated! Do you think you'll be safe down in your ports?"

"No, I don't. We'll try to strike up a new deal with the colonies. I would suggest you do the same, but I don't think they'll forgive you after your many transgressions."

Karl again felt the pull of his pistol, but there were just as many soldiers from Louisiana in the room as his own; if he pulled his weapon, bullets would fly in all directions. They would destroy each other before the colonies had the opportunity. He turned to the radio operator, listening to the dozens of footfalls leave the warehouse. The room was silent as General Ubel left, and then Liam whispered, "Karl, sir, what are your orders?"

Karl didn't respond. He grabbed the headphones off the radio operator's head and pushed the man until he stood from the chair. Then he sat and listened for many minutes.

"What the hell are you all doing standing around?" Liam said to the many blinking eyes. "Get back to work. Man the defenses, make sure the missiles are deployed. Double the scouts outside the gates, set a one-mile perimeter, and make sure they're watching the bridge." The crowd dispersed. Karl listened to the various radio channels, switching from one to the other. The air attack had obliterated the vessels off Alice's coast and was now dropping precise bombs on the inner workings of Alice and the defensive line. An overwhelming ground force had circled the perimeter, and any of their fleeing or surrendering soldiers were cut down indiscriminately. A screaming report came over the wire, *"They're not taking prisoners! They're executing our men waving white flags! Jesus Christ, it's a slaughterhouse ..."* Another report told of the barracks targeted in a bombardment, killing flea, bedbug, and man alike. There was nowhere to hide and nowhere to run.

Before Alice fell, he dreamed of its destruction, despite knowing that it would serve him best for it to remain intact. Now, his anger seethed that he was robbed of the opportunity to set the torch. And there was something beyond anger ... Jealousy. He was jealous. This war had consumed his life, put all other campaigns on the sidelines. And now, in under two hours, his newly acquired navy was destroyed and his allies defected. Could he still win this war? It occurred to him that the colonies had the opportunity to overwhelm Alice and burn it to ash. However, that was not what they were doing. They were flexing their muscles, dropping precise and decimating bombs.

The radio grew quieter, and then a report came in: *"We've received communication from the colonies… we're being told to rebel… we're offered absolution if we … take down the leadership …"* Karl exchanged a worried glance with the radio operator. Further reports followed from various sections of the defensive perimeter and from the offices and homes; battles, small and large, were waged. The aerial bombardment had ceased, and in its absence, the soldiers—*his* soldiers—had taken up arms against each other. Karl pressed the headphones to his ears, listening as a sergeant on the front line attempted to keep order. *"Backup, we need backup!"* The background noise was a boil of gunfire and screaming.

This isn't possible, Karl thought. *My men would never disobey me.*

But all indications told another tale. Alice was burning, and it was his own men holding the torch, but Karl had not issued the command. The flames were searching for those loyal to the Red Hands, especially himself.

Karl removed the earphones. "Cut the lines," he instructed the dazed-looking operators. "Cut all lines with Alice. No more reports coming in or out."

His attention was stolen by Liam, who was shouting at a radio operator, his face red, the veins on his thick neck protruding.

"What is it?" Karl asked.

"They're leaving," Liam said, not looking over. "Our soldiers are fleeing Hightown with Greg."

"How many?"

"About a company's worth, maybe a little more."

Karl stood from the table. "And Alice is gone." He took Liam's shoulder and led him away from listening ears. "We don't have much time until the colonies advance on us. First, they'll make a display of their might, and then they'll make the same proposition as they offered the soldiers in Alice—amnesty, in exchange for our heads on a stick."

"Our men will never—"

"They already have. We need to cut off all communication with Alice, keep Hightown in the dark for as long as possible."

"They're already fleeing. The colonies will never accept them, never absolve them."

"No," Karl said. "Not for our men. It's a false promise. However, you heard what Greg Ubel said; he's going to attempt to make a reconciliation with the colonies, and what do you think that agreement will entail? How will he be forgiven?"

"Jesus," Liam said in a low grumble. "We have to muster those most loyal to us and salvage what we can."

"Yes," Karl muttered, rubbing his forehead with his thumb and pointer finger. He knew what he had to do—must do—but making the call, saying the words, was nearly impossible.

Chapter Thirty-Nine
Low Tide

Simon, Bethany, and Brian gathered gear from a makeshift supply tent while discussing strategy. Simon's plan to sneak in slow and undetected was scratched. Time was not a luxury they had. Once Alice fell, the planes would come shrieking across the sky to Hightown, and the colony's combined army would circle the front. The rumor of General Driscoll's survival was not enough to stop the initiative—however, together with news of the Red Hands showing a reluctance to blindly follow Karl's orders, the plans were altered.

Simon felt the heft of the flak jacket, the water bladder, the grenades, ammunition, and his rifle, and doubt crept into his mind that the gear would weigh him down, be more of a hindrance than a help. But Brian convinced him that it was necessary. There was no time to scout, to go swift and silent into Hightown. There was a real possibility that they were heading straight into gunfire. The flak jackets were a must.

Carolanne said little as they prepared. The man she loved so dearly, who had returned from a presumed death, was leaving her once again. Less than an hour after his return, the medical tent was a scramble of activity as soldiers gathered.

"Simon, Brian," Richard Jarrett said. "The Rangers are gathering supplies and will be here shortly. As General Winters ordered, thirty men are joining the initiative, all on volunteer basis. If General Driscoll is alive, we're ready to bring him home. What's the plan?"

"Richard," Simon said. "I can't thank you and the others enough."

General Driscoll was presumed to be held captive in Karl Metzger's private quarters in one of the homes overlooking the bay. Over half of those buildings had been destroyed when the Red Hands invaded, so finding which home belonged to Karl was narrowed down. The easiest way was to come by the water, on raft—try to remain undetected, just as Brian had done when fleeing. But that would take time, and boats, of which they had neither. Richard drew a quick map by hand, and it was decided they would advance upon the topmost corner, closest to their position, where the wall hit the water, and then—if they broke past—they would travel fast along the bank, taking the old trails which navigated the shoreline, back when their purpose was for sea-gazing and leisurely strolls. This would take them to the steep coast with the homes above. They'd have to find the least vertical inclines to ascend in the dark. There was no way to know how much resistance they would encounter, so the incursion had to be fast, although intelligence reported Hightown was left lightly defended. Perhaps, if they were lucky, Karl was dead down in Alice, and with the lack of leadership, confusion would follow.

The rest of the brigade arrived, applying dark makeup to their faces and checking their ammunition and supplies. The plan was rehashed, and Simon and Richard spoke to the Rangers, offering handshakes and words of support. Then Brian checked his watch and made eye contact with Simon. "Ready?" he asked.

Simon inhaled and exhaled. "Never been so ready in my life."

***

They parked the two transport trucks a mile outside of Hightown's walls as all the while, the bombs were dropping on Alice, and the first reports of defection among the enemy's numbers were given. Soon, dawn would turn the sky a pale shade of blue, and with it would come the targeted aerial bombardment, and the inevitable war. Either the enemy in Hightown would defect, like what they had seen in Alice, or the United Colonies would bomb and burn the territory to the ground. Either way, it would soon be hell inside Hightown's walls.

Simon couldn't help but reflect that he had traveled all that distance, from British Columbia to the East Coast, to find his family. What he found was a new home, a new family, a new reason to keep moving forward. And now, he would again be marching, fighting, to find yet another home. Wherever that new home may be, he would be at peace if he had Bethany beside him, and to that end, he would have to tap into that animal he'd become on the lawn of Nick's mansion, to assault, brutalize his way through the Red Hands' front gate if needed, to where her uncle was kept captive.

He breathed in and out, in and out … *In and out* … The woods were thin, and they progressed fast, remaining quiet as each man observed the terrain, looked for enemy movement. When would clarity return, as it had the last time he'd fought, when he ran through the trenches, his body moving so fast it was as if he were not doing those evil things? Shooting, hacking, bludgeoning the enemy soldiers with a swiftness unknown to his skillset. He breathed, he tried to focus … but all he felt was fear and revulsion.

There was movement ahead.

The soldier in the front held up a fist, and everyone fell to a knee. Two, three … maybe five people ran fast toward them, seemingly unaware of their presence. Simon watched them filter through the trees, closer. His finger brushed the trigger of his rifle, his eyesight blurry down the wavering sights, sweat dripping from his forehead. Bethany crouched beside him, rifle up. He could hear her labored breathing. Someone shouted, "Hold up!" and the advancing men froze, aiming their rifles in the direction of the voice, searching.

A reply came. "We don't want to fight." A man in the lead turned his head and said, "Guns down," to his entourage. "W-we give up." The man put his rifle on the ground and raised his hands. Others did the same, or averted their aim.

For a moment, no one moved. An enemy force fleeing, thinking the soldiers they encountered were part of a larger brigade, an advancing party. Slowly, one of the men in Simon's group stood, and then others followed. They walked, weapons pointed, sidestepping the surrendering troops. The enemy soldiers seemed to understand, and with slow, deliberate steps, they continued on their way.

After a few yards, they moved quicker toward Hightown, and they came to another flock of deserters. A handful at first, then more. The walls were in view. Another dozen followed, and then a steady stream exited the gate. The advancing party made eye contact with the fleeing men, each one surprised, scared. These men knew end times had arrived. They knew death awaited any who stayed to fight. No one wanted to get caught in a shoot-out, not with escape a possibility.

The filthy, weary faces of the enemy passed, and when they came to the open entrance, the defenses were abandoned. Mounted machine guns were left with ammunition belts fed in the chambers. Lookout towers with no snipers. Floodlights dark. Richard turned and said in a whisper, "I can't believe this. They're retreating—they're giving up."

No one replied as Simon's party moved fast toward a small beachfront, where they found the trail skirting the shoreline. They encountered no more enemy soldiers as they progressed, and the paved trail was easy to navigate. As they ran, the only sound other than their panting breaths came from the gentle and rhythmic water lapping at the shores, calm and beautiful—the symphony of nature. The dark water, cast in shadow, reflected a million moons upon each crest, the water at low tide moving back toward the shore. It dawned on Simon that it was possible General Driscoll was gone—taken from Hightown in anticipation of the coming bombardment and moved elsewhere. Perhaps executed.

His hope was renewed as they neared the steep banks, and far up, obscured in the distance behind trees and homes, came the obvious illumination of a lone house running electricity. All of the men noticed it as they slowed, catching their breaths. Richard, Simon, and Brian took lead to find a suitable place to scale the bank. A little further on they found a long, narrow staircase leading from the trail. They spoke with hand signals alone, the men taking to the steps one at a time, until they were gathered on top. "All right," Simon said, his words coming out in huffs. "I'm scouting ahead. Wait here." All of the dark faces, smeared with camouflage and dirt, nodded their approval. The one belonging to Bethany stared back at him. Her stern demeanor broke, and her mouth opened, presumably to state that she was going to join him, but then she regressed and nodded.

Simon went slowly, despite his adrenaline pumping so hard that he found it difficult to move with precision. *When will I tap back into the warrior?* There came no answer.

Though his movements were not as graceful as they could be, Simon managed to stick to the shadows as he neared the edge of the building. He heard voices before he saw faces. Heard vehicle engines rumbling. When he peered out from around the corner of the house, he saw six or more soldiers standing outside the front door of the illuminated home. Four smoked, and all were listless. There were drivers in the three waiting Hummers. From his distance, their words were murmurs. Simon waited a moment longer, then backtracked, carefully selecting each footfall before placing his weight down. When he neared the huddled mass of his men, he whispered, "Six or so outside. Don't know how many inside. They're waiting for something, ready to take off."

"Okay," Richard said. "I don't see any way around this. We're going to be quick, take them by surprise, and storm the door. With any luck, they're the last of the vermin left in Hightown, although that's doubtful. We have to find the general and get the hell out before more show up."

"Rodger-dodger," one of the soldiers said.

With that, a quick plan was made to strike from either side of the adjacent home. Four men would remain behind, entering the neighboring home and offering covering fire from the second-floor windows.

"Ready?" Richard said. Everyone nodded. He looked to Simon and Brian. "You're on point."

Simon inhaled, nodded to Brian, and said, "All right. Group one, on me."

He turned toward Karl Metzger's home and led his soldiers to battle.

Chapter Forty
Never-Ending Sea

Brian's knee was killing him. It wasn't bad when they were sneaking through town, or running on the trail; it was in the pauses, when they stopped and knelt down, that he felt it inflame. He was weaker from his ordeal in the jail cell than he'd realized. The euphoria of escaping captivity and embracing Carolanne, his face pressed to her fragrant, thick hair, had overshadowed his injuries. Plus, while there was still strength left in his fingers, there was no way he'd let Bethany run off alone to face the enemy and save the man responsible for protecting him from the war and disease when it first blanketed the earth.

Adrenaline continued to fuel him onward, and it wasn't until they were past Hightown's perimeter and in the heart of town that he realized just how fatigued he was. When was the last time he'd slept more than a few aching minutes, cold and miserable, half-starved and shivering? But now the end was in sight. Crouched low, his knee on fire, his mind and body running on the fumes of stress and anxiety, Karl Metzger's home was just around the corner. His uncle, alive or … not … was close.

The light from the house shone out from around the bend like the sun about to eclipse over the horizon, and the night was so quiet that the running generator along with the engines of the idling trucks eliminated any noise the soldiers made as they crept along the siding of the neighboring house. He and Simon led the first group, and Brian now wished he was farther back, not out of fear, but out of concern his stiff knee and woozy mind would slow him down and cause injury to the soldiers following his lead.

But these thoughts, these pains, had to be suppressed.

The earphone in his left ear clicked once and then twice. After a pause, it clicked three more times in even intervals. Then the clicking repeated in four. The first clicks came from the team in the adjacent home, pressing the receivers on their radios. They were in position and ready for the assault. The next came from the group on the opposite side of the home, led by Richard Jarrett, and the last was emitted from Simon. Everyone was ready, waiting for the first shot from the team inside the home, signaling the rest to move out.

Bethany was beside him, her arm pressed against his, like a spring ready to pop. Mental images formed of her as a child, smiling as only children do at the simple wonders of the world, building miniature dams with him and Steven in the creeks around the wooded sections of Nelson. He remembered her at her wedding, a grown woman, and so happy. He saw her in the bunker, skinny and pale, animalistic, with Carolanne at her side. He saw her embracing Simon Kalispell, her mind at ease despite her tough persona—

The first bullet shot rang out, followed by another.

Simon sprang forward and Brian followed. All notions of personal distress vanished in a moment as he turned the corner, the bright lights of the home before him burning like a torch at sea. It took a moment for the scene to materialize, to spot where enemy soldiers were ducking for cover and returning fire. He ran forward, fanning out, aiming his rifle and pulling the trigger. The drumming of his heart dictated his panting breath as he fired at the side of the truck, the driver inside hiding below the door, shooting a pistol blindly out of the window. Others were also aiming at the vehicle, and the entire side became peppered with symmetrical holes as high-caliber ammunition battered the metal. Greasy smoke appeared in a thick cloud from under the hood as the tires popped, and the truck fell to the rims.

The returning fire ceased.

A line formed as the men from Richard Jarret's unit met with their own. Gunfire erupted from two of the windows, and the returning fire was short and precise, the men aware that inside that home lay the valuable reason for this incursion. An explosion flashed at his side, followed by another, at what Brian guessed were hand grenades lobbed down.

Richard was first at the house, his back pressed to the siding as he changed the clip to his machine gun, letting the empty magazine fall. He pulled back the bolt as the soldiers gathered, and he turned fast and kicked in the front door. Another soldier followed, and Brian was third. The light from inside was shockingly bright—and then there was a blinding flash and a roar, along with a force akin to being struck by a moving car. Brian felt his body become airborne as he was thrown violently against the far wall. The force of the blast was familiar enough, despite the confusion of the explosion, since after all, he'd been thrashed by a hand grenade in the past.

***

Simon was behind Richard and four other men when all at once the entry room erupted in a quick and violent explosion, the glass shattering outward from windows near his head. The men at the entrance were kicked with such force it appeared they'd vanished.

Simon fell to his side, shielding his eyes with his free hand. He looked around, saw Bethany behind him, safe. Someone grabbed his arm and pulled him to his feet, and he stormed inside with the rest of the brigade. Men were at the stairway, others moving from room to room, securing them in a fast, tactical formation. Simon knelt over one of the men fallen in the blast. The side of his face displayed the force of the shrapnel, and the man clasped desperately at his neck. Before Simon could find a bandage, he was already dead.

Richard Jarrett was getting back on his feet, but then fell forward, catching himself on his knees. Another soldier was beside him, holding a bleeding laceration somewhere on his left arm. Richard was saying, "Son of a bitch!" loud. Across the room, Brian was covered from head to toe in white dust and debris.

"Brian!" Bethany called out, rushing to his side. Simon followed, and brushed pieces of wood splinters and chunks of drywall off Brian's body.

"Brian," she repeated, "Are you okay?"

Brian didn't answer. His eyes shone bright and wet from his mask of dust, and he coughed. His lips were red with blood, but still he was getting to his feet, looking down at his body, trying to decipher if anything was missing or not working. Simon repeated, "You okay?" and helped look him over. A red spot had formed on his chest and leg, but Brian replied, "My gun …," looking around. The harness that kept it attached to his chest had been torn.

Simon found the rifle, covered in the same white dust and mixed with debris. Brian moved the slide but it was stuck, the metal displaying a shiny slice and indent. He tossed it aside and unholstered his pistol. Coughing, he said, "Let's go," and grabbed Simon's shoulder as he faltered his first step. Tears trailed from his red eyes, washing rivulets across the bothersome white dust. He rubbed his face, seeming to make it worse.

"Hold up," Simon said, and took his canteen from a pouch. "Tilt your head." Brian did as instructed and Simon ran the water over his eyes and face, and then ripped off the sterile wrapper from a bandage to wipe away the dust. Brian took the canteen and swished water around in his mouth, spit out a gritty red trail, and then they moved to the stairwell. The gunfire had ceased, and as they neared the top stair, they heard, "We got him!" yelled from down the hall.

They passed open doorways as they went, scanning each room with rifles pointed. Two were empty, a third had been shot up with a body on the ground, riddled with bullets, and at the last door, with the frame broken in by a hard kick, they saw him.

My God ... Simon froze at the doorway, the rush of emotions a mixture of torment, exhilaration, and relief. Bethany rushed forward; Brian hobbled after her. She said, "Uncle Al!" and buried her face in his shoulder. His old age had caught up with him during the ordeal, and then some. He looked frail, disheveled, his dry lips pursed, his voice coming out in a rasp. "Wh-what are you doing here, Beth?" And he began crying, sobbing, his back convulsing. Brian reached his side, and when his uncle looked up, seeing his ghostly figure, he cried again and grabbed at Brian's arm, pulling him in.

A soldier inspected the clasp around the general's ankle. The redness of his torn skin was visible behind the tattered cloths he'd wrapped behind the metal buckle.

Then Uncle Al broke off his embrace. "We need to get the fuck out of here."

"Shield your faces," a soldier said as he aimed his gun to a link in the chain. After a loud pop, the chain split.

"Come on," a soldier said. "Let's move!" Bethany took her uncle under his shoulder, helping him to his feet. Brian attempted to hold his other side, but his knee buckled at the weight.

"I'm fine," Uncle Al said. "Give me a gun."

But he was barefoot and faltered as he took a step. Simon handed him his pistol, and took over for Brian on Uncle Al's opposite side. Two soldiers remained in the rear as they proceeded down the stairs. Gunfire erupted again from outside as they entered the front room. Richard knelt by the door, his uniform cut back at his shoulder, and a hasty bandage and sling wrapped around his arm. He held a pistol in his free hand and was aiming out the door. "Move!" he said, addressing the group behind him. "We got a mess of 'em coming!"

***

Karl issued the order to retreat. It was the first time he'd uttered the words, and it hurt him to his core. It went against his instinct to keep the men on the line and fight until they were all dead. But with warplanes coming against him … It wouldn't be a fight at all. His soldiers would be turned to smoke in a blink of an eye. And furthermore, his men's weakness had become apparent as they turned on one another down in Alice. On Liam's council, he issued for his Red Hands to abandon their posts and flee to Odyssey, where they could regroup.

A large number of his men in Hightown had already disavowed their oaths, shedding their uniforms, with the handprint prominently displayed on their chests, as they escaped. If any of those miscreants thought they could do so and still enter Odyssey, they had another thing coming. They'd be added to the line of corpses decorating the road into town.

There was a good chance that most wouldn't make it back anyway. By all accounts, the enemy colonies had come in mass, and probably had soldiers waiting to cut down the deserters. His army … it was defeated, for all intents and purposes. Alice was gone in a flash. All he had fought for … all he had sacrificed; evaporated in a blaze. The army he'd raised from the depths of Haddonfield Maximum Security Prison, to Marianna, gathered from Mark Rothstein's brigade, and the Priest's underground silo. All of it gone. Dietrich too—he'd been in Alice when the bombs fell and the men rebelled. His officers were dwindled down, his army a skeleton crew. Rage boiled, and he bit his tongue against the temptation of taking what few soldiers he could muster and making a final charge into the oncoming wave of enemy troops, to kill as many as possible before bullets found them.

There was a good chance that his army would never recoup, never be strong enough to go up against the colonies again. He would have to take what he could get, keep the few who remained loyal, and with Liam's help, survive. He didn't know how he'd do it, but he would. He was Karl Metzger, and if they hadn't killed him yet, they never would.

The transport was driving him toward his home where he had men waiting. Liam had gathered the trusted few, the soldiers who they knew wouldn't turn on their vows. Several were from Haddonfield, and had fought since day one. Others were acquired along the way, such as Jacob, who had been expelled from Alice in years past, and held such a hatred for Tom Byrnes and Alice's citizens, that Karl knew the man would never turn on him.

A report came in over the radio. "You hear that?" Liam said as he drove.

"Yes," Karl replied. "I heard it. How many soldiers do we have mustered?"

"Fifty or so. We staying on course?"

"Oh, Mister Briggs, we most certainly are. Radio for the men to expect a bit of sport upon our arrival." He inspected his rifle, checked the chamber. The report indicated that right at that moment an insurgence of the enemy's soldiers had made it into Hightown, to his home, and were trying to steal his prize, the only possession he'd taken after the many fruitful raids, other than drink, food, and weapons. General Driscoll wasn't the prize he wanted; it wasn't the prize he yearned for—he yearned for his Bethany. The girl with fire in her eyes, a deep rage that he could feel in her glare, witness as she cursed and fought against the soldiers trying to sedate her in Nick Byrne's underground room. One day, he could coax her into seeing the world his way. If that would happen, oh Lord, even he would be terrified.

The colonies had taken Alice. Reports told of the gardens destroyed. The barracks reduced to rubble. Homes and offices, Alice Elementary, set ablaze by his own men. Hundreds, thousands, dead. The colonies left his organization a splinter of its prior potential—but they weren't going to take his one and only prize.

"Hurry up," he told Liam.

"I'm going as fast—" he began, then said, "Yes, sir," as they drove into the skirmish.

***

Someone grabbed Brian's shoulder and pulled him forward, toward the door. His uncle was in front of him, helped along by Bethany and Simon. "Go, go!" someone shouted, and before Brian knew it, he was outside. He found a machine gun on the ground next to a dead Red Hand, and holstered his pistol. Headlights glared, and bullets whacked into the earth, making the soil appear to be boiling. He fired at the headlights, along with everyone else. A hand reached out again and pushed him. His legs gave out and he was pulled back up. Then the person grabbing him, pulling him, dropped in a shocking mist of red. The neighboring home with the machine gunners on the top floor was taking heavy fire, the whole side of the building torn to pieces of broken timber and shards of glass as pockets of fire erupted. Hand grenades were lobbed from either side, and tufts of earth rose with each concussion. He shot his gun through bleary eyes and felt heat around wounds on his torso, stomach, and legs. New hands pushed and pulled him, and voices shouted commands, but his ears rung from the explosions, and all he heard was mumbling.

The line of fleeing soldiers was being cut down, blown up, and those who remained were forced to the steep side of the property where the ground dropped off to the trail and shoreline below. He lost track of his uncle as the men vanished over the side, sliding, tumbling, as bullets pelted the branches above. Brian's footing faltered on a slick layer of dead leaves and branches, and he skidded and dropped, rolling for a moment before hitting against the hard side of a tree.

"Brian!" a voice yelled, and he looked up to see Simon grabbing his shoulder, pulling him to his feet as he also helped Uncle Al, who, without shoes, had also tripped and fallen in the brush. "Come on, get up!" Simon yelled.

Brian's reserves of adrenaline kicked in, and he got to his feet. A sensation like he was plummeting from the top of a tall building caused him to falter again, but onward he went down the hill, falling until he hit the paved trail. *Oh Christ,* he thought as his vision strobed white. *Carolanne, all I want is to be with you ... I'm no use here.*

A few men had made it to the bottom and more were crashing through the brush, firing up the hill where the enemy was gathering, following them down, tossing grenades. Luckily, the brush and trees stopped most of the explosives from reaching the bottom.

Brian managed to regain his footing and hobbled onward. Simon and Bethany were in front of him and going faster, dragging Uncle Al along. Bethany looked over her shoulder. "Brian, come on!" He tried to shout back that he was coming, but his breathing was too labored to make words audible. With each step, the pain in his leg became more debilitating, and his knees buckled. He fell and pushed himself back up. His shirt was soaked with his own blood, and a thought came zapping into his mind: *I'm not going to make it.* They were still far from the town perimeter, and they had to sprint if they were going to outrun the soldiers on their heels.

Brian inhaled and exhaled, trying to regain his limited breathing and force himself to stand. Simon and Bethany were out of view around a bend. The last two of their soldiers ran by. "Come on, Brian—get up!" one yelled as they passed.

"Yeah …" Brian said, and got himself to standing on shaky legs. "I'm up."

Bullets pelted the paved trail, and one of the soldiers was struck down a few feet in front of Brian. The man fell off the trail, landing on the large boulders bordering the water's edge. The other man ran on. Brian looked at the dead soldier and then up to the distant horizon, where dawn had cracked, forming a magnificent deep orange and red slit where the water met the sky.

Brian moved to the boulders and removed two grenades from the dead man's belt, pulled the pin from the first, and threw it into the slope of earth where the enemy was appearing, then pulled the pin and threw the second. As the detonations erupted, he aimed and fired his machine gun while walking toward the approaching Red Hands. Two bodies tumbled to the pavement, killed either by the grenades or his bullets, and Brian fired until the chamber clicked empty. He tossed the gun, picked up another dropped on the path, and sprayed the thicket.

A piercing hot sensation rocketed into his arm as a bullet found him, but he continued to fire. Three men emerged from the brush, and Brian was quick to aim in their direction. All three dropped, but not before firing a few rounds; his same arm was hit again, and his thigh burned from where a bullet grazed his skin.

The second rifle clicked empty. He dropped it and unholstered his pistol, and with his nearly immobile left hand, he unsheathed his combat knife.

Flashes of Bethany as a young girl crossed his mind … Steven and himself back in Nelson, flipping burgers and serving beers on busy weekend nights in Hendrick's Bar and Grill … having a beer after hours with old Ben and Nancy Hendricks, her talking to him and Steven in gentle words, "I appreciate you boys more than you'll ever know," and Steven smiling his goofy smile as she rubbed his giant paw of a hand with her small, fragile fingers … Carolanne in his arms, her hair, God, how she smelled like the ocean, like countless waves, the freedom of a never-ending sea …

Brian felt something pop and grind in his knee as he ran forward, meeting another of the Red Hands as he crashed through the brush, and dropped the soldier with a shot to his chest. More appeared along the trail, and another bullet pierced his side. A wide man stood before him, and Brian plunged the knife forward. The man grabbed his wrist, but the knife managed to sink an inch into the man's side. The man wailed, and as Brian lifted his pistol … he saw Karl Metzger rise from the rear, his expression stony, his gaze narrowed. "Move!" the terrible general commanded.

Brian aimed over the wide man's shoulder to Karl, but the soldier was fighting back, despite the blade still implanted. They twisted and turned as Brian pulled the trigger, the shots wild. He saw Karl jerk to his side and grab his right shoulder as a bullet came within inches of his head. The wide man managed to break free, the knife falling to the ground, his hands at the wound. Brian pulled the trigger again, but before he could see where it struck, three sharp stabs of pain walloped into his chest, and the world turned black before he hit the pavement.

There he lay, on the trail by the shoreline, his unflinching gaze turned to the sky and horizon as his life drifted out over the water, and his body was finally at peace.

Chapter Forty-One
Devil Fingers

Bethany kept looking over her shoulder as they fled, saying, "Where's Brian?" but no one answered. Simon looked back, but the trail turned around too many bends. Once they neared the border and the path ended, they cut through the same section of town they'd traversed when entering Hightown, only now there was enough early morning light for them to no longer be invisible. Still, the town was deserted, more so than when they'd entered.

"We need to move," one of the soldiers said, despite that the party was running as fast as they could, out of breath, with Uncle Al dragged along and his bare feet striking rocks and branches. There were five of them altogether, and two of the soldiers were injured, one with less serious wounds to his chest, and the other with a bleeding arm beneath his shredded sleeve, which he held close to his body. They were close to the perimeter when Bethany said, "Wait—we have to wait for the others to catch up."

"There are no others," the man with the injured arm said.

"How do you know?"

"I was the last out of the house. There's no one behind me." He shook his head. "We lost them."

"That's not possible. There were at least three soldiers behind us—I saw Brian."

"I'm sorry," the man said. "Last I saw Brian, he was holding them up on the trail."

She craned her neck in the direction they'd come from. The weight of Uncle Al, along with the injured soldiers, made their escape slow, and by now, the enemy should have caught up. There was nothing to suggest that they were still followed. "He'll be right here," Uncle Al said.

No one replied. Simon removed his thin jacket and cut strips for Uncle Al to tie around his feet. The material he had wrapped between his ankle and the metal cuff, still trailing some links, had slipped away, and the skin beneath was battered.

"We can't leave anyone behind," Uncle Al said.

Bethany got to her feet and checked the chamber of her rifle.

"Where are you going?" the man with the injured arm said.

"I'm getting the others."

"Wait," Simon said, reaching for her arm. "Beth, hold up."

She pulled away. Her face was stern, set to the horizon. "I'm not leaving him."

"We have to get out of here," the man with the injured arm said.

"You all go on then," she said, and looked at Simon. "If something happened to him, if Brian didn't make it, how could I tell Carolanne? How could I explain that we just left him without knowing? He might be alive, injured … or if not … we owe it to him to find out."

The man with the injured arm cut in, "In about five minutes the jets are going to start dropping bombs, and the homes on the ridge are on their target list. Not to forget that we were chased here by a large brigade. You're crazy to turn back." With that he stood and started toward the gate.

"Wait," said one of the uninjured soldiers, a tall man named Sam. "They haven't caught up to us—chances are they fell back. I know Brian, we worked together for a short time in the kitchen. I'll go. I'll sprint there and back, check the trail. Beth, you owe it to your uncle to stay at his side."

She paused. Sam stood and checked the magazine in his assault rifle.

"I'm going with you," Bethany said.

"No, you're not." Uncle Al looked up. "He's right, Bethany. I've lost so much, everything I've fought for since before the disease reared its head. Please … don't leave me too."

"I'll go with him," Simon said. "We'll meet at the vehicles."

She looked at her uncle and then Simon, and nodded. "Go fast. Hurry. If they're still there, if it's an ambush, don't stay and fight. Run. Run back to me."

"I promise." He hugged her hard and fast, and then kissed her long and slow. They separated, and he turned to Sam. "Let's go." With that, they turned and ran.

***

"What do we do?" Sam asked.

Simon didn't answer.

The trail was deserted. Karl and his men were nowhere to be seen, but all around lay the destruction of war: bullet shells, splinters of blown trees, pools of blood. There appeared to be no pain in Brian's expression as his clouded eyes stared toward the horizon.

In the far distance came the thunderous roar that could only mean one thing—the planes were coming.

"We have less than five minutes," Sam said. "We can't carry him back, we've got to move. Chances are, here by the edge of the bay, him and the others who died on the trail will be spared from the bombing. We'll send a recovery team."

Simon looked at his friend, lifeless on the ground, remembered the things Bethany had told him: Brian's journey with Steven from Nelson to Aurora, Brian saving her life when a group of filthy men seized her and began dragging her away. He killed them all. One with a knife, and he got injured in an explosion while doing it, knocked unconscious while defending her life. How was Simon going to tell her, tell Uncle Al, that their last remaining family member was dead …?

… he would tell them of the serenity in Brian's expression, the lack of pain, his placid gaze watching the sun rise.

"Simon—"

"I know," he said. "Let's go." He paused for another moment, debating whether to close Brian's eyes. But then he turned and ran back up the trail, letting Brian watch his final sunrise alone.

***

Simon said, "Down—*get down*."

Sam turned from the road they were skirting and fell into the brush at the side of the pavement. The roar overhead was so close it tickled the inside of his eardrums, and near deafening explosions emerged from the bay, where they had witnessed the first bombs dropped on the warship docked in the water, turning the sunrise into a horizon on fire. But there was another rumble that did not come from the planes.

Lying on their stomachs in the brush, rifles aimed, they watched two Hummers and two pickup trucks drive fast toward the exit. There was just enough time to take a mental snapshot as they passed. The backs of the pickup trucks were full of men, dour-looking faces black with dirt and soot, uniforms frayed. Simon saw one with a bandage wrapped around his head. A shade of red seemed to envelop them all.

Once the vehicles passed, Sam said, "That was them, wasn't it?"

Simon nodded. *Karl Metzger survives,* he thought, and tried to decipher how far out of town Bethany and the soldiers would be by now. If they stuck to the same route as they had taken when coming in, they should be far enough away in the brush to remain hidden.

"Let's get out of here," Sam said.

They stood and ran as fast as they could. One of the ammunition warehouses must have been bombed, for at that moment an explosion cracked so loud it caused them both to turn and witness a pillar of fire blossom over the trees and buildings, thick, black veins of acrid smoke like devil fingers tickling the sky, and streaks like fireworks bursting in every direction.

"Jesus Christ!" Sam shouted.

The road opened up to a paved lot before the gated exit. Sam and Simon sprinted, sweat falling from their faces, their fingers, as they jumped over the ruins of a fallen guard tower, turned … and came upon the body of the soldier with the injured arm whom they had been fleeing with. He lay dead, barely recognizable. The exit was a few feet away. Simon halted.

"Simon—" Sam said, before seeing the body. "Shit …"

The other injured soldier lay with his face pressed to the pavement in a pool of red. And the same went with the uninjured man. They were dead, all of them.

"Beth …" Simon muttered, then louder, "Beth! *Beth!*" He looked all around.

"She's not here," Sam said, his voice urgent. Another ball of fire erupted like a geyser from hell. He grabbed Simon's shoulder and pulled him. "She made it to the vehicles—she must have."

They ran through the exit and onto the outside perimeter, searching for her. "Beth! Beth!" Simon yelled as loud as he could. "Albert! General Driscoll!" And then he saw him—the mighty general from the north, Albert Driscoll, the founder of Hightown and Alice, responsible for saving countless lives. The old man sat slumped over against the wall beside the door, shoeless, surrounded by piles of broken rocks. There was a hole in his forehead and a pool beneath him. On the wall above was a terrible splatter from where the bullet used to execute him hit concrete.

Sam said, "It-it was all in vain …"

The terrible realization hit Simon like a frozen spike at the base of his skull. *They have Bethany. Karl Metzger, the Hummers and trucks …*

And that was when he knew that Karl Metzger's fate lay in his hands and his hands alone. Even if they found Bethany safe and alive at the escape vehicles, he was going to end the miserable duration of Karl's reign with his own two hands. He would track him to the rim of the universe and push him over the edge, or die trying.

No more … he thought, and ran, sprinting over the pavement in the direction of the fleeing enemy vehicles.

***

When they reached the vehicles, they were both doubled over, panting. Simon held on to hope that she'd be there, waiting, or maybe one of the trucks would be missing. But she wasn't there, and the transports were parked as they'd been left. Simon took long sips of water between labored breaths, and the liquid seemed to absorb into his body the moment it passed his lips.

Sam climbed into the driver's side door of one of the transport trucks and turned the ignition. "Come on," he said. "We have to redirect troops to follow Karl. They must be fleeing to Odyssey. There's time to catch up."

Simon paused from drinking, his breathing still ragged, and wiped a trail of water from his chin. He removed the flak jacket and gear, letting it drop to the dusty ground, and finally felt free. His sweat-soaked shirt underneath was cool, and he said, "No."

"What? Come on, Simon."

Simon shook his head. "If the colonies catch up to Karl, they'll obliterate everything within a ten-foot radius of him. I'm going to get Beth back my way." He shook his head slowly. "No more following orders. I'm doing this alone. I'm doing it now." He walked to the opposite transport.

"Wait," Sam yelled. "I'm going with you."

"No," Simon shouted back. "Go back to the colonies and tell them Karl survived. They need to know. They need to turn their sights on Odyssey faster than anticipated. But I have to get there first."

Sam seemed to think it over in the silence as Simon tossed his gear inside the transport and turned the ignition. The engine was loud and the seat rumbled. He leaned out the open window and shouted, "Don't forget to tell them where Brian fell … and all the Rangers who died. I don't think Richard Jarrett made it far from the house."

Sam nodded and turned the wheel. "Good luck," he shouted back and saluted.

Simon put the truck into drive and wheeled onto the main road. Following Karl's path would be tough, but with the help of a map, he was reasonably sure he could decipher their route to Odyssey. He would bring ruination to what remained of the Red Hands.

Chapter Forty-Two
Perilous Decisions

Karl and a force of thirty men followed behind the insurgents as they sprinted down the trail by the water and turned around a bend. Liam staggered a few steps and dropped to a knee, clutching his side. "Go on," he said. "Jesus, that guy stuck me good."

On a stretch of trail that was long and straight, the water lapping the shore, the enemy was out of sight around a far bend, lost behind a wall of trees and seagrasses. Still, his men fired into the brush indiscriminately. At this point, if Albert Driscoll were to die, Karl would at least feel a sense of completion, justice for this terrible infringement. The gall of these men to breach his home and take what he possessed—the only possession he'd acquired from his years of warfare. The injustice was intolerable.

The reeds rebounded and evaporated into airborne puffs from the feathery plumes as bullets continued to follow their getaway. His soldiers sprinted on, panting, sweating as they closed the distance of the long stretch, and the curve beyond led to a small beach and the end of the trail.

"Are there any men left on the line?" Karl asked, the words difficult to say between labored breaths. "Well?" No one replied. He looked over his shoulder to the men fanning out as they took to the streets, running in the direction of the western gate. "Is anyone manning the line?"

The men looked at one another. Someone said, "I don't know, sir."

Karl gritted his teeth and ran. *Fucking Liam had to go and get himself stabbed. I'm left with morons.* "Find out! Call it in!"

A man got on his radio, and after a moment said, "We got a handful just south of the gate, on their way out. I called them back."

"Tell them to mind the old man."

"Yes, sir."

Karl continued pursuit, but the group slowed and a few doubled over, holding stiches on their sides. Karl looked back. "What are you waiting for?"

None of the men moved quickly. "Jesus, come on!" Karl yelled.

"Sir," one of them said, his cheeks burning bright beneath the layer of grime that seemed a part of his skin. "The colonies are on their way. We should get back to the trucks, flee while we can. If we go running after them it will take longer to get back to the vehicles. If we turn back now, we can at least drive to the gate, meet the others."

Never did the men speak so directly. *The fucking brashness of this one!* There were a million injuries Karl wanted to hurl, a million punishments, but for the sake of time, he swung his rifle into his hands and pulled the trigger. A bullet whacked into the man's chest and he fell to his back. The other men recoiled. Karl aimed another shot at the man's head and fired.

"Anyone else have any fucking opinions?"

He gazed from one soldier to the other, waiting for the typical, "No sir," but what he saw was something else. A few gripped their rifles tight, and some gazed back. Anger. They were angry.

Holy shit … I'm losing them.

There was a pause, and in that absence, the men sweating, unsure which side they would choose if Karl aimed another shot, he thought that the dead man was probably correct. The colonies would be arriving at any minute. With them would be the extreme force of their ground troops, surrounding the perimeter. There was a good chance they were out there already, and escape was futile.

"Perhaps ole headless there had a point," Karl said, cracking his lips into a thin smile. "Back to the trucks. We'll get to the gates as the others deal with the insurgents. Let's get the hell out of this dump."

There seemed to be a collective sigh as the men loosened the grip on their rifles and turned back the way they'd come.

***

The vehicles came to a stop outside the exit, and the engines remained idling as the men aboard the pickup trucks dismounted and fanned out to form a loose perimeter. Karl opened the door of his Hummer and stepped out. Liam remained inside, tending to his wound. The former king stood against the wall, a beaten old man, his clothing frayed, his hair matted with filth.

He approached his soldiers recalled from their escape. They'd managed to meet the small group of insurgents as they exited Hightown, and stomped their folly.

Karl smiled as he walked toward Albert Driscoll. "Oh, sir, how I've missed you so—"

He stopped short … was it possible? There on the ground, kneeling before a circle of his men, was a girl, a woman, strands of her long dark hair fallen from the tight bun, her helmet cast aside. One of his men gripped the top of her hair in his palm like a rope.

"You …" Karl said. "By all that's holy, I'd just about given up on you." He smiled and let out a deep chuckle. "It's fate, my dear."

She met his gaze, fire in her eyes, and he'd never felt more enthralled, not even in the final stages of battle. "Fate?" she said. "Fate! You fucking—" She moved forward to jump at him, but the man holding her hair yanked back, and she fell, grabbing her head.

"Get your fucking hand off her," Karl said, looking at the soldier.

The man let go without hesitation. "Sir," he said, stepping back.

She lay on the ground in the center of the circle of his men. "My dear Bethany," Karl said.

He saw movement to his side as the old man took a step forward. "Don't touch her," Albert Driscoll said. "You have me, so let her go. She's no use to you."

Karl didn't turn to face the exiled king, but rather stared down at Bethany. All those nights fantasizing about her capture, dreaming of her beauty. She was the one who was supposed to be kept in chains in his bedroom, not this grumpy old bedfellow. He turned to Albert Driscoll, unholstered his pistol, and aimed. The general raised his hands before his face, said, "Kar—" before the bullet shot cracked loud, and the old man's head jerked back.

Bethany jumped to her feet, screaming, *"No!"* and arrived at Karl, swinging her arms. The soldiers around stepped forward to intervene, but Karl just smiled, absorbing the punches with feet planted. Her holster was empty, her sheath held no blade. All she had were her fists, and even those tasted sweet to be coming from her.

A voice shouted from the idling Hummer. "What the hell are you all doing?" Liam leaned out the open door. "Let's get the hell out of here!"

"Indeed, Mister Briggs," Karl said. "Indeed."

He grabbed Bethany's collar and gave her a stiff shove, then issued quick instructions to the men, and everyone dispersed to the vehicles. Karl patted his front pocket for a cigar and found a thin one with a crack down the side, battered from the recent exertion, but still he struck a match. The frayed tobacco sputtered in flame, and after another two matches, he got it burning. He took another from his pocket and offered it to Liam across the opposite seat. With a rumble, the vehicles proceeded away from Hightown.

"Don't know how you're so relaxed," Liam said, slumped in his seat. His face was pale and clammy. The wound in his side was a puncture an inch or so deep, nothing to be concerned about.

"You don't want it then?"

Liam looked over. "Yeah, give it here. Sir." He winced as he leaned to take the cigar, one hand holding his side. The roar of the fighter jets reverberated through the cabin of the Hummer. Karl looked at the driver's side mirror and saw the reflection of fireballs licking at the sky in the distance, far over the trees. Hightown was gone. Alice was gone. What remained of his empire was held together by threads. Back at his home, as the men ran to the vehicles to escape, he'd witnessed the bombs dropped on his warship in the bay. Despite the order to evacuate, the vessel ran into trouble trying to navigate out of the shallow waters, and it was bombarded with a full crew of men.

"How many escaped Hightown?" he asked Liam.

"I … don't know, sir. Not many."

"If you had to guess."

"Maybe, I don't know … a hundred, two hundred, tops. Some are radioing in. The ones with vehicles should manage to flee. The ones on foot, there's nothing to be done. They'll most likely be rounded up."

"Did they rebel, like down in Alice?"

Liam cleared his throat. "Y-yes, sir. There were reports of aggression in the warehouses. Word of Alice's mutiny spread, and limited radio broadcasts reached the men before we cut the lines. They were offered amnesty if they took up arms against those loyal to our brotherhood. And just now, while you were dealing with Albert Driscoll, the men fleeing the eastern line came up against General Ubel and the soldiers from Louisiana. They've turned on us, as expected."

"The colonies will never offer them redemption. It's a ruse."

Liam shrugged.

Karl watched the landscape flow by out the window, and gazed at the flames in the rear window reflection. He inhaled and exhaled.

"What's the plan when we get to Odyssey, sir?" Liam asked. "How are we going to regroup?"

The smoke felt good in Karl's lungs—hot, stinging. He wished he had a taste of whiskey to further the burn.

Liam didn't repeat his question. Instead, they sat in silence. After a pause, Karl said, "We're not going to Odyssey, Mister Briggs. By my estimations, the colonies will be marching to their gates next."

"Where do you aim to take us?"

Karl let an exhale of smoke drift from his lips, then leaned forward and told the driver the new destination.

"Should we radio for the soldiers in Odyssey to depart?"

Karl exhaled a cloud of smoke. "No," he said. "And the others who are fleeing Hightown, don't mention a word. They'll be followed. Let the colonies think that all who remain are in Odyssey."

A flutter of ash flew backward into the trunk of the Hummer. He looked back. "Sorry, my dear," he said to Bethany. Her wrists were bound. Her ankles too. A gag was tied tight in her mouth. He would reward the soldiers who'd captured her. He would honor the few who remained loyal.

Chapter Forty-Three
Someday Soon

With Connor and Winston at her side, Carolanne watched the lone troop transport return. A stab of pain struck her heart, and then a deep foreboding as one solitary man stepped out from the driver's side door. She waited for the other transports to appear, but they didn't. A small hand gripped her own.

Jeremy and two officers spoke to the man who returned, and a medic looked him over, despite being waved away. Her eyes were already tearing as she approached him. Once the officers broke off their conversation, the soldier caught her eyes and a look of distress crossed his expression.

"I'm sorry," was all he said, and Carolanne understood. She'd understood before Brian had returned from capture. She knew it after the first battle in Alice. It was the way he talked, the sound of his voice, the distress in his eyes. A part of him died back in Nick's mansion when Steven expired in his arms.

She wiped her cheeks and asked, "How did it happen?"

The soldier told her a rushed tale and what he knew of Brian's death. "It appeared to be quick, if that brings you any relief." He bit his lip and then added, "I'd imagine that it doesn't."

"And Beth? Simon? Where's Uncle Al?"

"Beth … I don't know. Our guess is that Karl has her. Simon is following them. I tried to go with him, but he wouldn't have it. Albert Driscoll … he didn't make it."

She shook her head. "It was all in vain. Brian died for nothing."

Sam had no reply.

***

The dead were interred in a field outside of Alice, where the soil was soft and easy to dig. The orderly fashion of the colonies working in unison was staggering. In preparation for casualties, long trenches were dug before the bodies arrived, and each was lowered in turn as soldiers kept inventory. The casualty rate was far less than estimated, as the air support doled out heavy losses against the Red Hands and caused them to fight among each other, toppling Karl's reign. In the end, his own men brought about his decline, and they slaughtered each other in brutal fashion, burning much of Alice during their hostilities. An unexpected mass exodus followed in Hightown, and those who fled were being rounded up as they headed west toward Odyssey.

The graves were to be used for fallen allies only. The corpses of the Red Hands were left where they fell. It was still under consideration whether Alice was too heavily damaged to repopulate. If the colony was to be abandoned, the town would serve as an open-air tomb for Karl's fallen army. It was declared by the officers that none of the deceased would be brought back to California, Texas, or Albuquerque. This was true for officers as well, and the corpse of Nelson Barnett was found, along with Richard Jarrett and Casey Edmunds. They were lowered in the pit unceremoniously as a man in fatigues wrote their names in a ledger and inscribed their numbers from ID tags.

Despite Carolanne telling Connor that he didn't have to witness Brian's burial, the boy was adamant that he be there. However, once they reached the field, she wished that she'd been more insistent he stay behind. The sight was horrific, despite the small number of casualties, and the smell worse. Rigor mortis. Severed limbs. Decapitations.

Winston's ears perked up as they neared the grave, and his nose wrinkled. Connor called his attention. "No, boy," he said. "Stay with me."

She asked Connor, "Are you all right? You don't have to stay."

The boy answered, "I'm fine," despite a waver in his voice.

The residents of Alice did not use ID tags, nor did the non-military personnel or the citizens who joined the colonies after their inception. When Brian's body was brought to the grave, the soldier marked his name in the ledger, and the pallbearers—who wore dark green, rubber coveralls—paused before the pit when they saw the waiting party. They lowered the stretcher to the ground and walked away, making brief eye contact with Carolanne as they offered a thin smile.

Brian looked much the same in death as he did in life, despite the ashen color of his skin and the layer of grit on his face.

When Carolanne fell to her knees beside him, Connor rushed to her side. The colonies were moving out in twenty minutes. She had to say goodbye to everything she had once held dear, her loved ones, a home, an actual life. This was the world she lived in—one of constant heartache, infinite battles, strife.

She brought along a cloth and a canteen of water and washed away the dirt on Brian's skin with trembling hands. Then she combed back his matted brown hair. Her fingers touched his handsome face, his muscular arms. The world would never change, and the fault did not lie on Karl Metzger's shoulders alone. Each survivor of this new dawn moved within the circle of violence. The public execution of Nicholas Byrnes. The roundup of the Dragoons, all strung up by their necks. The dozens, perhaps hundreds of surrendering Red Hands who stumbled out of Hightown, injured, surrendering—murdered.

She carried the helpless feeling of loss in her belly like a rotten meal, a terrible rock in the pit of her stomach. The military precision of the colonies was just as much to blame for the eternal war as the enemy. Someday soon, there would be no one left to kill their fellow man. Someday soon, humanity would perish. Kneeling there beside her beloved Brian, it was impossible to foresee a future in which the human animal would crawl out from under its rock of ignorance. After the last battle, when Brian returned from the fight on Nick's lawn alive and healthy, she believed that a day would come when hostilities would cease. She believed that someday soon, peace would prevail and wars would end. Now, she wasn't so sure.

It seemed like she was there for only a minute or two when shrill whistles cut through the air. The burial crew tasked with filling in the graves were nearing the spot where she knelt.

Carolanne stepped away and looked over at Connor, who was doing his best to hold back sobs, yet tears streamed down his face as he kept one hand on Winston's back. She put a hand over the young boy's shoulder, pulling him to her side, and said out loud, "Goodbye, Brian," but the words carried more weight than a simple message. She was saying goodbye to her love, her home, the life she once knew.

Chapter Forty-Four
Ten Gallons

The knife wound on Liam's side wasn't as bad as the man was making it out to be. A scratch. A superficial puncture that bled more than it warranted.

"Never been stabbed," he said. "Shot twice, but never stabbed." He kept pressure on the bandage beneath his fatigues. "Hurts like the devil."

Miles passed, and with them Karl smoked a cigar and didn't utter a word. He sat in the back seat, Liam at his side, moaning and going on about his wound. The driver and passenger said nothing, which was the smart thing to do. Karl felt their questions in the silence: How many of their people survived? Did he think the colonies were going to go after the small remaining settlements? Was it all lost; should they give up now and hope to keep their lives? Should they disband and scatter in the wild? What would they do … what would they do—*what would they do*?

He couldn't rightfully answer.

The world … I had it. I held it in my hands.

As far as surviving, Karl had little concern. He'd been through hell and back, his body torn, burned, blown up. He would survive. As far as a plan to keep what remained of his army running like it had before … impossible. How the hell did the colonies get fighter jets? The defenses of Alice and Hightown, once thought to be impressive, did not have the slightest notion of opposing high-altitude aircraft.

An hour passed in silence. Numbers went through Karl's mind. Numbers, tallies, strategies. First thing first, he must remain in the present moment and deal with their current situation. Mustering what remained of his men required his survival over all others, and in order to survive, they had a long drive ahead of them, and with that came the urgency of fuel.

"How much fuel we got in reserves?" he said to no one in particular. The three men were taken aback by the break to the silence, and the driver cleared his throat. "Got pretty much a full tank now, two full five-gallon canisters, and a few empty cans if we come to some fuel."

"Come to some fuel?" His voice rose. "We just left a fucking city of fuel, and you didn't think to bring as much as we could carry? Empty cans?"

"S-sir," the driver stuttered. "It was, I … I didn't get the fuel, sir. We thought we were going to Odyssey. Brought more than enough to get us there."

Karl rubbed the bridge of his nose and looked at the back of the man's head. "It's Jacob, right?" he asked.

The driver nodded. "Yes, sir."

"Do the other vehicles have the same amount of fuel onboard?"

"Um, yes, sir. By my reckoning."

Karl spied Jacob's messy nest of hair. He fought the compulsion to shoot him right then and there. "Pull over," he said. "Order the others to pull over."

There was a pause, and Karl said, "What the fuck are you waiting for?"

"Yes, sir."

The order was relayed over the radio, and the driver navigated to the side of the road. Karl gave them a rushed plan and said, "We have to be quick about it." The driver and passenger exchanged worried glances. "You want to survive?" Karl asked.

The passenger replied, "Yes. Of course, sir. We're ready."

The doors opened and the men got out. Liam stood hunched over, holding his wound, and called out, "Out of the vehicles! Let's go! Hurry up!" He separated them into two groups.

Doors opened on the idling trucks and Hummers. The men in the beds of the pickups stayed where they were.

"You too, all of you!" Liam yelled, organizing them out of the vehicles. "We need a head count and inventory. General Metzger has something to tell you, so line up!"

The men did as instructed. There weren't many of them. Out of Karl's army of thousands, he now had a lousy string of miserable eyes waiting upon his words. He stood before them, patting his pocket for a cigar, then realizing he didn't have any left.

"All right," he said to Liam, "let's get on with it."

Liam raised his machine gun, and so did Karl, Jacob, and the passenger. The gunfire tore into the confused faces like a tsunami over ants. A few attempted to run or aim their rifles, but the automatic fire cut them down in a matter of seconds. Alive and then dead. Just like that. One half had been spared, the group on the left, who were aiming their rifles back and forth between Karl and their dead compatriots.

"As you can see," Karl said to the group on the left, "you've been spared. We now have enough resources to see us to our destination, so be thankful that you were standing on the correct side."

Everyone looked down at the bodies. Some moved, twitched, made gurgling noises. "Start siphoning the fuel," Karl said. "Gather their weapons, and see if any of them got tobacco. Be quick about it." He started walking back to his waiting Hummer, but then paused and turned. "Remember," he said, staring at Jacob and the passenger. "This wouldn't have happened if you'd brought enough fuel." Then he turned, opened the rear door, and got in. As he'd fired his own gun at his men, his eyes looked to his side, to Jacob. The man had not pulled the trigger. He aimed his gun, but he didn't fire a shot.

Karl rubbed the bridge of his nose and sighed. He'd deal with Jacob later.

"Ahh," he said, and turned to Bethany in the trunk, her puffy eyes opened to slits. "I'll get you home in due time. Don't you worry."

Chapter Forty-Five
Shadow Pursuit

The receiver volume on the console was set as low as possible. Simon wanted silence. He needed to absorb solitude, let the wind rushing in through the open window wash away the streaming chain of negative thoughts and emotions coursing through his mind. When he first began his pursuit, a familiar voice spoke over the airwaves, calling his name. It was Jeremy, imploring him not to follow Karl into Odyssey. The town would be decimated, he warned. There was no emotional connection and little strategic value in perhaps one day rebuilding Odyssey. It would be burned to the ground, the ashes bombed to dust, the dust ground to powder. The same was true for Karl's other settlements, the recently discovered docks, and the prison in Texas.

Drones had inspected the docks and, finding it lightly guarded, the warplanes alone dealt with the area as the ground army prepared to march to Odyssey. As the planes soared overhead, the enemies on the ground fell back into the ships, all of which were monitored by the small drones. The jets destroyed the ships in the harbor before they managed to fire off any large munitions in defense, and they now lay at the bottom of the sea.

Simon told Jeremy to scratch Winston's head for him and to help console Carolanne, and that this time his decision could not be swayed. He was going to face Karl alone, how it should have been done since the beginning. Use stealth and clarity, not direct force. Reluctantly, Jeremy wished him good luck.

And then a feeling came rushing over Simon. Deep anguish, loss and guilt.

The death of the Rangers who tried and failed to free Uncle Al. Bethany, captured. Brian, who had fought at his side and helped him retake Alice in the battle on Nick Byrnes' lawn. Alice's collapse, the failure of everything he had traveled so far to attain when leaving the cabin deep in the woods of British Columbia. It seemed like another lifetime. The cabin. Alone with Winston, losing his mind during the heavy snowfalls, aching for his parents, his brother. Then that night when he went to his truck and found the pictures of his family and ran out into the snow, howling mad in despair, only to come face to face with a moose who reared in surprise, snorting plumes of steam into the moonlight.

Did it really happen?

All he wanted was to find home, find his parents, his old bedroom … but it was gone. His youth was erased. Alice took its place, and his purpose in life became scouting forays and teaching the citizens tidbits of survival training. It occupied his thoughts. Bethany occupied more. She overwhelmed his desire. She became the life he was longing to find, and together in Alice, his happiness increased.

And now Alice was gone. Smoke and rubble, the gardens burnt. His life taken from him again, his friends killed. So many people dead or in despair, and this time, the disease wasn't to blame. The fault lay on one pair of shoulders, one man—Karl Metzger. The sound of his name caused anger to flash through Simon's veins in hot pulses.

War would never end, it seemed. What the disease did not erase, the remainder of humanity would attempt to destroy. Was there an answer to this? Was there a way out, a new method of governing, a bright ideology? Simon didn't think so. Perhaps future generations, but he knew that future generations learned from the old ones. Why was fighting so deeply engrained in the human psyche, to allow one person to commit barbarities and atrocities against another? Was it so tightly woven in our genetic code, that to be without war would spawn the next step in human evolution? Perhaps someday soon, but certainly not in his lifetime.

Simon didn't have the answer for any of these thoughts. They had been debated for centuries by brighter minds than his own, with no solutions to be found. For now, he had to deal with the present moment, stay focused, feel the wind blowing in through the window, watch the pavement flowing by under the tires.

A map lay unfolded on the passenger seat. Simon glanced over, half expecting to see Winston in his rightful place beside him, and his heart ached to scratch the happy panting face of his old dog. But instead, he studied the map during long stretches of the drive, and examined the positioning of abandoned vehicles. It was not unlike stalking a deer and inspecting the brush for indications of an animal's trail: a snapped twig, disturbed leaves. During the first two years of human inactivity on the roads, weeds had sprung wild in every crack and vined out over long stretches. Those first plants died with the seasons, and their residues formed thin layers of soil, hastened by mosses and fungi, over the pavement. Interstates became camouflaged back into grassy fields, and difficult to decipher if not for the rusting shells of cars and buses. Karl's retreating Hummers and pickup trucks left trampled turf, bent grasses, broken vines, and automobiles nudged out of their way. Much the same as the tracks an animal leaves in the wild, but on a larger scale, and easier to detect.

He was on the right track. A few miles behind, he judged, since they would stop for longer periods as they navigated the terrain and moved stalled vehicles and rubble. It was critical to remain just out of sight, make sure he didn't advance too quickly. If he were to be seen, then his pursuit would be futile. He wouldn't stand a chance taking them on face-to-face. He kept a slow enough pace to not worry about catching up. At times, he had to park and get out, inspect the terrain close up to follow the tracks.

If he was going to eliminate the Red Hands and take Bethany home, he would become a shadow. If he wanted his life to have purpose, he would remain vigilant. Flashes of what could happen crossed his mind: him and Bethany tending a garden. Him and Bethany waking up together, unhindered by the awful stress and strain of warfare. The two of them keeping warm by a fire on a cold night, Winston curled at their feet in blissful content. Teaching Connor how to hunt with a spear, stalk and survive, so that the boy could one day pass the teachings on to future generations. Help the child deal with his mental state after the countless deaths he'd been forced to witness. Romantic, idealistic raptures. It was possible, though. But to achieve happiness, he would have to abandon all prior notions of what home was, of what it could be.

With her, it could be anywhere.

With her, he could find comfort on a rock.

With her, the terrible cycle of violence could cease.

They could live in peace.

But first, he had to get her …

… and to do that, he must kill Karl Metzger.

Chapter Forty-Six
Jackknife

Karl never thought he'd miss the words of a holy man, but his mood was brightened imagining the throaty tunes of Priest Dietrich singing out over the troops in hymnal battle song. These thoughts lasted mere moments, as he knew he would never hear his psalms sung again. Never witness the apocalyptic form of his army marching to its tune, singing and mumbling along like summoned ghosts from the rocky deserts they trod and defiled.

It was over.

Out of the carload, the only one he could trust was Liam, who had the opportunity to take control of the Red Hands back when Karl was presumed dead after the first battle in Alice and failed to act. Liam would live and die at his side. Their fates were intertwined, to live and fight together, forever. The rest of them, not so much. Their loyalty extended to the amount of food Karl held in the palm of his hand. Once empty, they bit. Once threatened, they rebelled.

"How are we in terms of supplies?" he asked Liam, snapping the man out of a daydream.

"Ah, um, to what regard?"

"Food. Water."

Liam thought for a moment, then said, "Let me call it in. Numbers might have altered since the last report."

"Sir," Liam said. "Can I speak frankly?" His voice was meek.

"Of course."

"What is it, sir … about her?" He motioned his head toward the trunk.

"What do you mean?"

"I've never seen you enchanted by anything other than the pressing need to further the gains of the men, to conquer new territories and expand our growth. The same with her uncle. I've never seen you so possessive over anything other than food, water, whiskey, and tobacco."

Normally, Karl would not let the conversation proceed. All Liam had to know was where to march and when to gather the troops. But with a new survival tactic came a change of persona, perhaps, and Karl nodded for him to continue.

"I mean," Liam continued, "back in Hightown, our remaining men followed their escape rather than flee as the bombs fell. Then when you saw her, Albert Driscoll became dispensable. In all of our time together, you've never … I mean, I never saw you so passionate. Is it … because of the other one? The girl you told me about, years ago?"

Karl digested what he'd just heard and disregarded the mentioning of the other girl. He had told Liam of her in folly on one drunken night, camped out on a prairie far away. She belonged to another lifetime, his youth, a world that no longer existed, and he tried not to dwell in the past.

He told Liam, "I don't know what it is about her." But his actual thought was that prior to Bethany, all his desires remained in the compulsion for gain, land, and goods—survival. He wanted the world, and he wanted it served on a silver platter for him to devour at will. General Driscoll was part of that world. The man had been allowed to live under Karl's authority. But the general was not a proper trophy. He was not a real plaything. Bethany's spell had pervaded the depths of his imagination. Back when he was in the clutches of Doctor Freeman, in his labyrinth underground, drugged and injured, it was the image of her that stoked fire in his heart. It pushed him to press on, to demand the loyalty of the dockworkers and fight to conquer both Hightown and Alice. What he did not realize until he had her in his possession was that the distress over losing his army, his command, was curtailed. With her the world was his own. She was, in essence, the final victory he'd been longing for.

***

The miles passed swiftly despite the inhospitable condition of the roads, with some grown so wild it was easier to drive off the pavement. They shared ration bars and water, which they had plenty of. Karl loosened Bethany's gag and put a bar in her bound hands, but she didn't budge to take a bite. Not even a sip of water. She lay there as if dead. He would revive her spirits when they were alone and at home together. There, he would work on rehabilitating her attitude.

They stopped twice to fill the gas tanks, and with each stop the men got out to urinate beside the vehicles. The men in the pickup truck also took the opportunity to stretch and refuel. Karl again offered Bethany a chance to relieve herself, but she didn't respond when asked. If it wasn't for the occasional blinking and the movement of her chest as she breathed, he would have checked her pulse.

The high-calorie survival bar that he gave her dropped to the bed of the trunk. He picked it up and took a bite, noticing that she was lying in a pool of urine. The bar had grown dryer, brittle, closer to a solid chunk of flavorless wood.

They drove all through the night, stopping occasionally to navigate troublesome terrain. Communications came over the radio, but they were few and far between, not the constant clatter that had once come from commanding thousands of troops. Karl closed his eyes and let the vibration from the truck lull him into the deep realm of fantastical dreams, some pleasant, many not.

He awoke with a start, realizing at once where he was, and fearing the blade of his men to challenge his command. They were stopped, and the driver and passenger were outside refueling.

"Where are we?" Karl asked Liam, who appeared to be awake despite his closed eyes.

The man cracked a smile. "Close," he said. "Two miles back we turned off Interstate Forty."

"You don't say?" This was good news. If they continued on Forty, it would bring them closer to Odyssey. This crossroads of sorts was now pointing them farther southwest. The trunk had been opened for Bethany to get out to relieve herself, but she stayed inside.

Karl and Liam opened the rear doors and stretched. "She hasn't said a word," Karl said.

Liam shrugged. "Got nothin' to say."

They walked off to urinate by the side of the road, and when they returned, Jacob was at the trunk. Although it was hard to see from his distance, Bethany's mouth was moving. Jacob closed the trunk, made quick eye contact with Karl, and went back to the driver's side. His cheeks were crimson.

Karl hummed a nameless tune and returned to his seat. They drove off with Karl tapping his knee, his eyes going back and forth between Jacob in the driver's seat and the rearview mirror, where he could almost see the side of Bethany in the back.

A few miles went by, and beneath the loud rumble of the truck he whispered to Liam, who was falling asleep. "Listen," he said, "I've been thinking that it's perhaps time for us to change tactics to ensure our continued survival."

Liam's eyes opened. Karl leaned in and spoke a confided plan. After a moment, Liam said, "All right."

Karl never took his eyes off Jacob and the rearview mirror, and when another ten miles went by, Liam spoke to the car, "Gotta take a leak again. Pull over."

They relayed the message to the pickup truck, and the Hummer came to a stop. Jacob and the passenger stayed in their seats.

"I might as well go too, while we're stopped," Karl said, opening his door. "Top the fuel off."

"Sir," the passenger said. "We filled the tank last stop. We're still full."

"Let's keep it that way. We're pulled over, so top the tank off. Both of you."

Jacob and the passenger exchanged glances, then they turned off the engine and opened their doors. Karl stretched in the brilliant daylight. There was a slight chill that felt wonderful. He opened the trunk, looking down at Bethany with a wide smile. She looked tiny, disheveled. "Go on and relieve yourself." Karl looked around at the expansive and overgrown fields on either side and added, "There's nowhere to run. We'll give you privacy."

He walked near where Liam stood on the side of the road. "Mister Briggs," he said. "I believe my presumptions are correct. But even if they're not, it is still the best course of action. You and I," he said, tightening his belt, then motioning to Liam and himself, "are the only ones who can trust each other."

"Yes, sir. I agree."

With that, they turned to the Hummer. Karl eyed the two soldiers standing beside the trunk, the passenger holding the bright red container. "Ready, Mister Briggs?"

"I follow your lead, sir."

Karl flashed his wide set of teeth at the two soldiers and said, "We're making good progress."

"Yes, sir," the passenger said. They'd finished refueling the tank and were strapping the fuel to the roof.

Liam walked to the pickup truck as the men climbed back aboard. He leaned into the driver's side window, and a moment later, the truck made a turn in the road and headed back to Interstate Forty, and to Odyssey beyond, where Liam had ordered them to travel.

"Where the hell are they going?" Jacob asked, looking at the leaving truck.

"I sent them on a task," Karl said, issuing another smile. "It's of no consequence."

Jacob swallowed visibly and exchanged a quick glance with Karl. In that fraction of a moment, each man understood the other's ambitions without speaking a word.

Liam swung his rifle up first, and Jacob and Karl were fast to unholster their sidearms.

All three men pulled their triggers. The passenger flinched and grabbed his rifle, but a bullet struck his torso, and he fell over fast and hard. Jacob managed two shots until a bullet pierced his chest and he spun to land facedown in the dusty road, his pistol falling from his grip.

Karl reholstered his firearm, all while whistling a tune.

"Fuck," Liam said with a grunt. "The fucker got me!" Karl looked at his lieutenant standing behind him. The man grabbed at his bicep, thick red emerging between his fingers, and more red spreading from his thigh.

Karl walked toward him and caught his lieutenant as he stumbled to his knees. "Let's get you to the Hummer," he said.

"Shit," Liam said. "Hurts something fierce." He hobbled on one leg as Karl held his shoulder.

He was helped into the passenger seat, and Karl grabbed a medical kit. "Start bandaging," he said. "I'll be right back."

Jacob was still alive, moaning and moving. Before dealing with him, Karl went to the trunk. Bethany's eyes were large, her mouth in a grimace. She leaped forward like a jack-in-the-box, a folding knife in her hand, the small blade reflecting the sunlight. Her ankles were still bound, but she'd managed to cut the ropes from her raw wrists.

Karl was not surprised by the attack, and he stepped back fast. After hours of being tied in the trunk, her muscles had fatigued, and her movements were slow. Karl leveled his fist and struck a quick blow to her face. She fell backward, and the knife dropped from her hand. Blood emerged from her nose, and her eyes teared up as she covered her face.

"Now, now," he said. "It will be all right. It's not broken; I would have felt the bone snap."

"F-fuck you," she said. Then louder, "Fuck you!"

"In due time, my dear." He retied her wrists, pulling the cord tight. Blood trailed down her cheek as he slammed the trunk shut, cutting off another "Fuck y—"

He turned to Jacob. "Not yet expired, I see." He pushed the man onto his back with the heel of his boot. Jacob groaned, his hands over a deep wound on his chest. Blood trickled from his lips and he coughed a deep, fluid-filled rattle.

"I'm disappointed, my boy. I had hope in you. But you're a special type of stupid, aren't you? You shot my best officer. Twice." Karl shook his head.

Jacob didn't reply.

"Did you really think she'd slice my throat with that little toy of a knife? Then what? You two would ride off into the sunset?"

Jacob looked into his eyes. Then he laughed a low and trembling laugh. "It's o-over, Karl. It's all over."

"For you, yes. But I'm still standing."

Jacob shook his head, coughed again, and struggled to inhale. Then he said, "Death will find you. It's a matter of time, a-and you've r-run out of t-time. We-we all h-have ..."

Karl unsheathed his combat knife. "No, my boy. I do not think so."

He swiped the blade across Jacob's throat and walked toward the front of the Hummer.

"It's been a while since I've driven, Mister Briggs. How is your wound? Did the bullet hit bone?"

Liam sat in the passenger seat, a mess of bloody bandages on his lap and around his feet. "N-no," he said, struggling to wrap a strip of gauze around his arm, where it quickly became red. He was sweating, pale.

"Here," Karl said. "Let me help you." He took the medical bag and removed more gauze and duct tape. The bullet hole in Liam's arm went straight through the fleshy part. It was nothing serious. Karl cut away the material on his leg, and Liam let out a wail. "Easy now," Karl said, inspecting the damage. The bullet appeared to still be lodged somewhere near his groin. "Not so bad," he lied. "Barely bleeding."

"I-it's near the artery. Shit, I can feel the son of a bitch in there." Liam gritted his teeth, his skin blanched. He reclined his seat to lying down, and Karl secured a bandage as best he could, with Liam hollering in pain and squirming in the seat. After he wound enough duct tape to hold the gauze, he started the ignition.

"Thank you, sir," Liam said, his eyelids heavy.

"From now on, you address me as Karl."

"Yes, sir," Liam said, and then scratched at his beard with his good hand, seemingly puzzled on how to do this.

Karl took the radio off the receiver and called his men in Odyssey. He reported that they should await his arrival and defend the town from the reckless force of the invaders who were fast at their heels. He explained that the colonies were set to slaughter them all, so they had to fight like their lives were on the line, because they truly were. He knew many would flee. But that was of no consequence as they drove onward, a half day's ride away from their destination.

"Hold tight, dear," Karl yelled back to the trunk. "Tonight, we dine waterside."

Chapter Forty-Seven
Beacon

The recent mass execution on the side of the road was a sure indication that Simon was on the correct path. His first thought was that a brigade from the colonies had caught up to the fleeing Red Hands, but after calling it in on the radio, he learned they had nothing to do with the carnage. This brought on a strange and sudden emotion, the realization that he was all alone, away from the others, and that he was vulnerable. He was reminded of his trip from British Columbia to Alice, and the sensation that he was a tiny speck upon an earth covered by a crushing, dark force was troublesome.

As he inspected the bodies for the face of Karl Metzger, his heart beat with trepidation, praying to his own gods that Bethany was not among the dead; but neither friend nor enemy lay among the corpses. Two out of the four vehicles he'd witnessed fleeing Hightown were parked on the side of the road, the gas caps hanging from the open valves.

Fuel. The things people kill for.

The pavement twinkled with bullet shells reflecting the sun, but there was no indication of a battle, no bullet holes in the vehicles, no retuned fire from the line of men. This was an execution, through and through, and by all appearances, committed by their colleagues.

The area seemed tainted, inhabited by corrupt spirits, and despite the press to move onward, Simon first checked the two vehicles. He found what he'd been hoping for: one of their radios. The keys were still in the ignition, and when he turned the electricity to life, he grabbed the receiver. As expected, a code was needed to access the frequency the Red Hands used. He turned the radio off and went back to his truck.

Deciphering the route became more difficult now that he was trailing two vehicles instead of four. As night approached, he abandoned the pursuit, partially because seeing the slight nuances of bent grasses, broken twigs, and nudged vehicles was exponentially more difficult in the dark and inside the cabin of the truck, but also because he felt exposed with his headlights beaming against the crushing shadows. As it became too dark to see without the lights, he found a thicket of stalled vehicles and parked alongside them, to make his home for the night among the dry old corpses occupying the neighboring cars.

With the absence of light, he found the only activity to distract his thoughts from the demons in his mind was to attempt deep meditation. The task was impossible for long durations, as his mind wandered to Bethany, to Karl, to Brian, to Winston, to Connor, to Carolanne, to Jeremy, and to the idea that this entire rescue pursuit could be in folly. A romanticized vision … a heroic endeavor … his death.

The strength he carried dissolved at night in lows, and then was brought back up again by focusing his attention to his breath, letting his gaze wander on a glint of moonlight on the dashboard. *Remain in the present moment,* he told himself. *Do not think of the future, the past, what could come, what might never occur …* It was impossible at times.

Despite the outward negative forces, he'd been trained for this. The two years spent in isolation in the cabin, the thousands of mental demons he fought when trapped inside for months as the snow fell. He breathed, in and out, and focused on the absence of thought, on nothing and everything. Soon, he realized he could sleep. His brain had burned to the last of its fortitude, and if he wanted to continue this hunt with a rational mind, in folly or not, he had to put aside his racing trepidations and manage at least a few hours of sleep.

***

When the sun rose, with the green of the grass vibrant again, the sky pale forms of yellows, blues, and reds, the urgency of the plight arose. Simon filled the fuel tank while eating a high-calorie survival bar and continued the journey. Miles upon miles of nothing but destruction, overcome by dust and earth. It had been two years since Simon's last journey far from Alice, and the world had decomposed into a crumbling trash heap. That's what humanity had become: trash. All garbage. Thousands of vehicles parked wherever they stopped, plant life clinging to their rusted sides. Bodies overcome by flowering greenery, their bones woven through by creeping weeds like threads from a needle.

The interstate was becoming a forest, trees obscuring street signs and dilapidated rest stops. In another year, two tops, it would be impossible to determine much of the landscape as not belonging to a jungle. This could be humanity's chance to right itself, to begin fresh. There was enough fertile land to support flourishing plant life, enough edibles found in the wild to help people endure.

The path went straight for hours, and with them Simon thought about the craziness of this all, that he was driving across the country to save one person and eliminate the others, while seeing how nature found a way to bounce back better than ever with the absence of human life.

His trail of thought was cut off as a crater enveloped half the road, relatively new judging by the young sprouts inside the blackened pit. In the center was a strange mass of machinery, twisted and burnt. A round, half-broken section the size of a small car, and then a longer cylindrical device double in length. Small sections of bright metal emerged from the wreckage, reflecting the sun. A satellite, no doubt. Simon wondered about radiation or spilled chemicals as he passed, but his worry subsided knowing the wreckage was old.

It wasn't the first downed satellite he'd seen—there was one west of Alice that he'd viewed through binoculars, but this was the closest he'd been to one. Close enough that he could have read the country of origin if it had been written on the side before its fiery downfall.

Then something strange occurred; the tire tracks veered off Interstate Forty. Simon stopped and took a long look at the two roads ahead—the interstate and the exit. The long grasses over Forty moved delicately in the wind, unbroken and untrod. The map didn't give a good indication of where the exit could lead, but it was no longer heading toward Odyssey, unless Karl had knowledge that the road ahead was undrivable.

He turned onto the exit, following the tire marks, and came to a town. The vines of thousands of plants had reduced the façades of the buildings to rubble, slowly weaving themselves through bricks and mortar, until the structures became little more than dust. The trail of the fleeing tires followed to the opposite side of the town, where at the end, a large warehouse construction store had a tree emerging from a collapsed roof.

No more than a mile further, two dark forms lay on the side of the road. Simon slowed, looking out the window at the lifeless bodies. New corpses to blend with the old. Both were male, and neither was tall enough to be Karl Metzger, so Simon didn't bother to stop and inspect them closer. For whatever reason, the Red Hands were eliminating their own, shedding their skin to emerge as a new form of the same snake.

God, I wish I had Winston here to keep me company, he thought as the hours went by, and the sky began to dim. He didn't want to spend another night in the truck, without a fire, alone with his thoughts.

Judging by the map and the signs he could read through the overgrown brush, he had entered the northern border of Texas a little time ago. The Lone Star Colony was far to the south, near the water, and he had no reason to believe he was traveling there. By his current perception, the line of pursuit might take him to Haddonfield Maximum Security Prison, where he knew the Red Hands had a stronghold. It was the logical assumption.

The grassy terrain was changing to dry and arid soil, and blown sand overtook the road. Soon, he'd have to stop for the night, park the truck in another thicket of ...

... was that a light?

Up ahead ...

He pulled over and killed the engine, spying the faint flicker of illumination. There was no smoke to give the indication that it was a fire. By all appearances, it was artificial. Simon opened the door, enjoying the warm breezy air and the smell of desert sagebrush.

He hugged the side of the road, rifle in hand, and climbed a small hill. The land all around was flat, and the small incline provided adequate vantage. Through his binoculars he saw a wall, more of a fence, the color of which resembled the arid soil. The light emerged from somewhere inside, and although it was hard to properly determine in the fading evening, it looked as if the tire tracks followed straight to this walled-off city.

Then the light turned off, and the area was again shrouded in the developing starlight.

Chapter Forty-Eight
Passenger Seat

In Karl's long absence, Marianna had fared better than he had anticipated. Left without the stern leadership of one of his top officers, like Liam Briggs, Captain Black, Bishop, the Priest, Sultan, or Mark Rothstein, the soldiers had kept reasonable order.

They arrived before sunset into a deserted land. All the men had been ordered to retreat to Odyssey, where they were told to await Karl's arrival. Odyssey, though, would soon fall. It was inevitable against the overwhelming force of the colonies. Karl's new hope was that all of his men would perish. Better they be dead than left alive to interrogate, to give rumor that perhaps he was alive within the walls of Marianna. If he wanted to survive, his notion of the world he had once longed to possess must change. For now, this meant a warm meal. Plenty of water. Copious amounts of hard alcohol and tobacco. And an eternity to spend with Bethany.

He parked near the warehouse and said to Liam, "I'll get her to bed. You get a meal going." He motioned with his head to the trunk, but Liam was still asleep. "Liam …" he said, then spied the blood-soaked floorboard by his lieutenant's feet. "Shit," Karl said, and shook his head. "Sorry, old sport." He patted Liam's shoulder. "The ride must have bumped something loose." He checked Liam's pulse just to be sure, but could tell by the temperature of the man's skin that he had expired at some point in their drive.

Karl opened his door and stepped out, stretching his back. He let out a yawn, then opened the trunk and stood smiling down at Bethany in her disheveled form.

"Good morning, sunshine," he said.

She blinked rapidly behind the dark circles around her eyes, but didn't speak. Her gag had been off for hours, but still she didn't say a word. Not a sound. She hadn't eaten or had a lick of water.

"Come on now," he said, sliding his hand around her bicep. "Easy does it, come on out."

He helped her to her feet, and she faltered, her eyes fluttering up in their lids. He caught her and was about to lay her on down to let the blood rush back to her head, but then she regained her strength and her eyes opened.

"You need food, water. Come on."

He cut the binds around her ankles, and they began walking across the dusty lane.

"What," her voice squeaked out, barely audible, "do you want with me?"

"Come again?"

"What …" She licked her chapped lips. "Why are you doing this?"

He smiled. "You're special to me."

"Special?" Her voice cracked into something close to a laugh, but a tear had formed and slid down her cheek. "I'll never love you … I'll never feel anything but repulsion at the thought of your hideous face."

His grip tightened around her arm.

"Oh, I understand. It will take time. Years, maybe. And love is such a silly word."

"Your army is gone. You're all alone. That piece of shit in the passenger seat is dead, and you don't even care. Was he a friend of yours? Are you capable of feeling any human emotion other than joy at seeing people die? And what makes you think the colonies don't know about this place? They'll find you. They'll kill you."

"Look who's suddenly chatty?"

"It's true, you can't hide from them."

"I intend to do just that. At least for a duration, until this whole thing blows over."

"Blows over?" Her voice was incredulous. "Blows over! You've killed thousands, you've murdered, executed, kidnapped—"

"I've done no such thing. I've *survived*. With survival comes obstacles and tribulations, all of which I've risen above. Some things, such as my deceased officer in the vehicle … well, those things come with survival."

They were on the far edge of town, with the central pond in view around a cluster of buildings that were more like shacks.

"You can't keep me forever," she said. "You can't keep me locked away like a toy."

He didn't respond.

"Have you ever been with a woman? I bet you haven't. I bet—"

"You remind me of Charlotte." He paused, waiting for her to ask who Charlotte was, but when she didn't, he continued. "I was twelve … no, thirteen. She was the same age, give or take. I had served a duration at a juvenile detention center; I believe that time was for robbery, but I do not recall. Anyway, I was released. My mother and father came to sign me out. Pick me up. In the parking lot, me holding my backpack, when we were far enough away from the detention center, my dad turned and gave me a swift punch. It wasn't the first time I felt his knuckles, but it was the worst sting of my life up to that point. 'Walk,' he told me. 'Walk home.' My mother was crying, shaking her head, saying, 'How did such a monster come from my body?' They got in their car and drove away.

"So, I began the five-mile journey home. I remember the day like it was yesterday, the spring air both cool and warm at the same time. The blue sky without a puff of clouds. The way my legs and feet took to the pavement, three miles in, feeling strength in my muscles. It was wonderful. After two months of staring at cement walls, allowed outside only in a trampled muddy lot where the boys got into fistfights, angry over the physical and sexual abuse from the counselors and guards, this walk was glorious. I was free to explore parks, gardens … the world was open, mine for the taking. I was a mile away from my home when schools were getting out. And then I saw her, my dear Charlotte."

"I don't care about your twisted ex-girlfriend," Bethany cut in.

"She was so much more than that. The moment my eyes glanced upon her slender frame, her pale complexion, jet-black hair, the fire in her eyes … I knew she was mine."

"I ain't her, so you can—"

"Would you like me to find that gag again?"

Bethany didn't answer.

"For weeks, once I was again reintroduced to the public-school system, I would sneak out when I could, run two towns over to watch my Charlotte leave her school. She'd laugh and talk with her friends, books in her arms, her long black hair blowing in the breeze. She was the depiction of teenage innocence.

"My father spent a duration as a carpenter, when he wasn't too drunk to operate the tools. But mostly, his gear sat around collecting dust in the garage. The back of our property bordered on woods, where I spent my youth climbing trees and hunting small animals with BB guns and knives. One day I got my dad's shovel and started digging a hole. I realized later that somewhere deep in my subconscious I knew what I was doing, but at the time, I rationalized that I was just having fun, being a boy. I dug and dug, and then used my father's saws and hammers, and strips of timber he'd brought back from job sites. I fortified the walls. Had a nice little room underway. All of this when I was thirteen. You should be impressed; most boys are still playing cops and robbers."

"I don't want to hear any more," she said.

"Oh, but you do. You need to understand the way things are. So, this little underground room was shaping up, tall enough for me to stand in. In the meantime, I watched my Charlotte from afar. Followed her bus one day. Saw her home. For many evenings, I stood outside her windows in the night, watching her eat dinner with her family, everyone smiling, laughing. She had to be mine. I still told myself that little room was all for fun, a hideout, but I knew that it was for her and her only. There was no way around it. Our fates were intertwined, the same as mine and yours." He motioned between them.

"In hindsight," Karl continued, "I was not able to make it hospitable enough for her to survive for a long period, despite my best efforts. At night, before I fell asleep, I would fantasize about having her out there, if only for a few days. It would be my crowning achievement. I was waterproofing the room when my father found it. He saw his tools covered in a tarp, dirty, his wood cut to size. When I got home from school, he greeted me with an open hand across the cheek. "Don't touch my tools," he said. "What you diggin' that hole for anyway? A place for you to bury more of the neighborhood cats and dogs? They'll lock you up for good, you go off doing that again." He marched me out in the woods, made me pour gasoline in the pit, absorb into the wood, and stood sipping a beer as he passed me the matches. "Do it, or I'll knock you silly," he said.

"At night, I still fantasized about Charlotte, possessing her, having her close by, alive or dead, flesh or bones. I would start a new room somewhere else, a better bunker. I spent the summer finding a spot, to no avail. When school started back up, well, Charlotte was gone. Nowhere to be seen. I watched the kids go in and out of the building, day after day. My only guess is that she moved."

"You're a sick fuck, you know that?"

Karl opened the door to a small structure, half cabin and half plywood walls. The interior was a single room with a cast-iron stove and three cots against the walls. It was littered with empty bottles and food wrappers. He moved a cot aside and felt along the floor until he said, "Ah-ha, here we go." He pried up a loose floorboard and placed it aside. Beneath was a circular doorway. "I haven't had the chance to witness this marvel yet," he said. "It was discovered after my departure. Whoever made it and when they made it remains a mystery." He opened the circular doorway and said, "After you."

Bethany shook her head. "No." Her voice trembled. "There's no way I'm going down there."

"From what I've been told, it's rather impressive. Enough room for a dozen. More than enough storage for food and water. Once we hear that Odyssey has fallen, we can spend a few weeks below the ground, waiting for the colonies to search Marianna. They will find it deserted, and after they travel back to their homes, many, many miles away, you and I can start our happy family, together forever. Perhaps one day I'll let you out to breathe fresh air, but that's yet to be seen. Come now."

"I'm not going down—"

"Did you not learn the lesson from my story? I will never allow for another Charlotte, do you understand? I will not spend years fantasizing. You're going down there where it's safe. You belong to me, and I will never let you go."

Chapter Forty-Nine
Marianna's Fate

I am the wind. I am the rock. I am the tree, and my roots grow deep. I am the wind. I am the rock. I am the tree, and my roots grow deep ...

Darkness set in, and with it, Simon sat in the brush and observed the walled town from afar. There was no movement, no lights in windows, nothing to suggest that the settlement was populated. But it was. Bethany was behind those walls. Karl too.

At what he guessed to be close to two in the morning, a faint glow emanated from somewhere deep within the town. Simon removed his boots, jacket, and shirt. He fashioned a pair of shoes made from strips of leather, not unlike moccasins, which allowed him to move with stealth. He holstered his Colt .45, passed down from his father and his grandfather before, used during the war of his generation. Two spare clips were stuck in pouches, and his knife was sheathed on his side. Without using charcoal, since lighting a fire was foolish, he rubbed dirt and sand all over his body and hair. He wetted his back by dripping water from his canteen and spread more grit over every square inch of flesh.

He took another breath, in and out, the clarity of the world coming into focus. He was the tree, the wind, the hunter, the warrior.

It was time.

He proceeded to the wall in slow and deliberate steps, despite feeling reasonably sure there were no lookouts. The moon cascaded a silver hue upon the ground, making the late hour seem magical.

Once at the barricade, Simon followed the curve, not hearing a sound from within. He could climb it easily, but was afraid of making noise. Although he wanted to avoid the entrance, he found himself nearing it, walking with deliberate steps. He inched his face closer to the chain-link fence until he was looking within, could see the outline of a sandbag wall. No faces looked back. For many minutes he remained there, and then he touched the cold metal. It began to slide open. Not much—a few inches, about a foot. The opposite end was held together by a chain and lock, but not tight. Crouching, he moved across the space and sucked in his belly as he slid inside Marianna.

***

"You can't keep me down here, you son of a bitch!"

But he could. And he was. Bethany refused to accept the reality of her situation. Alone, underground in a cement bunker, the cold walls dripping with perspiration. Her ankle was shackled, but her hands free. This devil killed her uncle. Her brother. He'd taken her away from the people she loved, the world she knew. Brian was probably dead too. Adding further to her torment, she hadn't eaten or drank anything for … days?

Dim light came through the open hatch door across the room as Karl brought box after box of supplies into the bunker. It took him hours, and with it, the humming of the generator began driving her crazy.

Is this my fate?

If the colonies believed that Karl was dead after they bombed Odyssey, and her with him, they would all go back to their respective lands. Simon would mourn. Carolanne … Jesus, she had more to lament than anyone.

As night fell and sunlight no longer cascaded down the entry shoot, Karl had filled the bunker with enough boxes of emergency rations and water to last months. He explained to her that if the colonies did inspect Marianna, they would take whatever was left in the warehouse. What they had there, deep underground, would have to last. Before Karl turned and left, he told her, "Reports are in: the colonies have reached Odyssey. I expect that it will fall before dawn. Tomorrow, we will be one happy family down here, where the soldiers will never find us." He pulled two bottles of brown liquor from a box and said, "Tonight, I sleep among the stars for the last time in a duration.

I will leave the hatch door open for you to enjoy the fresh air." And with that, he turned off all of the power except for one small, glowing red light near the hatch door, and the generator which continued to hum.

For hours she sat in the dark, her mind spinning. She inspected the clasp around her ankle, the chain, and where it was bolted into the hard floor. How long could a person be kept chained up before losing their mind?

Faces flashed before her eyes: Uncle Al, Steven, Brian, even Winston, but mostly Simon.

She'd lost him.

She'd lost everything.

She would not allow Karl to win. She would not permit him the satisfaction of keeping her boxed up, become the Charlotte that he could never attain. She wouldn't allow it.

When she'd first been brought down there, she saw it, but didn't say a word. Most likely, Karl had seen it too, but thought nothing of it. A metal washer, about an inch in diameter, a perfect metal circle, in the corner nearby. She picked it up and felt the slick metal sides, then began rubbing it on the cement floor, grinding and grinding, beside the bolts attached to the chain. After ten minutes, she felt the warmth of blood where the metal rubbed into her skin. She stopped and inspected the floor. The cement had barely a scratch, yet the metal was grinding down. It was hopeless.

She paused for a moment, whispering to herself, "I ain't gonna cry, damn it." Then she began grinding the washer against the ground again, keeping it at more of an angle. She stopped to feel the edge, test the sharpness against her thumb, and then went on grinding. Her knuckles hit the floor and scraped, but still she went at it. It didn't take long until the edge was sharp enough to cut.

She wanted desperately to slash the blade against Karl's throat, watch him drown in his own blood, but knew the chance of getting one clean sweep was impossible. In the end, if she even managed to hit him, he'd be mildly injured, and he would never make the mistake of leaving a metal object near her again. Perhaps he'd kill her. But she wouldn't let that happen; she wouldn't let him decide her fate. It wasn't his choice to make …

… I am not your Charlotte …

With that, she tested the sharpness against the soft patch of skin on her wrist. The pain was electric, but she fought back the tears as the wound began to bleed. *I ain't gonna cry … you don't win, Karl Metzger.*

***

Marianna was small compared to Alice and Hightown, yet large enough that it would have been difficult to enter with stealth had there been soldiers guarding the walls. Simon moved in the shadows, always looking ahead, envisioning himself several paces beyond.

There were noises now. Faint, but detectable. They came from the direction of the pale light. The homes and buildings were shacks, mostly plywood, with some crudely fashioned out of cement and bricks. He kept his back to walls as he slid from shack to shack, firearm in hand. Not far in the distance, he heard the static and chaotic noise of a radio broadcasting voices.

Karl Metzger.

His heart drummed against the wall of the building; his vision throbbed crimson.

I am the wind. I am the rock. I am the tree, and my roots grow deep. I am the wind. I am the rock. I am the tree, and my roots grow deep …

There was another noise, a mechanical hum, a few yards to his side.

He remained behind the far walls of the homes until he came to the source of the noise. A generator was running outside one of the buildings, blurting out black exhaust, with a power cord trailing inside. He followed the cord to an open hatch door in the corner of the room. A bunker. First, he listened. It was possible there were more of Karl's men down there. He attempted to look down, but couldn't see a thing, and debated for a moment over whether to inspect the bunker or go and face Karl Metzger … then impulse overtook him, and he begun descending the ladder.

The darkness was like swimming in ink. Crawling, he tried to let his eyes adjust, but couldn't see anything other than stacks of boxes. A little red light shone like a beacon, and he inched further inside, seeing the rectangular outline of what looked like a light switch on the wall. He stood and placed his fingers on the switch, ready to spring on anyone who might be sleeping down there.

He counted.

One …

… two …

… three.

A fluorescent light flickered and came to life.

Beth …

She looked back at him, terrified. Covered in dirt, he appeared to be more of a monster than a man.

"Si—" she said, huddled in the corner. Simon rushed over with a finger over his lips.

"Bethany," he whispered. There was blood around her. Her eyes were distant and wet. He grabbed her tight, and saw something small and metal in her fingers. Blood was trailing out of her wrists, not fast, but trailing nonetheless.

"Oh my God," he said.

"Am I …" she mumbled. "Is this …"

"*Shh*," he said and went over to the boxes, looking from label to label, until he saw one with a large red cross painted on the side. He tore it open and placed packages of supplies on the ground until he found large bandages and a suture kit.

He ran back to her; her eyelids were languid, but her consciousness was still there. "Is that really you?" she asked, her lip trembling. He opened a bottle of water and held it to her lips. She drank it in like a dehydrated sponge.

"I'm here. You have to be quiet." His fingers were slippery with blood as he tore into the packaging. As long as he could stop the bleeding, she'd survive. "This is going to hurt," he said.

"I'm-I'm so sorry, Simon. I just couldn't …"

"You don't have to explain yourself."

His fingers trembled with adrenaline as he punctured the sharp point of a needle into her skin. She flinched but did not cry out.

"I'm so sorry."

"You're alive, that's all I care about. How many people are here?"

"Just him. Karl." Tears fell to the floor. "I'm so ashamed."

"Stop that."

He managed to get a few stitches in, despite being poorly done, and wrapped the gauze around her wrists, going around and around …

… then it hit.

Like a burst of bright light, all the held-back rage came sweeping in, his eyes flashing large, and he turned, fast.

"Simon," she said, holding the chain around her ankle. "Get me out of here."

Chapter Fifty
A Million Shards of Broken Glass

The airwaves were full of voices being mauled, shot, destroyed, as Karl sipped at his bottle and smoked his cigar, listening to it all fall to utter ruin.

The night was magnificent, the sky full of a thousand sparkling flecks and reflecting over the gentle sways of the pond. Despite the serenity, his mind wandered to the never-ending list of chores still necessary to ensure his survival. First thing in the morning, he had to get rid of Liam's corpse. That would be easy enough. He could drag it waterside and tie a few rocks to the man's feet before bringing him out to deeper waters. He should probably get rid of the Hummer too, with the front seat drenched in his lieutenant's blood. It was also possible that the colonies would be able to track it from belonging to Hightown's armory. Maybe he should leave now, drive the Hummer ten miles into the desert and set it ablaze?

No. Not tonight. Not now. This was his last night of fresh air. Karl bit his cigar and closed his eyes, letting the sounds of crickets fill his perception—

There was a noise behind him—footfalls.

He stood fast and turned as three pops fired off in unison. "Jesus!" Karl shouted and half stood, grabbing at the pistol in his holster, which was draped over the back of his chair. A sharp pain stung at his thigh.

***

Simon ran right at Karl, sprinting, an effigy of pure nightmares. Bethany was behind him holding his rifle, but she was injured, and Simon wished she would have listened to him and stayed behind. Simon held his pistol before him, aimed, and—there was a crunching noise behind him, and Simon didn't have to glance behind him to know that Bethany had taken a knee and was ready to shoot. Without hesitation, Simon pulled the trigger.

"Jesus," Karl let out, the gap between them narrowing. The man had moved quickly upon hearing the slight noise of Bethany kneeling, disturbing a small tuft of sagebrush, and was lifting his own pistol. Simon fired off the remaining rounds in his clip and tossed the pistol aside. Loud pops continued from behind him as Bethany continued to fire. Karl fell on his back, hard. He never managed to get off a shot.

"Oh, fuck—" was all Karl got out before Simon jumped on top of him, his legs straddling the man's body. Karl's back was in the water, a lapping tide crossing his face, choking off his words. A dark pool emerged from Karl's chest, and Simon could feel the warmth of the man's blood soak into the fabric near his thigh. A bullet had pierced the criminal, the monster, the butcher, close to his heart.

Still, Karl's long arms grasped at Simon's throat, tried to find an eye socket. Simon wailed his fists down, striking over and over, waiting for Karl's strong fingers to relent.

Bethany was calling out from behind them, "Move, Simon!" He guessed she couldn't make a shot with them so close together. Then he felt her reach his side, bump into him, grab something from his belt. His knife. The side of a blade caught a glimmer of moonlight before Bethany plunged it down, sending the pain of a million deaths to explode inside Karl's chest.

Karl's eyes shot large, and his breath escaped his body in a long, fluid-filled exhalation.

Karl reached for the handle, but Bethany and Simon held it firmly in place. They stared at each other. "M-mister Kalispell," Karl said, blood trailing from his mouth. And then, to Simon's horror, a laugh bubbled past the man's lips as he said, "S-s-o you will b-be my assassin. You've m-managed to k-kill me. Yet, in me lives the basis of human ideology, and you cannot kill ideology. Through that, I will live forever. You cannot kill me. You n-never could, and you never will. No one can k-kill Karl Met—"

Simon pulled the blade free, and Karl's eyes again shot large as thick red surged from the wound. Simon grabbed Karl's shoulder, and Bethany gripped the other. "I've heard enough of your fucking poison," Bethany said.

They dragged him fast into the deeper waters, feeling his body convulse. Simon had heard that the sensation of breathing in water was akin to inhaling shards of broken glass. Through the dark water, the shadowy form of Karl Metzger grew still, and he rested along the murky bottom, where his body would remain to mix with the bones of those slain in the water before.

Chapter Fifty-One
Concentric Circles

Simon opened the door to a warm breeze and walked across the yard to the stump with his axe stuck in the top. If they wanted to remain comfortable through the winter, they'd need much more wood. Thankfully, he wouldn't have to chop it all himself. He was positioning a smaller log on top of the larger one when he heard the rumble of an engine. The sun's position in the sky indicated that it was about the correct time in the afternoon for a visit. He brought the axe down and collected the splintered pieces before walking to meet the workers.

Two jeeps parked, and the soldiers got out. They greeted Simon, saying, "Sir," and walked around to the other side of the cabin where work was being done to add additional rooms before the winter.

Simon went inside and said, "The workers are here."

Bethany was eating a bowl of granola at the table. She looked up. "I heard them," she said with a smile. "I'll give them a hand in a minute."

"Where's Connor?" he asked, and walked over to kissed the top of her head.

"Checking the fish traps."

Simon nodded and took a seat on the couch.

"You okay?" Bethany stood from the table and put her empty bowl in the sink.

"Yeah, just tired. I'll be out to help in a few."

"Take as much time as you need."

"Carolanne didn't come this time."

Bethany nodded and took a seat beside him on the couch. "I figured. She'd of come inside by now if she had."

"She's going to work herself to death."

"It's just the way she copes."

Simon was about to tell Bethany that she coped the same way, but decided it was best to remain quiet. They'd both implored Carolanne to join them at the cabin, retire from the busy life of the colonies, but in the end, she couldn't be swayed. She would, for now, do everything in her power to help others in the hospital. If she could save one life, then perhaps her own life would again have purpose. And by all accounts, she'd saved dozens of lives.

Simon closed his eyes and let his mind ease. Bethany stroked his hair lightly, then said, "Rest for as long as you need. I'll go help the workers."

"Sounds good." The cushion rebounded as she stood, and he heard her footfalls lead to the door. It was hard at times, closing his eyes. That was when the memories returned. But he'd managed to overcome much of his anguish. It didn't happen all at once. Days passed with minimal conversation between himself and Bethany following the escape from Marianna, with her in the back seat of a truck once belonging to Karl, speeding fast out of that wicked place. They found Liam slumped in the passenger seat, cold and stiff, and Simon pushed him to lie on the dusty ground.

The entire experience was too much to discuss, too much to rationalize. The relief of Karl being dead was diminished by all the atrocities they'd endured because of that vile man. In the end, Karl did not die in an elaborate shoot-out. It wasn't like the movies Simon had seen growing up, or the scenes he'd read in books. The good guy and bad guy didn't exchange a dozen blows. There was no long, drawn-out fight. Karl died quickly. They watched the light fade from his eyes before allowing his form to disappear into the dark murk of the pond. Simon didn't speak to him, didn't voice the thousands of insults he had wanted to hurl at the man. At that moment by the edge of the water, Simon had become the warrior, the beast, the thing of dread that he needed to tap into in order to plunge the blade into Karl's chest without a moment of hesitation.

After telling Jeremy the tale of Karl's last stand, it was decided to leave Karl's bloated corpse in the water rather than have the soldiers sift through the bottom. Perhaps some good would come of it as the fish fed on his body.

There was no pleasure in killing Karl, only a sense of completion.

Once back with the colony, as the soldiers celebrated Karl's demise, some crying, Simon and Bethany found Carolanne, Connor, and Winston—who was the happiest of all to see them—and after a tearful embrace, they located a lone tent and lay inside for hours, a full day, being brought food and water. They didn't talk much, just held each other. Simon realized many things at that moment. He realized that the home he had been searching for was long gone. And not just a physical structure, but a place for mental security and familiarity. Sometime after he'd left his parents and lived in the wilderness of British Columbia, he'd undergone a change. His life up to that point had ended, and his new life was in the woods. What he'd longed for back when he'd traveled east, alone with Winston, was for the past to stay in the present; for his parents to be alive, for his brother to be home. None of which was possible.

They were taken to Albuquerque, where Simon was treated like a mystical god for killing Karl Metzger. When word came that settlements had been discovered far to the north, unrelated to the United Colonies, Bethany, Carolanne, and Connor listened to Simon's proposition. In the end, in their constant despair and worsening depression, they agreed it would be in their best interest to live alone, away from war, away from what has and always will be society's idea of surviving. All except for Carolanne, who said she would go crazy living in the woods. She needed work. She needed to be making a difference in the world. She needed to be part of the system.

In an effort to link with the northern colonies and establish treaties, Jeremy was happy to send soldiers to erect compounds near Simon's cabin in British Columbia, and workers regularly stopped by to lend supplies, and sometimes stayed to receive wilderness training. Simon, Bethany, and Connor would remain a part of the United Colonies, but they would do so alone.

Simon opened his eyes and took in a long, sweet breath. A mug half full of coffee remained where Bethany left it on the table, and Simon finished it in one long sip. Before leaving, he let his fingers brush the cool side of the cast-iron fireplace.

He would be back shortly to help with the construction, but he wanted to check on Connor first. He spied the gardens as he went, examining the ripe tomatoes that needed to be picked and the thick green beans. They could do that later, after the soldiers left. They would do it just the three of them, enjoying the quiet evening and the warm vegetables, baked in the sun.

He paused by the waterside, his hand on the tree with the mess of roots at the base which fit his body so well when he meditated. The bark felt nice and scratchy on his palm. Connor was out in the water, swimming leisurely toward one of the traps. The boy was good. With more practice, he would one day become a better stalker than Simon could ever dream to be. The boy had, after all, been raised in this hellish world. Simon smiled, and then walked a few steps over to the mound of short grass and developing flowers. A rock lay on top, the name *Winston* carved in deep.

"Well, boy, I got you home," he said, and patted the rock. "You're a good boy, aren't you, dummy?"

Simon kicked off his boots, removed his shirt and pants, and proceeded down to the water in his underwear to spend his afternoon in peace.

Epilogue

After four months of solitude, he was let outside into daylight. The guards had a soft spot for the old man, battered, nearly dead—should be dead, but he wasn't. At night, every night, he hummed a quiet tune. In time, the guards began asking him questions, and were delighted in his heartfelt responses.

The first burst of fresh air on his skin was like being reborn, and he told his guards as such. He fell to the ground in tears, an old man crying over something so simple and wonderful. A breeze. Sunlight.

His words held wisdom, enough for soldiers to visit the man behind bars. Six months into his imprisonment he was authorized to attend church services, fully shackled. A few weeks later, the shackles were removed, but the guards remained at his sides. He repeated "Amen" louder than all the others after the minister issued the words, and was lost for hours at a time in deep prayer.

Always he smiled, even in the blackest of cells. Eventually, he was given additional blankets, an extra pillow, better rations.

Then one day, a soldier from the colonies told him that the minister was sick, and would he like to fill in?

Priest Dietrich smiled and said, "Of course. God bless you, son."

The soldier told him he'd return in an hour for service.

The Priest adjusted his eye patch and smiled, humming a gentle hymnal tune.

www.BrandonZenner.com

www.amazon.com/author/brandonzenner

Thank you for reading *The After War Series*. Sign up for Brandon Zenner's email list on his website to be kept informed. You will also receive a free short story, "Helix Illuminated," when you sign up. As always, the best way you can support an independent author is by leaving a review on Amazon. Each and every review is read and appreciated by the author, both good and bad. The Amazon link above will take you there. Please read on past the Acknowledgments for a preview of Brandon Zenner's novel, *Whiskey Devils*. For those of you who want more, check out Brandon Zenner's blog site here: https://brandonzennerblog.wordpress.com

From the Author

I was having a beer with a friend a few weeks ago, and a song came on the jukebox that I'm a big fan of, but my friend had never heard. The verse builds with a slow instrumental beginning, and crescendos into crashing lyrics. I told my friend that the song held some inspiration for me while writing *Whiskey Devils*, in a particular scene involving a biker gang going into a deadly shoot-out. The song remained vigilant in my thoughts while I structured the narratives, pacing, and settings. My friend had read *Whiskey Devils*, and was surprised and happy that I provided the insight. That song was "Gut Feeling" by Devo. If you've never heard it, well, you should.

That got me to thinking about how important music is in creating and shaping not only my own writing, but countless other novels, pieces of art, and just about everything that we as humans do. I'm an avid runner, which helps me clear my mind and create the scenes and narratives in my books, and the music pumping through my headphones has a big effect on my mindset while putting the miles underfoot. I thought I'd use this opportunity to share some of the music that has helped create my novels, and which continues to inspire me.

After reading *The After War Series*, it should come as no surprise that classical music is important in my life. There was a brief period when I wrote in silence, back when my office was temporarily in the basement of my old house. It was cool, dark, and quiet down there. But outside of that short period, classical is and always will be in the background as I write. I prefer sonatas, piano and violin pieces over full orchestra, and I keep the volume low, and headphones on. Right now, I'm listening to Mendelsohn. Other composers that are commonly playing include Camille Saint-Saën,

Tchaikovsky, Dvorak, Chopin, Debussy, and of course Beethoven. There are more, but those are my main guys.

That isn't to say that classical music is the only genre that impacts me, but it's what I prefer to listen to while writing. Various other songs and artists have inspired my words. Here's a strange one for you: "A Minha Menina," by Os Mutantes, out of Brazil. I don't understand the lyrics, but the playful harmony sums up Evan Powers and Nick Grady's relationship in *Whiskey Devils* perfectly. And to be honest, I actually enjoy and prefer not knowing the words. At the end of the novel, I mention that "Box of Rain" by The Grateful Dead played a strong hand in creating the scenes, and that remains true for just about every Grateful Dead song.

Outside of *Whiskey Devils*, I recently went through a Pixies revival, and when I was first outlining *Butcher Rising*, I was mowing my lawn while listening to "Wave of Mutilation," loud, on a hot summer day. Some of the key components of the story came to me in that moment, and I named the lake and the town of Marianna after a lyric in that song. I do also like using soft, feminine titles for towns and colonies to offset the violence which occurs behind their walls, such as Alice.

Aside from my Pixies revival, I've gone back to listening to the Doors after a long absence, and have found Jim Morrison's haunting lyrics superb while debating scenes and structures in my mind. There are several nods to the Doors in this novel. Catch them if you can. Believe it or not, my five-year-old daughter was the first to pick up on one of the biggest clues. That was a proud moment in fathering for me.

While speaking of haunted lyrics, "Breathing" by Kate Bush had a big influence while finishing up the rough draft for *The After War*. I grew up listening to her eerie melodies, and whenever I hear it, I envision Brian and Steven in utter despair traversing the dismal post-apocalyptic terrain during their journey to Aurora, and Simon and Winston's long trek from British Columbia to the East Coast of the US.

There are countless other songs that influenced me, but for now, that's all there is to share.

I want to thank you for reading *The After War Series*. It's been a long journey, both for you, the reader, and for me in writing and creating these books. When the idea first came to mind back when I was sixteen, I had no clue that it would blossom into a three-part series. Even when I wrote the first rough draft, over ten years ago, I didn't know the scope of where it would take me. It's so hard to say goodbye to my beloved characters. They are a part of me, and I am a part of them, no matter if they're fictional. I put them through hell. I led some to death, others to redemption, and just about all to despair and depression. For that, I am sorry.

Goodbye, Brian Rhodes.

Goodbye, Simon Kalispell.

Goodbye, my good buddy, Winston. You're such a good boy …

All the best,

Brandon Zenner

Acknowledgments

In no particular order, the following people deserve my full appreciation for their help and support in creating this novel: John Zur, Hal Zenner, Margarette Shields, Stephanie Parent, Deborah Dove, and Jason and Marina Anderson over at Polgarus Studio. Of course, my wife and daughter, Mallory and Sadie-Mae, have supported my career from the start, and put up with my long days and early mornings spent tucked away in my office. This book would not have been possible without the help and support of everyone listed. As indicated at the beginning of the novel, this book is dedicated to my parents, Hal and Natalie Zenner, who have been huge supporters of not only my work, but of the arts in general. I had previously not wanted to dedicate such a violent book to them, but with this tale ending a three-book series which has taken me over half of my life to complete, I felt it was time to give them proper acknowledgment.

Preview: Whiskey Devils

"A large marijuana growing operation, Russian mobsters, undercover drug agents, and a biker gang, wraps up with a series of unexpected and shocking plot reversals that brings the book to a violent, surprising, and powerful end." (BookLife Prize in Fiction, by Publishers Weekly)

Chapter 1

Spring, 2003

Weaving through the crowd, I passed my exhausted coworkers, their faces gaunt and ghostly pale in the fluorescent lighting. All of them were salivating before the punch-out clock like a pack of ravenous hounds eager to tear into the flesh of that Friday night. They leaned from one leg to the other, purses in hand, sunglasses dangling from open collars. The din of conversation lessened as I neared the clock, and all eyes were cast upon me.

They were thinking, *Is he really going to do it? Is Powers leaving early?*

The receptionist's sharp stare burned with scorn from behind her blonde bangs, but I ignored her gaze and approached the clock. My time card was in my hand, "Evan Powers" scribbled on top. The paper glided effortlessly through the punch-out machine, making a slight mechanical noise as it stamped out the time, 4:47. The clicking noise echoed in the now-silent room, and I hightailed it to the door, daring my eager coworkers to follow.

Warm air cloaked me in all its glory as I flung the door open. My flesh tingled—honest to God, tingled—like the sun was drawing out some poison from the office's artificial cold air.

As I crossed the parking lot toward my car, I resisted turning to look through the wall-length window of the manager's office. Kim would be staring up from a stack of papers on her desk, watching me in disbelief as she checked the time on her watch. No one left before the clock struck five. No one.

Yeah, I did it. I left early. But fuck it—I quit. So there was that.

The well-traveled engine of my Buick rumbled to life, sputtering out clouds of gray exhaust. I backed out, put the car in drive, and sped the hell out of there.

A cigar was waiting for me in the glove box, and I clamped it between my teeth as I loosened the collar of my button-up shirt.

I laughed out loud, feeling a bit like a madman who laughs alone at the world, thinking, *I'm free, you fuckers—I'm free!* A cloud of cigar smoke was sucked out the window, replaced by the clean springtime breeze.

Traffic was already forming on the highway, but I had managed to beat the mass of cars that would stretch on for miles only minutes after five o'clock. The landscape gradually changed to an immense array of blossoming trees and flat wilderness as I distanced myself from town, driving deeper into the heart of the New Jersey Pine Barrens. My housemate Nick and I rented a nice piece of property: three acres of trees and land, with many more acres of wilderness in every direction. Our nearest neighbor was old Mr. Patrick, or Grandpa, and we didn't cross paths with the man too often. We invited him over whenever we had parties, but Grandpa rarely showed up and never stayed for long. He was cool with us, but when our parties got going, and a handful of ragged hippies turned into twenty, thirty, forty, sixty—whatever—he would take off. Not before schooling us all in a game of horseshoes, of course, and drinking about a six-pack of beer. The man could put them away.

I drove past Grandpa's mailbox and our driveway soon appeared. Nick's work truck came into view as I pulled in, and way out in the back of the yard I spotted him standing beside our massive garden. Nick had been living in the rental house for fifteen years. Our good friend, Darin Long, had been a housemate with us for the past five years, but due to his mother discovering that she has cancer, he had moved back home to Montana. Now it was only the two of us, all alone in that low ranch in the middle of the woods.

Hippie Nick, he was sometimes called, or more recently, The Old Man. It was a term of endearment. The guy had lived through the cultural revolution of the '60s and '70s, which meant that for most of our friends, myself included, Nick Grady was the closest thing to a legitimate hippie that we would ever encounter. The guy followed the Dead, marched at civil rights protests, and did all that fun stuff that made him practically a sage in the eyes of my stoner friends.

I got out of the car and passed Nick's work van on the way to the house. The *G* and *R* in Grady Construction and Repair on the van's side were barely legible, faded with time.

Our front door was unlocked, and I went straight to the kitchen. We had a strict nonsmoking rule indoors, for everything other than herb, so I had to be quick with my still-burning cigar. I grabbed two beers from the fridge and went out the kitchen door to the backyard. Nick was under the apple tree next to the garden, swaying with a beer in hand. The Dead blared from his portable CD player, the extension cord trailing all the way back to the house, lost like a snake in the grass.

Water droplets rained down from the sprinkler over the budding tomato plants, zucchinis, peppers, and everything else we'd planted only a few weeks ago. The corn stalks were already about two feet tall.

Nick moved to the music, barefoot, with his wrapped hemp necklaces and beadwork bouncing on his gray-haired chest. The only article of clothing the guy ever wore at home was a pair of cutoff jean shorts. When he saw me approaching he nodded.

"Hey there," I said.

Nick smiled a crooked smile, a rubber band stuck between his lips as he pulled his long hair out of his face. A cooler was out there next to the few battered Adirondack chairs, and I could tell by the look in Nick's eyes that he was already a few beers in. I handed him the beer I had brought from the kitchen anyway. Sierra Nevada, always Sierra Nevada. It was the only beer the guy would drink if given a choice. However, if he didn't have a choice, he'd drink most anything. Especially bourbon. We went through the stuff like it was water.

The song ended and he yelled out, "Yo, Powers! What's up, man?" He was evidently in a great mood.

"Nothing, Nick." I tried to be nonchalant, but my lips cracked into a smile. "I did it."

His eyes lit up. "You quit?"

I nodded.

"Ha!" He bounced over on quick feet and hugged me with his strong, skinny arms. "I'm so happy for you, brother. I know that job was dragging you down."

"Thanks, man."

"Want to call some people up, get the bonfire going?"

I shrugged. "I wouldn't mind having a few beers."

His face was radiant, and I knew he was swallowing back the question he'd been asking me for years now. The words were trying to burst free from his mouth, but I was going to wait a little while longer before letting him know that I would work for him full time. And I wasn't talking about his handyman service; as good as he was at repairing cabinets, replacing shingles, and even doing some landscaping for a handful of local Pineys. I was talking about his *other* job. His real job.

"You doing some shooting?" I nodded toward the small arsenal on the coffee table: his old Western-style six-shooters. They were a hobby of sorts, first for him, and then for me. After all, we did live in the middle of the woods. Not to mention that the house one over from old Mr. Grandpa's was the fire chief's, and the man was a regular at our parties—as clean-cut as he was—and he kept an eye on the police radio for call-ins about noise. I consider myself clean-cut as well, in comparison to most of the transients who pass through our doors. My hair is short, I wear nice pants and shirts, and I keep myself in decent shape. Ever since I met Nick, I've been trying to get the guy to go running with me, or use the weight bench in the basement. But he always declines. "Look at me," he says. "I'm skinny enough. There won't be nothing left of me." It's true. The guy's a rail: skinny and strong. A lifetime's worth of hard labor made it impossible for him to ever be a pound overweight.

Nick looked to the black powder pistols. "Knock yourself out," he said, and went back to swaying with the music, mumbling along with the words while looking out over the sea of vegetables glistening from the sprinkler water.

As the sun began to set and the beer in the cooler dwindled, we loaded and fired the six-shooters at a wide tree stump across the yard. The process of loading a black powder revolver was tedious, but that made shooting them all the more enjoyable. We had to work for our fun.

While we were shooting, the house phone rang several times, and soon our driveway became illuminated by headlights. A few people showed up with more beer, weed, and various low-grade narcotics and hallucinogens. Ritalin, Adderall—that sort of thing. Most everyone, myself excepted, got stoned the minute they crossed onto our property. Weed was never my thing. I rarely smoked, which was in contrast to the company I kept.

This guy named Mario showed up tripping on mushrooms, sitting a foot away from the blazing flames in the fire pit, his bright orange hair seeming to glow in the flickering light. I thought about asking him for a few caps, but decided against it. Ever since Darin moved out, Nick and I had to be on the lookout for people fucked up on the more serious drugs, like cocaine, heroin, and even speed. That was a big no-no at our home. Darin used to be our enforcer of sorts. He was a strong guy, although his short and stout build made him appear youthful, especially with his long dark hair kept up in a ponytail. Ex Army, believe it or not. But that life wasn't for him. Darin was a feel-good stoner who liked lounging around the house shirtless, just like Nick.

But Darin was gone, so it was up to Nick and me to watch over our guests. Just last party I found a guy taking a line of coke in our bathroom. He was so strung out that he forgot to lock the handle, and when I told him to get rid of the shit he started spewing vulgarities at me through his clattering jaw. Before his erratic mind thought it was a good idea to throw a swing, Nick and I had his arms behind his back, and we did the old heave-ho out the door, holding the back of his belt and his collar. I learned long ago in my bartending days to never let the other guy swing first. Unless of course the other guy was so fucked up that he couldn't hit the side of a wall. Or if the guy was a lawyer. Never hit a lawyer first. But back at my old bar, the local clientele were far from lawyers.

Lucky for us, the crowd was mellow tonight as the alcohol and marijuana flowed. At some point the fire chief showed up, wearing a big grin. He disappeared with Nick inside the house, and when he came back out, he was baked out of his mind.

"Hey, Powers," he said, his red eyes sparkling.

"What's up?"

"Check this out."

The fire chief swung a canvas duffel bag around from his shoulder and opened the zipper. A copious amount of fireworks lay inside.

"Cool, huh?"

"Yeah." I smiled. "Cool."

The night wore on and the fireworks were ignited to thunderous ovation from the enamored crowd. The fire chief kept his radio turned up in case the noise got called into the cops.

Maybe fifteen people were gathered in the backyard when I saw headlights approach from down the driveway and stop short of the house. I checked the time on my watch. It was impossible to see in the darkness, but I knew the headlights belonged to the black Plymouth Fury Gran Coupe that had been arriving at our house at that same time every week, for years now. I looked for Nick in the crowd and spotted him by the fire.

"Hey," I said, approaching.

When Nick looked at me, I tapped my watch and nodded toward the car. His face soured.

"Motherfucker," he muttered, and swilled back his beer.

Nick went to the house, and a moment later he emerged from the front, walking toward the car. He opened the passenger door, illuminating the car's interior while stepping inside.

It wasn't long until the passenger door opened again and Nick got out. The Plymouth reversed out of the driveway, not bothering to swing around the circle. Nick had told me in the past that the man didn't like it when strangers were at our house during his stops. But then he had gone on, "If he makes his stops on a Friday, it can't be avoided. Fuck him."

When Nick got close, I handed him a beer. His face was set in the same crazed anger that always overtook him after leaving the man in the Plymouth. I silently prayed that he wouldn't start hitting the bottle hard, like he often did after the man's visits, and go off on one of his insane rambles. Not now, not tonight. Tonight, I was celebrating my new life. My new path, as twisted as it might become.

"You okay?" I asked.

Nick took the beer and our eyes met. His face softened. "Yeah, man." He patted me on the shoulder, and we walked into the yard to join the circle of people watching the fire chief light off the last of his fireworks.

And there was Becka. Her fair complexion illuminated in bouncing shadows from the fire, her dark, somewhat curly hair pure black in the night.

"Hey," I said, walking up to her. "When'd you get here?"

She turned and smiled at the sound of my voice. "Hey, Powers. Just a minute ago. I was looking for you."

She patted the grass beside her and I took a seat, making it a point for our thighs to touch.

"I did it," I told her. "I quit."

"The office?"

"The office."

"Powers," she exclaimed. "That's wonderful, man!"

She reached over and wrapped her arms around me, burying her face in my chest.

This was good. This is what I needed. I needed Becka, her arms holding me tight all night long. When was the last time we'd hooked up? A week ago? Maybe more. Nick jokingly referred to Becka as my girlfriend, but we were nothing like that. Just friends. Two people in their mid-thirties who had been in terrible relationships, much like all the other loners out there who find themselves still single past their twenties. We just wanted to keep things cool. Sure, we liked each other, but we didn't want to make our relationship something more than it needed to be. For her birthday last year I bought her a small oval locket. Nothing fancy or expensive. I regretted giving it to her the moment I saw the surprise and uncertainty on her face. She did wear it, though, up until recently. She said she misplaced it, put it down somewhere, and that it's got to be around. Probably at home. Probably fell from the kitchen sink. She'd find it, she told me.

But who knows.

Becka had been friends with Nick for years longer than I'd known either of them. I originally thought that Nick and Becka had a romantic past, but Darin later set me straight. Besides, their ages are decades apart … not that that would stop either of them.

As the last explosion filled the air, the fire chief turned to the crowd. "That's it," he said, displaying his empty duffel bag. "That's all she wrote."

Nick stood a few feet away from the crowd and we caught each other's eyes.

"Hey, Becka, you gonna be here for a few minutes?"

She looked up at me with a smile and then back to the fire. "I'm not going anywhere."

I hugged her shoulder and stood. "Be right back."

"Hey, grab me a beer while you're at it?" She displayed her near-empty bottle, the light from the fire making it transparent.

"Of course." I smiled, walking toward Nick. "Be right back."

Nick and I stood apart from the group as the fire chief shook out a few stray firecrackers into the fire, turning the duffel bag upside down and shaking it out.

"Hey," Nick shouted over the roar of our friends laughing and jumping away from this madman dumping explosives over the open flame. "We gotta talk."

"Yeah," I said. "I know."

"You give my proposition some thought?"

I nodded, not that he could see me with his eyes transfixed on the fire. With Darin gone, Nick was shorthanded. He'd been asking me to work full time at his operation for years, but I always declined. I was too clean-cut for that life, I used to think. I was better off as a part-time employee. But after spending three years stuck at a cubicle in the stalest environment that I could possibly imagine, wasting away the best and most productive time of the day—between nine and five, when the human mind and body is at its best— I was starting to see things in a different light. Plus, he was offering me more than just hours—he was offering me a management position. Small responsibilities at first, but they would grow over time. But the real benefit, I thought, was that Becka and I would be spending more time together.

"Yeah, Nick, I've given your proposition a lot of thought. I'm in. I'm all aboard."

He turned to me. "Seriously?"

"Seriously."

He extended a hand, smiling like a little boy. "Oh, brother, you are most needed!"

We shook, and then of course he hugged me.

"Man, this is going to be great!" he shouted, arms out in the air, holding his beer aloft to the night sky. The light from the fire flickered dancing shadows all over his body.

"We'll start tomorrow," he said, taking a swig of beer and bouncing on his toes.

I smiled.

He tossed the empty straight into the roaring flame, and grabbed two cold ones from the cooler. He popped the caps and handed me a bottle.

"Cheers, brother," he said.

We clinked glasses.

"Cheers."

He took a long pull, and I again prayed to myself that he wouldn't get too fucked up. I didn't need him screaming crazy shit at our guests, crying, sobbing, and making no sense at all.

"I think it will be best if we start late," he said after a burp.

"Agreed."

Sipping my beer, I watched Becka transfixed on the fire, a smile on her radiant face as she swayed to the music. As much of a free spirit as she was, Becka had something about her. She had class, and an amazing mind that I wanted to keep discovering. She wasn't the type of person to lay her cards out on the table; I had to keep guessing what was in her hand. Her beauty was the type that tongue-tied men, but there was more between us than sheer attraction. We had a chemistry that couldn't be put into words, but only felt as a throbbing heat in my chest. It was intrigue that kept me coming back for more; it was her quiet, pondering eyes that displayed indecipherable emotion. Simple words from her lips carried the weight of the world and affected me like I imagine poetry inspires minds greater than my own.

Her shadowy form beckoned me to approach and sit with her on that lush field of grass for as long as eternity would allow.

Turning, I grabbed two beers from the cooler. I was about to tell Nick that I would be back, but he had seen the rapture in my eyes and had begun to drift away, chatting with the fire chief.

"Welcome back," Becka said, looking up to me as I approached. There was longing in her eyes.

Feeling a bit drunk, I smiled coolly and took a seat beside her to watch the roaring bonfire.

Tomorrow, my life would change—for the better, I thought. I would be managing a productive and quite illegal drug operation. But now, in the present moment, I didn't want to contemplate the future or lament the past. I wanted to stay stuck in time, right where I was.

Continue reading here:
https://www.amazon.com/dp/B01AHI307Y
Or here:
http://www.amazon.com/author/brandonzenner
Or even here:
http://www.BrandonZenner.com